Crown & Thorns

J.L. SPOHR

THE REALM SERIES by J. L. Spohr

Sword & Shield
Heirs & Spares
God & King
Crown & Thorns

Crown & Thorns

BOOK III OF THE REALM SERIES

J. L. Spohr

Plum Street Press

Crown & Thorns

J. L. Spohr

Printed in the United States of America

Plum Street Press
1037 NE 65th St., #274, Seattle, WA 98115

For more information about this book visit: www.jlspohr.com

Edition ISBNs
Hardcover: 978-0-9986277-1-7
Trade Paperback: 978-0-9892173-9-2
E-book: 978-0-9892173-5-4

Cover design by Kelly Leslie
Book design by Morgana Gallaway
Author photo by Karly Lee

"To His Love When He Had Obtained Her," by Sir Walter Raleigh, fair use
"The Shepherd's Praise of his Sacred Diana," by Sir Walter Raleigh, fair use

For my readers—
Thank you

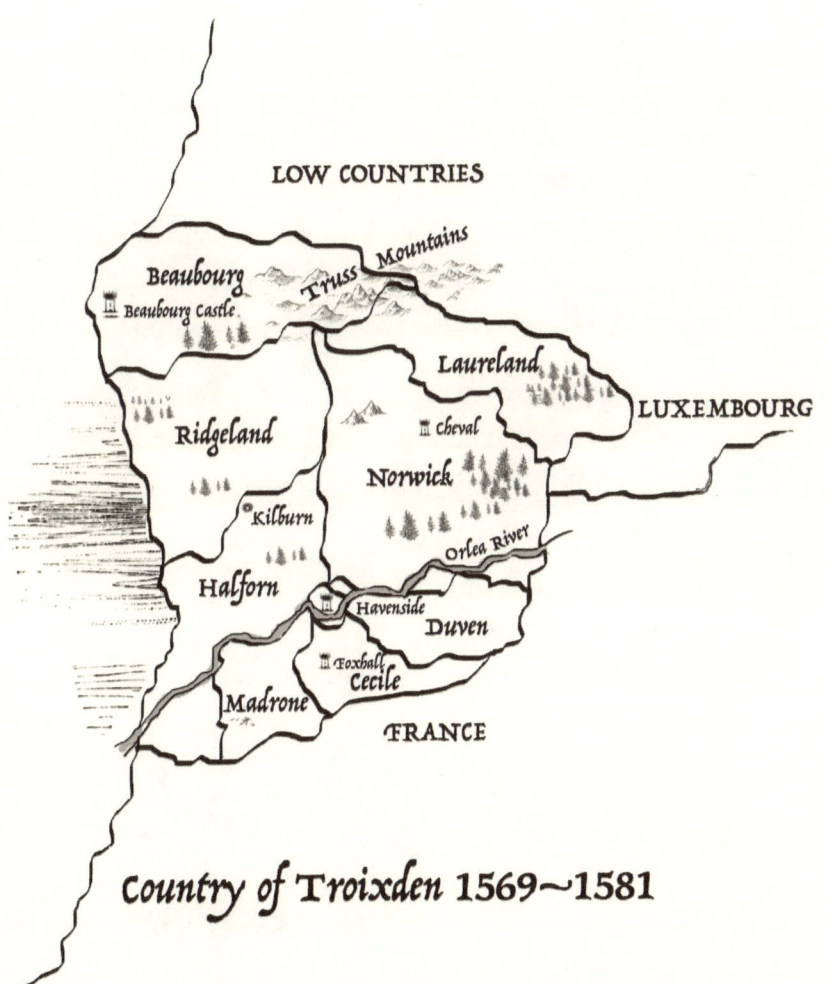

LOW COUNTRIES

Beaubourg

Beaubourg Castle

Truss Mountains

Laureland

LUXEMBOURG

Ridgeland

Cheval

Norwick

Kilburn

Orlea River

Halforn

Havenside

Duven

Foxhall
Cecile

Madrone

FRANCE

Country of Troixden 1569~1581

Set me as a seal upon thine heart . . . for love is strong as death; jealousy is cruel as the grave: the coals thereof are coals of fire, which hath a most vehement flame.

– Song of Solomon 8:6

A king's wrath is like the roar of a lion; he who angers him forfeits his life.

– Proverbs 20:2

Chapters

CHAPTER 1

1575

William, King of Troixden, frowned down upon the wiry Frenchman. Courtiers and diplomats swirled about in the Great Hall, but the king focused on the self-satisfied ambassador before him. So, the French would not aide Troixden's cause. William would see about that. He put his hands on his hips, short cape expanding like wings.

"Norwick," he called over his shoulder, "show the ambassador the rose garden. He apparently enjoys flowers. And pricks." The ambassador's pursed lips turned into a scowl.

Robert, Duke of Norwick, slid his black eyes to his cousin and king. "By all means, my liege." He strolled the few feet between them, giving William a tight bow. "Shall I request entertainment as well? From the ladies perhaps?"

"Oh, I believe his lordship will be quite content viewing beauty of a botanical nature alone. No need to distract him with—how did you put it, milord?" The king licked his lips. "'Inconsequential advantages.' We'd hate to put him to such pains as the ministrations of our fine ladies of court."

The ambassador harrumphed, sneered in Robert's general direction, and muttered something unflattering in French. Robert gestured for the ambassador to take the lead and, while passing the king, gave William a long-suffering sigh. But William's mind had already turned to a new strategy. With Spain, the German states, and possibly England playing Troixden's allies at day, only to swallow his country whole in the night, this blow from the French was formidable.

The French knew Spain wanted Troixden for its own. All the better to launch their attacks on England and shore up their control in the Low Countries. It didn't matter that Troixden was Catholic. Troixden was land—land needed to keep all Protestants in check, to complete the vise that would squeeze the French power out of existence. So why would France's new King Henry invite the Spanish fox into his henhouse? Was France running low on funds? Why could France not fight its own war against its own pesky Protestants? Did Henry not see the lunacy in leaving Troixden dangling as a secondary Spanish prize? Though not if William had anything to do with it. Troixden was a small, but mighty.

"We may be inconsequential to France, but not to Spain,"

Daniel, Duke of Cecile said, his pallid hand clapping William's shoulder.

"And therein lies the problem." William looked to the ceiling, studying the massive gold-leaf eaves. Carved and painted heads of jolly courtesans stared down. The eavesdroppers. If only he could be as well informed as those wooden busts. He shook his head. "We'll have to see what England has to say about all this."

"The enemy of my enemy is my friend, I suppose." A look of metal glinted in Daniel's pale eyes.

William gave a mirthless laugh and turned to join his bedeviled cousin in the rose garden, but barely made it two strides.

"Majesty, if I may, a moment of your time." It was the Earl of Ridgeland. Tall as the king, but lanky and light. Fierce in a joust, horrible at cards.

"Of course, Ridgeland." William bent his head, only half listening to the earl. It wasn't so long ago William enjoyed the press of court—the whispered intrigues, the flirtatious laughter, the riot of colors, the cacophony. But his distaste had grown with time. He would much rather be in his chambers with a select group or, better yet, alone with his queen. Or holding the princess in his lap, her silken head resting under his chin, reading him her Latin verses. He closed his eyes and breathed deeply, focusing on the air as the earl droned. As if a lazy summer breeze curled a propped window, the timbre of the hall changed. William glanced up in time to watch a sea of curtsies and bobbed heads cascade toward him.

Inhaling again, his heart began to pound. Waiting. Wanting.

The waters parted and there stood his queen, swathed in shining royal blue with golden sleeves, diamonds and emeralds dripping from her crown, her neck. There was fire behind her brown eyes as they locked on to his. His blood quickened, ready to know what secret they hid.

Ridgeland prattled on, unaware of the king's inattention. The queen made her way to William's right, dropping an elegant curtsy, never releasing his eyes. Her brow arched and a half smile graced her face. He took in her scent, thick with lavender.

"Majesty," she said, not breaking pace. He seized her wrist before she passed, squeezing it.

"Milady. Do not tarry this eve. Come to me at your earliest."

She nodded, her smile deepening, and continued toward the doors and the sun, taking all peace and pleasantness with her.

"Well the king's in a right foul mood," said Mary, Annelore's matron of honor, huffing along on the way to the queen's private garden.

Annelore jutted her chin toward the rose garden. "And I believe that's why." She could just make out the French ambassador's plumage, blowing atop his silk cap. Shielded from view as he was, by precisely trimmed Cyprus hedges that formed the rose garden walls, she could neither see his face nor hear his words, but by the look on Robert's face, Anna guessed the conversation's content. As much as she loathed the king's cousin, she pitied him now, cornered by thorns and blue ostrich feathers.

"But 'tis nonetheless peculiar, my dear," Mary said, pulling Anna back from her bustling ladies and over exuberant hounds.

"The king's always been one to shake off such slights. At least in public."

Anna frowned, turning away when Robert's eyes met hers, a question on his dark brow. "He's not had to deal with a threat on this scale before." Anna lowered her voice. "If France abandons us to the Spanish, we've no choice but to plead with the heretics of England. And where does that put us in the eyes of our countrymen?" Anna held her head high and beckoned Mary to join the rest of the entourage. "The king will rally as he always does. And he will solve it with as little bloodshed as possible. Now come," she gestured to the garden gate, twined with a riot of sweet peas, "we must needs replenish our doctoring kits. The alum is at its peak."

Mary nodded, but didn't smile as usual. "And with any luck we'll have some plump dandelion root to boot."

Anna wished Mary had said nothing. She didn't want her afternoon ruined by thoughts of wars and invasions, theology taken to extremes, and her husband, her beloved king, ground beneath it all. No. She would keep this place sacred.

Her ladies parted to allow her first entry to the garden. Stepping inside was like stepping into another world. A world of peace and harmony, of bluebells and berries, of fairies and fireflies, bees and buttercups. Towering delphiniums joined with juniper to shade the gravel path leading to the heart of her escape, the medicinal garden. There she grew the plants she and Mary, and half the Havenside physicians and apothecaries, used to heal and soothe and all manner of other things. She'd lost count of how many love draughts she'd made for her ladies, smiling at their superstition and sighing at their youthful hope, remembering her own failed attempts at evoking love with such potions.

She removed her long smock from a hook and breathed in the warm, bursting scent of a June afternoon. Pushing up her sleeves, she strolled deeper into the gardens, letting the chatter of ladies and the twittering of birds fall away. She trailed her fingers along the flowers, squeezing the tips, releasing their fragrance. Coming finally to her destination, she stopped short.

Not twenty feet from her, sprawled in a garden chair, chin on her chest, bodice laces loosened to accommodate her blooming, baby-filled belly, was Margaux, Countess of Mohrlang, snoring. Upon her head sat a halo of a hat, made of fine straw with a hole in the middle, exposing her blindingly blonde head to the elements.

Anna cleared her throat. "Countess?" Margaux stirred with a grunt, blinking her eyes at the bright sun.

"Good Lord in heaven," Yvette said, pressing past Anna with a hurried curtsy, a grim look marring her smooth face. "Take that ridiculous contraption off your head."

Margaux jumped up, uselessly pulling her bodice together. "'Twas a gift from Francesco de' Medici. 'Tis all the rage in Florence."

"Your hair is light enough without the Medici's getting involved." Yvette snatched the offending *solana*.

"Quite so, Countess," Anna said. "And I doubt your husband, nor the king, would take kindly to you accepting beautifying gifts from the Grand Duke of Tuscany. We've enough diplomatic problems as it is."

Margaux closed her laces with a jerk. "With my husband

away from court on so many occasions, I've all the more reason to keep my beauty fresh for his return." A smirk tugging at her lips as her eyes raked Anna, pausing on the grungy smock . . . or was it on the stubbornly flat womb? "Wouldn't you agree, Highness?"

Anna nodded at Margaux, ignoring the jab. She didn't wish to start another battle of wills with the woman. Especially over something so trifling as a ridiculous and ineffectual hat. As if Margaux needed any help being the most beautiful woman at court. Thank the Lord in heaven William was immune to her charms.

"We just fought a civil war to keep our land Catholic. A war that ended only on the terms of a shaky truce. What does Your Majesty think the Laurelanders would do if we put in a plea to the Queen of England? Simply sit and watch—keep terms?" The king's grand master general darted his sharp eyes about the men at council, demanding a response, demanding they take sides. Robert returned the man's plea with a stony stare. He knew the king was in no mood to be pushed. Besides, if anyone would do the pushing, it would be Robert.

"Patronizing your king does not further your cause, sir," William said, matching the general's glares with well-practiced calm. "Besides," he smiled, "does not this recognition from the pope buy us a little grace—and a little time?" He gestured to the fine parchment on the table, dangling with thick wax seals the size of fists. "If I'm officially a Defender of the Faith, what is a friendly letter to the English going to do?"

"I'll tell you what it will do." This was the Archbishop of Bartmore now, his ever-present sneer pronounced. "It will stir up the Laureland heretics yet again and spread more than imagined fear through the rest of your people. There will be fighting in the very streets of Havenside."

"Which you would be more than happy to champion?" Robert leaned into the broad table. "Or would you turn tail and run again, Your Eminence?"

Bartmore had returned to court, oily grin on his face, five long months after fleeing, amid fear the previous war would turn Troixden Protestant. It didn't take long for Bartmore to weasel back into his seat at Council Table. As the highest-ranking churchman in the country, concessions had to be made. But that didn't mean Robert had to like them.

Bartmore sniffed, stared down his hawk-like nose at Robert. "And what side would *you* fight for, Your Grace?"

"Enough!" The king's patience was at an end. "Much like before, you all seem to want to whip everyone into a false frenzy. The truce with Laureland still stands, and, with the earl possibly on his deathbed, there will be no rallying of anyone. If Spain swallows us whole, it does not matter what any of our countrymen believe, for they will no longer be our countrymen." William rose with a heavy sigh and began to pace. "Since the French have thrown us off, we have a better chance of diffusing the Spanish interest if we reach out to England."

"But what if that makes the Spanish even more intent on making us their own personal port for an attack?" the general said.

William ran his hands through his close-cropped hair.

"At least it will do something to get them all to show

their cards. The French, the Spanish, the English, even our own Laurelanders. We are stuck in a morass of guesses and hunches." He slammed his fist into his open palm. "'Tis just a letter."

"Quite so," Robert said, happy at the thought of dispatching a small entourage to England, with him at the head. "What shall it contain?"

The king snapped his fingers in Daniel's general direction. "Cecile, isn't she negotiating with France again for the hand of the Duke of Anjou? We can make it a pretense of congratulations."

"I believe you're correct, Highness," Daniel said, quill scratching across the page.

"Draw something up. Have it ready by week's end." The king returned to his chair, leaning upon its back, face weary. Robert wondered, not for the first time, if the queen's powers to soothe him had begun to fade. "And with the royal tour headed south in a few short weeks, we can perchance play one off the other."

"My liege," Daniel said, "I highly doubt the French will meet with us. After what the ambassador said . . ."

"Can't imagine why they would either," William said, "but there will be eyes and ears at the border—that is a certainty. We must look our most resplendent and magnanimous. Thus our dear cuz shall lead the way."

The men at council chuckled; even the archbishop smirked. Robert tried not to wince at their mild mockery. He knew the king wasn't being cruel. Indeed, this was nothing compared to their private ribbings. But that was it—those were private. William didn't need to take his foul mood out on Robert.

Or perhaps Robert was the one in a foul mood. He hadn't seen Yvette in days, Margaux grew more haughty and mouthy at pace with her belly, and the thought of having to tag along with court like a well-dressed lap dog—in the highest heat of the summer—didn't bode well for his spirits.

"Yes, well, I do have a reputation to uphold," Robert said.

"Then, gentlemen, if that is all, 'tis late," the king said, "and we have prettier things to look at than the glum faces of you dour lot."

The men rose as one as the king took his leave. Robert grabbed his papers and rounded the table to intercept Daniel, who was most likely headed to bow and scrape behind William. Robert pulled Daniel almost inside the horse-sized fireplace.

"Is there no way to dissuade the king from this trip south?"

Daniel's brow crinkled. "You know it has been planned for months. For years even, as the king and queen were supposed to take their royal tour there directly after the wedding."

"And it's really of that much import that I travel as well?"

"You heard the king." Daniel searched Robert's face. "Whatever is the matter, friend?"

Robert stared over Daniel's shoulder, the lush green of the rolling hills beckoning through the window. He wasn't sure if he was speaking to himself or answering Daniel when he said, "As much as you may not believe it, I miss my home. I miss my boys."

"Then why not ride to them now?" Daniel laid a hand on Robert's arm. "Go. Take care of your estate business, then come back to court rested and ready to take on the French and the English and God knows who else."

Robert nodded, smile growing. "I do believe I shall, Your Grace. I do believe I shall."

Robert didn't know what inner compass drew him to the nursery. Perhaps the thought of heading home to see his boys compelled him to see his littlest cousin, or perhaps he thought she might bring him solace. Regardless, the greeting he got put all his brooding to bed.

"Uncle Robert!" Cate threw herself at his chest, barely in time for his open arms to receive her. She nestled her chin on his shoulder and whispered, "You are my favorite."

He pulled back with a cocked brow. "Surely not above your Mama and Papa?"

Her face grew serious, and she shook her head slowly. "Not above Papa. But Mama sometimes makes me mad."

He laughed and whispered, "Me too."

Her eyes widened so he could see the whites all around her hazel irises. "You won't tell."

Robert put on his most serious court face and held up two fingers. "I swear it upon the hairs of my chin." Then he tickled her until she squealed for him to stop. "Right then. With that covered, what shall we up to?"

She took his hand and pulled him to the window seat. "Stories," she said, and clambered up to rest in the nook of his arm.

"You're like your auntie, always wanting stories," he said, smiling down at her auburn curls.

Though really, she wasn't like the first Cate. Everyone else seemed to think so, and she did resembled her late aunt, with her long lashes and bow lips, but her brow was more William, her cheekbones her mother's. And her eyes. Her eyes were nothing he'd ever seen in one so young. Sometimes they flashed keen intelligence, lacking all naiveté. As if she could read one's very heart, as if she were seeing something others couldn't. An old soul returned to earth to teach them all a thing or two.

Robert began a fable, for she liked stories with lessons, looking down her nose at tales of knights and princesses.

"Well look at this pretty picture."

Both Robert and Cate glanced at the door to find Daniel bowing in.

Robert bent to Cate's ear. "Do you like me more than him?" he teased.

She flashed those eyes at him, but then they softened back to a child's. "Don't tell."

He held her gaze and brought two fingers to his chin. She pursed her lips, hiding a smile.

"Cecile," Robert said, "what brings you down to these frivolous parts of the palace?" He poked a finger into Cate's soft side, making her kink and giggle.

Cecile looked at them, uncertain. Robert thought Daniel carried himself as though Cate might bite his ankles, yet he also seemed drawn to her . . .probably that resemblance to Will's sister.

Daniel smiled placidly at Cate. "I've come to speak to the princess's maids in regard to the trip south. We want to make sure she stays cool, rested." A sadness swept Daniel's face, and

Robert knew he recalled the Realm Review that in all likelihood had killed the princess's namesake.

Daniel paused, then set off to speak with Cate's entourage.

"That reminds me," Robert said, with a kiss to Cate's head. "I leave tomorrow at sunup to see your boy cousins."

"But can't I go with you?" she asked, twisting in his lap.

"I'm sorry, my pet, but I've business to attend, and besides, your parents would never allow it."

She jut small fists into her sides. "But I only see them at Christmastide!"

He gathered her into a hug. "You stay and keep your parents company, and I'll see if I can't bring the boys back with me. How would that be?"

He felt her nod against his neck, her arms tightening around him. She released him and busied her hands in her hair. Finally extracting a blue velvet ribbon, she handed it to him in all formality.

"Then you shall have my favor." She kissed it then lay it across his palm.

He brought it to his heart. "Then I shall indeed have a most pleasant journey."

"Again, Papa, again!" Cate hopped on the balls of her silk-slippered feet, sparrow-brown curls bouncing about her round face.

William's smile broadened at her pleading. Every day her face matured into her mother's high cheekbones. Every day her language grew more proficient, eloquent even. Every minute she seemed taller. And with all of it, William's heart winced. His baby girl was certainly not such anymore. He glanced across his chamber to Anna, sitting in her favorite deep leather chair, her eyes clouded even as she smiled at the princess. Maybe her thoughts turned the same way as his, but he couldn't tell like he used to do. Her face used to be unsuitably readable for a royal, as if he could hear the thoughts running through her mind before she even opened her mouth. But royal life had changed her. The mask he remembered seeing on his mother's face, broken only in private moments with him and his sister, now covered his wife's.

He harkened back to a time when Anna was so open, so guileless. He'd known even then it would change. It had to change if she—they—were to survive as king and queen. But as husband and wife . . . he regretted the reserve that shadowed her now, so hard for her to shake, even in his company. He sighed, returning his attention to Cate.

"If you insist, my pet." He jumped up, grabbed her under the arms amid much giggling, and foisted her high in the air, catching her to him as she fell back to earth. Giving her a swift kiss on the head, he set her softly down on the bearskin rug. "Now that's it, Princess-pie. No more. For it makes Mama nervous."

Anna's smile was tight. "Oh, I know you'd never hurt our Catey."

"But you're nervous all the same." He strolled to his wife, cupped her chin in his hand. Ah, there it was, the true face of his love—free, eyes twinkling, waiting to jest. He bent down and kissed her long and sweet. Releasing her, he straddled her chair arm and sat. "All mother's hearts quicken at the sight of their children in peril, even if the peril be naught."

She patted his thigh. "And how would you know so much of mothers?"

He shrugged. "I'm a keen observer. I do recall a certain someone who would not be farther than twenty feet away from the princess for about a year . . ."

"And there was another certain someone who would not be farther than fifty feet . . ." She nudged his leg with her elbow, trying to keep a straight face.

"Ah, but the someone I speak of would not even let our fair Daniel hold said princess . . . Robert I can understand—I mean, the man can break a rock by looking at it cross-eyed—but Daniel . . ."

She laughed now, holding out her arms for Cate to climb into. "Indeed, I was fairly horrible to both men. And it wasn't a year . . . only a few months."

William whistled, shook his head. "A lioness has nothing on my queen." He kissed Anna's and Cate's heads in turn.

"Now, Catey, 'tis time for bed." Anna gave the princess a final squeeze. "Off with you."

"But I haven't recited my Latin." William knew that pout. How Anna could withstand it was beyond him. Big eyes wet with the start of disappointed tears, mouth open in disbelief.

"One night will not erase all your lessons. Look, Nurse Claire is here." Anna nodded toward the door.

"But, Mama . . ."

"No buts, my dear."

The princess turned her charms to William. "Papa?"

He had to look away, giving his answer to the room at large.

"Now, Catherine, a princess must follow the instruction of her queen to the letter. And at the first."

"But—"

"To question in order to understand is all well and good, but to question to forestall the inevitable is folly." She scrunched up her face at this, whether in confusion or umbrage, he couldn't tell. "Besides which, you must obey your mother."

"Goodnight, princess." Anna shoved her charge off her lap. Cate shuffled away. "Is that any way for a lady to walk?" Cate stopped, mumbled something under her breath, then lifted her head and walked as though she floated. Upon reaching her nurse, she turned and gave her parents a perfect curtsy.

"Good eve and good morrow, Majesties."

She still spoke with the lisp of the young, and it took everything William had not to run across the room, scoop her up, and hold her captive the rest of the evening. Instead he nodded. "Good eve and good morrow to you, Your Highness."

"And the sweetest of dreams," Anna added.

With Cate collected and off to bed, William and Anna were alone. It felt like weeks to him, even though it had only been three days.

"And you, my queen?"

"And me what, my king?"

"Shall we also to bed and share the sweetest of dreams?" He glanced down at her, watching her eyes, trying to read her again, the shadow-mask flitting across her face. She leaned over and kissed his knee.

"That sounds like a perfect end to a perfectly frustrating day."

"A perfect end to most days, I'd venture."

She rose and came to stand between his legs. She took his face in both her hands, looking him up and down.

"Ah, Wills. If I didn't have you I . . ."

"What?" He peered into her dark eyes. They began to glisten, tears gathering at the corners. Before any could fall, he wiped them with his thumbs, kissing away the salty wetness. "If you didn't have me . . ."

She drew his face to hers, pressing a warm, smooth cheek against his scratchy stubble. "Tell me I'm enough for you."

He laughed, low in his chest. "Good Lord in heaven, Anna. Enough? You overflow. So much sometimes I can hardly stand it."

She nuzzled his jaw, and he felt his groin tighten. But he knew her sentiment wasn't some flirtatious bid for attention. He must nip this in the bud if his plans for the evening were not to be thwarted. He took her face and gazed into her eyes.

"The murmurs of courtiers have no place between us, Anna." She gave a sad smile. "You must know by now that I don't give a damn who's pregnant, or how many sons Robert has, or any of it." She flinched. "And if you give me a fleet of daughters . . . or never give me another child, there is nothing—not a thing—that will take me from your side." And now her smile was true, those stubborn tears gone from her eyes. "You keep me sane. You remind me who I am. You speak to me out of love rather than duty. And you grow more beautiful to my eyes every day." He smoothed her cheeks again. "Now, does that about cover it?"

She sputtered a laugh. "Dear Wills, do you make my heart skip beats simply to get me in your bed?"

"Well, I daresay it has worked many a time before." He grinned back at her, and all traces of her sorrow fled.

"Rogue."

"Saucy minx."

"I'll show you saucy." She arched a brow and coaxed him forward, but before he could grab her she jumped, giving chase. He watched her flit about the room, laughing as she sought to hide in various uncooperative locations. He stood, slowly unlacing his shirt.

"Sometimes to catch the mouse, all the cat must do is set a trap."

"Indeed?" She brought a hand to her chest, catching her breath. "What trap exactly, my feline friend?"

He yanked off his trunks, stepping out of them as he went to the bed. Grabbing a glass at the bedside, he filled it with the summer fruited wine he knew she loved. He held it to his lips and took a long drag.

"You'll have to do more than tempt me with libations, for those are easily obtained by other means."

He nodded, contemplating. Then he tore off his shirt. She gasped, unabashedly staring at his naked form. Picking up a tray of grapes, salami, and cheeses, he slid it to the center of the bed, then grabbed his glass and climbed in.

"I've got all night," he said. She chewed the corner of her lip, eyes narrowed.

"Damnable man." She headed to him, shaking her head. "You know I can't refuse when meat and cheese are involved."

"And with such endearments, how could anyone refuse thee, my sweet?"

She burst out a good, hard belly laugh, one he hadn't heard

in ages. She came to the side of the bed, swiped the glass right out of his hand, and drained it.

He gaped at her, falsely incredulous.

"Well, the mouse must be fortified when dealing with the cat," She said, then took a cheese knife and handed it to him. "Here." She turned her back to him. "Since you're clearly in the mood for ruining clothing again." She looked over her shoulder with a sly grin. "I never cared much for this one anyway."

As he sliced through her bodice laces, seeing her breath quicken with each snap, he wondered who exactly was the cat.

Robert's eyes roved the prone form of his olive-skinned lover. He wanted to hold this picture in his head, remember the feel of her beneath him, next to him, see the curve of her mysterious smile, the dark depths of her eyes. He would be at Norwick nearly a month, and he certainly couldn't take his mistress with him. Other men were that bold, but Robert held to a certain sense of decorum. As much as he would miss Yvette, he wouldn't so easily disturb the fragile calm he had taken pains to create at his homestead.

He leaned forward and sucked her shoulder. She turned her head and kissed his temple. "Now tell me," she said. "For you are never so sweet and so gentle as when you have bad news to share."

Robert laughed and rolled on to his back. "Sometimes, my dear, I fear you know me too well." She didn't laugh in return. "I am away to Norwick until court leaves for the south."

"That's an entire month." She hoisted herself up from the

thick rug, Robert ignoring her displeasure and watching her move. She was panther like—sleek, muscular.

"Admittedly, I generally only stay for a fortnight, but, if you will recall, I have yet to return this year. There is much business to attend to."

"Meaning the duchess." She cinched her robe about her waist and poured a glass of wine to the brim.

"And my lords." He reached for the poured glass. She snorted and sucked the drink down herself. "Come now, you would not begrudge me my sons." He roused himself and joined her by the table, poured his own wine, and grabbed a bunch of green grapes.

"Oh, your sons I can abide, even take pleasure in. But you must imagine it does not excite me to have you sharing your wife's bed."

"You do realize how that sounds?" He gave her a mischievous smile and she cracked a little.

"Of course I do."

He cupped her cheek in his palm. "And you do know I bear no love for my wife, save that as the mother of my sons and the kindness and patience she gives me."

She rolled her almond-shaped eyes. "Come now, Robert— we've been at this before. Love does not play into it for us either, remember?" She put down her glass, avoiding his gaze. "Whenever you leave court, your sister becomes unbearable, and the king irritable."

"Well, you'll have to encourage the queen to help him take his leisure more often." He took a long swig of the rich wine. "As for my sister, ignore the woman. I certainly do."

"Ha! Like when you ignored her last week as she flirted with every man at court, and all were whispering yet again about who might be her babe's father? Or when she ignored your warnings to stay away from that horrid Westerville when he rode into court last autumn on his high horse?"

"Touché." Robert put his glass down and faced her. "All the same, your main concern should be getting the queen into the king's bed as much as possible."

"I thought you didn't want the threat of another heir."

"The queen's womb has not proven fertile." He sauntered to her, sliding his hands beneath her robe, around her hips. "What I want is a happy, pliable king. And nothing makes him more so than when things go well with him and the queen."

She watched his hands. "And you think more bed-sport will make me happy and pliable too?"

He tilted forward, gently bit her chin. "I do not know about you, but it will certainly make me so." She tried and failed at a frown as his hands traveled up her back. "Think of it as a going-away present."

"Mine or yours?" The corners of her mouth curved into that luscious smile.

"Both."

CHAPTER 2

Entourage

The height of July sent the palace to sweltering. And Anna knew heading south would be even worse. She stood amid piles of gowns and accouterments, deciding what was appropriate both for an official royal tour and for the heat. The answer was apparently nothing and everything. She pushed aside a mound of kirtles and flopped on the bed, head in her hands, ladies swirling about, tittering and gossiping while the court musicians played softly from the window seat.

Yvette held up sapphire earbobs for Anna to consider. The late King Charles of France had gifted them to her after Cate's birth.

"Would it do to remind the new French king of his father—would it somehow offend him?" Anna shook her head. No matter how long she'd been queen, she couldn't get used to the fact that her wardrobe could have political import. "They're small, to be sure. Might as well pack them."

"Then you'll be wanting the blue and green gown from the silks Queen Catherine sent," Yvette said, almost in a grumble. Robert still hadn't returned from Norwick, making the normally composed lady tight as a wound clock. And it made William touchy too, as if Robert took part of the king's joviality with him to his far-off estate. The last few nights had ended with mild bickering between the king and queen instead of their tradition of fondness and, well, more than fondness. She'd been racking her brain for a way to smooth things out with him, something other than the princess to give them a mutual purpose.

"That's it!" Anna sprang from her seat. "All this time and it was right under my nose."

Yvette turned back to Anna, with a barely restrained look of burden.

"All the while, the king and council have been trying to deal with Henry and his ambassadors—not the Queen Mother. Yet she's the one who pulls the strings."

Yvette nodded. "Which means they've really been dealing with the queen the entire time."

"Yes, but not outright." Anna started to pace, thoughts on the edge of something—something that could crack the nut of these cowardly Frenchmen. "It's all been cloaked in language to Henry. Perhaps if we—if I—started a cordial correspondence with Catherine. One queen to another. Woman to woman . . ."

Yvette kept packing. "Henry's policies are de facto Catherine's policies."

"Yes, but not acknowledged by anyone. If I appeal to her vanity, joke about how the men sputter about . . ."

"Our king don't sputter about," Mary said, hauling a pile of shifts from the bed to an open chest. "And I doubt he'd take kindly to ye spoutin' it to that Medici woman."

"Of course he doesn't sputter," Anna said, frowning. She was simply thinking out loud. Mary of all people knew the habit of hers. Lord she was sick of everyone's testy moods. "I wouldn't say it so bluntly. Besides, he'd be in on the whole thing. In fact, I shall tell him of my thoughts at once. He can help me formulate them into a more coherent strategy."

"I cannot believe I'm saying this," Margaux piped in, "but Mary is right. It confuses me as to why you would want to paint your king and husband in such an unflattering light."

"I didn't say that, Countess." The king would be sure to hear of her slip, no matter how she broached it with him, and would no doubt be hurt by it. Blast all. And here she was hoping this could be something Wills and she could do together . . . She was about ready to respond with a more witty return when her caller announced a visitor.

"His Lordship, the Earl of Mohrlang!"

Mohrlang? What on earth was Margaux's husband doing here?

In he strode, his gait that of an assured courtier, no longer of a blushing, shy boy. Almost twenty, he had grown nearly as tall as William, his orange hair now a rich copper. Gone was the childish chub of his earlier days as Margaux's husband. Here stood a young man, all tautness and high chest and cleft chin to prove it. Looking at him again after all these months, Anna wasn't so sure Margaux would have cuckolded her husband this time around.

"Majesty, ladies." He bowed low to Anna. "I came back to court as soon as I could." He turned to Margaux, took her hand, and kissed it with devotion. "My darling, you must not travel with the court and must fly back to Mohrlang with me."

Margaux looked both vexed and entranced. "Whatever for? Frederick and I are nearly packed for—"

"Perfect," the earl said, a broad smile on his face. "We can send the trunks with us and waste as little time as possible here at court."

Margaux lowered her voice to no avail, annoyance clear in her eyes. "Why must we away from court and from the south, my lord?"

"Have you not heard?" He looked about the room, stricken. "Why there is plague about, even now crawling toward Havenside, surely to bloom in full in this sweltering heat."

Mary clucked, pushing past a pale-faced Lady Jane. "The heat's got nothin' to do with it, milord." Lady Jane clutched at her skirts, eyes flitting to the doors, worry creasing her brow. Surely she too would want to stay back with her son John, or flee to the north.

Mohrlang frowned at his wife. "All the same. I will not put my sweet wife, my heir, and our unborn child at risk."

Margaux cast desperate eyes at Anna. If there was one thing Anna knew Margaux hated, it was being cooped up, away from court. Even if her jailer was a comely and obviously doting husband.

"Indeed, my lord," Anna said, happy for an excuse to be rid of the meddlesome woman. "We cannot risk the countess's health, nor that of any sons of Troixden." Margaux's eyes grew wider, if that were possible. Anna was sure to pay for this in some petty way.

"Then 'tis all settled!" He grabbed Margaux's hands again and kissed them both. "Besides, I have dearly missed having you all to myself, wife."

"But do you not, dear husband, give a care for their majesties and the princess royal?" Margaux slipped out of his hands, face innocent. "Should they not as well seek shelter with us?"

"I . . . uh . . ." His face colored. "My apologies, Majesty. 'Twas thoughtless of me. Of course the court should come west. While we are not yet prepared for such a large undertaking, I'm sure—"

"You are too kind, my lord," Anna said with a smile, "but the court must needs attend to politics in the south, plague or no plague. We will of course take the utmost precaution, and perhaps I shall send the princess to Beaubourg to be safe. I'm sure my father would be delighted."

"Of course, Majesty, if it is what you prefer." Mohrlang bowed again.

"I'm sure the countess will take pleasure in her stay with you. And what a joy to have your child be born in your own estate, with you there to care for your wife in her recovery."

Mohrlang's eyes danced with pride. "It will be my privilege and honor." He turned again to his stunned wife. "We will leave on the morrow. Anything left can be packed and sent along after us." He smiled. "I never thought news of a plague would bring me such joy."

Margaux dipped a small curtsy. "And I, my lord."

When he left, Margaux refused to look at Anna.

"I assume you will want the evening off to attend upon your lord, Countess?"

Margaux gave a curt nod, rubbing under her eyes. "If it pleases your Highness, I shall finish with this last trunk and see to mine own packing."

Anna felt a twinge of guilt. She didn't realize Margaux would take being sent away this harshly. While her presence was a daily reminder of Anna's barren womb, alongside all the woman's haughty looks and flirtations with the king, there was no reason to punish the countess. In fact, Anna almost wished she were going west as well—anywhere but south in this horrid weather in a long train, staying in close quarters in relatively small estates. Ah, well. By the time they all returned, Margaux would prob-ably have another baby boy to croon about.

"And Countess?" Anna said, Margaux finally meeting her eyes. "Know I wish you all health and gladness in the birth of your babe." Margaux blinked, face stoic. "Believe that we will eagerly await the news of your safe delivery. To that end—Mary?" Mary bustled over, moping sweat from her brow. "Would you please send three bottles of your birthing draught as well as a large vial of oils to the countess's rooms?"

Mary nodded and headed to her stores.

Margaux curtsied, the smallest hint of a truce on her face. "I thank you, Highness."

As much as there was no love lost between them, Anna always held the health of a mother and child as sacred. And Margaux could leave now, with the olive branch of coveted birthing tinctures tucked in her pocket.

That evening, Anna took supper with the king in his private dining room, but privacy was not to be had. Servers and tasters and other attendants were present, including a smattering of her ladies, and a handful of courtiers, Daniel and Ridgeland among them. Anna felt the heat of their stares, the lick of their whispers. She would be unable to see the king privately later as he had business, so she swallowed a last bit of bread, cleared her throat, and smiled.

"I've been thinking about France."

"Oh?" William put down his fork. "And here I try my best not to think of them."

She kept smiling and plunged ahead. "It seems to me, perhaps if I reach out to Queen Catherine, queen to queen, perhaps there might be a way to garner their support, militarily and otherwise, should another uprising occur." He stared blankly back. "Or, at the very least, smooth things over a bit."

"My dear Queen," William sat forward, leaning his chin on steepled fingers, "we've been negotiating with Catherine for years."

"Yes, but through the king. I understand it's all artful diplomacy, but I thought I might be able to coax her into a softer side. You know, commiserate about men mucking things or whatnot."

"Mucking things?" William's face changed, though his voice stayed even. "I'm mucking things?"

The room was silent, and she swore her pounding heart could be heard all the way to the kitchens.

"Will—Highness, you know I don't mean that."

"But you'd like to have a little laugh with the Queen Mother of France about it?" He shoved up from the table, crossed his arms over his broad chest, and paced. "And this will help them to see us as a country to take seriously? When our queen mocks our king?"

"You misunderstand." She rose to meet him. Damn her thoughtless mouth! "She sent me silks a while back, and I had a dress made of them. I thought I'd send her the sketch of the design and thank her. Tell her I'll be proud to wear it on our visit to the southern border . . . small, unimportant feminine things."

"There is not a feminine bone in that woman's body." His face relaxed a hair. "And how is speaking of clothes going to get her to send us ten thousand men in case the Spanish or Low Countries decide to invade?"

Anna moved in close so she could speak without being overheard. "For once it's you who are overreacting and not me." She touched his tense arm. "I don't see what's wrong with striking up a correspondence—"

"Overreacting?" His deep blue eyes turned to a steel rarely directed at her. "This is not some courtier we're talking about, not some wealthy widow who melts at the first flattery. Why, 'tis rumored she plotted to kill the Queen of Scots on numerous occasions."

Anna swallowed her own frustration. "Again, you shoot down my efforts at diplomacy before even hearing me out, before even talking it through." Someone, probably Daniel, cleared a throat. William's eyes did not leave Anna's. She was pinned like a specimen on a needle.

"Leave us!"

With much shuffling and murmured "Majesties," the room cleared in haste. All the while, Anna's shallow breath heaved with offense. He knew she wasn't trying to insult him. Why did he have to be so patronizing about what was a very sensible strategy—the beginnings of one anyway?

When the room emptied he grabbed her upper arms, his face even closer. "Why would you say such a thing to me in public? It's like you were crowned yesterday, Anna."

"That I would dare to think I could be a help in negotiations with France?" She narrowed her eyes at him.

"*You* are aggrieved?" He squeezed tighter. "You just told a room full of gossips that I was mucking things with France and that some paltry pleasantries about clothes would solve all. You made both of us look like right idiots! And what's worse, you made me look weak. You might as well have chopped off my balls with your steak knife!"

"That's ludicrous and you know it." She wrenched her arms free. He turned from her and strode back to his drink. "No one thinks you're weak, or an idiot—"

"Apparently my own wife does!"

"I'm trying—"

"Well stop bloody trying, Anna!" He downed his entire glass in one slug and slammed it down to pour another.

"You have transformed a casual supper conversation into the apocalypse. Why can't we—"

He stilled, turned. "And do you remember the last time you had a slip of the tongue at a causal meal?" His voice was like flint. She could count on one hand the number of times he'd spoken to anyone, let alone her, in that tone. "It caused a riot in the city. People were killed—including one of your fellow midwives if I recall. Houses burned. Then we went to war."

"These are not the same." She shook her head. "And if your wounded pride would quiet, you'd also remember that it was by my actions the riot was quelled."

His mouth twisted in retort, but pounding at the door stilled him.

"The Countess Cariline," the caller announced.

"Send her in," William said, retreating back to the table.

Cariline had previously served as one of Anna's ladies-in-waiting, but as she had grown children of her own, Anna had sent her to be Cate's governess and nurse. The compact and lithe woman, her dark hair graying at the temples, took a loving, yet no-nonsense approach to her duties, a needed counter to Anna and William's constant indulgence.

She gave an abbreviated curtsy. "Majesties. I knew you would want to know. The princess has taken to bed with fever."

Without a word, William strode past both Anna and Cariline not caring whether they followed, not caring what else the woman had to say.

"Majesty, wait," Anna called.

"I will to my daughter without delay," he said, his voice booming down the hall.

He heard Anna and Cariline hustling behind, crisp skirts crackling.

"Tell me more, Countess," Anna said.

"She hadn't been feeling well all day, saying she was hot." Cariline's words were clipped, focused. "We thought 'twas the heat. We brought her in to lie down and be fanned around three o'clock. She slept. And has not wakened since."

It was now ten o'clock.

William continued to walk a few paces ahead, grinding his teeth.

"We finally saw fit to feel her head and she was burning up, her cheeks flush . . ."

They arrived at the door as Mary was opening it. Her mouth dropped open in surprise. She wiped her hands on the apron that covered her working dress. She must have been there for some time. And no one had come to fetch him? Mary strode forward, arms stretched in front of her, waving her hands.

"You can't be here, Majesties," she said, forgetting to curtsy.

William glanced to his daughter's bed, but all he could see was a mass of women swarming about her. He pushed past Mary and started for Cate.

"Majesty, wait!" Mary yelped, following him with Anna right behind.

He turned, eyes blazing. "You will tell me the issue, Madam. Now."

"'Tis the *scarlatina*, Highness." Mary crossed her arms over her chest, as if that settled matters. Anna released a strangled cry. Despite their arguing, he depended on Anna, especially with illness. She was always so confident, so determined to whip whatever sicknesses or blights came their way. But the look on her face now . . . it undid him.

"Where are the physicians? Why were we not told immediately?" The nurses cowered under his wrath. All except Mary.

"Majesty, the physicians have been here. Since there's nothing you an' the queen can do, we wanted to wait until—"

"Wait!" He charged the matron, who finally flinched. "Dammit, I will not be kept ignorant of my daughter's health!"

He heard a tiny cough from the bed. "Papa?" came a croak.

He started toward her again, but both Anna and Mary blocked his path.

"Highness," Anna said, hands on his chest, holding him at bay, "if it's indeed *scarlatina* you cannot go to her. If you were to contract it—it runs worse in adults." She searched his face.

He saw the pleading in her eyes. He knew she wouldn't hold him back for a trifle. He knew the danger. But he didn't care.

"I will not be put away. Not this time." He glared at Mary, memories of just such an encounter bubbling within him. "For I am king now, no mere prince."

Anna brought him away from Mary, out of the sight line of the bed.

"Wills, please," she whispered, her eyes reddening. "What will become of us if you . . ."

He got closer to her, voice low, urgent.

"Anna, don't ask this of me. You of all people. I will not leave our daughter to die alone. No matter the outcome."

"I will stay with her day and night. I'll send you word every half hour if you desire. You've got to think of the realm—"

"Do not presume to tell me how to be a father as well as a king. If you can't stand it, I suggest you retire to your own chambers until the morrow. I will not leave my child."

She bit her lower lip, nodded, then released him.

Taking a deep breath he strode to Cate's bed, flanks of nurses curtsying and parting at his approach.

Catey lay with a damp cloth on her forehead, hair splayed about her pillows. Her cheeks looked as though someone had smacked her, or that she'd been too long in the sun. The scarlet blotches reached down her neck and onto her exposed flat, tiny chest.

"Papa," she said, hoarse voice barely above a whisper. Her hand reached for his over the sheets, curling her fingers over his forefinger in a loose grip.

"Shh, darling," William said, reaching a hand to stroke her head. "Hush now, sweet pea. Papa's here."

Her eyes rolled back, her fingers relaxed, and she was gone to the world in a deep, sweaty sleep.

It was well past two in the morning when Anna rose from Cate's bedside to again replace the wet cloth on her forehead. William sat across the bed from Anna, head between his hands, occasionally murmuring soft prayers or pleas. Neither had slept. She couldn't help but worry, and now for her husband's health as well. Anna had *scarlatina* as a child—though not a case this severe—and knew she could no longer catch it. William was another story. He prided himself on his robust constitution, claiming he'd never been ill a day in his life. Hyperbole certainly, but it did mean he must have never contended with any serious illness, else he would remember it well. He felt himself immune. But Anna had nursed many a strapping man of Beaubourg cut down in his prime, permanently crippled or sent to an early death. Disease paid no heed to age or station.

She wrung out a fresh cloth set to cooling by Cariline and the other nurse still present. Anna had dismissed all but two, allowing the rest to take shifts, Mary only persuaded when Anna promised to wake her personally to take the next shift. Countess Cariline too refused to leave Cate's side and stayed on, quietly readying more cloth, stirring serums, and preparing teas.

"Thank you, Countess," Anna whispered over tinkling of water.

Cariline nodded. "She is a sweet, precocious, imaginative girl. And she's a fighter that one. Takes after her mother." Cariline honored Anna with one of her few, quick smiles. "She will pull through this, 'tis certain."

Anna nodded in return. "At least her fever has not increased, though I would dearly like it to break."

The countess laid a hand on Anna's arm. "Highness, you of all people know this sickness has no fast healing. The fever may not break tonight, but it will break. Mark my words."

Anna pressed Cariline's hand. "Let us pray you are right." She tiptoed back to Cate's bedside. Before replacing the old cloth, she kissed her daughter's forehead. William stirred, face haggard yet hopeful. He seemed to Anna like one of the palace wolfhounds, exhausted after a day of unfruitful hunting, eyes weary, face shaggy, but alert to any movement that might prove a triumph.

She shook her head in answer to his silent question and sat back down, eyes drifting over her sleeping child.

"Is there anything more we can do?" William whispered, desperation in his eyes.

"We must watch and wait." Sensing his need to do something, anything, she said, "It may be time to change the wraps at her feet. Would you like to do so, my liege?"

"Absolutely. Anything." In two long strides he reached the foot of the bed, hands covering Cate's mummified feet.

Anna went back to the table arrayed with supplies. Collecting two long strips of fresh cloth and two poesies of lavender, mint, and broadleaf sage, she joined William, brushing her arm against his. Despite them pulling together for their daughter, she still felt the prickles of their argument, felt the dense storm hovering.

She placed the herbs on the bed, readying the wrap.

William rubbed his thumbs over Cate's covered ankles. "I wish she would wake."

"Her long sleep, while distressing to us, is restorative to her."

William grunted. Anna slid her hands over his, skin tingling with the contact, her body aching to be wrapped in his arms and told it was going to be all right—Cate, the politics and plotting, their marriage, all of it. She rested her hands on his longer than necessary, feeling the roundness of his knuckles, the hardness of his rings, the tickle of sparse hairs, then reluctantly pulled his hands aside.

"So then," she said, taking the tail end of the old wrap, "let me show you how to change these out." Gently, she lifted Cate's feather-light leg, nesting her daughter's foot in her palm. The foot was barely the length of her fingers. She swallowed the catch in her throat, hit again by the princess's frailty. This tiny appendage reminded her she wasn't dealing with a young lady, but her barely-not-a-baby girl.

Cate was loquacious well beyond her years and tall for her age. And she would come up with the most dizzying questions. Certainly anything beyond what Anna remembered pondering as a child. Not but a month past, Cate demanded to be given grace when she had stuck out her tongue at the French ambassador and was sent from the king's presence. "What do you mean you want grace, Catey?" Anna had asked. "Grace is something good you don't deserve," Cate had answered. "I was bad, but I want to stay with you and Papa. So you should give me grace." William and Anna had laughed about it that night together by the fire, William quipping that of all the courtiers who deserved a stuck out tongue it was surely the French ambassador. Bartmore being a close second. Then they had self-indulgently marveled at what a startling child they had made together. Recalling the rest of the evening brought a blush to Anna's cheeks and a different kind of pang to her heart.

She glanced sidelong at William, watching as he imitated her movements on Cate's other leg. Then, taking a wet cloth, she wiped away the sweat-drenched herbs from the bottom of Cate's foot, concentrating on her task to slow her heart.

"Blast it all, I forgot the rosemary water." She went quickly again to the sideboard and, turning back with a carafe of the herb-scented water, she halted. William was bent low over Cate's feet, one hand easily cupping them both. He was kissing her toes, a tear glistening on his cheek, oblivious to anything but their girl.

Anna came back slowly, not wanting to disturb the scene. When she reached his side, he reverently handed a foot to Anna. With her free hand, Anna soaked a sponge in the water and drew it up Cate's leg and back again, washing away the stink, replacing it with soothing coolness. William covered Anna's hand as she had his, thumb swiping slow along her pinky's spine. He then drew the sponge from her, water trailing over her knuckles.

"Like this?" he said, following Anna's motions exactly.

She nodded, but he was absorbed in his actions. When finished, he looked to her, expectation on his face, a soldier of healing, ready for the next order.

She held up the poesy. "We'll put these on the bottoms of her feet as they were before. Arrange the leaves to cover as much skin as possible."

William took up his own bunch of herbs. "What does this do?"

"Well, in the best case, it helps draw the sickness out of her body through her feet." She placed the herbs and began to wrap.

"Huh." William twirled the poesy in his fingers, eyeing it with suspicion. "I suppose at least the scent is pleasant."

"I suppose." Anna finished her task. "Now your turn."

He deftly held the spread leaves on Cate's foot with his thumb and forefinger, using the other fingers to help work the wrap around her foot. Anna leaned in, checking his work. As she suspected, the wrappings were too tight.

"Just a moment, Wills—we need to adjust these." She snaked the end out of his hand and folded it over Cate's ankle loosely. "If they're too tight she'll swell. Her skin needs to be able to breathe. Here, feel."

Instead of simply observing Anna's work, he came behind her, covering her, chin over her shoulder, his body heat pressing in, creating a cocoon around them. He took her hand again, reaching around to feel the light tension of the cloth. He nodded. She began again. As she reached mid-calf, he slid his hand over hers, callouses brushing along her fingers, and gently took the remaining cloth from her. She cradled Cate's leg as he finished the task, his free hand going casually to Anna's waist, his thumb stroking her dress ribbing. She tried not to tremble.

Anna set Cate's leg down and, for the second time that evening, didn't want to break the bittersweet spell.

"I'm sorry," he whispered, his breath tickling her ear. She turned in his arms, facing him, both his hands now circling her waist. "At supper . . ."

She searched his eyes. "I am sorry too. I get ahead of myself—heedless. And as much as I try to watch my words, they do not obey when I'm riled."

Taking a hand from her waist, he clasped her head to his chest, pulling her in. They swayed together, relieved tears streaming silently down Anna's face. He brought both hands to her cheeks, wiping them, then brushed his lips against her forehead.

"Your passion is what I so love about you. And your faithfulness—to me, our daughter, our realm." She leaned up on her toes and let her lips meet his. They tasted salty and mildly of wine. Breaking away, she gave him a timid smile of contrition.

He moved to sit on the edge of the bed, pulling Anna beside him. "I've been so . . . on edge as of late. 'Tis not fair of me to take it out upon those who love me best."

"And 'twas not fair of *me* to put you in such a position in front of observers," she said. "I know your mood has been dark these past weeks, and I shouldn't have antagonized you."

He snorted. "I'm not a bear, to be treated with tenterhooks, my dear. Though I must admit I do feel caged." He held her hand in his lap, tracing her fingers. "I received a letter from Elizabeth today. 'Twas typical. Coy, noncommittal. A brief thank you and well wishes on our travels. It seems we shall have no succor from any of our neighbors. Neighbors we buffer from each other, I might add." He sighed. "She no more wants the Spanish taking over Troixden than I do, but all she gives us is disregard."

"Is that not some hint though, her mentioning our travels? Not something she would concern herself with if not of some import."

"Indeed. Daniel and I agree she's making a pointed dismissal there, showing us she knows we head to France. And even though she flirts with a betrothal to Anjou, she only does so to keep the beast to heel." He pushed up from the bed.

"For heaven's sake, if anyone has the right to take umbrage, it's us to England," she said, watching him head away from her then back, thumbnail caught between his teeth. "They've never stopped wanting a piece of France, especially after losing Calais, and as Calais's closest neighbor, we have much more to fear from the English than they of us."

"Ah, but 'tis those with the most power who have right to take offense. Not we 'inconsequential' states." He came to sit next to her.

"Do not let these other haughty monarchs make you feel powerless." She patted his knee. "Remember Socrates's gadfly, who 'all day long lands in all places, fastening upon you, arousing and persuading and reproaching you?'"

"Yes, my love, but they swatted that gadfly flat, if you recall."

"The point still stands. We may be a small country, but we have the loyalty of our people and the strength of our king."

William shook his head, but smiled all the same. "For now."

Robert lifted his face to the sun, soaking in the mild heat, pulling its energy into himself. He would need all he could get for his reappearance at court. This was his last day at home, and he would savor it.

Giggling broke his meditations and he opened his eyes to find his youngest son, Gerard, diving through a hedgerow. A second later his middle son, Thomas, followed suit, hollering threats, his wooden sword aloft. Robert smiled.

The vast garden was kept in tight, clean rows, as it had been in his father's time. Robert had never bothered to change it, since he was rarely at Cheval Castle, and if changes were to be made, the strolling gardens would be well down on the list. Besides, the boys enjoyed them, giving chase, holding make-believe jousts, racing from end to end to see if Thomas or Gerard could ever beat their oldest brother's record.

Even so, each time he saw the close-cropped rows, erect as palace guards and equally taciturn, he had to remind himself his bastard of a father was dead. Only then would his chest unclench and breathe clean air in peace.

His mother had loved gardens, but her tastes ran more toward the current queen's, flowers spilling over unkempt boxwoods, all manner of exotic herbs, and bees. Always the bees. She had a mound of lavender to keep them happy and two hives from which poured the sweetest honey he'd ever tasted. Once witch-hunting priests murdered his mother, the first thing his father did was plow down her treasured plants, crushing the indignant insects with it, only to plant yards and yards of unchanging hedges. Maybe that was part of the reason Annelore bothered him. She could plant and midwife and doctor, but no rumors stuck to her. No, she was exalted, the people's queen, while his mother had been hauled away.

But never mind all that now. Now he had to start thinking of his strategy for when the court sidled up to the French border. Daniel had been less than forthcoming in his correspondence, pretending as if nothing of interest or import was happening at court. Daniel was smart, but he couldn't sniff out a plot if it came up and grabbed his bullocks. He was far too trusting, far too buried in his own quick mind to think how others weaved deception. Oh, certainly he knew everything at court was politically motivated, from the type of flat cap worn to the false smiles over a feast, but the inner workings of subterfuge? Well, Daniel certainly hadn't figured out when Margaux had forged the queen's hand, never even sniffed a hint that the queen's protracted bareness years ago was due to Margaux's aborticides.

But Robert had. Because he knew how a miscreant's mind worked. And while he would use his deceptions for saving his beloved country from the clutches of bloodthirsty Catholics, for finagling his eldest son Rob to be William's heir, he knew those artful powers could be used for evil. Something he'd learned early on from his father.

"Your Grace?" His wife's lilting voice carried on the breeze. He turned as she minced across the pink gravel, holding her lilac skirts aloft. She was, after all, very pretty. Fair, like Margaux, but where his sister was all hard edges, his wife was soft, delicate, like the tasseled silk pillows she decorated the house with. There was not a place to sit in the entire estate without a pastel pillow. Even the blasted stables had them. Who the hell needs a silk pillow in a stable?

"Yes, my dear?" He strolled to her, not wishing her strain. She wasn't a woman of much exercise. Taking the air was for men, and for stout country women. He smiled remembering the look of horror on her face when he told her of the queen's proclivities for riding and stomping about. "Well, those Northerners are all savages," she had said, prim as you please.

"There is a gentleman here to see you, Your Grace. A Lord Westerville."

"Dammit all to hell." He kicked the pebbles, causing his wife to jump back.

"My apologies, Your Grace. I didn't realize he was unfit to be received."

Robert took Marie's arm a bit too forcefully, but she didn't protest. "He is indeed no gentleman. Where did you put him?"

"Why in your study, where you take all your visitors."

He increased his pace. He'd rather have the man between his wife's thighs than in his private study.

"Tell me you did not leave him there alone."

"Of course not." A servant opened the French doors as they approached. "There are two guards outside, and I sent for refreshments. Besides, he had a man with him."

"Who?" They had only passed the east wing, a good hundred more yards of turns and hallways yet.

"He—he didn't say. Oh my liege lord, I beg you not be cross with me!"

"'Tis not your fault," he managed, swiftly kissing her knuckles, "but you will retire to other rooms. I wish to see this Westerville alone."

"As you command, husband." She curtsied and scurried off. Probably to go cry into a silk pillow somewhere, airing her sorrows to her minuscule French dog. He didn't have time to worry about that. No matter what transpired between Robert and his visitor, if the king heard the man had been allowed inside Robert's walls, there would be hell to pay.

Westerville was right where Robert expected him to be, the bastard—standing behind Robert's desk, pretending to read the book spines on the shelves lining the wall, humming to himself.

"Ah! Your Grace." Westerville smiled broadly, rubbing his hands as if Robert were encroaching upon his hospitality rather than the other way around. "So good of you to see me."

Robert narrowed his eyes at the bulky man, taking in his

stoop, his bejeweled fingers, his carved ivory walking stick leaning proprietarily against Robert's desk. Robert advanced upon
him, forcing him to move from his place.

"What the devil do you want, Westerville?"

"Well you be in a fine mood this afternoon, my friend."
Westerville shuffled in front of a chair facing Robert's desk and
bent at the knees, making to slowly lower himself into the cush-
ioned seat.

"Did I say you could sit?" Robert said. "For you will not be
here long enough to make the effort worth your while."

Westerville laughed. "Touchy, touchy! And here you don't
even know what I've to say."

"Get on with it, then get out." Robert leaned over his desk,
arms spread wide, holding his weight. He scrutinized the surface. Certainly he wasn't the fastidious Daniel, but even among
what others would see as a mess, every paper, pen, blotter, and
weight had its place in Robert's mind. He could tell if anything
were disturbed, even by a breeze.

"Do you really think me so daft as to riffle your things,
Norwick?"

Robert cocked a brow at the man. "You are not known for
your intellect, to be sure."

Westerville smiled. "Then we have something in common."

"Spit it out, Westerville." *Before I beat you with your own cane.*

"I hear England has snubbed the king." His smile didn't
fade. "As have the French." Robert continued to stare ice at
the man, though he wondered how Westerville had heard of
an English snub and Robert hadn't. William should have sent

him personally to Elizabeth instead of a letter. He was much more to her preference, if his past visit there was any indication. "That makes our fair realm a great piece of meat for the hungry Spanish dogs . . . unless the Germans would like a piece of us first."

Robert stood to his full height and rolled his eyes. "Your skills of deduction are dizzying. Unless you wish to tell me something that half the country doesn't already know, I suggest—"

"What, can I not pay a visit to my old friend and speak of current affairs?"

"We were never friends."

Westerville's smile faded. "Partners then?"

"Are you drunk?"

"Fine, fine. I can see you're busy." Westerville gestured at Robert's attire of a loose shirt, no jacket, and simple trunks. "The Laureland lords are restless. Even with the earl on his sickbed, or perhaps even because, they see this as a perfect opportunity to woo support from the neighboring Low Countries."

Robert slammed his fist on the desk. "For the sake of Mother Mary and all the angels, none of this is news, you coxcomb!"

All false joviality was wiped from Westerville's face. He leaned forward on his cane. "And did you know they are planning to strike whilst the king and court are in the south?"

Doubt flashed through Robert's eyes, but he kept his manner. "And you know this how?"

He waved a pointer finger in the air. "Tsk, tsk, Your Grace. One never reveals one's sources."

Despite his heart and mind racing, Robert sat in his deer-hide chair, leaned back, and propped his feet on his desk. "Supposing I did not already know this, and supposing I actually believed you, why are you telling me? Why not go directly to the king?"

"Why, Norwick, despite our mutual dislike, I thought we were on the same side. I thought you would rejoice at this news."

Robert was up in a flash, rounding the desk, his seal opener quivering at the flesh of Westerville's chin. Westerville's man, who had been standing silently in the corner, startled, eyes huge.

"Don't you ever presume to speak of treason or heresy in my presence," Robert said. "You've only ever been on the side with more money."

Westerville didn't flinch. "Which happens to be the king and his coffers. At present."

"Get out of my sight, before I finish what his majesty started in that barn."

Westerville held up his hands, retreating as if from a stalking tiger. "Know that when Laureland comes calling—and they will come calling—'tis me you have to thank for the forewarning."

"I'll give you thanks in hell, Westerville."

"Suit yourself." He turned to go. "But I'm sure the king will want to know what on earth we've been gossiping about up here together."

"Out." Robert started toward the man.

"Oh I'm leaving, Norwick."

Robert watched him go, his man stumbling behind.

"One more thing." Westerville poked his head back in the room. "I hear your fair sister is soon to give birth."

"What business of that is yours?" Robert feigned disinterest, choosing to inspect his fingernails with his now purposeless seal opener.

Westerville chuckled. "Oh nothing. Remember, my eyes are brown, the king's are blue, and I believe her husband's are . . . hazel? Yes, something greenish." Before Robert could hurl another insult, the man was down the hall, his laughter bouncing off the high walls and rolling back to meet Robert where he stood.

Damn that man to hell. And his inconstant sister too.

William sat at his desk, eyes glazed, as Daniel talked. A hot breeze blew in from the open widow, and even though he had finally bathed, he felt sticky and worn. There had been no change in Cate. Even though Anna and Mary kept reassuring him that sleep was important, he feared the princess was slipping away.

". . . Ready to leave at week's end." Daniel finished his speech and looked expectantly at the king.

"Pardon?"

Daniel cleared his throat and began again. "By week's end all of court shall be ready to depart."

"I will not leave to go make eyes at the French across the border when the princess lies near death."

"Forgive me, Majesty, but none have claimed her illness to be as severe as—" The look on the king's face stopped Daniel. "I only mean to say she will certainly recover . . ."

William watched his friend flounder. Maybe he *was* that bear, to be treated with caution, with little lies to curb his temper. He felt it now. The boiling in his veins. And for the first time in his life, he actually understood—though without sympathy—why his father was the brute everyone remembered. Maybe that hadn't been his father's true nature. Maybe being king brought it out in him. All the fawning people, all the wealth, the power to wound with a look, crush with a word. The constant strain of everyone's expectations. Perhaps he'd simply played into the role until the role consumed him.

William squeezed his eyes shut. He would not become that man. He owed it to his wife, his people, himself.

"Even if she does recover quickly, departing four days from now is much too soon. Besides, shouldn't we wait for Norwick?"

"Countess Cariline of Mounds!" The guard's voice rang out in the room.

"Highness," Cariline said, hurrying in. "I beg your pardon, but the queen sent me right away. The princess is awake."

"We'll continue this later, Cecile," William said, shoving away from the desk. He strode down the stairs, not looking back. "In the meantime, recall Norwick to court. With haste."

As fast as was seemly, William took the short hall that lead to the nursery. He rounded the doorway into her room and there she sat, legs tucked underneath her, head on Anna's chest, beatific smile on her miraculously pale face. He rushed to them, embracing both, careful not to crush his fragile daughter.

"My sweetest girl," he released them so he could get a good look at the princess. "How do you feel?"

"Tired." Her voice was weak, scratchy. "My belly hurts."

He felt her cheek with the back of his hand. "She's not as warm. And the rash is fading."

Anna nodded. "But I worry about her stomach." She turned her head away. "Sometimes there's stomach upset with *scarlatina*. Sometimes not. 'Tis too soon to tell. We've been giving her broth and soft bread . . ." Anna stroked Cate's hair, the curls coiling back into place with each pass.

"Mama," Cate said, dread in her strained voice, "I don't feel good . . ."

Suddenly, her whole body convulsed with a retching sound far too loud for such a small girl. William jumped to intervene, but in one quick movement, Anna had a chamber pot ready with one arm and Cate positioned over it with the other. A flock of nurses rushed to them as Cate gave up her stomach's contents. Once, twice, three times, she heaved, barely able to weep between each bout. Then the pot was taken away and replaced with a fresh one, while Mary wiped Cate's mouth and hands with gentle care.

Cate sniffed and curled up like a snail in Anna's lap.

"If I could only do something . . ." William dragged a hand down his face.

Cate was now staring up at him, hazel eyes huge in their sunken sockets. "Don't worry, Papa."

He raised his brows. "Is that so?"

She nodded, solemn. "The angels told me so."

He laughed and reached for her hand. He could fit three of them in his palm alone. "Well, who can argue with angels?"

She stretched away from Anna and crawled under her bed-clothes. William pulled the sheet taught, folding it across her chest.

"And my brother said so too."

He stopped mid-fold. "Your brother?" He laughed again. "You've a very bright imagination, Catey."

"He came and talked to me. While I was asleep."

William glanced at Anna, whose face had paled. "Did your cousin Frederick come by?" Yet they both knew Margaux and her son were well on their way to Mohrlang.

Cate shook her head. "He was with the angels. He said he tried to come down before, but had to wait."

Anna's hand leapt to her belly. Was she too remembering the little prince who died in her womb? But surely Cate was making up stories . . .

"Sweetling," Anna said, leaning in, whispering. "All this talk of angels and brothers is not proper."

Cate gave a wistful smile. "He said you and Papa will get really mad, and he can't come play with me unless you believe each other."

"What do you mean, Catey?" William had heard of the very ill seeing things that weren't there—not just crying out to loved ones, but believing those loved ones were present. But this?

"Not now, later." She yawned.

"Later what?" William watched as her eyes fluttered.

Anna grabbed his forearm and shook her head. "Don't encourage this."

"My brother. He said he'll come play later. After the battle. Papa needs to believe in Mama." She turned on her side, eyes shut fast as if unconscious of her parents.

Anna rose abruptly. William came around the bed to meet her, guiding her to the window, away from the attendants.

"Who has been telling our daughter tales?" Anna said, worrying her bottom lip.

"She's seeing visions. How else would she know of her brother?" William said.

"I will not believe my daughter's a soothsayer." She shuddered beneath his hands.

"People see visions in Scripture all the time."

"We can tell no one of this. No one, Wills." Her eyes darted about the room.

"I, for one, want to know more of what she saw," he said, thrill in his voice. "What battle, for instance? What does she mean 'believe each other?'"

She gaped at him. "Are you telling me that you, who barely acknowledge the church, are ready to believe the ravings of a fevered three-year-old?"

"When you put it that way . . ."

"You know what people will do to us—to her—if anyone finds out."

The image of Robert's mother being dragged to the stake flashed in William's mind. He had been only eight when it happened, but he could never forget her face. The betrayal, the fear, the desperate longing for her children.

"No one will find out." He shook the picture from his mind. "And if they do, we pronounce it a gift from God."

"People do not need one more reason to think us heretics. Or worse." She searched his face, her eyes full of worry. "Promise me, Wills. No more talk of this, especially to Cate. It was all a fever dream. Nothing more."

But Cate had mentioned a son. A son who had come and

would come again. He didn't care if the messenger was from the dark or the light. The message itself was clear: he would finally have his heir. Yes, it was straw to grasp, but straw was all he had.

He nodded, despite his inner tumult. "I must see to Daniel and council, but do not hesitate to fetch me if her state changes." He kissed her forehead. "I love you both."

And with that, he left his ladies, comforted in the knowledge that Cate would recover.

CHAPTER 3

Of Horses and Men

*A*nna's head ached from all the jostling. She tried to rest against the velvet-padded carriage walls, but inevitably the wheels would hit a rock or pothole. She was exhausted after the sleepless nights of watching over Cate, amplified by the beating sun baking her in this gilded oven. Cate had been blessedly out of bed and chasing the dogs in the gardens before the royal entourage departed, and Anna wished she herself were as buoyant.

Conversation had long since fled, as both her carriage mates were similarly sullen. Yvette and Brigitte stared out the windows, scrunched up against the walls so tightly, their skirts barely touched.

Mercifully, the carriage halted, and the door was wrenched open by none other than the king himself.

"My queen, we've arrived at Cecile's humble abode." He thrust a hand inside for her to grasp. Steadying her as she climbed out, he whispered, "Perhaps while the train unloads you and I might take the shade by one of the lakes?"

"Nothing would please me more." She smiled up at him. "But allow me to change."

He looked her up and down. "Indeed, Madam, for your attire is much too complicated for my intended purposes."

"You amaze me, my liege. You ride all day in the heat and dust, yet you thirst for more sport?" He led her to the bowing horde of servants spread along the courtyard of Daniel's vast Foxhall Castle.

"A thirst that is never quenched, my dear—only restrained for duty's sake." He pressed his lips to her temple, an errant hand sliding up her side. Despite her own sticky skin and throbbing head, her blood quickened with his touch.

"Then I shall not tarry long in my preparations."

Bernard had traveled with them and guided her to her chambers for their brief stay. In allowing Margaux, Jane, and Mary to remain back, she was all the more gladdened by his impeccable service. A fortnight previously, she'd caught him studying the layouts of each castle and manor they would stop at, teasing him for his meticulous preparation. But she was grateful now.

All this reminded her that she must ask William for a permanent nurse for Lady Jane's boy, John. He remained sickly and thin, with a constant dry cough and pasty skin. While Anna wanted Jane to feel as though she could tend to her son, Anna felt Jane's increasing absences, both in service and in friendship. And since the lady was from Cecile, perhaps she would be comfortable with a nurse from here.

But that would come later. As Bernard led her into her charming rooms, she glanced at the bed and remembered who and what was waiting for her.

William let the cool lake water hold his limbs, the small currents arcing around him, arousing his senses, refreshing his mind. This swimming hole was his favorite. Daniel had only come into the property as an adult. Foxhall had been one of William's mother's castles, her August retreat. William and his siblings, plus the Norwicks and Daniel, had spent many a day in this very spot, picnicking under the same giant oaks at the water's edge, trying to dive to the depths of this pocketed cove, jumping from the wide, flat rocks that had seemed like cliffs to his child's mind, but were merely boulders now. He dove again, eyes shocking to the cold, chest clamped in its fight to hold air. He could see the soft sand covered in a layer of green sludge. If he kicked a little more, reached a little farther . . . but it wasn't to be. His burning lungs sent him surging upward, breaking the water's surface with a gasp.

And just in time. Through the trees he spied horses approaching. Anna. His body twitched in expectation. He watched her approach the idyllic scene, blankets, furs, and pillows spread on the sun-dappled grass, baskets overflowing with fruits, meats, wine. She dismounted, a riot of color, deep green and brown, slashed with gold, as if she were part of the very forest, a woodland fairy.

He swam closer to shore but had no intention of getting out. He wanted her to come in.

"You've far too many clothes on, Highness."

He could see her blush from where he bobbed. She glanced at the blankets, spying his discarded attire.

"And you've too little, Highness."

"I will not hesitate to soak you were you stand," he called.

She shook her head, smiling. "If it counts at all, I only have one set of sleeves on."

"It doesn't, but valiant effort nonetheless." He took a mouthful of water and spit it like a fountain. "Send your attendants away and take the water with me."

Not that she needed to say anything, as their servants were used to the privacy the king and queen insisted upon. Brigitte, Yvette, and four guards were already making their way to the encampment he'd set up for his own small entourage, with plenty of victuals and entertainment to keep them all happy.

She walked to the shore, hands on her hips, shaking her head. "You're incorrigible."

"You like me that way." His feet finally touched the lake's silky bottom, and he walked to shore, water rippling down his shoulders, his chest, his thighs. He watched his wife's eyes grow larger the farther he emerged.

"'Tis considered rude to stare," he said, stopping a few feet from her.

She lifted her gaze to meet his and a shot went through him, straight to his groin.

"Are mine eyes not part of my body?"

He raised a brow. He noticed she wore a simple front-lace gown, more appropriate for a merchant girl than for a queen. She loosened the tie at the top.

"And did I not vow, 'with my body I thee worship?'"

He closed the space between them, hooking his fingers through the laces. "You move entirely too slowly." He yanked, drawing her to his bare chest, body throbbing against hers.

"Is that so?" She flung her arm around his neck, pulling his lips to hers, her tongue seeking his, her other hand finding his manhood. He hissed, tried not to bite her lip.

"Dammit, woman." He stopped working on her ties, picked her up by the waist, and tumbled down to the embroidered blanket. She laughed, lightly dragging her fingers up his spine. He took her mouth again, sinking into the pleasure, the anticipation, the ache, and wondered, not for the first time, why the hell they didn't do this more often.

Anna sank into the comfort of the earth, William's fingers combing through the hair at her forehead. She stared at the cloud-dotted sky, wishing she could hold the moment a little longer, all the while feeling duty pressing in.

"What's the matter, my Anna?" William said, resting his chin atop her head. "Methinks we had a lovely time of it. Or two. Or three." She could hear the grin around his words.

"I'm just thinking."

"How many times have I told you that is an unfortunate pastime?"

"You're right." She rolled to her belly, leaning on her elbows, chin on his still-bare chest. "In fact, I was thinking how lovely this was because we were away from all the chaos . . . and that made me think of the chaos."

He grabbed her head with both hands. "Well, stop it then. Swat those buzzing bees of worry away. For this place is holy ground. The holy ground of thoughtless pleasure-making."

"If you insist, my liege."

"Oh I do." He pushed up onto straightened arms. Anna also readjusted, sitting beside him, legs tucked under her skirt like a girl, observing the still, emerald water. "For me, this place is like your meadow in Beaubourg. I came here as a boy with my mother when she wished to fly from court. We would spend weeks here, like now, in late summer and fall. She was never happier. I was never happier." He tipped to her and kissed her cheek. "That is, until I forced you to marry me at sword-point."

She turned, catching his lips. "Thank you for bringing me here. I shall not taint it with my womanly worries."

"You couldn't taint a thing, even if you tried." William again reclined on his arms.

Anna looked at him sidelong. "That's not exactly what you said a fortnight ago."

He waved this away like a bothersome bug. "Oh tush, my dear. You know I don't mean it when I growl and snarl."

She swallowed. She didn't want to ruin their rapport, but if she didn't ask, she wouldn't know. And it would haunt her. That look in his eye the night Cate was sick, that glint of loathing . . .

"'Tis my worry, Wills, that in your growls you hint at the truth."

He sat up fully now, frowned. He considered her for an interminable amount of time, his thick lashes blinking with his breath's slow rhythm.

"Anna . . ." He sighed. "Indeed, you anger me at times. But if you didn't anger me, it would mean you were not the woman I love." She frowned. "If your mind were not so sharp, your passion for our family and our country so deep, there would be nothing at all for us to argue about. Nothing to make my blood boil. If you were some placid, amiable woman . . . or worse, some plotter like Margaux, I wouldn't love you like I do."

"Oh come now, Wills. If you married one of Halforn's girls, or Duven's sister, or Helena of Laureland, you would have a much easier time of it . . . and probably more children."

He lifted her chin with a forefinger. "And I would be bored out of my mind." She looked into the blue depths of his eyes, as serene as the water beside them. "Do I, at times, wish you were more compliant, would think before you speak—especially in public? Of course. But would I make you so and then lose the queen I see before me?" She smiled, shaking her head at him. "Pliability is all fine and good, my love, but it does not make a queen. And it does not become my wife."

She kissed him then, lips and tongues tangling until she left him gasping.

"You're just trying to get under my skirts again, aren't you?"

He laughed, a gut laugh that echoed off the slate slabs enclos-ing the cove.

"Aye. I am always, without a doubt, trying to get under your skirts. But what I said still stands." He pulled her to his chest and lay down again, taking up their earlier position, her head in the crook of his arm, him stroking her hair.

"Speaking of children, Bernard sent word right before I left for the pond." She rubbed her knuckles along his side. "A swift rider delivered a message from the palace. Cate is out of bed today and teaching her toys mathematics. Apparently, it's all Mary and Cariline can do to keep up with her."

The king smiled. "That's my girl. I hated to leave her, but I see now it was the right decision."

"Sometimes Daniel can be right," Anna said.

"Now don't go letting him get an enlarged head."

"He's got Robert to keep from that ever happening." Anna took his free hand and knit their fingers together. "Why does Robert tease him so?"

"Robert doesn't understand him. And he mocks what he doesn't understand."

"Which is why Robert is more suited as jester than as Lord Privy Seal, second only to the king."

William sighed. "Let's not start arguing about Robert again."

"But you just said you liked arguing."

He laughed. "I didn't say I liked it—I said I wouldn't change it. That's quite a difference."

"Touché." She poked his side, and he laughed all the more.

"Though I am concerned that he didn't return to court in time to leave with the train." He clasped his hands behind his head, using them like a pillow. "Didn't even send word. 'Tis strange."

"Do you think him unwell, or dare I detect some niggling of doubt about the motivations of your dear cuz?"

He shook his head. "Nothing like that. He's just . . . been different these past months—distracted almost, jumpy. I catch him staring out the windows in council instead of eyes observing, calculating each man's words and storing them up for God knows what intrigues."

"So you admit he's plotting?"

William rolled his eyes. "Come now, we both know he's always plotting. You think he's plotting to lob off my head, and I know he's plotting to somehow best the Catholics. And while that is worrisome, 'tis nowhere near the regicide you imagine."

She frowned. "You speak of the Catholics as if you were not one."

"There are Catholics, and there are those of us who would worship God in our own fashion."

She sat upright, color draining from her face. "You speak like a heretic!"

"Whoa!" William rose to meet her, holding up his hands. "I do not speak of changing my faith, our country's faith—I speak of politics versus belief. Surely you of all people see the difference."

"Indeed." She took a steadying breath. "But the phraseology you used was frightening, Wills. You sounded like that dogmatic Calvin."

He circled her in his arms, nuzzling her ear. "And how would you know what those heretics sound like, hmm, my queen?"

"If we do not know our enemy, how can we fight them?"

He gave her cheek a peck. "Exactly."

Yvette and Brigitte were finishing Anna's coiffure for supper when Bernard rushed into Anna's borrowed chamber with barely a knock.

"Highness." He did his jig bow with sharp efficiency. "Another message."

A glance at the blue seal told the queen it wasn't from Havenside. Blue was the color of Beaubourg, the color of home. "Bring it here, Bernard." She waved him over, wondering whether it was Bryan or her father who wrote.

Yvette offered her an opener and she popped of the seal, unfolding the short letter, immediately recognizing her father's beloved hand. She scanned the note, her smile growing. "My father is to come with us to the border."

"That's cheering news," Yvette said, placing a last pearl.

"He was in the south trading horses for the king's stables. He will bring the horses to meet us in Madrone for the king to survey."

"Surely an excuse to see you, Majesty." Yvette gave Anna a tight smile. William wasn't the only one troubled by Robert's absence. Anna nodded and turned to her steward.

"Thank you, Bernard. You may have the evening free to enjoy the estate as you please."

"You are most magnanimous, Majesty." He bowed low and scooted out of the room backward, still bent at the waist. If he wasn't so serious about his duties, Anna would have laughed out loud at the sight.

Anna rose and beckoned Yvette to follow her to the tall, thin window alcove. "My lady," Anna said, resting a hand on Yvette's forearm, "you seem more troubled than I would imagine. Is it only Norwick, or is there more?"

Yvette pursed her lips, looked down at her hands. "We are all women, are we not?" She flashed her almost black eyes up to Anna's. "Begging your pardon, Highness, but you as well are no stranger to jealousy. Though yours be wholly unfounded."

Anna snatched back her hand. "And yours is not whispered of every day and all around. Imagine the taunts his wife must live with."

"Do you not think that rips at me? The shame of it?" Yvette's face was stone.

"I didn't mean to scold." Anna shook her head. "I know Robert doesn't care for his wife as the king cares for me, and yet 'tis hard at times for me to have sympathy for a mistress. Even one I count as friend."

"And that is the crux of it." Yvette needlessly smoothed her skirts. "Because he has strayed from his wife, it means he can—and probably will—stray again."

"Certainly he will not take another mistress under his own roof if he does not allow you therein."

"And how do we know he is still at his castle? The king could not get word to or from him before we left. Does that not strike you as curious?"

"You have a point," Anna said. "But surely he is not so stupid or flagrant."

Yvette took Anna's hand and squeezed it. "Thank you, Madam. 'Tis more than I deserve, as you rightly say."

"Oh, Yvette, I think we women deserve quite a bit more than what we get in this world. If you have found love, who am I to judge you?"

"And that's what I can't stand." She turned to the window, frowning out to the horizon as if she could conjure Robert on a steed riding down the slopping hillside. "I'll never have him all to myself. He will always have another mistress. More powerful than a woman to be sure."

"What do you mean?"

"Revenge is his mistress." She snapped her head back to the queen. "Revenge and cunning and politics."

Anna took hold of both Yvette's shoulders, trying to calm her worst fears. "Who does he want revenge from, my lady?"

"Everyone and no one." She shook her head again. "The world."

Anna released her and straightened. "I see."

"Do not take my self-pitying complaints to heart, Majesty. They're just the words of a slighted mistress."

Anna nodded but felt her stomach coil. Surely Yvette didn't mean to hint at danger to the king, yet both the lady and William could be blind to Robert's ways. Yvette's worries of another woman were not of concern. Anna saw the proprietary way Robert looked at Yvette, the way his bored eyes flitted from lady to lady until they fell on Yvette, as his whole body came alert. She'd seen the panic in his eyes when Yvette had gone missing for a day, saw the pain nestled in the corners of his mouth when the two were at odds. No, Robert wouldn't stray from Yvette. But he would certainly stray from the king if it were in his best interests.

"Let us speak of happier things," Yvette said, tone brightening, "like the fact that your courses are eight days late."

Anna froze. Surely not. But with Cate sick and all the packing . . . "I thought they were due to start tomorrow at the earliest."

Yvette took Anna's arm, walking her to the sideboard, whispering, "You must know your ladies track your cycles like hawks, for there is nothing so important to your person as another child."

Anna put a hand to her stomach. She had felt rather off the past day or so, her breasts heavier, tenderer, getting out of bed in the morning harder to do. And hadn't Cate said something about a brother? No, she wouldn't put stock in a child's fevered musings, even if it confirmed her and William's most desperate hope—the realm's most desperate hope. An heir . . . Surely this was ladies' gossip, and her calculations were the correct ones. It was her own body, for heaven's sake. She should know when she was due to bleed again.

She pressed her fingers to her temples. "I would thank you to speak of this to no one, milady. Even if, as you claim, the other ladies have already guessed, we should not jump to conclusions, especially as this prior fortnight has been especially trying."

"As you wish, Majesty."

"Yvette, I mean it." She turned to the woman, staying her with a stare. "I will not raise the king's hopes, the country's hopes, to dash them a week hence."

Yvette curtsied. "You have my word."

"Thank you." At least Margaux wasn't here. A secret this big wouldn't be one she would hold. But Yvette's stock in trade was secrecy. Without it, and surely without Robert, she had not a leg to stand on.

William paced the vast balcony overlooking Cecile's rolling hills, sunset turning their golden tops to pinks and purples. Daniel's castle was more diminutive palace than defensive structure, with low outer walls allowing the upper floor's wrapped balconies providing a view of tidy cypress trees and checkerboard crops. When in Umbria or the hill towns outside Florence, William was always reminded of Cecile. No wonder he'd found reasons to stay in those regions when he'd been in exile. He took up a goblet of summer mead he'd left on the parapet, drank the whole thing down, wiped his mouth on his sleeve, and waited for Daniel. He walked to the far corner, looking south, catching a glimpse of the forest that hid the swimming hole. His body warmed as mead and thoughts of the queen filled him. She was luscious, ravenous. Like their early days. He closed his eyes and pictured her there, naked and laughing and flush and spent. If Daniel didn't hurry . . .

"Majesty." William turned to find his friend in a low bow.

"Daniel, come, pour yourself some drink."

"I hope you have found everything to your satisfaction, and that nothing has ruined the good memories you have of the place." Daniel brought the pitcher out to William, filling the king's cup and splashing a trifling in his own.

"The memories have only been enriched. I'm sorry we are away on the morrow."

"Duty calls." Daniel tipped his glass to William's. "And I'm sure the queen is anxious to reach Madrone and her father, what with her—" Daniel reddened to his ears and coughed. "These Arabian horses Beaubourg brings should be a boon—"

"Out with it," William said, eyeing his friend.

Daniel swallowed. "Out with what?"

"About the queen being anxious." William put his hands on his hips and faced Daniel.

He flitted a hand. "A slip of the tongue."

"Your tongue never slips."

Daniel grimaced into his drink. "'Tis really nothing more than conjecture."

"I will be the judge of that."

"Truly, Majesty, please—"

"Oh, enough with the Majesties and get on with it."

Daniel pursed his lips and shook his head.

"How does the queen seem to you?"

"Jesus, Mary, and the devil to boot, what the hell are you on about?"

Daniel winced, as if William would box him about the ears. "I think she may be with child."

William blinked.

Daniel held up his hands. "'Tis merely a rumor. You know how they are."

"Explain."

"One of the nurses who met with the queen to gain employment for Lady Jane hinted that the queen was in bloom, as it were."

"Hinted how?" William advanced on his friend. "The queen would not have spouted such to a stranger before bringing this news to me."

"That is not for me to say, sire." Daniel shrugged. "If 'tis true the queen spoke out of turn, she must have her reasons."

"Enough of this speculation!" William stormed back into the castle, determined to find the queen's chambers without Daniel's help. He only took two wrong turns before he burst through Anna's shuttered doors to feminine gasps of alarm. Anna was in her night robe, reading at the windows, her ladies in various stages of undress. He ignored them.

Anna's joy-filled face soon fell as he came to her, glaring down, anger and happiness warring within him. How could she not tell him, yet tell another? And if it were true . . . thank Holy God! He leaned in so only she could hear.

"How could you tell a stranger something so . . . intimate?" There was another round of gasps, followed by two stifled male apologies. Daniel and Bernard had entered the fray.

"Whatever are you on about?" Her face scrunched as she patted the window seat beside her.

"I shan't sit." He looked her up and down, trying to divine what a nurse might see, but she looked unchanged to him. Nor had her appetite altered. He rotated his jaw. "Daniel told me you're pregnant and—"

"You can't know that." Her eyes grew huge, her mouth hung open.

"Ah, but I do know that." His voice was raised now. Surely they all heard, but he couldn't help it. Her silence was too wounding. "Thanks to the prattling lips of a nurse you felt at liberty to confide in, it seems the whole kingdom will know before your own husband!"

"Majesty," came Daniel's mumbled protest.

Anna rose, the force of her flashing eyes pushing him to step back.

"Thank you, Cecile, but I believe you've done enough." She brushed past the king. "Here are the actual facts, Your Highness." Even though she addressed him, she clearly spoke to the room. "Some of my ladies calculate that I am late in my courses. By *my* calculation, if I am late, it be by merely a day and 'tis more than likely I be not late at all. It may be the gossip among my ladies that has reached the ears of our ever-fastidious Cecile." She turned her scornful gaze now to Daniel. "Now, for the 'prattling lips' of this strange nurse I can give no light, for nothing of my health other than to toast it was spoken in my interviews."

Daniel's face was red, whether in embarrassment or anger or both, William couldn't tell, but all any of the men in the room could do was gaze at the floor like scolded children.

"Furthermore," Anna strolled to Daniel, head tilted like a curious bird. "It pains me to hear that Cecile would take this idle gossip to Your Majesty without first checking its veracity."

"Be not angry at Cecile, My Lady. In truth I drug it from him," William said, well censured. Daniel bowed his head in silent acknowledgment of his defense.

William came to Anna's side, resting his hand on her shoulder. The velvet of her robe felt soft, and his heart panged. If she was right in this, they remained far from another child.

"And I'm sorry to have accused you." He turned to the room

at large and noticed the ladies were properly covered and huddled in a dutiful pack. "You ladies as well, please accept my apologies for barging in upon your toilets. You serve us both well and should not be mortified in such service."

As one they acquiesced. "Yes, Your Majesty."

Anna rubbed his arm and leaned in. "How could you think for even a moment I would keep such splendid news from you?"

"I so want it to be true." He bowed his head. "I'm sorry for being such a charging bull. I don't know what's wrong with my moods as of late. I seem like a woman, changeable as the winds."

"What a romantic thing to say." She pursed her lips into a smile, and he returned it.

"Ah, so you think you are not as changeable? Must I point out examples? For they are many."

"You are lucky you had your way with me this afternoon, for I do believe I am good and shuttered."

He grinned. "And my point is made complete."

She laughed at this and rose on her toes to kiss his cheek.

"It pains me to interrupt, Majesties," Daniel said, looking anywhere but at the pair, "but there was another matter I wished to speak about, sire."

"By all means, Cecile, speak your peace."

Daniel flicked his eyes to Anna. "The queen's chamber is hardly the place to discuss state craft, begging her pardon."

"Clear the room," William said. He steered Anna to a comfortable chair. While her protestations of pregnancy were valid, there was still a chance, and he would take as much care of her as he could.

"Majesty," Daniel said, "the queen need not be troubled—"

"I am not troubled, Cecile."

"It's merely a tying up loose ends of the day. Surely, sire, we could retire back—" There was pleading in Daniel's eyes, but to shut Anna out now would lose William any ground he'd just gained. Besides, she'd wheedle it out of him later with her feminine wiles.

"I may be retiring right here, so you may out with it." Daniel nodded at this. "You know I have no secrets from the queen." Anna took William's hand and squeezed it, rubbing her thumb over the top of his knuckles.

"'Tis about Norwick." Daniel released his breath, deflated, defeated. He looked only at William when he spoke. "I've had word that Westerville was seen leaving Cheval Castle two days before Norwick was due back at court."

"I hope he was leaving with another knife in his back," William said.

Anna's grip tightened. William mentally damned himself for not taking Daniel's hint. The last thing he needed was another bone for Anna to gnaw on about Robert.

"What of it? What more?"

"I was informed he only stayed a short time, not even an hour. He rode with four men, one entered with him."

"That's it? That's all you have to tell me?" William released Anna's hand and rose. "For God's sake, Daniel, Westerville's tried to visit me and been shown the door. What of it if he's trying to ply his tricks with Robert and had a similar result?"

"If the result were the same, why is Robert not here with court?" Anna stood as well, completing the circle.

"He was detained." William threw up his arms.

"By what, by whom? With no word to his king? This sounds like proof of—" Anna said.

"Proof of what?" He turned from them.

"I'm sorry, Highness," he heard Daniel move closer, close enough to touch him, "but there's more. Within an hour of meeting with Westerville, Robert sent messengers, to each of the lower lords—two of whom returned to Cheval with knights."

Anna came to face William. "Wills, don't you see, don't you finally see his true intentions?"

William wanted to roar, to hit things, to break them. Most of all he wanted his friend, his cousin, at his side making jokes and raising a glass. He looked his trembling wife up and down.

"You're both jumping to very hasty conclusions. All you've told me is Robert's guest list. Perhaps he was fêting his lords on his last night, or—"

"But it wasn't his last night. If it was his last night he would be here, now." Anna's face was white. He wanted to shake her, to stop her from speaking the treasonous conclusions his own mind was coming to. Robert couldn't. He wouldn't. Something must have spooked him . . .

"Highness, I do not know what happened on the battle-field at Laureland, when you were taken, what was said. But Westerville was certainly under the impression at the time—"

"You're right, Daniel," he spun around, "you weren't there, so you would have no impressions. Robert thwarted that son-of-a-bitch and saved my life. He is not planning on taking it now."

"Perhaps it's not your life he wants," Anna said.

William snorted like a warhorse on charge, his mind flicking through scenes of that wretched night. Westerville in that stable, his cocky grin. Saying to William, 'The only other person who knows you're alive is Norwick. And he's not telling.' Bryan crying out before fainting, 'He's not your friend!' Robert's startled, almost disappointed reaction to William's return. His focus returned to Daniel.

"You truly think *Robert* would conspire against me in such a way? And with Westerville?" But he was really asking it of himself. Had Anna been right all along?

"Perhaps Westerville finally gave him the means," Anna said.

Blinking away her comment, he strode to his friend. "Daniel. Look at me. This is Robert we're talking about. Robert. Our cousin. Our blood."

Daniel closed his eyes, exhaled, and gave a slight shake of his head.

"He could just as well be sending the alarm that Westerville is up to no good." William said, convincing himself as he tried to convince the other two. "Surely we will hear more when we cross into Madrone on the morrow."

"But if we're wrong," Anna took William's hand again.

William shook off her hand. "If we don't see this ridiculous flirtation across the border through, there may be no realm for anyone to rule."

Anna faced William. "You always say to me not to pay heed to Robert, that Daniel is the smartest one at court, and here Daniel is, shy of accusing the man himself—"

"I trust him!" He didn't mean to yell. Didn't mean to cause

that look on her face. He closed his eyes, resigned. "I trust Robert." Opening his eyes he saw a tear hovering near the tips of her lashes. His heart sank.

"Daniel, leave us." He waited until footsteps faded and doors closed. Then he rushed to her, taking her face in his hands, wiping away any tear that might fall. He took her mouth, seeking, finding, felt her body slacken and released her, bending his head to look into her eyes.

"Do you not see? That when you try to pit me against him, when you rail against his loyalty no matter what I think, 'tis you who do not trust me? You do not trust that I too worry over my throne and my head and the fate of my family. You think that in the six years of knowing him that you see him better than I, who have known him my whole life."

"Wills, I—"

"You don't think I know that he plots, that he's power hungry, that he hates the pope almost as much as he hates Bartmore for burning his mother—"

"His mother? I-I didn't—"

"And that he spies on us both, weaves his web to be seen in the best light, to catch any fly he can—yes, I know all of this." He moved his hands to her neck. "I know all of this and I still trust him with my life. And yours. Because he knows I would be destroyed if anything were to happen to you, despite his enmity toward you. And I need you to show him the same courtesy. I need you to trust him because I trust him."

She lowered her head, he could almost hear her thinking through those auburn strands.

"If you cannot bring yourself to say you trust him, say you trust me."

She looked up, swallowed. "Unequivocally."

He nodded. "That is enough." Moving his hand to the back of her head, he drew her forehead to his lips. "It is enough, my Anna."

Robert patrolled his study at Cheval, checking the windows on each trip round the room, hoping to see men. Any men but the two lords sitting in his chairs before the fire, contentedly filling themselves with ale and sweetmeats.

"What is taking so damned long?" Robert again strode to the windows. All he saw was the graveled path lit by blazing pillared torches.

Henrich, Earl of Mounds, brushed crumbs off his golden, yet graying, mustache. He was Countess Cariline's husband, fifteen years Robert's senior and holder of an estate on the edge of Robert's duchy. He and his wife had served the last three kings with patience and loyalty. He was mild mannered and had no secrets. Thus, Robert disliked him.

"You know many are away from their estates and lands this time of year. We'll be lucky to have even two more lords and their men at arms," Mounds said.

"'Tis a wild goose chase if you ask me," Lord Bolstad added. He was Robert's distant cousin, skinny as an arrow and as sharp. "Since when do you take to such bold action based on rumors delivered to you by one man—and a traitor at that?" He popped a honey-dipped fig into his mouth.

"So why are you here, Bolstad?" Robert turned on his heel, bearing down.

"When one's duke calls one to arms, one responds. If one likes one's estate. And head."

Mounds covered his chuckle with a well-timed cough.

"So it would not matter why I call you to arms? You'd fight for me regardless?" Robert strolled to the table of refreshments and poured himself a glass.

Bolstad shrugged. "You sent messengers—I came."

"We live to serve, Your Grace," Mounds said.

"That is what I like to hear, gentlemen. We'd better hope the rest of my lords feel the same."

"Nothing like a good excuse to get off the estate to be sure," Bolstad said, surely thinking of his ten children. "Whether it be fool's errand or no."

As Robert let the silence deepen, he could feel the shift in Bolstad's manner. Both men knew Robert was no fool, or at least not someone to trifle with. And the last thing Robert needed right now was fewer men. He would let the remark go.

"Let us indeed hope it only be a summer airing then." He placed his glass on the table. "But I have a feeling the blood of our countrymen will be shed by this time tomorrow."

The sound of many hooves churning gravel reached them.

"Finally," Robert breathed in relief. "It has begun."

The route to southern Madrone and the French border took four days of winding through small, exuberant towns, festooned in welcome to their passing king and queen. Outside each village, Anna would arrange herself on horseback, if she were not already there, and she and the king would ride side by side, smiling, waving, and blessing their people. But other than these staged moments, silence reigned. It was as though a pall had fallen, not only on the royal couple, but on the entire train.

As they neared the southern town of Lesché, Anna's mood lightened, for she would see her father, the Duke of Beaubourg, for the first time in months.

The royal palace at Lesché was rarely used, especially in the summer, as it was smaller and older than all the others, but its keepers had outdone themselves, adorning the place with new gilt and paint, bursting gardens, and a courtyard fountain spouting red wine. By the time the royals arrived, most of their belongings had been unpacked, lending the place a feel of home that Cecile's fine estate had not.

Impatient to get to the stables and see her father and his Arabian horses, Anna sat unceremoniously on the edge of the bubbling fountain. She dipped a finger in and sucked. The oaky, smooth taste of Troixden's famous Madrone curled around her tongue.

She leaned back on her hands as Brigitte, Amelia, and Stefania settled themselves beside her, murmuring their impressions of the palace. Anna saw three men scurry to Daniel, handing him various scrolls, leaning in to whisper accounts. She didn't know her husband's whereabouts, and his absence prevented her from leaping up and snatching the scrolls from

Daniel's hands. She told William she would trust him concerning Robert, but there was a fine line between trusting William's actions and trusting Robert's. As Daniel strode into the palace depths, she fought the urge to follow. She would show William she meant what she'd said. She willed her eyes closed.

"A rather incongruous posture for a queen, hmm?"

Her eyes flew open at the sound of her father's teasing voice. Not even allowing him to bow, she flung her arms around his neck, his chain of office digging into her breastbone.

"Oh, Father, how I've missed you."

He chuckled. "I couldn't tell."

She released him. He kissed her ring, bowed, then tucked her arm under his and strolled to a side arch that led through the gardens to the stables.

"You're buttering me up so I'll show you what I've brought the king."

She smiled. "It does give me some small delight that I shall see them before the king, but not even a thousand splendid horses could delight me more than seeing you."

"You make an old man blush, Daughter, but I've got sorry news for you." Anna's grip tightened on her father's arm. His tone was teasing, but she'd known him to affect such a demeanor when delivering truly bad news, to soften the blow. Was he ill? His beard did seem less full and more gray, his eyes deeper in their sockets. "You will not be the first, as the king has already inspected the horses and is in the stables as we speak."

She laughed her relief. "Well, he has a habit of being the first at most things."

"The advantage of kingship."

From the stables came the horses' neighs and nickers and William's voice, whispering sweet nothings to his new charges. Her eyes needed time to adjust as they entered, but she could see William's sword hilt glinting from the back of the stable. The smell of hay, manure, leather, and sweating beasts put her at ease, reminding her of her own childhood stables, where she'd learned how to care for and ride horses. She also recalled nestling herself atop mounds of fresh hay in empty stables, hiding from duties or punishment, cradling a book of high adventure. She'd never dreamed of the adventurous life she now led, and how constricting it would be.

She turned to the first stall and was met with a snort by a deep brown bay, her black mane curling the width of her neck. She threw her head back, haughty as all, completely unimpressed with the queen standing before her.

"Hello, princess," Anna said, holding out her palm. The horse stamped her feet but edged closer. "That's right, my beauty." The mare snuffed again, then nuzzled into Anna's palm, nostrils flaring, sucking skin. Anna reached out her other hand to stroke the horse's neck. "What a noble one, Father. So nimble yet strong of character and will."

"The same might be said of you, milady." William had silently approached and was leaning against the stall.

Anna gave the horse a final pat. "And I'm willing to bet she also dislikes restraint." The mare neighed as if in agreement. Anna plucked an apple out of a nearby barrel and fed it to the horse.

"Shall you never be restrained then." William took her hand. Hadn't they spent the previous weeks arguing about just that? "These horses are magnificent, Beaubourg." He guided Anna further into the stables, nodding at each specimen. "I will surely take the lot, and any more you can arrange from your tradesmen."

"I'm so glad you approve. The horses are legend and only need to be seen in person to tell the legends are true," her father said, two steps behind them. "Shall I take one in the ring for Your Majesty? They are beautiful to behold in a canter."

"Please," William said, eyes dancing like that of a boy with his first practice sword. "In fact, take the bay the queen was admiring."

"Right away, Majesty." Her father bowed then turned to the stable hands. "Come, let us prepare Sheba."

The men hurried to the first stall, leaving Anna and William well away from the commotion.

"I feel like I need to apologize for something," William said, looking up at the rafters, "but I don't know what it is."

Anna clasped his hands. "'Tis nothing you've done, Wills. Everything is so tense. Even without the question of Robert—"

"Not him again—"

"I'm saying there's much more to worry on. Putting our best foot forward with France without causing England umbrage, leaving Cate behind after she was so ill . . . and what if she starts talking about visions—"

William loosed her hand and slid his up to her cheek. He shook his head. "Cate will be fine. France, England, Robert . . . all will be well, if only I know it is well between us." She bit her lip. "I hate this feeling of distance that has unfurled between us. I don't know if I put it there or we both have a hand in it, but I want it gone, love. If I cannot fix whatever is off-center between us, how do I have any hope of ruling a country?"

She nodded and felt her heart thrumming to the soft clip-clop of hooves exiting the stable.

"I do not know how it got there either, but we shall abolish it. Together. For I loathe it as you do."

Almost before the words left her mouth, his lips were on hers, hard, his body pushing her back into an empty stall. When his hands sought her skirts, she broke away.

"Wills, here? Now? There are men, including my father, mere feet away—" He kissed her again, sucking, a hand finding her bare thigh.

"Then we'll have to be quiet, won't we?" He gave her a devilish grin, but she stopped his next onslaught.

"You think we can mend what's wrong between us by coupling in strange locales?" She gestured to the walls, the hay.

His hand traveled upward, and she stifled a moan. "I think it's a damn good place to start."

William managed to escort the queen out of the stable and into the training field without a smirk. Her face was flush, but other than that, she gave no hint. Guiding her up to the viewing platform, he whispered, "This reminds me of a tour of the library I once gave you."

A smile tugged at her lips. "At least this time, half of court is not present to see if I can keep my composure."

William waved this away. "Come now—we had them all

fooled." He sat her down and grinned. "At least we can pretend we did."

She laughed, and he could feel her relax again. She was right that lovemaking wasn't going to solve their disputes, mend the rift that kept opening between them. For now, he would savor her company and her joy.

"And do you think we fooled them this time?" She nodded to her father and the stable hands, trotting Sheba in a wide circle. He sat beside her, still holding her hand.

"Well, we certainly didn't fool the horses." Her blush deepened. He kissed her knuckles, taking in her smell, mixed with leather and horse and hay.

Beaubourg approached the stand. "Majesties, I will take her through her paces now. Then, if you prefer, you shall mount her and see how she rides."

Anna giggled and turn away, as even William had to look down to regain some semblance of royal dignity. He cleared his throat.

"Thank you, Your Grace, but I've had enough riding today." Anna bit the knuckles of her free hand. Oh, this was too good. "I'm famished from the pounding. For now, I would simply like . . . to watch."

When her father was safely back to the center of the ring, she exhaled. "Wills, I could kill you!" But there was levity in her eyes, and she burst out in contagious laughter.

"Well, would *you* have wanted to go riding after that performance in the stable? Riding a horse, of course. Me, I'm ready to be ri—" She swatted his arm.

"Be still before I can take no more."

"That's not what you said—" She smacked him again and he held up his hands. "I surrender, I surrender! Stop thwacking me."

She leaned over to him. "And that's not what *you* said, either."

It was William's turn to laugh, but Beaubourg's sharp whistle sobered them enough to watch the sight before them. And what a sight it was. The bay circled the field in a wide arc, its tail aloft, tendrils trailing in the wind like a mythical creature. It would be insulting to say the horse galloped, for she verily floated, speeding across the ground like a cloud in a storm.

"Oh," Anna said, eyes wide, as entranced as he was.

One more whistle and the horse halted mid-stride with hardly a grunt.

As Beaubourg approached again, William saw Daniel hustling across the stable yard, a handful of scribes trailing him.

"Your horse has rendered us speechless, Beaubourg," William said, rising to meet the duke above the railing.

"With a fleet of these for our cavalry, people would surely think twice before instigating a fight," Beaubourg said, squinting up at the king.

"We dare think just watching them run would daze our enemies," he said as Daniel reached the rails, bowed, and gave William a look. Thank God he'd had some consoling time with the queen earlier. "I shall ride on this Sheba tomorrow when we inspect the borderlands," William said. "Have our knights ride the rest out. Let's give these changeable French something to talk about."

"Perfect, sire." Beaubourg bowed, then winked at the queen. "Then I must leave you both and prepare."

"We shall see you at supper, Father," Anna called.

William returned to her and helped her rise. Daniel cleared his throat.

"I both see and hear you, Cecile." William took his time walking his wife off the grandstand. "And I cannot say I'm in any hurry to give you an audience."

"I've word from Norwick."

"Right to the chase then, hmm?" William narrowed his eyes, wondering where Daniel's discretion had gone. He didn't want Anna hearing any more wild rumors about Robert's fealty—or lack thereof.

Daniel glanced between king and queen, then seemed to look over Anna's shoulder.

"Excuse me, Madam," Daniel said, making a plucking motion with his fingers. "It's just, there seems to be . . ." He grimaced. The queen brushed off her shoulder, quizzical. "No, in your hair. There's . . ." All of them tensed as he reached forward and stood back holding a short stalk of hay. Anna's cheeks reddened. "My apologies, Majesty."

"I would not fault you for attention to detail," she said, head high.

Daniel rolled the hay between his thumb and forefinger. His eyes widened a fraction and he dropped the hay, wiping his hands together.

"About Norwick . . ." William prompted.

"The news is strange," Daniel said, snapping to attention. "The afternoon before his scheduled departure from Cheval, it was made known to him of a plot by Laureland to seize Palace

Havenside in the court's absence." Anna gasped. "He says it sounded like gossip, but he roused a few dozen men just in case, and heads to the palace to leave his men, doubling the guards, with reinforcements from Ridgeland meeting him there. He plans to arrive here in Madrone in two days' time at the latest, with hard riding the entire way."

"So that's what Westerville wanted," William said.

"Which makes me wonder why Westerville, who is in league with Laureland, would tip off Norwick to such exploits," Daniel said.

"Whether or not he is in league with Laureland is the real question. That man's loyalty is for sale to the highest bidder." William took Anna's arm and started for the castle, the small entourage following. "But I can't see Norwick paying him for the information . . ."

"Perhaps he wanted future reward, should Norwick route the scheme," Anna said.

"Or we're all being played." William stopped in the courtyard next to the drunken fountain and gestured for a glass. "And it seems our dear cuz is ahead of the game." After a quick sip by his taster, the glass was placed in his outstretched hand. "He took necessary precaution, but did not leap into undue alarm. I think we should follow his lead and do the same."

"But if it's true . . . the princess is in danger, not to mention the people who serve us." He could tell Anna was trying to stay calm, focused.

"If I thought for a second Catherine was in danger, we would be away at once, with a call to thousands of men to arms." He rested a hand on her shoulder. "And Norwick would do the same. He loves the princess, and what's more he loves the realm. He would not risk either."

"But even he says he doesn't know the veracity of Westerville's story. If it's true . . ."

"If it is true, Highness," Daniel said, "we would have heard word of movement long before this. Most of the men who fought for Laureland were mercenaries and farmers, a scrabble of barely disciplined men. They couldn't move on the palace without notice. And they would have had to start any move-ment before our own departure. We would have heard—we would have known."

"Yet isn't it the opposite?" Anna said, looking at them is if they were daft. "Farmers traveling for summer markets, hiding weapons under their wares, mercenaries hired along the way, populating the pubs of Havenside, waiting for the court to leave? It would be much easier for that 'scrabble of men' to hide in plain sight. We may think our enemies bumbling, but they would not simply march into town."

William flicked his eyes to Daniel. Her argument was not unreasonable, and worry crept into his veins.

Daniel waved away his stewards and edged closer to the royal pair. "Rest assured, Madam, if there were fresh mercenaries and disgruntled farmers making pilgrimage to Havenside, we would know. I would know."

"You stake the safety of the princess on the scant word of your spies?" Anna's accusation hung in the air, the gurgling of the fountain the only sound.

Daniel's face tightened. "I would never do anything to cause or allow harm to the king's family, least of all to Ca—the princess."

"The queen does not question your loyalty, Daniel," William said. "Nor do I, but I share her concern. Laureland has had three years to stew about their situation. And if they think we are basically abandoned by all our allies, why would they not try something bold, catching us unawares?"

"Because they know it would be a slaughter." Daniel drew closer to them both, his body inches from them. "Let's think of the worst. Say they took the castle. Robert is on his way—"

"With only a handful of men!" Anna had pulled her gold chain from beneath her bodice and fiddled with the rough-cut ruby.

"With Ridgeland's to follow. Word would not only be sent to us, but sent with fleet feet to all corners of the country calling to arms. By the time we would arrive back at the palace, even the blood of the Laurelanders would be cleaned from the stones."

"Not if they have leverage." William turned cold, even in the courtyard's sweltering heat. "Not if they have the princess."

"Blast and damn!" Robert paced the upper floors of the unremarkable inn he and his men had commandeered outside Havenside's walls. He had ordered them all to halt after a young court page was found, horseless and panting.

"Your Grace! Thank God!" The boy's livery was torn, caked

with mud and heaven knew what else. "The palace . . . invaded—you must send men."

Bile rose in Norwick's throat. He dismounted and knelt at the boy's eye level.

"Tell me what happened."

"'Twas the middle of the night. I don't know how they overtook the guards. They herded everyone into the dungeons," the boy said, hands on his knees as he gulped for air. "I think I'm the only one to have escaped, Your Grace."

"Who? What did they want?" Robert scanned the horizon behind the boy as if the enemy line were there, ready to fight.

"I'm sorry, Your Grace—I don't know. I heard the screams and the orders for people to go below. And so I, I fled to find help. One of the dying guards said to find you . . ."

Norwick stroked his goatee, pursed his lips. Even though he'd prepared for this very thing, he hadn't imagined it would actually happen. Westerville was such a braggart, one could hardly take him seriously. But Robert was forced to now.

"And how was it you managed to slip out?" The boy looked at the ground, shifted his weight. "Well, out with it."

"I was in the kitchens . . ."

"Helping yourself to some cakes perchance?" Norwick ruffled the boy's hair.

"Cook said I could have some, I swear!"

"Tell me then—what did you hear? What did you see?"

"I heard screams, like I said, and clanging metal, and orders for everyone to go below to the dungeons." The boy started to shake. Robert retrieved his saddle blanket and covered the boy's shoulders. "I hear 'em coming to the kitchens, and I ran into the garden, hid against the wall. When I couldn't hear 'em no more, I waited some more and stole my way through the stable yard and I saw . . ." His eyes glistened, his face gone pale. He was barely older than Robert's eldest, whom he'd left safe and well fed, dreaming of gallantry, with no thoughts of murdered stable hands and guards left in bloody heaps, fleeing for his own life.

"'Tis all right, my boy. You needn't speak of it." Norwick went to his horse again and took out a hard-crusted loaf and some cheese. He brought the boy to the inn and Davey, as he was called, fell asleep peacefully in Robert's own bed.

Bolstad had since ridden to the city to discover what he could. Luckily, the rebels hadn't yet taken the city walls, but the people were frightened. Bolstad wasn't able to confirm whether or not people were in the dungeons. Worst of all, no one had heard word of Princess Catherine's whereabouts.

"Is Westerville with them?" Norwick asked. Bolstad shrugged his ignorance. "Dammit man, of what use are you? No princess, no Westerville. No idea of numbers even!"

Bolstad was unfazed. It was unsettling. "Do you wish to wait for Ridgeland's men before we try to communicate with the aggressors?"

Robert shook his head. "Have Mounds take his men to reinforce the city walls. When Ridgeland gets here, we'll send more. Go yourself with two men and a white flag to find out what they want, who's claiming leadership." The boy stirred, mumbling in his sleep. Robert lowered his voice. "And find out what in the hell they've done with the princess."

"I'll see to it, Your Grace." Bolstad bowed and left.

Robert returned to the little desk he'd been sitting at before being interrupted. With next to no news, what in God's name could he write to William? Yet write he must. Not only to the king, but to every lord in the immediate region. He would make damn sure that when the king returned, this rebellion was well and put down. For if he were ever to win his own case against the Catholics, ever to turn the king to his side, he must never be connected to this rabble. And until Troixden's Protestants stopped acting like drunken children, Robert had no hope of convincing his cousin to see the light. At least not through diplomacy.

"Blast and damn!" he said again, pounding the table. Laureland's little stunt had set his plans back years.

Chapter 4

Siege

*R*obert's call to arms was heeded by the time Bolstad returned that afternoon. Men from the outskirts of Havenside, and many within, were gathered in the fields behind the inn, practicing their swordcraft as tents popped up like dandelions in spring.

Bolstad found Robert inspecting the horses. "Your Grace." He bowed. "I've much to tell, but we should away from the stables."

Bolstad's tone irked him. He should be the one requesting privacy. But Robert was too impatient to hear word, so he strode to the back of the inn and rounded on the man.

"What news? What of Catherine?"

"There are eighty to one hundred men, Your Grace, and while an army could certainly best them, with the men we have here, plus needing to protect the city wall—"

"And they have the advantage of the protections inherent to the castle . . . Dammit!"

"I fear if we wait for reinforcements, they may take more drastic actions."

"The princess?"

"They claimed to have her, but they would not show her to me, nor would they produce any of her nursemaids."

"So they're either lying, or—" Robert wiped a hand down his face. His gut knotted.

"I don't think she's dead. They'd have no leverage with the king if she were." How could Bolstad speak so calmly about it?

"So they're bluffing, or they have her and are trying to draw us in."

Robert surveyed the gathered men—only eighty or so with Mound's men now at the wall. It would be slaughter if they tried to take the castle outright. And if they waited, there was no telling what would happen, who would be sacrificed. And once the king returned, if these rebels had Cate, what then? If the full force of Troixden's amassed soldiers moved to storm the castle, that beautiful, precocious, sweetling of a girl would lose her life. The king would give up his throne to protect her . . .

"What were their demands?" Robert unconsciously put his hand to his sword hilt.

Bolstad worried the corner of his mouth, sun glinting off the red in his hair like a halo. "She was not very clear about them—"

"Wait, she?"

"Yes. The Earl of Laureland is dead. His daughter, Helena, sits on the throne, self-styling as queen."

"Get my horse! Now!" Five men jumped at Robert's command.

"Do you think that wise, begging Your Grace's pardon?" Bolstad eyed him, wary.

"If anyone in this land knows how to coax a lady," he said as he pushed past the man, "it sure as hell is me."

The palace yard was eerily quiet. Robert noticed about ten men flanking the outer walls, two manning the gates. They hadn't bothered to tidy up. Among the dead he counted three stable hands, eight guards, and a horse, flies buzzing about their bodies. Robert dismounted, leaving the horses with his man, bringing two other men with him.

The rebels guarding the courtyard gate snapped to attention, eyes wide when they saw Robert. One moved to stop him, but a glare put the man back in his place. Some other rebels loitered in the courtyard, gaping at Robert and his men. Amazingly, the Great Hall doors were open, drunken hoots floating out. Striding through as any normal day at court, Robert halted, stunned by the scene.

Men, mostly mercenaries from the looks of them, trolled about, hunting frightened kitchen wenches, smacking serving boys' heads, spilling wine, snoring in corners. The hall was rank with vomit, urine, stale wine. It reminded him of William's father's court, though less clothed and gentile.

A man bolstered by a pillar leered at Robert. "Top of the morning t' Your Grace." He drew out Robert's title, sounding like the snake he surely was.

"'Tis well nigh five o'clock, you drunken fool." Robert grabbed him by his soiled shirt.

"Ssso ye says."

"Where's Helena? Where's Princess Catherine?" The man cackled, his rotted breath making Robert wince. "Tell me, dammit, and I'll let you live."

"You're one t' talk! Ha! I should be killin' yous . . ."

Robert gave him a good shake, sending the man's head lolling. "Your choice is to tell me now or soon see the contents of your intestines." Though Robert and his men had been disarmed at the castle gate, his guard unsheathed a dagger hidden in the back of his trunks.

The drunk considered the matter. He jutted his head at the throne room. "In there, the lot of 'em."

Robert released the man, who fell to the ground with a soft thud. "If you see 'em, tell 'em they still owes me m' pay!"

That was a welcome piece of news. Either Helena didn't have the funds to pay this horde, or she was waiting until she got what she wanted. Probably both. A mercenary wouldn't last long in serving Helena without a jingle in his purse. And Robert, well, he had jingles to spare. Ignoring the curious glances from the rest of Helena's band of killers, Robert strode to the throne room as if it were his rightful place. Which it was. Two guards tried to stop him at the doors, but he jabbed his thumb at the white flag his man carried and continued on his way. He was stopped again by the drastic transformation of the room he knew so well.

Someone had placed large fire urns burning around the throne dais, making it much harder to approach. Two candelabras were lit, and with the sun casting the castle in shadow, the room was dull, funereal. He heard the soft murmurs of men whom he could only assume were behind the dais, as Robert couldn't see them. Helena sat not on the king's throne, but on the queen's, petting a downy, snow-white cat on her lap, its fur marring her black silk mourning costume. It had yellow eyes and looked down upon Robert as if he were a mongrel. But not Helena. In her eyes, he saw fear.

"Lady Helena," Robert smiled, but didn't bow. "This is indeed a surprise." She nodded, eyeing Robert's two guards. Robert chuckled. "Certainly, to see you sitting on the queen's throne, but also to see the disorderly and disrespectful mob of men you have ransacking the hall. I would have thought a religious woman like you would have more, shall we say, honorable men about her."

"Those men got me where I need to be, and I will not have you disparage them." What she lacked in conviction she made up for in volume.

Robert took two steps closer. "Ah, so you've become practical rather than pious since your father's death—my condolences by the way. May he rest well, etcetera." *Wherever he's resting.* "Oh no need to take offense, milady, for I too am a practical man. The only issue at present is that our practicalities be not aligned."

"And you are here to align them?" She looked directly at him for the first time.

"If possible." One more step. He felt like a boy playing halt-and-go. "But first I need to know where Princess Catherine is and how she fares."

She swallowed and looked down at her cat, whose tail waved like a pendulum against her thigh.

"You would think me so cruel as to harm an innocent child?"

"I don't think you cruel." He was almost to the flaming urns. "But those men out there, drunk with beer and victory . . ."

She kept swallowing, her strokes increasing in speed. "I'm sure the little girl be fine." Her voice warbled, and Robert's stomach plunged. She was lying, hiding something . . . if anything had happened to Cate . . .

"Apologies, milady." He fought to keep his voice casual, conversational, "but I must see her highness with my own eyes."

"What," came a male voice from behind the throne, "you don't trust the word of your new queen, Norwick?" Westerville sauntered up the stairs, gloating. He leaned his arm atop the king's throne. Robert wasn't sure what to think. Why would the man tip off Robert about the invasion and then head up the thing himself? It made no sense. Though Westerville rarely made sense.

"Ah, Westerville," Robert said. "We meet again so soon."

"What does he mean so soon?" Helena whispered.

Westerville ignored her. "I always like to have a man right where I want him."

"Interesting," Robert said. "I tend to say that about a woman, but to each his own."

"How dare you insult my—"

Westerville's guffaw cut her off. "Well, you know me, Norwick—always looking out for the best available partner."

Westerville had to know he wouldn't get out of this alive. So what was the man's angle?

"Enough of this, Westerville. Where's the princess?"

"Princess? Oh, she's not a princess any longer."

Robert's skull pounded, quick flashes of auburn curls mixed with blood assaulted him. He wanted to vomit.

"What in the hell did you do to her?"

"Me?" Westerville chuckled. "Why nothing. Like the queen said, the girl is fine. She's just no longer a princess because her papa and mama are no longer king and queen."

"You know as well as I do that simply commandeering the castle and sitting on the throne doesn't mean a damn thing."

"Oh, we'll get Bartmore to comply with a coronation. Just as we'll get an abdication from the king." Westerville's eyes fell on Helena. "Whether 'tis peaceful or not depends entirely upon you."

"I thought you were daft before, but you are categorically insane," Robert said.

"You have insulted my betrothed enough!" Helena said, reaching out a hand to grasp Westerville's. "You will show us the respect we deserve."

"Betrothed?" Robert stumbled back. Westerville and horse-faced Helena? "You can't be."

"Of course we can." Helena sat up taller and squeezed Westerville's hand. "Since I renounce the so-called king, he has no authority over who I can and cannot marry."

"I don't know what poison Westerville has been feeding you," Robert inched forward, flanked by flames to match his own ire, "but you are about sixty-fifth in the line of succession."

"I was brought here by God!" She slammed her fist on the arm of the throne, sending her cat scampering off her lap to slink through the shadows. "It is God who puts me on the throne—no man and no rules of man."

"And yet 'tis the church who sanctions those rules of men." Robert's feet touched the first step. "Hasn't the king been nothing but kind to you? What has happened to that sweet, blushing girl he almost made his queen?"

"That girl has grown, and blushes no longer." Though her face belied this statement. "I've seen my kinsmen struck through by the king who swore to protect us, to let us live and worship in peace."

"The king did everything in his power to stop the war—you know that."

"I know nothing of the sort." She gazed into the flames. "All I know is death and loss and oppression." Silence hung in the air, like a ghost holding its breath. "I had a vision from God. Like Joan of Arc. That I would win the realm for the true religion." She blinked as if coming out of a trance, then looked up to Westerville. "And now, my dearest has helped me to fulfill God's promise."

"Then why the hell am I here," Robert bit off each word with a near growl.

Westerville left his so-called betrothed's side and strolled down the stairs. "Who was it that said history always repeats itself? Was it that dear old Machiavelli or some ancient Greek?

No matter." He came to stand next to Robert. "You're here so we can negotiate."

"About what exactly?" Robert said. "About whether or not my men slaughter all of you now, or I wait for the king's army to do it?"

"You're looking at it all wrong." Westerville snorted. "Lady Helena is merely holding the throne until the new king is installed."

"You?"

He waved this away with another guffaw. "Lord no, I'd never want that job. Too constricting for my taste."

"But, Joseph, you said—" Westerville held up a hand to stop Helena's outburst.

"You are here, Norwick, to finally do what you couldn't on the battlefield." He inched closer to Robert. "To finally have the revenge you've always coveted. You, on the throne, cutting all ties with the pope, making yourself ruler of the Protestant church in Troixden. With all the glory and power that entails."

Robert cocked a brow and swallowed hard. "And what's in it for you, for Lady Helena?"

"Why, what I've always wanted. Money, land. A dukedom. A seat at council—perhaps your old seat." Westerville was inches from him now.

"And what of the king and queen and princess?"

"Stop calling them that," Helena said, with a lack of conviction.

"My dear Norwick," Westerville smiled. "Here you are yet again, in the enviable position of taking the throne away from your cousin, and this time, without having him killed. So what will it be?"

Robert's eyes locked on Westerville's. "Show me the princess."

The man's grin became maniacal. "You would so easily sell your friend and cousin for a simple glance at a little brat?"

Robert curled his fingers around Westerville's jacket, pulling the tall man down to eye level.

"I will not agree to your terms until you show me Catherine—alive."

Anna didn't know whether to scream or wail, hurl something or hurt someone. The news was too much to bear. William's face was stone and even Daniel stood silently, waiting for one of them to speak.

"We leave now," William said, heading for the door of their shared chamber. "The queen will stay and oversee the packing—"

Anna dug her nails into her palms. "Nothing on earth could keep me away from our daughter, not even an order from my king."

William whirled around and seized her. "Anna, if you come with me it will only put you in harm's way. And keeping you safe will distract me from what needs to be done." She bit her lip hard to hold back tears, tasting the metal of her blood.

"With respect, Majesties," Daniel said, "Norwick's report is quite vague. He only says that the castle is taken, but since he has his men and Ridgeland's, everything could be very well in hand."

"And that communication is two days old!" William let go of Anna and whipped around to face Daniel. "For all we know everyone we love and hold dear are already dead."

"More likely they are already victorious." Daniel lifted his hand in a calming motion that only riled Anna more. "This is Norwick we are talking about. Not only is he a master of diplomacy, he is also an expert at strategy and warcraft. He would never endanger the princess's life."

"Norwick does not have the authority to negotiate on the king's behalf," Anna said, smoothing her skirts to keep her hands from trembling.

"But the Laurelanders don't know that," Daniel countered.

"Are you trying to convince us the king should not ride immediately?"

"It could be a trap set by Laureland to lure him, to capture him. Westerville has done such before." Daniel seemed like a mournful hound begging its master not to leave the fireside.

"I have over seventy knights and guards, not to mention lords with fighting experience, surrounding me as we speak." William eyed him incredulously. "How exactly do you think I will be at risk?"

"Because you will want to negotiate with them face to face." Daniel's rarely seen frustration was manifest. "Because you will ignore wise counsel to not go inside the palace, because you—"

"Are you calling me an imbecile?"

"I am calling you a devoted father!" Both men's faces were flushed as they stared each other down. New terror gripped Anna's heart. Daniel was right. William would do anything, even abandon the throne, forfeit his own life, to protect

Catherine. They would bring him to his knees and use their daughter to do it.

"You're right, Cecile. I am a father." William's voice was lower, but not calmer. "And I will not stand here a moment longer and risk the life of my child on conjecture. The surest way of knowing the truth is seeing it with mine own eyes."

He again made to leave, but Anna grabbed his arm. "I'm coming with you."

"You're staying." He tried to shake her free, but she wouldn't relent.

"You just said we have seventy men and more for protection. I won't do anything rash or get in anyone's way."

He turned to her. "I couldn't live with myself if something happened to you. It's just too dangerous, too distracting for me."

"And I couldn't live with myself if I wasn't there to hold my child after this trauma, if I were not there to be the first arms she came to." She cupped his face with her hand, feeling his rough stubble, imploring his stormy eyes. "You cannot keep me from my child. And from my husband's side."

He inhaled deeply and bowed his head. "Only if you promise to do as I command. In this, I am not merely your king—I am also your general. Do you understand?"

She kissed him quick and hard. "Thank you, Wills," she whispered, "you won't regret this."

"I hope to God I won't." He released her and strode through the door, Daniel in his wake, scowling. "Be ready to ride in half-hour's time. We ride through the night."

Anna ripped at her stays and ordered her shocked ladies to find her hunting costume. Thank the Lord for the new horses her father had brought. The king and his company would need all the speed they could get.

Be brave, my sweet girl. Mama and Papa are coming for you.

Robert knew William was coming. It didn't matter that he'd had no word. The king would ride harder and faster than any messenger. Robert had little time.

He was back in his own palace chambers and hadn't seen Westerville and Helena since his audience with them the day prior. They ignored his request to see Cate, but he was able to sneak around the palace and had visited the dungeons. No princess. And none of her nurses either.

The other prisoners called to him, overjoyed to see a familiar face, begging for food, fresh rushes, buckets of human waste to be emptied. He promised he would do what he could, but he wasn't sure what pull he had with their captors. He knew the deplorable conditions would horrify Helena, and Westerville wouldn't give two figs. If he were to help these people, and for his larger plan to succeed, he needed to get Helena alone.

The scene in the Great Hall was subdued compared to the previous day. Most likely people were sleeping off their drink—some had even taken to the benches at the long tables to do so. The foul smell, however, remained. Robert winced as he strode through, heading to the throne room. Finding it empty, he snuck up the stairs to the royal apartments and heard humming from the queen's chamber. The real question was, did Helena truly believe she was queen, or was Westerville creating a part for her to play?

Hoping to God she was alone, Robert crept down the hall. The queen's chamber doors were open, with only one barely conscious guard defending the woman. Robert slipped by him and silently crossed the threshold, peeking through the arches at the self-styled queen. She held one of Annelore's gown's to her body and twisted side to side, her eyes fixed on the mirror. But she didn't smile. As much as she looked a girl pretending to be a princess, the joy of such imaginings registered nowhere on her person. If his recollections were correct, it was the same gown Annelore had worn at the Festival of Harvest months after becoming queen. It was the color of wheat, with moss green velvet and fur at the cuffs. He remembered thinking the gold made her complexion sallow, the ensemble itself too thematic, as if she were dressed for a part in a masque, mocking the whole tradition. Robert crept to the final pillar.

Helena stopped humming and sighed. She reached over to the queen's toilette and grabbed a pair of gold sewing scissors. The humming began again, but this time sounded forced, louder. Taking the scissors, she cut through the intricate embroidery at the dress's neckline. She lifted the dress again by hoisting up her breasts, giving herself a critical eye.

"Whore," she whispered, her face contorted, cheeks blotched. "You little *whore*! That's how you won him. You lifted your skirts and shoved your chest in his face. You let him pant like a dog for meat, drooling all over your nakedness, while you both yelped in sick pleasure."

She spat at her reflection in the mirror, but whether she spoke of the queen or herself, Robert couldn't tell.

"You don't deserve him—you deserve the fires of hell!" Suddenly, she ripped the dress down the bodice with a primordial scream, thrashing her head as if she were in pain.

Frozen, Robert was unsure whether to slip out or make his presence known. When she finished mutilating the dress, she fell in a heap to the floor, weeping. Robert tiptoed backward toward the door, unseen by Helena. The guard, now fully awake, gave him a wild look, one that either said "How in the hell did you get here?" or "What in the hell is that woman on about?" Whichever it was, the guard made no move to stop Robert.

As much as Robert wanted to flee the scene, he knew this was the best chance of winning his cause. He took a steadying breath and pounded on the door.

"Knock, knock!" he called in his most convivial voice and strode in. He heard her sniff amid a rustle of fabric.

"Your Grace, I—"

Seeing her clutching at the strips of the queen's gown, he hurried to her, face all concern.

"My lady, whatever is the matter?" Her reddened eyes darted about. "Come, come—sit. This whole thing must be so trying for you."

She nodded, still in a daze. "Yes, trying, very trying."

He situated her on a tufted chaise, gently pulling the gold silks from her hands. "What can I do? How can I help you?"

Her faced mottled, her brows furrowed. "You will help me wrest this realm from the hands of those Catholic sinners." She grabbed his hands. "I know you sympathize with our cause. Don't you see? I don't care about being queen. Queens are just painted whores. But you, you could be king. And you could make it so, just by your word!"

He stroked her hand and smiled. "But you are a wise woman. You know 'tis not that simple."

"Oh, but it can be." She squeezed his fingers. "You just proclaim it so, and it will be so."

"But I must overthrow the king first."

She chortled. "'Tis a trifle! He'll do whatever you say when you have his daughter."

"And when he gets his daughter back?" Her grip tightened and Robert fought not to gasp.

"He won't get her back. That's just it. You keep promising and promising, but don't give her back, no, no."

"Is that what you and Westerville are doing now?"

"Wouldn't you?" She loosed his hands, folding her own on her lap.

"But I've already told you I would do what you ask if you simply show me the pri—the child."

She made a dismissive gesture. "She is quite safe and happy, milord."

Robert winced inwardly at her demotion of his title. He needed her respect, her devotion. He needed to wrest her from Westerville. He picked up her hand, kissing her knuckles.

"I know you would never, even in your wildest imaginings, harm a child. You are too good, too virtuous and God fearing a woman." She let him pull her hand to his chest. "But I have to admit, I worry about Westerville. In the past, he has been known to do rash things. Cruel things."

"Oh, my betrothed would never go against my wishes." She snatched her hand back but stared at it, blushing.

Robert turned his face to the window. The sun blazed down upon the stables, and he saw a flash of blue livery and blonde hair duck behind the stable's shadow. One of Ridgeland's men? Blue . . . *Focus, dammit!*

"I shouldn't be telling you this," he said.

"Telling me what?" She bent toward him. He could feel her looking his face over.

He turned, catching her right in her muddy eyes. "But I would hate for your innocent heart to be deceived." He sensed her quickening breath, saw her bosom flush.

"Your betrothed shamelessly chased my happily married sis-ter about court last winter. Some say . . . no. I can't it. 'Tis too horrid."

"You must tell me!" Her face was so close. He closed his eyes.

"I'm sorry, Madam. You should not be subject to salacious court gossip."

When he opened his eyes, hers were wide, her lips moist. He knew what that look meant. But if he took her in his arms, he would turn himself into a sinful adulterer in her eyes. No, he needed to be the confidant, the one looking out for her best interests. He licked his lips and sat back, breaking the spell he'd cast on her.

"When last he was at court, he was with my sister." Robert shook his head.

Her face turned stony as she rose. "I will take this under advisement," she said. "I thank you for your visit, but now you must leave."

"I'm sorry if I upset you, but I implore you—be on your guard. You don't need him to get what you want, but he certainly needs you." Robert stood and bowed low. "If we are, as you say, to bring the realm joyously into reform, I will need your knowledge on how to keep us a sovereign nation, and not simply swallowed up by other Protestant states."

"Indeed, Your Grace." She stepped over the pile that had been a royal gown and offered Robert her hand. "You may kiss my hand to show your fealty."

He took it, mouth hovering over her fingers. "All I ask is that I see my little cousin, make sure Westerville hasn't disobeyed your orders and intentions."

"By all means." She smiled. "You shall go straightaway to the nursery and find her there, plump and happy."

He kissed her hand, lingering, flicked his tongue on her knuckle. Not enough to be lewd, but enough to make her flush again. And with that farewell, he went to find Cate.

Robert couldn't help but be proud of his performance. While he had a minor twinge of guilt at manipulating an obvious lunatic, that guilt was appeased by knowing that Helena committed treason and put him, his cause, his friend, and his little cousin in danger. Whistling as he went, he played the different scenarios in his mind. Certainly he could contrive some excuse to seize the throne, rally his men to his cause and do away with Westerville, but that still left the problem of William. Though the king had muttered about taking the queen and princess to some remote estate, maybe back to Beaubourg, and living out the rest of his days in peace and quiet, Robert knew William wouldn't simply prance away with a toast to King Robert. If Wills was anything, he was doggedly loyal to Troixden. As little heed as he paid to God, he felt it was He who put the crown on his head, He who charged William with defending, tending, and keeping the peace.

Yet was it completely out of the question that he would cede the throne? If Robert made clear he was only pretending to be king to keep Cate safe, and once William had a taste for freedom, would he relent? William had once said he didn't trust Robert to rule. But if he saw Robert in action? *Oh, come off it. Stick to the task. The end is not me on the throne, the end is breaking with Rome.*

"Why, Norwick!" Westerville, lounging in an overstuffed chair in the middle of the hall, grinned at him. "Whatever brings you to this part of the palace?"

Two mercenaries stood outside Cate's door with three more, armed to the teeth, surrounding Westerville.

"Just here so you hold up your end of the bargain. Producing the princess. Unharmed." The guards outside her door shifted, stiffened.

"She is indisposed at the moment." Westerville picked at his fingernails.

"Lady Helena says you don't have her." Robert kept his eyes on those guards. If anyone would accidentally reveal the truth, it was them.

Westerville laughed. "And she probably also gave you the keys to the dungeon cells."

"We had quite a . . . cozy conversation, she and I."

Westerville's smile faded. "Isn't that nice for you both?" He crossed a foot over his knee and went back to inspecting his nails. "I find it interesting she would have anything to say about the princess—or should we call her the lady—as Queen Helena has not laid eyes on the girl. I personally saw to Catherine's protection, as well as the comfort of her nurses."

"Enough games, Westerville—just let me see *the lady* and you get what you want. I'll even see you ease yourself gracefully out of your obviously unwanted betrothal."

"And why would I want out of such a match?"

"Because she's barely gentry. And you aspire to, shall we say, nobler pursuits?"

Westerville clapped his hands. "Bravo, Norwick. Why, you are full of favors. I wonder why."

Robert rolled his eyes and made to shoulder past Westerville's guards but was grabbed by the back of his jacket.

"Not so fast, my friend." Westerville stood and faced him.

"The only reason you will not show her to me is that you do not have her or you have harmed her." Despite being restrained, Robert was in the man's face. "Either of those circumstances means my men, and half of Troixden, descend on this place and rip you to mincemeat."

"Would you really like to see what happens when you test

that theory?" Westerville signaled to the guard at her door. The man swallowed, then pounded twice. A young girl's shrill cry pierced the air, turning Robert's blood cold.

"Goddammit, Westerville, if you hurt her—"

"You listen to me now, Norwick." He jabbed a beefy finger in Robert's chest. "If you simply do what you're told, the girl will come to no harm. But if you don't stop your trickery, your manipulation, it will be you—by your actions, not mine—who turns her to mincemeat." He looked to the guards holding Robert. "I believe His Grace could use some air."

They led him away, back down the hall and the stairs, and eventually tossed him into the courtyard. What on earth could he do now? They had Catherine. Which meant they had everything. Anxious and annoyed in equal parts, Robert wandered to the stable yards. He should ride out and check on his men, see how many more had come, what kind of shape they were in to form an attack.

The stable guard was snoring on a bench, a half mug of beer dangling from his hand. At least he wouldn't have to make up some story about why he wanted a horse. Robert entered and walked slowly, searching for his own horse, covering his nose at the stench. The least these people could do is release the stable hands long enough to care for the beasts. What a gang of idiots. About halfway into the stable he heard a soft but distinct whistle from the stall behind him and to his left.

"Who's there?" Robert spun around.

"Your Grace, thank God!" A blonde head popped over the stall. Robert fought the urge to roll his eyes. Not this knave again.

"Why, Sir Bryan, to whatever devil do I owe this meeting?"

Bryan scrambled out of the stall, wiping hay from his blue and white livery. So this was whom he'd seen from the queen's chambers. Sir Bryan the bumbler.

"I came right when I heard the castle was taken. I was in Kilburn and—"

"With all due respect, sir," Robert held up his hand, "the last thing we need right now is a knight with a vaulted sense of valor and a permanently injured fighting arm."

"I'm not here to fight." His unspoiled face was full of wounded pride.

"Then what on earth are you here for?" Robert turned away from him, continuing his search for his steed.

"I know where the princess is."

William was as good as his promise. They had ridden hard, with him at the front of the train of knights, Anna in the back surrounded by men at arms. But even with the fleet of Arabians, the horses and the men needed rest if they were to stay in fighting shape. They stopped well after dark a mere half-day's ride from Havenside and made a meager camp—only one tent for her and the king, and everyone eating what they had in their saddlebags.

The going had been rough. Madrone's wide southern plains and soft hills narrowed to rocky crags filled with switchbacks one-horse wide. Going around would've made for an easier ride, but added more time to their journey. At least the crags provided some shadowed relief from the unrelenting sun.

Anna's mind kept jumping between worry for Cate and worry about what the French would think of their hasty departure. Having Daniel stay back and be his diplomatic self would help, but she couldn't shake the feeling that the Medici queen and her puppet son would somehow use the situation to their advantage. Finally laying her weary bones on a pallet in their tent, she pulled her cloak closer around her. They had stopped to camp on a high, exposed meadow, wind whipping around them. Her lips were chapped, her cheeks burned, and every inch of her was sore. William was out conferring with someone or another about strategy for the morning, but she had neither the strength nor the heart to demand to be part of the conversation. She laid her head down on a rolled-up saddle blanket and tried to rest. But sleep wouldn't come. Not without knowing where her daughter was or whether she was in some state of pain and fear.

The tent door flapped open and William entered, face sun-scarred and stoic. He pulled a leather-belly flask from a bag and took long gulps. He heaved a great sigh and crouched beside her. With one hand he stroked her hair, with the other he offered her a drink.

"It will help you sleep, love."

"Having our daughter back will help me sleep." But she accepted what he offered, taking tentative sips of the strong, bitter liquid. She could feel its warmth spreading from her belly to her chest. She drank more, desperate for the oblivion of sleep.

William kicked off his boots and climbed behind her, pulling her close to his chest, nestling in. He kissed her on the tender spot right behind her ear. "They will not have harmed her.

I'm sure of it." She winced. "There is nothing to prevent their wholesale slaughter if they do anything to harm her. She's their only advantage."

"That's exactly what I'm afraid of, Wills." She could feel the liquid working on her body, slowing her mind and speech. "She's not some pawn in a game, a piece to be played."

"As you and God are witnesses, my queen, our daughter shall not be endangered." He smoothed her hair and rested his chin on her shoulder, his overgrown stubble rubbing her cheek. "I would give up the throne first."

Though her heart leapt in protest at this declaration, the potion stemmed her response and she fell into a hard, blackened sleep.

Robert managed to ride out of the palace stables, Bryan at his side, with nothing but a nod and confident smile for the half-drunk mercenaries at the gate. It was well after midnight, but he was sure his lords would be waiting for him.

The inn where all had gathered was ablaze in light and activity. When he entered, a collective hoot and hooray went up, with much backslapping and mug clanking. The young messenger boy ran to him, offering an ale. He ruffled the boy's hair and took the drink.

"Ridgeland, Mounds, Bolstad—come upstairs with me, would you please?"

The three men and Bryan followed Robert back to the

cramped room he hadn't seen in two days. He motioned for Bryan to shut the door.

"Sir Bryan, tell these men what you told me." Robert sat, threw his feet up on the writing desk, and steepled his fingers.

Bryan made a quick head bow and began. "I've just come from Kilburn. It seems Mistress Mary and the Countess Cariline felt it would do the princess good, after recovering from her illness, to get some fresh northern air, and set about to take the princess to her grandfather in Beaubourg, along with Lady Jane and her boy. They had not written to tell him of this visit, wishing it to be a surprise. When they arrived, they found the duke was gone on business south. Not wanting to trouble the servants longer, they stayed a night and set out to return to the palace. They stopped at Kilburn for the next night. That is where I found them safe, sound, and with no news of what had taken place at Havenside. I told them to hasten back to Beaubourg, telling no one of their destination. I sent word to my wife and brother to call together the Beaubourg castle guards, who surely now have the princess encased in the utmost security and none the worse for wear." Bryan finished, breathless, and sat on Robert's bed.

The men gaped. Then all eyes turned to Robert.

"Which of course means, my friends, we've nothing to keep us from charging the castle and stringing up every last one of those bastards."

"For God and for Troixden!" Ridgeland called.

"Our goal is for as few of our men to fall as possible. We don't want to come at them screaming. We do this by stealth."

In the next hour, the men hammered out their plan, and if all went accordingly, Robert would welcome the king home to a palace as good as new, to sit on the freshly fluffed throne. The thought gave him only a pause before he fell into a peaceful sleep.

The riders arose before dawn. As much as William hated to wake Anna, and frankly himself, he couldn't help the urgency to be home. So they woke and readied themselves for the final few miles. Soft murmurings of road-weary men floated about the camp, clouds of breath streamed from horse nostrils, leather straps squeaked. The fast approach of hooves from the north broke through the tension and a dozen men unsheathed their swords.

"I come in the name of the Duke of Norwick for the king!" the rider called. "I've an urgent message from the palace."

William removed his gloves and retrieved the note from the now dismounted and kneeling messenger.

> *HRH,*
>
> *We attack at dawn under cover. Though we have many men and they only eighty or so, we wish no casualties of the palace staff and fear these mercenaries would simply slaughter those in their custody if they caught wind of our intention. If need be, we will form a full assault.*
>
> *But be of good heart: I have it on true authority that the princess is right now safely in Beaubourg, surrounded*

by her grandfather's guards and none the wiser to the siege. 'Tis a long tale, but Catherine is well and truly safe and has not been in danger at any point during these ghastly proceedings. Our men encamp at the inn on the northwest side of the city wall. The wall remains open with the help of fresh men.

By the time you read this, we will have already begun our attack. If our goal is accomplished, you will see our griffin standard flying high once again. If there is none, guide your forces to the meadow by the inn, where we will start anew.

Wishing you quick return.

Yours ever faithful and true, my dear friend and liege, Norwick

"Where's the queen?" William called, turning. He had sent her again to the end of the train, farthest from harm's way. "The queen!" went mimicking calls down the line. Not bothering with protocol, he ran down the long line of mounted men, Robert's news flapping in his fist. He finally found her, encircled by men, warming her hands around a metal mug. Seeing the look on his face, the paper in his hand, she dropped the drink, steaming liquid spilling at her feet.

He crushed her against his chest. "It's all right, my love." She started to shake in his arms. "Anna, dearest, she's safe. They don't have her. She's safe."

"What? How can . . ." she reared back, unbelieving.

"I just got word from Robert. She's been in Beaubourg this entire time."

He felt her knees begin to buckle, but he held her fast. Her hands found her rosary beads under her riding cloak.

"Thank you, thank you, Lord."

He hugged her again, kissing the crown of her head. "Robert is already laying siege to the castle—he may even be finished by the time we return." She crossed herself.

"Now," he said, touching their foreheads together, "let us ride not in fear but in confidence of swift victory." She nodded, making his head nod too. "I hope this finally redeems our fair cousin in your eyes, my dear. For 'tis he who routes these rebels, not leads them."

She inhaled, holding her breath for a moment. "I am fully ready to apologize for misjudging his motivations in this case."

"And you will give him proper lauding in victory?" The edge of his mouth twitched as he goaded her. Her eyes were sly as she looked at him through her lashes.

"I will give your fair cousin all hail he deserves, my liege." He could almost hear her mind add *in public.*

A thin, dull yellow line pierced the horizon as Robert crept along the castle walls near the kitchens. When Piedmont Cathedral's bell tolled six, each group of ten men would stream into the palace at various points of lazily guarded entry. The rebels at the gate had been easy to subdue, thanks to Bryan's special brew, sold to them the previous evening by an enterprising blonde, blue-eyed merchant.

Mounds was set to recapture the dungeon, while the rest of

the groups were to herd the rebels into the Great Hall. If they resisted, they were to be slain on the spot.

The aroma of baking bread wafted through the open windows, which didn't help the state of Robert's anxious stomach. *Dong!* The first toll echoed off the palace walls, shaking his bones. He gripped his dagger hilt and held up his hand to stay the men pressed beside him against the wall. Four more tolls. He sucked in his breath and in time with the final toll, unsheathed his weapon and flung himself into the bakery's warmth, his men following quickly and silently.

A wrinkled woman, elbow deep in dough, yelped but held her tongue as Robert put his finger to his mouth. Only three other women were working, all wide eyed and trembling at the intrusion. The old woman jerked her head to the rear and left, indicating the hall. Robert could see the back of a gigantic bald man.

Robert pointed at his tallest man, gestured at the guard, then made a slashing motion across his neck. The man nodded, and without pause, snuck behind the giant and slit his throat. The bald man fell to his knees, gurgling and spewing blood. The women screamed.

So much for stealth. He divided his men down the two hallways that exited the kitchen, as he took the one the convulsing rebel lay dying in. He heard faint footfalls, echoing calls of alarm as those ensconced in the palace became aware of the assault. At the top of the stairway ahead, a woman screamed.

"Come any closer and I kill her," a gravel voice said. Another male voice answered, but Robert couldn't make out the words. Then the first man said, "I'm not going anywhere with you chits." Robert tiptoed up the round staircase, clasping his mail to his body to keep it from swinging. He heard scuffling feet and the woman yip. At the final turn, Robert could see the man's head and shoulders, his back to the stairs. "I said back off!" The man retreated to the top of the stairwell, wrangling his hostage. Robert bound up the stairs, dagger ready to bleed the man's kidney, but the man twisted around, revealing a girl no older than ten, mouth covered by a massive, hairy hand, cheeks slick with tears. Robert was inches away from gutting the girl through.

"Not so hasty now, are we?" the man said as he sized up Robert. He held a small pistol to the girl's temple. "Do ye take us for imbeciles? As if we wouldn't be ready for some trickery? Not one of these men sleeps without one eye open." He briefly removed the gun from her head and waved the firearm about, as if to indicate the rest of his ilk.

Get him talking. Keep the gun away from the girl. "So why have we already captured and killed half your men?" Robert said.

The man laughed, again pressing the barrel against the girl. "You've done none-such."

"Really? Look about you. Listen. What do you hear?" Robert inched closer. "Running. Screams—male screams. Screams of panic and surprise and death."

The man sneered, his grip tightening on the pistol handle. "Cowards."

"And what do you call a man who uses a mere girl as a shield?" Robert could tell the man felt cornered, must have realized he had no escape. If he killed the girl, they would kill him, and if he released the girl, they would kill him. The longer his men spent with this one rebel, the slower and bloodier the rest of the siege. Robert cursed himself for not bringing his own pistol, but such weapons were too loud for a surprise attack. Besides, Robert preferred steel.

"I'd call that a man of business," the man said, as if trying to haggle a better price for apples.

Robert lolled his head with an exaggerated sigh. "Fine. Go."

"What?" Disbelief contorted the man's dirty face.

"You're wasting our time. One mercenary slipping through our fingers is certainly not worth losing ground over." Robert gestured to the stairwell with his dagger. "Go on now."

The man, dragging the girl, relaxed his grip on the gun, shuffling in the direction of the stairs.

"Get out of my—" Robert's command was cut off by a great howl from the man, who doubled over, dropping gun and girl in the process, landing on the floor curling into himself. The girl ran down stairs to safety. Robert looked for blood. A couple of the men started to laugh. "She knocked her elbow where it counts," someone said.

Robert allowed himself a small grin. "Bradley, put him out of his misery."

"With pleasure, Your Grace."

Robert and the rest of his men continued to the Great Hall, the death yell of the hostage taker following in their wake. They checked room after room, finding no one, as shouting from the Great Hall increased. He entered the controlled chaos through the corner by the chapel. The balcony was lined with archers, bows at the ready, arrows pointed down into the sunken floor. Tables and benches were overturned, and Robert's men surrounded groups of rebels in various stages of undress. A scattering of bodies littered the floor. He counted two from Ridgeland, one of Bolstad's. The rest were rebels. Handfuls of shaking, crying women, also in various stages of undress, were sprinkled throughout. A quick survey didn't reveal Helena. Or Westerville.

"Where's Lady Helena?" he asked the room at large.

Bolstad stepped forward. "She is holed up in the chapel, Your Grace. Claiming sanctuary."

"Now isn't that just perfect?" No wonder three of his men guarded the chapel doors. He'd thought it was to keep people out. Apparently it was to keep Helena in.

"I will see to her myself. In the meantime," he raised his voice, "let all these poor women go. Bolstad, check on Mounds in the dungeon. Let our people out, but make sure they avoid the Hall until we've taken care of this lot. Bradley, Bryan—take ten men and find Westerville. Dead or alive."

Robert sauntered to the chapel and down the short, intricately tiled aisle, each of his footfalls heavy and distinct. Helena was kneeling, plastered against the golden altar, her eyes crazed as she followed his progress.

Robert clucked his tongue. "My lady. If only you'd listened to me and surrendered yourself and the princess when you had the chance."

"You said you would be king—you said you would save me." Her voice was high and strained.

"I said you had to give me the princess first." He reached the altar rail and leaned against it.

"We never had her! I swear it—I would never have hurt her!"

"It's too late for confessions now, milady." Robert shook his head. Her arms were stretched out, imitating the Christ hanging high above, her hands clutching the carvings, one palming what looked to be some sainted friar's head. "What are we going to do now? I told you not to trust Westerville, and look where his scheming has gotten you."

"I claim sanctuary." She gripped the golden monk's head harder. Robert crossed his arms over his chest and sat on the rail.

"Helena. May I call you Helena?" She didn't respond, just trembled. "First of all, you cannot claim sanctuary against the king in his own palace—"

"But this is still holy—"

"And second, a woman who claims to be as pious as you, so fervent in her Protestant beliefs, would not use papish laws to protect herself, now would she?"

"You can't let them kill me!" She released the altar, clasping her hands together. "I didn't mean—"

He held up his hand. "You will come to no harm from my men. But you can't stay in the chapel. You must know that."

"The priest will care for me until I am absolved of all fault." She seemed to think this was as obvious as the air.

"You may either come with me now and be situated as befits your station in Stone Yard, or you may wait until the king arrives. Though if you ask me, 'tis the queen you should worry about." He inspected his boots. "Nothing like the fear of a mother for her child to rile one into a frenzy."

"But I am a woman. The queen would never—"

"The queen would kill you herself with her bare hands given the opportunity, milady." He stopped pretending disinterest and bore his eyes into hers. "What is it to be, Helena—the Yard now, or the queen by sundown?"

She swallowed, then smoothed her crimson skirts once, twice, three times, and staggered to her feet.

"That's better." He offered her his arm. She was hideous, treasonous, and insane, but he still pitied her. When they'd gone a little way down the aisle, she stopped and looked at him.

"Where is Luther?"

"Is that some code I'm supposed to understand?" Was she now threatening him with her own accusations of treason?

"My cat, Luther." Tears gathered in her eyes and Robert breathed his relief. "Do you know what has happened to him?"

He nudged her on. "I can assure you of one thing. Wherever he is, 'tis a far better place than where you're headed."

Sending her off with guards to the Yard, Robert returned to the Great Hall to find Bryan rushing in.

"He's gone," the knight said. "But he can't be far."

"Goddamn!" Robert reined in his desire to punch something. "Go after him, take more men, and spread out! Then bring that bastard to me."

High atop Palace Havenside, the golden griffin undulated in the wind, as if ready to take flight. The siege was already won. William pulled his horse to a stop, beckoning a few of his knights forward, shielding his eyes from the noonday sun.

"Let us take twenty men to the palace. The rest and the queen shall continue to the inn. Once we've made sure everything is in order, we can send for them." The men bowed their agreement, and William rode to the back of the line to find Annelore squinting up at the flag.

"Then 'tis finished?" she said.

"So it seems. I will ride in with some men to see where we stand and send for you once I know the palace is secure."

"I want to come with you." She twisted in her saddle, a frown on her face.

"I know you do, but believe me, you don't want to see what horrors surely lay in wait."

"You think I am not stout enough of heart? You forget I have treated the dying my life entire. Have severed limbs, drained abscesses, birthed babies, and nursed all manners of wounds and pestilence."

"Look at me." He steered his horse close enough to hers that he could take her hand, kiss it, and cover it with his own as he wished to cover her. "You do not want to see this. Not in your home. You do not want the memories to fly at you unbidden when you walk the halls. I don't doubt the stoutness of your heart, but I would keep the reality of the battlefield forever from your eyes."

"As you wish it," she said, bringing her eyes to meet his. She reached up to stroke his cheek. "But be quick. And be safe."

Giving her palm one last kiss, he rode off to the main palace gate. Before he even reached it, a great hurrah burst from the walls, with shouts of "Long Live the King!" He waved as he passed into the courtyard and was immediately greeted by two gaunt and bruised stable hands in filthy livery, their existence giving William hope. His men surrounded him, and they made their way into the Great Hall. The stench hit first. Bile rose up his throat at the metallic smell of freshly spilled blood, mixed with lye, sweat, urine, and stale beer. Thank God Anna had heeded him for once. Not wishing to show hesitation, he strode forward. The sun cooked the stones of the palace, making even the airy Hall an oven of horrors. The marble tiles were smeared wet with blood, bodies were stacked against the far wall, and female servants scrubbed on their hands and knees, pulling steaming buckets of reddened water behind them. Two men dragged a corpse between them and heaved it atop one of the teetering piles. And there, his back to William and in fresh silks, directing the men in their chore, was Robert. He looked like some wealthy woodland sprite on holiday to see what the devil was up to. William shook his head and smiled.

Feverishly working people stopped upon recognizing their visitor. Some gasped and hid their faces, and the body bearers fell to their knees. Robert spun around and opened his arms as wide as his grin.

"Majesty!" He came forward, remembered himself, and swept into a ceremonial bow. "We'd hoped to have the palace a bit more tidy before your arrival."

William clasped Robert's arm. "That you have cleared the hive of heretical wasps is more than sufficient, dear cuz."

"And I am just glad you're here in one piece, though now it seems the detour from your plans is all for naught."

"France was being coy." He patted Robert on the back, steering him to the throne room and away from the putrid scouring. "I don't think the trip would have come to anything anyway."

Giant urns filled with ashes surrounded the dais and William gave Robert a questioning look.

"Helena saw fit to be encased by fire—for all the good it did her." Robert scratched his goatee, observing the scene as if he were surveying new hedgerows.

"Helena was behind this? Quiet, docile, blushing Helena?" William had heard her father the earl had died, but never in his wildest imaginings did he think she would be capable of this. Robert shrugged. "Why, she could barely look me in the eye for nerves five years ago."

"I do believe she was nudged by a certain kidnapping lord along the way." Robert plunked himself down on a stair, resting his elbows on his knees. It was only then that William noticed the sunken purple under his eyes.

"I thought Westerville came to see you."

Robert's eyes briefly widened. "That he did. He came to tip me off. God knows why."

Out of nowhere, two kitchen boys and a royal taster appeared, laden with a large tray of fruits and bread, cheeses and miniature meat pies. They balanced the tray on one of the urns, placing pitchers of ale on another.

"What did he offer you, Norwick?" William said after the boys had finished and moved away.

"Nothing." Robert hoisted himself up and poured a mug. "Not at first anyway. He just dangled this piece of potential plot in front of me back at Cheval. I don't know if he was goading me, taunting me, or what, but it got my attention enough to gather a few of my lords to detour here. And thank God we did." Robert drained his drink and met William's eyes, as if challenging him to see a lie.

"But why would he warn you of a plot he instigated?" While William's stomach growled, the smell of death still hung about him and he couldn't eat. Instead, he settled into his throne. He didn't mean to imply ownership, being weary of body, but if asserting his sovereignty helped straighten out Robert's story, all the better.

Robert nodded up to William, wry grin on his face. "He wanted my arse in that chair, cuz. That's why. Thought if he used Catherine as leverage you'd just roll over and let me rule."

"Not a bad plan." William tapped his fingers on his thigh. "And were you not tempted to do just that?"

Robert was about to toss a grape into his mouth but stopped and looked William right in the eyes.

"I would never have used Cate against you. I may be a greedy, twisted man, but I would never harm that little girl, or any child. Even if my own life depended on it."

Silence hung between them. Then William nodded, cognizant that Robert hadn't precisely answered his question.

"So how is Helena wrapped up in all this?"

"I don't know." The grape finally reached its mark and he spoke over his chewing. "But I think he needed legitimate influence in Laureland, so he got himself betrothed to her, filled her head with a bunch of ideas about God calling her to lead Troixden out of the false religion. She's . . . well, you'll see for yourself, but these past years have not been good to her. Especially in the head."

"So they're in the Yard?"

"Just her. He's gone." Robert shrugged again. "The bastard."

"Dammit!" William pounded his fist on the throne. That man was more slippery than a river trout.

"I've got men combing the countryside for him," Robert said, as if reading William's mind. "But there's no trace. And Helena doesn't have any idea where he'd be. Not that she'd give him up if she did."

William shook his head. "Am I really going to have to kill a woman?"

"Well, as I say, she is wrong in the head. You could easily show mercy based on that." Robert's mouth twitched. "You've shown mercy for less in the past."

William rolled his eyes. "Yes, and the knave, as you like to call him, has saved my life at least twice."

"Actually, you can thank him for Cate's safety as well. He's the one who told me he'd seen her in Kilburn. Told them all to hole up in Beaubourg and sent the duke's men to guard the place."

"The knight in shining armor rides again," William sighed.

Robert walked up the stairs and sat next to William, in Daniel's chair. "Takes one to know one." Robert elbowed William, grinning.

"Not that I did much this time around." William considered his friend. "So what exactly was in this for Westerville?"

"He said when I was king, he could be me—sort of second in command. Money, land, and the respect money and land buys."

"Second in command, hmm?"

"His words, not mine."

For the first time in nearly a week, William laughed, his friend joining in.

CHAPTER 6

Traitor's Hill

Anna snuggled under the sheets of William's bed, cheek on his chest, his heartbeat steady and strong beneath her. "'Tis all settled. I shall leave tomorrow to fetch Catey."

"It will take more time that way. Robert has already sent word that it's safe for her return, along with half the palace guard. She'll be here in three days' time." William combed his fingers through her hair, the sensation drawing her toward slumber.

"But if I leave tomorrow, I see her in two days' time." She yawned.

"Which means I see her in four."

She looked up at him and found him pouting. She gave a sleepy laugh.

"I surrender, Wills. I will wait right along with you. And by then, the rest of the palace shall be put to rights and most of my ladies will have returned."

"'Tis a shame about your chambers—if I would've known, I wouldn't have let you see them."

She shuddered, remembering the scene. Ripped gowns lay in heaps like landed flotsam, filleted kirtles and charred underthings littered the fireplace, and the bed, with curtains tattered, was riddled with stab wounds, feathers and straw strewn about. Oddly, the only thing untouched was Anna's toilette. Her brushes, combs, oils, and powders were all perfectly aligned, as if Bernard had just been there.

"You don't really have to execute her, do you? She's not of right mind."

William kissed the top of her head then rolled to his side, curling around her.

"For once in my rule, I do not think it behooves me to show mercy, as much as it pains me."

"That poor woman. It should be that damned Westerville's head on the block, not hers."

"Would it be so. Though I don't think the block will be her fate. Women convicted of treason are burned."

She loosed herself from his arms and turned to face him. "Surely not! She's the daughter of an earl—if she's killed at all it should be a private execution with the axe."

His forehead creased and he looked down at his now empty arms. "'Tis not simply justice, but politics we must be mindful of.

To kill her quietly does not serve our interests." He sighed, then flicked his eyes to hers. In the dim candlelight they were the color of the sea in a squall, filled with regret and resolve. "We must show Laureland that we deal seriously with their treason, and we must show the rest of Troixden that we deem her not only traitor, but heretic. We can't simply dispatch her—we must use her justified execution to tell a story to our people. And to the outside world as well. Our court, our country, is not to be trifled with."

She nodded and cupped his cheek, rubbing the thick stubble with her thumb. "I hate this."

"I do too, my queen." He turned his lips to her palm. "But I love your compassionate heart."

The king, Robert, Daniel, and a smattering of men who'd returned to court sat around Council Table, faces grim. A steady rain had started that morning, and an incessant drip plunking down the giant fireplace was the only sound in the room, pounding a hole in Robert's skull. He wanted to run from the room, but instead he drew his thumbnail across the grain on the side of the table, a habit from boyhood. His father would always pull his ear when he did so, with his mother right behind to kiss away the sting.

Bartmore broke the silence. "She is a heretic. There's nothing further to discuss. Heretics burn." He held up his right hand, palm facing upward. "And females committing treason burn." Up went his left, balancing with his right, like a scale. "She is both."

The Duke of Halforn cleared his throat, adjusting his bulk. "'Tis still a delicate matter. She's not of sound mind."

"Isn't it more merciful then?" Bartmore said, gloating down the table. "If she is crazed, she should be put out of her misery."

"That's an incredibly cruel thing to say," Halforn balked.

"Cruel or not, 'tis truth." Bartmore folded his arms.

"And you call yourself a man of the cloth! "Robert had never seen Halforn apoplectic before.

"Gentlemen." Daniel rapped his knuckles on the table. "This issue is fraught with concern on many sides. We only wish to do what is best for Troixden while also seeking to respect the mental state and sex of the prisoner."

Apparently the king was content to let them debate, for he frowned out the window at the rain lashing against Stone Yard.

"I was the one who saw her," Robert said at last. "She was misled by Westerville, and, judging by the state of the queen's chambers, certainly lunatic. If we must kill her, let it be the axe."

"Yet the axe gives her more than she rightly deserves," Ridgeland said. "Her treason was too bold."

"Which, again, is why I see no reason to belabor this," Bartmore said. "The woman must burn. And in all haste."

Robert went rigid. He was eight again, watching a fresh-faced priest mumble in Latin, pretending to call out the demons of his mother's soul, her screams echoing through the ages.

"And why are you so quick to burn women, Bartmore?" Robert said with barely restrained rage.

"Enough," William said, eyes still fixed in the distance. "We all know it must be done. Woman or no, sane or no. I want it finished before the princess returns. Norwick, you will stand as proxy."

"First light tomorrow then," Daniel said. The king finally broke his gaze with a nod, rose, and made to leave.

"Begging your pardon, Majesty, but what method have you decided upon?" Daniel sat with quill poised. The king glanced at Robert.

"The axe." He strode to the door. "In public."

As if the entire room had been holding its breath, it now exhaled, and Robert's heart slowed. If Robert was to be proxy, as was his duty for all executions, he wouldn't have been able to face a burning. And William knew it.

Now, if only he could find Westerville.

Anna lounged in her window seat, staring through the rain-washed glass at a glint of light emitting from the top of Stone Yard. Helena was up there, in the same cell Bryan had lived in for a year. What must she be thinking? Did she know death was upon her, or was she oblivious, still clinging to the faith that God had called her to make Troixden Protestant, and therefore, she couldn't possibly be dying on the morrow?

Her curtain rings chimed softly. Her ladies murmured around her as Bernard directed servants to replace the last bits of her decimated belongings, returning her chambers to order.

Anna's heart was weary, her only bright spot the knowledge that Cate would be back in her arms the next afternoon.

Bernard cleared his throat, shocking her out of her swirling thoughts. "Majesty," he made his complex bow, "I want to make sure the adjustments to your chamber meet with your approval. Though we had to reuse some materials from past royals and other noble apartments, I assure you that fresh linens are on the bed and new curtains have been ordered."

Her chambers had previously been decorated with a crimson and gold theme that she'd never warmed to anyway. Now her bed was draped in ivory, covered in delicate violet flowers, spring-green vines, and gold thread. In place of the finials, lavender and ivory ostrich feathers spread their plumes. Even the tapestries were brighter, pale yellow-backed scenes of Adam and Eve, frolicking woodland creatures, a unicorn rearing in an undulating meadow of wildflowers. If she couldn't feel delighted, at least her chamber would give such an impression.

"Bernard, you have outdone yourself yet again," she smiled as widely as her mood allowed. "I love how light it feels now, how verdant and pretty. You need not replace a thing."

"I was inspired by drawings from the French court," he said, trying to hide a smile of pride. "I felt our queen deserved chambers less dreary and mannish. Opulent, but not gaudy. Beautiful and bright, to reflect the occupant." She caught the hint of a blush on his cheeks.

"Well you have captured it, and in such little time, under such trying circumstances. You are a true artist."

His color deepened and he bowed low, making to leave. "I almost forgot!" He pulled a letter from his pocket. "This came today from Mohrlang."

It must be news from Margaux. She called her ladies over to

hear, for it surely was an official announcement, nothing personal for the queen.

> Year 6, WR, August, 25, 1575
> To Her Royal Highness, Queen Annelore Matilda,
>
> It is with great joy that I announce the birth of my son, Lord Henry William James.
> Your Majesty's presence is humbly requested for the rite of baptism this Sunday next, at Piedmont Cathedral.
> It is our hope Your Highness will stand as Godmother, that Lord Henry may have the purest, most faithful to guide him through his life.
>
> Your Loyal Servant of God and King,
> Eustace, Earl of Mohrlang

Amid the delighted squeals about her, Anna's heart turned cold. Another boy. Of noble blood. She glanced down at her own barren belly, her courses having started when they left Madrone. Dear God in heaven, why could she not conceive a son? With Norwick's boys, and now Margaux's, the lines of succession overflowed with her enemies' sons.

And the audacity of asking her to be godmother. Of course, it was proper for the queen to stand for children of nobles, but it was as if Anna's nose was being rubbed in Margaux's continued fertility.

She sat on the end of her freshly fixed bed, desperate to relieve her tangled worries in William's arms, but knowing he was in council, deciding poor Helena's fate. With dull eyes, she watched Lady Jane break from the crowd and approach.

"Highness," she said from her low curtsy, "I haven't had a chance to thank you for John's new nurse."

Anna managed a smile. "It was really more the Duke of Cecile's doing."

"Well, I thank ye nonetheless."

Yvette appeared at Anna's side as if from nowhere, two goblets of summer wine in her hands.

"I thought you may be in need of some refreshment," she said with a quick curtsy. She gave Jane a meaningful look and the lady took her leave.

Anna sipped the wine gratefully and patted the mattress, inviting Yvette to sit. "You know me all too well, my lady."

"You will have sons, my queen," Yvette perched next to Anna.

Anna laughed without mirth. "And wouldn't that just go against everything your lover has planned for?" Yvette startled away, her face pale. Anna sighed. "Forgive me, Yvette. I didn't mean . . . my mood is dark today, and you are correct in suspecting the earl's news does nothing to lighten it."

"I will not pretend my Robert does not desire his sons on the throne. What man would not?" She sipped her wine. "But he does not do so at the expense of the king and his happiness. Surely his recent actions prove it to be so?"

Anna studied his mistress's face. Robert had saved William's rule. She softened. "I shall not argue, for my head aches already." Yvette nodded. "It must be nice for you to have him back though. Norwick, I mean."

"It is more than nice to have him back." It was the first time Anna had seen Yvette look shy. "But he is changed somehow. Less vibrant, more urgent, as if he were trying to regain something that's slipping away." She waved this off. "I'm probably overthinking things. Being with a man after a long absence is always a bit strange at first."

Anna thought back to the times William had been away, during the war, after Cate was born. She understood what Yvette meant.

"It's like we are chasing a dream when we come together after so long," Yvette said.

A creak of hinges interrupted them, and the king stepped from their private passageway. He looked as if he hadn't slept or eaten for days.

"Come with me, won't you?" he said.

That was all Anna needed to hear.

For once, Robert dressed to blend in. A gray wool cloak pulled around him, his chain of office beneath, rather than on top, he made purposeful progress toward Traitor's Hill, Havenside's public execution sight. It was a grassy knoll, rising up near the south end of town, giving the condemned a view of the rooftops and a last glance at the palace. If a white and red flag were raised instead of the griffin, the prisoner was granted his or her life. No such mercy shined upon Helena.

During summer, the hill was peopled with families on picnic, young lovers sighing at the view, children rolling about, picking weedy flowers. While this day was gray, clouds hanging low and heavy over the city, the hill was no less populated. An execution was an event, the grisly horror of it designed both to keep people in line and to allow the crowd's sense of justice and vitriol to be thrown at the accused, instead of at the king.

A scaffold had been hastily erected, sawdust piled on the ground like anthills. As proxy, Robert sat in the stands built for the peerage and gentry, in the center of the third row so nothing could obstruct his view. From his vantage point, he could see people five deep lining the half-mile path Helena would take from Stone Yard to Traitor's Hill.

Sitting there, listening to the wave of mob noise flow to the hill, the memory of his mother's gruesome death etched deeper in his mind. And here was Helena, another woman betrayed, crazy and treasonous though she be. Betrayed by men and justice, as the true instigator ran free. But examples must be made. Calm must be maintained. For the first time since William had become king, Robert despised his own vaulted role.

The jeers grew louder, rising up the hill. Cowbells rang as she passed, people threw rotten food, and some spit. He could only see her white-capped head through the throng as she inched closer, the mob pressing in.

Bartmore and Moltmann, the bishop of Havenside, stood on the scaffold. It was tradition that the executioner stood behind a sheet, hung so the condemned couldn't see him. Once the prisoner was in place, the executioner mounted a set of stairs at the back of the scaffold. If the prisoner chose, he or she would never see the axe or the man wielding it.

As Helena crested the hill, the noise reached its peak as well, then faded into an eerie, ponderous silence. She was paraded past the nobles in the stands, her long chin jutting out, mumbling prayers to herself in German. Suddenly, she looked up, right at Robert.

"Your Grace!" she called, eyes hopeful. "Thank the Lord you're here! You will stop this! You promised me—" Robert focused on his shoes as the jailer shoved her forward.

"Norwick!" Her voice cracked on the last syllable, melting into a wail. The courtiers around him cleared their throats, adjusted themselves on their benches. Some peered at him, accusing or curious.

She could barely lift her skirts to climb the scaffold, so wracked with weeping she was. Moltmann scurried down the stairs to help her, whispered something to her, and she nodded, stumbling the rest of the way. The jailer lumbered behind her, cleared his throat, spit, and proclaimed her sentence.

"Lady Helena of Laureland, thou hast been found guilty of high treason against the king's person, of heresy against God and the One True Church, destruction and illegal seizure of His Majesty's property, and conspiracy to harm the princess royal. The law of the realm demands thy head smitten off until thou art dead, as is the king's pleasure. May God have mercy on your soul."

Bartmore stepped forward, swirling his purple robes for effect. Making the sign of the cross, he performed last rites in Latin with his ever-present scowl. He finally reached the section wherein the condemned confesses, and Helena, finally roused, stood on shaky feet. She balled up her hands in her skirts like a child would, but looked into the crowd.

"I do now confess any sins I may have committed against God and man, known or unknown to my person. It was our Lord Jesus Himself who called me to this particular service that I would render thee—freedom from the tyranny of Catholic rule." Someone booed. "Mayhap it whilst be in my death that you, poor peasant folk, will awaken to the new dawn, will reckon my death a martyr's, for—" She stopped and stared, seemingly straight at Robert.

"You said you would protect me! You would keep me safe no matter the ends!" Her voice was shrill.

People looked around, searching for the person she accused. Robert rose, unsure of what to do, but he knew he must stop her ravings.

"'Tis thou who shouldst be here in my stead, you leech!" There was jostling in the middle of the crowd.

Robert realized Helena wasn't cursing him, but someone in the crowd. People were flung aside with disgruntled shouts, and Robert saw a bulky, cloaked figure fighting his way out of the mob.

"Guards!" Robert called. "Seize that man!"

The man charged through the crowd at full speed, trampling anyone in his way.

"That's right, my love!" Helena cackled, clapping her hands. "Run! Run little chicken!"

He disappeared over the hillside, but the guards were closing in on him. While everyone's attention was drawn away, Helena picked up her skirts and tried to flee in the opposite direction.

The crowd, delighted with the escapades, let her through unimpeded. This wasn't the spectacle the king and council had hoped for.

The jailer, bereft of guards, rambled after Helena to the masses' hoots and hollers, but their delight turned to disappointed groans when back up the hill she came, struggling against the grip of two hulking townsmen. They handed her to the jailer, who shackled her and shuffled her back to the scaffold, her head bowed, tears and snot flowing.

In all the commotion, the executioner, black hood and all, had come out from behind the sheet to stand on the platform, leaning on his axe like one would a fence post. When Helena saw him, she screamed again. Moltmann helped her to her knees, blindfolding her with his own kerchief.

She turned her head, searching, and shouted, "I forgive thee!" Whether to the executioner, to the king, or to the crowd, Robert couldn't tell. As she was about to be bent forward, the guards marched back into view, Westerville at their center. Robert raised his hand to halt the execution.

"Bring him," Robert said. The people parted, letting the guards through and soon, a stone-faced Westerville stood before him.

"Why on earth would you come here, today of all days?" Robert shook his head.

"I owed her that much." He shrugged, belying his obvious distress. "Besides, I need to know she's dead—the only person who could prove against me." He smirked. "Or don't you feel the same, Norwick?"

Robert turned to the guards. "Take him to the platform."

"On whose authority?" Westerville said. "I should be tried and sentenced only by the king, not his power-grabbing lesser!"

Of course the man could be right. Robert was at liberty, vis-à-vis the law, to grant clemency to the accused, but whether or not that proxy power extended to executing another was the sticky bit. Yet if he delayed, if Westerville was tried, not only would it drag on, giving the man time to escape again, but accusations of treason would be laid at Robert's feet as well. It wouldn't matter that he gave his word to Helena and Westerville as a ruse. He had enough enemies at court, enough people who desired his downfall—the queen at the front of the line—to be immune to such recriminations. Damn. Where the hell was Daniel when you needed him?

"As proxy," Robert said, convincing himself as much as those around him, "I have the authority of the king in this place. Not only does the lady testify to your involvement and leadership in the plot, but I, with mine own eyes and ears, attest to your treachery. Believe me, what happens next is more merciful than the king would ever be." Without catching a breath, he yelled, "Take him! Under order of the king!"

The guards dragged Westerville away. "Then you should be taken too, Judas!" As Westerville thrashed against the guards, shouting his innocence, there was pointing and whispering. Robert only heard snippets. "Warned you" and "traitor" and "I'm not so foolish."

Robert stayed standing, in shock. A hand clasped his shoulder.

"I'll vouch for this, Norwick." It was Ridgeland. "All who were there will stand for you—your heroism and his treason."

Robert nodded. "Thank you, My Lord."

Westerville was now on the scaffold, held by four guards. Helena, still blindfolded and trembling, reached out a hand. "My love, clasp mine hand once more, I beg thee."

Robert nodded to the jailer, who bent her head to the block. "No!" She shrieked, her hand grasping at air. "Let me have a last human comfort!" Moltmann, again the angel of mercy, bent to her, closing his hand around hers as she sobbed.

Not even a child in the crowd made a peep as everyone watched, transfixed by the terror of this mighty lady, fallen. Helena turned her face to the platform, and the headsman took no pause. As soon as her much-maligned chin was pointing down, he swung, giving her less than a second to anticipate the blow. Her head was cleaved clean off.

A howl erupted from Westerville. Helena's body was dumped in the awaiting pine box, along with her head. The king thought it would elicit pity to display the thing on a pike.

Bartmore kept looking from the jailer to Robert, probably trying to determine his cue. Finally, the jailer stepped forward.

"Lord Joseph of Westerville, thou hast been found guilty of high treason against the king's person, and . . . other such charges. The law of the realm demands thy head smitten off until thou art dead, as is the king's pleasure. May God have mercy on your soul."

Sweeping forward, Bartmore began.

"I don't want your sniveling incantations!" Westerville said. Bartmore froze, mouth open, arm halfway through the sign of the cross.

"They won't help you where you're going anyway," Bartmore said, retreating to the back of the platform with a haughty glance at Moltmann. The young bishop stared at the blood pooling at the front of the block.

The guards forced Westerville to his knees in the same spot so recently vacated by his illegally betrothed.

"I get last words!" he roared.

Robert shook his head, and Westerville was forced onto the block.

"You'll pay for this, Norwick! You won't—" His words died on his tongue as his head left his body, rolling like a flour sack from a cart. It bounced into the crowd and the people pressed back, giving it room to finally rest on the trampled grass. A young man ran forward, grabbed Westerville's head by the hair, and thrust it to the sky. The people cheered. A surprise double death—it would be spoken of for years. As would the gossip of Robert's involvement. He knew they would be speculating in the pubs, wondering what Westerville was literally cut off from saying.

Already the crowd dispersed, talking excitedly. Robert went to the foot of the scaffold, careful not to step in the blood. Without a word, he handed the jailer and headsman a hefty payment. He took one last look at Westerville's headless body and left for the castle, swearing he would never again attend one of these spectacles.

William, arms crossed over his chest, pounded a path in the stone behind his desk. Daniel stood at the desk's end and Robert slouched in a chair, hand to forehead as if nursing a hangover. William had spent almost twenty minutes shouting at the man. A full day had passed before he could even look at his cousin, but he remained unable to tamp his temper.

"You had no authority, Robert!" William whirled to face him.

"So you would rather I simply let him traipse away as he always does? Evade justice, plot more treason? We had him, he was guilty—"

"That's the point!" William slammed the desk. "We had him! We could have questioned him, tortured him if need be, gotten names, money channels, sympathizers. The man was a negotiator—he would have given up his own mother for the right price."

"You can't just—"

"And now any information he had is dead with him! Because you were in such a damned hurry to see his head fly!"

"It wasn't like that, Wills—"

William flew around the desk, hauling Robert up by his jacket. "Don't you dare call me 'Wills' right now. I am not your relation, not your friend. I am your king." Robert glared at him, jaw tight. "Was this little show of yours to protect crown and country, or to clean up loose ends?"

William's logic told him he was overreacting, that Robert did what he thought he had to do. But William's outrage at losing potentially crucial information, as well as Robert playing king, to a bloody end, disallowed him from granting his cousin any leeway.

William released him and went back to pacing.

"With all due respect, *sire*," Robert said, straightening his jacket, "if you had seen the horror he made of your palace, the men he had killed without cause, the way in which he strutted about your throne room, spouting vitriol and treason, mayhap you would not be so incensed by his sudden demise."

"Dammit, Robert, of course we would have killed him in the end! But we needed every last drop of his dealings before he died."

"And you expect anything out of that man's mouth would have been true?"

"Actually," Daniel said, emerging from the shadows, "I don't think Westerville has ever been false. A manipulator, surely, but he had never brought us false witness."

Robert threw up his arms. "You're always taking your precious William's side in things."

"That's enough, Robert." William glanced between the two men. Daniel was red, Robert sullen. *Precious William?* The king shook off the jab. "It's true though, about Westerville. He warned you about the plot, he tried to warn me about you being a closet Protestant—"

Robert pointed at Daniel. "That's not—"

"Daniel's not an idiot. Of course he knows where your loyalties lie. But he prefers to look the other way as long as it doesn't infringe upon your fealty. As do I." Robert, defeated, sank into the chair. "All the man ever wanted to do was haggle the best deal for himself."

"He lied to Helena, lied to the men he led to certain death," Robert said, still frowning.

"But he never lied to us." Daniel had recovered his placid demeanor, though his voice was quiet.

"And you think when his life was on the line, he'd tell you the truth? He'd tell you what you wanted to hear."

"I would think that would be the absolute worst time to lie," Daniel said, fingertips resting on the desk, "when one risks one's life."

"It's obvious you've never been a party to torture, Daniel dear."

"I've been a party to more than you know," Daniel said in a strange voice. He seemed lost for a moment, then cleared his throat and turned to William. "There is certainly nothing to be gained now by arguing about the matter. The deed is done."

"And justice has been served—don't forget that in all your bluster," Robert said, rising and snatching his flat cap from William's desk.

"Did I say you could take your leave?" William bit off each word, unsure of what more there was to say, but sick of his cousin taking liberties.

"Begging your pardon, Your Majestic-ness, but I must pre-pare for my nephew's baptism," Robert said, one brow cocked. "Surely you haven't forgotten the newest noble, bouncing baby boy of Troixden?"

Dammit. The baptism was about the last thing he wanted to attend, not just because Anna would be in a foul mood. He huffed and waved Robert off. The man affected a foppish bow and nearly skipped out the door. How could Robert think he'd won this particular argument?

Daniel cleared his throat. "I'd best take my leave as well, friend, unless you'd like for me to stay . . ." He made a vague gesture at the scattered paper and overturned candlesticks on the desk. William clapped his back, escorting him to the door. "Pay Robert no mind," Daniel said. "You know how he lashes out when he feels cornered."

"And you also—pay him no heed," William said with a smile. Daniel nodded and ducked out the door.

"Gentlemen," William said, throwing his arms wide to the gathered grooms, dressers, and servants outside his doors, ready to puff him up for the service. "Have your way with me."

God knows, everyone else is.

Anna clutched Cate's hand as they left the queen's chambers for the Mohrlang baptism. She reveled in the smallness and warmth, the fidgeting fingers of her daughter, too excited to stay still. Anna vowed she wouldn't steal Cate's joy in this day, no matter how much Anna dreaded it.

Since Catherine's arrival the previous afternoon, the queen hadn't let the princess leave her side. Even William had stayed in Anna's chambers, lying in bed with them both, stroking his daughter's hair, studying her face as she slept. Once convinced Cate was truly, deeply, peacefully in slumber, he told Anna in hushed tones of the heinous execution. How Helena ran, how Westerville was found and killed on the spot. For once, Anna sided with Robert. The less time the fearful Westerville had on this earth the better. Before she was queen, before she was a mother, she would have chastised herself for such gratitude at anyone's death. But that man had threatened the lives of the two she held most dear. A mother, a wife, shows no mercy there.

Anna and her entourage were nearly to the top of the throne room stairs when Cate's hand broke free of Anna's grasp.

"Uncle Robert!" Cate ran to a frowning Robert, but when he saw her coming he crouched down, arms wide, smile heartfelt.

"Why, my delicious little cousin!" He scooped her up and nibbled her ears as she giggled. He stood, Cate straddling his hip, and approached the queen. Cate was running her finger through his groomed goatee.

"Majesty," he said with a head bow.

Anna was struck silent. Her insides were already a jumble at having to go stand with yet another of Margaux's sons, and here now was Robert, unwanted savior of her king and castle.

"Your Grace." Anna let him take her hand. He kissed her knuckles, and she instinctively squeezed his fingers in return. "Why, princess, it seems you have caught a wild beast to play with."

Cate gave her mother a serious look. "No, Mama, it's Uncle Robert."

Both Anna and the duke laughed, diffusing some of the tension. Robert set the girl down with a pat on her head.

"I don't think your mama would like you mussed," he said.

"Majesty, I—"

"Your Grace, it—"

They smiled awkwardly at each other.

"My apologies, Majesty," he said, a kind of sadness returning to his face. "Surely you wish to be away."

Anna took Cate's hand and nodded. She made to pass him but stopped. They were shoulder to shoulder, or rather shoulder to bicep, for Robert had a good four inches on her. She faced him. Lifting her eyes, she saw his, near black in the dim hall's light, searching her face. If she didn't know better, she'd swear he wanted to fall in her arms and weep.

"Your Grace." She took a deep breath. She could feel her ladies pressing in behind her. "I've not found the right time to thank you properly for . . . for what you did in the king's and my absence." His eyes narrowed as if he hadn't heard correctly. "And for the princess . . ." Emotion she thought she had hidden away swelled inside her and she had to physically swallow it down. "If you hadn't—if they'd come back to Havenside . . ."

His eyes flicked to Cate and softened. He spoke to the queen but kept watching the princess.

"I was merely fulfilling my oath—any man would have done the same." He nodded a bow as if to excuse himself, but Anna caught his arm.

"That may be so, but I didn't believe . . ." she felt his muscles tighten beneath her hand and freed him. He returned his gaze to her, some unspoken sorrow still lodged there. "Robert, I owe you an apology. For not having faith . . . not believing . . ." She shook her head, ashamed that she couldn't verbalize her slander against him. "You saved us all, so quickly and so well. If it weren't for—"

He clasped both her hands. "Majesty, while I appreciate your sincerity, I wish you to think nothing of it. You are all hale and whole and I would have it no other way, despite rumormongering to the contrary."

"And Westerville . . ." He winced at her words. "I would have done the same. Worse if my stomach could handle it."

He peered at her, then nodded, brought her hands to his lips, and kissed them again, closing his eyes as he did so.

She curtsied and he released her, his head staying down as she passed, her heart racing. Had she just made peace with the Dread Duke of Norwick?

CHAPTER 7

Gift of the English

As Christmastide approached, the court had mostly returned to normalcy. Even Margaux was in attendance, and, Robert noted with perhaps as much annoyance as the queen, took every opportunity to parade her boys through the Great Hall, loudly proclaiming what a time she was having trying to keep up with her hearty sons. But even his irksome sister wouldn't dampen his mood. The whole execution fuss was behind him, and his wife had decided yet again to only join him at court for the week of Twelfth Night, leaving him a whole month of freedom.

He sat in the throne room with Daniel and the king and queen, yawning through a slow privy court. An English messenger had handed over various papers, as the royals whispered and Daniel sorted through the missives.

"Apparently, the Queen of England has sent us a present of sorts," Daniel finally said, frowning down at the parchment in his hands.

Robert raised his brows. Perhaps this gift exchange would lead him to England's shores. After the palace siege debacle, he needed to garner Protestant support away from his cousins' watchful eyes. He drummed his fingers on his gilt chair.

"Is it bigger than a bread loaf?"

The queen pursed her lips, swallowing a smile. While her stilted apology had brought them to a truce of sorts, she was presently only useful to Robert for keeping the king in good spirits. And she was failing. He'd have to talk to Yvette about it. Again.

"It seems we are about to find out," William said.

The king gestured to the throne room doors. Standing behind the crossed pike axes of the king's guard was a man, about Robert's height and build, but a decade younger. He wore an unwieldy curled ruff beneath a well-groomed beard, with olive and gold trunks puffed out from his thighs like sweet rolls. Definitely English. They dressed as if they had something to prove. The young man glanced around, whistling to himself. When the guards pulled back their weapons, he flinched, then smiled to himself.

"Walter Raleigh, Esquire of England, to see their Majesties," the court caller shouted.

Raleigh entered, not so much as if he ruled it, but as if it were home.

"Majesties, Your Graces." He bowed and rose. "I bring you hearty greetings from Her Most Magnificent Majesty, Queen Elizabeth of England, Ireland, and France."

Robert snorted. William shot him a silencing glance. Raleigh continued, flicking intelligent eyes between king, queen, Robert, and Daniel, as if gauging who was truly in charge.

"She hath received word of your safe and peaceful conclusion to the strife at summer's end with much joy, and wishes me to tell you she is always at the ready to help her good friends of Troixden in any capacity that might suit both realms."

What on earth was the man on about? Since when were Troixden and England friends? Both were ever waiting to see who would blink first.

"We thank you for the message," William said, eyeing the admittedly striking man. "Her Majesty is most magnanimous in sending her message verbally as well as penned." Raleigh nodded. "I'm sure we will have fine greetings to return to her. In the meantime, what are your plans in our fair lands?"

"Why, Your Highness, I am the gift His Grace Cecile spoke of. Here for as long as you find me diverting." He walked forward, handing Daniel more papers.

"Yet we already have an ambassador," William said.

"And a jester," Robert added, struggling not to glower at the man. Who did he think he was, waltzing in the court to be "diverting?"

"Begging your pardon, sire, but you misunderstand." Raleigh flicked his eyes to the queen, gave her a once over, and returned to studying William. "Her Majesty wishes for me to explore the continent. Thought it would be beneficial for me to spend time at the various courts, to learn diplomacy. She said there was no court more quaint and kind than this." William's jaw clenched. "Nor a royal family more intelligent and lovely," Raleigh added quickly. The queen had the audacity to blush.

"That is all fine and good for your own interests, Raleigh, but of what possible use could you be to us? You've obviously no authority with Elizabeth, you're considered a heretic in our lands, and you've no skill we are in need of."

Raleigh kept smiling. "King Philip and his court didn't seem to mind all that."

"You're telling us you've just come from the Spanish court?" William leaned forward.

"Indeed. In fact, Her Majesty explicitly withdrew me from his court to come to yours, and I must say I do find yours much more charming." He turned to the queen and bowed. "Speaking of, Highness, I bring you happy greetings from the Viscount de Alba. He does not leave his own chambers or garden courtyard much these days, but he remembers you most fondly and keeps you and the king in his prayers."

"Thank you, Raleigh," the queen said. "While my heart saddens to hear his pace has slowed, I'm touched he remembers us well, as we do him." She looked at William with eyes like a little girl who has found a stray kitten she wants to keep.

"As I say, Highness, I am only here at your pleasure. Should you bid me be gone, I shall depart forthwith," he lowered his voice, "off to France and that hag of a Medici. Though after my time with the Huguenots, I doubt she'll bid me welcome." A hint of a smile pulled at William's mouth. "I beg your pardon, Majesties," Raleigh said. "Did I say that last bit out loud?"

William looked at Daniel, who shrugged. "With Christmastide upon us, we shan't send you stumbling out into the cold like the holy family. We've plenty of room for one more guest. You must stay at the very least until Twelfth Night."

"Wonderful," the queen said, clapping her hands. "Welcome to our quaint, but no less decorous, court."

Robert rolled his eyes. He needed another wolf at court like he needed another damned nephew.

"You are more than gracious, Highness." Raleigh bowed again, but his eyes didn't leave the queen. "I look forward to bringing you whatever services and pleasures I may—all you must do is ask."

As Daniel rose to make arrangements for the English invader, Robert leaned across the queen to harass William.

"Truly, Wills? This fop? After the brush we've just had with our own rebel reformers?"

The queen swatted a kerchief at Robert to bid him off her lap. "What, Norwick," she said, "afraid this young bon vivant will usurp your glorified place as court hedonist?"

"Hardly, Madam." Robert leaned back. "It simply strikes me that one so young and inexperienced, flitting about the courts of our so-called friends, could do more harm than good."

"You're probably right," William said, taking the queen's hand and rising to go, "but cheer up, cuz. 'Tis only 'til Christmas. How much damage could the man do?"

As much as Anna enjoyed the festivities of Christmastide, the enchanting decor, the continually full mugs of hot and spiced drinks, the palace was becoming claustrophobic. Each year it seemed the season stretched further back into December and with Christmas Day still over a week hence, she sought refuge in her favorite place—the garden.

Bundling herself and her ladies into winter furs, she trudged out into the snow-covered rose garden to collect the season's final rose hips.

"Why must we be a party to this excursion," Anna heard Margaux say to Brigitte. "Certainly there are servants for this chore."

"But then you would miss the sun making the snow like a field of diamonds," Anna called, determined not to let even Margaux ruin her day. "Or the plump red rosebuds dusted with snow-like marzipans, the bracing air instead of soot and moldy damp filling you with health."

Margaux mumbled something unintelligible, at which Brigitte tittered.

"Pay them no heed, dearie," Mary said, tromping beside Anna, her breath billowing clouds before her.

Anna threaded her arm through Mary's, pulling her close. "I feel as though she cannot hurt me anymore. Something about her having yet another boy—she's done her worst. She may flaunt her babes about, but she'll never get what she really wants."

"Well someone is feeling quite confident today. Seems you and His Majesty had an enjoyable evening."

Anna smiled, looking to the sky. "But more than that. We

spoke for a long while, as we used to in the early days. I feel as though something vital has come back to us."

"Perhaps that scare with the Laurelanders put you to rights."

"Perhaps," Anna said, releasing Mary to lift her skirts over the lip of the rose garden path, "but I think 'tis something more lasting than just an acknowledgment of our own mortality."

The garden glistened, with thorny stems hunched under dustings of snow. A single set of footprints led to the center and there, on a curved bench, his back to her, was Raleigh. Proceeding down the path, she called to him. "A fine morning, is it not?"

He startled, hastening to tuck something in his jacket. "Yes, Madam." He stood to bow, and she motioned for him to sit again, noticing a capped inkwell on the bench beside him. Before taking his seat, he dusted off the bench with his gloves so that she might join him. "Won't you take your ease with me?" His dark eyes sparkled, his smile broad and genuine. She couldn't help but smile back.

"'Tis kind of you, Raleigh, but my ladies and I are here to see to the last of the rose hips."

"Oh you don't mean to cut them, do you?" He almost jumped up again.

She laughed. "But of course! We need them for our medicines, as well as our scents and satchels."

"'Tis a pity," he said, reaching out to touch one such oranged globe. "For I have been admiring their beauty, their incongruity in the snow. Winter speaks to me of death yet these hips nearly burst forth, womb like, with life. As if a whole world is inside."

"How poetically you speak, sir. You should take your musings to verse." The rest of her ladies had gathered round, giving

Raleigh curious and flirtatious glances. Margaux looked ready to pounce on the man. Anna sat next to Raleigh, making sure her woolen cloak was tucked beneath her.

His high cheeks were red, either from sheepishness or the cold or both. "I will admit, Madam, I do dabble in the art."

She clapped her hands together. "Well then, 'tis settled—you must amuse us with your verse."

He shook his head, looked at his hands. "They are not so very well as to be heard by such an audience as Your Majesty."

"And I shall be the judge of that." She brushed her fingers on his forearm. "Were you not tasked with diversion? We ladies have a cold and long chore ahead of us. Surely you shan't refuse us this pleasure at passing the time."

"My words are ill formed—merely incomplete thoughts . . ." Despite his speech, he drew out a small leather-bound book from his jacket, flipping through half-written pages. "But I suppose I can read you my thoughts on your winter garden."

"I would be much obliged." She folded her hands in her lap and watched him expectantly. He cleared his throat, gave her a trepidatious look, and began.

> So frail all things as we see,
> So subject unto conquering Time.
> Then gather Flowers in their prime,
> Let them not fall and perish so;
> Nature her bounties did bestow
> On us that we might use them: And
> 'Tis coldness not to understand
> What she and Youth and Form persuade

With Opportunity, that's made . . .

He closed the book, face now almost the color of the roses. The ladies clapped and tittered. Anna nodded.

"That was remarkable, milord. I insist on hearing more as we work. If that one be not finished, pick another and more while we are about our work."

"You are too kind to a novice, Madam," he said as she stood. "They really are just bits and pieces."

"Well, Raleigh," she motioned for Mary to hand her a basket and shears, "your bits and pieces are much more pleasing to mine ears than the yips of our dogs chasing the winter hares."

He laughed, "May it never be said that I let such a fine lady be plagued so."

Though Raleigh pained himself to appear serious, he couldn't shake the vital buoyancy that shone through him. As if he were moments away from stealing one off on a grand adventure.

"To thy work, ladies," she said, turning from him. "The gracious Raleigh has submitted to our request for more verses." She headed to the bushes nearest him, and careful to avoid the thorns, grabbed the main stem and shook, producing a miniature snowdrift.

"Praised be Diana's fair and harmless light; Praised be the dews wherewith she moists the ground . . ."

Anna smiled again, feeling almost like a child, without a care in the world. Raleigh's voice faded as Anna concentrated on her cuttings, taking the plump, leaving the wizened, avoiding the pricks. It felt such an indulgence to lose herself to a common task in the bracing air, no statecraft to attend to, no worries of barren wombs or treasonous subjects—just the lilting, masculine voice, soothing her slow way across the garden. All too soon her task was done, but by the sun's height, she knew at least two hours had been whiled away.

She found her ladies sprawled about the benches surrounding the frozen over fountain, baskets in various levels of fullness. Margaux and Brigitte's predictably near empty, Mary's brimming, and Lady Jane's a respectable three-quarters. Raleigh had stopped reciting and was laughing with the women.

"Thank you, Raleigh, for keeping us entertained this morning." Anna sauntered back to the gaggle.

"Apologies if I was too distracting, Highness." He bowed his head, but the gleam didn't leave his eye.

"Quite the contrary. For I believe you got your wish." She gestured at their surroundings. "Many a rose hip remains. Enough, methinks, that you might finish your poem."

"Indeed!" He slapped his book of poems against his thigh.

"It will please me if you supped with the king and me this eve in His Majesty's dining chambers."

He stood and folded into a graceful bow. "The pleasure is surely mine, Majesty. I shall count the minutes."

She nodded, a smirk fighting to show. "In the meantime I leave you to your artistic meanderings. Ladies!" She clapped her hands, more like a governess than she'd intended. Women leapt up, dusting off snow and cold. "I believe we have earned warm refreshment. Let us leave this beleaguered man to his own devices."

She caught some of her younger ladies giving Raleigh little waves and snickering as they left, their elders shaking their heads in amused condescension. But even Anna had to admit she left the garden with a new lift to her step. After returning indoors, she would find William straightaway and sweep him up in her newfound spirit.

William was so preoccupied with pressing matters—the French and Spanish alliance, the rebels in his own land—that he'd almost forgotten young Raleigh was at court. But after Anna had surprised him that afternoon in his bedchamber, he wasn't ill disposed to her request that the man sup with them. Besides, Cate would be there, and he could never resist his daughter's presence.

Robert, Daniel, and Halforn rounded out the number, with a compliment of the queen's ladies and king's grooms standing to the sides of the room.

"The queen tells me you're a poet, Raleigh," William said, spearing a venison slice.

"Her Majesty is much too generous in her estimation." Raleigh raised a glass in Anna's direction.

"Come now, she tells me you kept the ladies entertained this morning." William refilled his own glass, glancing down the long table at Anna, who was watching their guest.

"I will admit only that it is something to which I aspire."

"So you don't see it as an amusement then?" Halforn said, affable as ever. "You wish your works to be widely read?"

William heard Robert snort, then cover it up by blowing his nose.

"I suppose so," Raleigh said. "Though what I truly long for is exploration. To see the vastness of the world, not merely the continent, but the New World, the Holy Lands, the Far East."

"Quite ambitious," Robert said. "Does your queen have such excess as to finance expansive exploration simply for pleasure?"

Cate, who had been dreamy-eyed during the conversation, cut in before more tension could mount, her innocent stare fixed on Raleigh.

"Will you write me a poem, sir?"

The man chuckled and smiled indulgently. "Anything for you, Princess. What would you like me to write about? Fairies? Knights? Ladies fair?"

Catherine shook her head, auburn curls bouncing. "I wish to be a queen. For I shan't be one in life."

Raleigh glanced at William, his eyes questioning. "Surely your king and father will marry you to a fine prince, and then you shall one day be queen."

"I mean queen for myself, like your Elizabeth."

Raleigh laughed again, while everyone else shifted nervously.

"Well in that case, perhaps you *will* be queen for yourself."

William stopped chewing, eyes blazing at the man. The entire room went quiet, and only Halforn's heavy breath could be heard. Raleigh looked around the table, realizing his offense.

"Oh, I shan't be queen for myself," Cate said with a sad sigh, "my brother will be king."

"Catherine—" Anna gave their daughter a silencing glance.

"I beg your pardon, Majesties," Raleigh said, glass raised again. "I didn't know congratulations were in order."

"They are not." William gave Raleigh a tight smile. "The princess speaks out of the wishes of us all."

"No, Papa, I told you—I met my brother and he will be here soon."

"She suffered recently from *scarlatina*," Anna said. "She had fever dreams—"

Cate knit her brows. "'Twas not a dream."

The gathered courtiers whispered, stealing glances at one other. Even Daniel and Robert exchanged a meaningful look. Anna had warned William of this, warned him how people would react when they heard of Cate's strange vision. Thank God her words could be swept away as a child's fancy.

"Catherine," Anna's tone was cold, clipped, "that is quite enough."

"But why—"

"Dear Princess," Raleigh said, "I will write you the most beauteous poem in coupled verse, of the strong, brave, and stunning Queen Catherine Annelore, ruler of all she surveys. It shall be my Twelfth Night gift to you. We could even make it into a masque—how would that be?"

"Wonderful, Raleigh," Anna said, relieved.

Cate clapped, all talk of brothers driven from her mind as she listened to her mother and Raleigh talk of costume ideas. But William's mind remained fixed. Cate wasn't one for daydreams and make-believe. Rarely did she pretend to be anything other than what she was, more content by her father's and mother's sides than in the company of peers, more delighted by books and study than by playthings. The way she talked of her brother, the way she still insisted on his birth, even months later, was unlike her. And despite everyone's misgivings, William clung to her prediction with the hope of a drowning man seeing land. He didn't care if it was witchcraft or necromancy or a vision from the Lord on High. He needed—the realm needed—Catherine to be right. He just hoped the next minor court scandal would soon eclipse her outburst, leaving William alone with his silly, desperate belief.

Finally, the ladies took their leave and the men retired to William's chamber for drink and cards, though Halforn gave his goodnights, offering to escort the queen to her rooms. William called the lute player in as well, and the men settled at William's desk, Robert sitting as far from Raleigh as possible. Daniel dealt the cards.

"So tell me, Raleigh," William said, "do you find it at all strange to be in the courts of England's enemies? France, Spain . . ." He eyed Raleigh over his cards. "And while we would not put ourselves in such a category, surely it poses some difficulties being in Catholic courts."

"I wondered that myself," Daniel said, sorting his hand, "for I'm told you fought fiercely with the Huguenots at the Battle of Moncontour."

Raleigh nodded slowly, addressing his fanned cards. "When one grows up watching his father hunted down, not once, but numerous times, barely escaping execution for only living out the edicts set forth by Mary's father and brother, one does tend to adopt a distaste for Catholic zealots. But yours is known as a peaceable country. You allow your Protestants to worship as they would."

"And yet they continue to try us," William said. "So I ask again, why exactly are you making a tour of Catholic countries?"

"Despite my beliefs, or my queen's, we both see the benefit of diplomacy, even amongst those most likely to come against us, perhaps even more so." Raleigh discarded and took a sip of ale.

"Yet you say you do not come as a diplomat." William watched the man's beard twitch as he swallowed.

"There is official diplomacy, and diplomacy of another kind altogether." Raleigh smiled. "That of friendship."

"And how is your *friendship* with Philip?"

"Close enough to know if he plans to invade. Is that what you mean?" Raleigh laid his cards on the table, ending the round. "Let's just say, Highness, I do not play my hand until it's a sure winner."

"If you're trying to be poetic," Robert said, "you're right—you're quite poor at it."

William pinned Raleigh with a stare. "Sir, at the moment I'm not sure I believe you have a hand to play at all, let alone any cards." Raleigh's cheeks reddened.

"But a man of strategy never shows his cards," Raleigh said, cheek twitching.

"A man of strategy does not presume to sit at the gaming table of the king if he brings nothing to it." William cocked a brow. "Such a man as that is sent packing."

Raleigh's eyes grew large. He worked his jaw as if to speak, but instead yawned.

"Begging your pardon, Highness, but the day hath caught up

with me. I beg to take leave. I promise not to be so ambiguous in the future, but I don't wish to give you incorrect intelligence."

William nodded, still holding his eyes. "Indeed. I will require direct answers in regard to Spain if you plan to be 'diverting' our court much longer."

Raleigh bowed and left.

"Good riddance," Robert said with a scowl.

"Tush now, Norwick," William said, throwing down his cards, "I thought you would take a liking to the lad. Seeing as you share, shall we say, some similarities?"

William knew he shouldn't provoke Robert's ire just to placate his own, but it was so easily done.

"Merely because the man's father was chased about by Bloody Mary's inquisitors does not mean we shall become boon companions." Robert shot out of his chair. "That man knows nothing of suffering, of striving, of loyalty. He's a child, a mere puppet of his queen, and you'd be fool to think anything else of him."

William stood as well. "Watch your tone, Norwick."

"Watch what you imply."

Daniel stepped between them, hands stretched to each man's chest. "Perhaps we should all call the evening to a close, lest we lose the hard-won festive cheer the palace has brightened with these last weeks."

"Cecile makes a sound suggestion." William gestured to the room at large, tone flat. "Let us leave off this eve. Go make merry with your women, so the morning may be all the more . . . festive."

The men hurried out, Robert still in a huff. William glanced at the door by his bedside. He hoped to take his own advice.

Entering the private hallway, he saw a faint glow of light beneath the door at the other end and something inside him unclenched. He strode to the light, waiting to be enveloped.

As much as Robert wanted to ignore any directives from William, he strayed into Yvette's chambers, fingering her various trinkets until she returned for the night from her duties with the queen. He didn't have to wait long.

Nor was she surprised to see him there. She came straight to him, face implacable, took his head in her hands and covered his mouth with hers, taking a long pull on his lower lip. Apparently he wasn't the only one who had been missing their visits.

"I cannot have you stay the night," Yvette said when they'd finished their tangle, hooded eyes watching him refasten his trunks. "I have the last night watch."

She was sparsely covered in a fur blanket, propped against the headboard. A smile twitched on his face, as did things further down. "That doesn't mean we can't have another go, now does it?"

Her eyebrow arched and he thought she would succumb, but then she yawned, stretching her arms like a languid cat.

"I'm glad to see I inspire you so," he said, throwing his shirt over his head.

"My apologies, Your Grace—it has been a long day."

He sat on the edge of her bed. "Yes, I hear the queen kept you all out in the cold." He crossed his foot over opposite knee to lace his boots. "But you were entertained by the English runt, so it must not have been so bad."

She threw a small, velvet pillow at him, but missed. "I don't see why you dislike him so. You two could get on quite well in your penchant for revenge against the Catholics."

"Why does everyone keep saying that?" He got up and frowned down at her. "Why must I like the prat, let alone want to plot some treasonous act with him?"

"My, my," her smile was mocking, "someone's a bit touchy on the matter."

He snatched his jacket from the back of a chair. He sniffed, trying to regain some composure.

"He's an English interloper with no power and a mouth for telling tales. Tales which we've no way of proving true or false. God forbid we hatch policies against our supposed allies based on anything he says."

She rolled out of bed, taking the blanket with her. "First of all, no one at council is that daft—even Bartmore. But second," she stopped in front of him, drawing her forefinger along his jaw, "he does hold power. And that is what is gnawing at you, My Lord." He scoffed, skin tingling with her touch. "He is handsome, he is charming, and he is full of boyish vigor. Not a woman at court, aged or youth, has not taken notice of this. Why, the queen's own chamber turns to a swooning mess anytime he is mentioned, let alone when he is present."

"And what of the queen?"

"Oh, she's too holy and loyal to turn from the king, but I tell you this. The man is gifted." She dragged her thumb across his lips.

He grabbed her upper arms and pressed her to him. "Do

you suggest we use this—take down the queen, leave William heirless?"

She turned her head away. "I didn't mean to imply that."

"Then what did you imply?"

"I—" She wrested free. "I've taken a liking to the queen. I would not want to harm her so."

He threw up his arms. "Mother of Moses, Yvette, you've got to focus on the future."

"She doesn't deserve it, Robert."

"You claim she is too loyal, too devoted to God and king. Let her prove it."

"Robert—"

"If she falls, it's her own fault. You'll only give her ample opportunity to make the choice between indulgence or fealty."

"Why must it be this? You would truly wound your so-called friend and king this way?" She turned from him to put on her shift.

"Better this than any other way. You think he would not be more harmed by a coup? Another war? In a few years' time, the princess will be betrothed to my Rob and eventually William will see the advantages of abdicating to Rob when he's of age."

He was surprised he hadn't thought of this earlier. It was the perfect solution. Robert would have to bide nearly a decade before William would even consider giving up the throne to Rob. No matter. This was an easy opportunity—he must at least try.

"Do you hear yourself?" She yanked her robe tightly around her. "You speak of maybes and conjectures, all the while making the very real demand of me to entrap the queen. You realize she could be killed for it? Especially if she becomes pregnant?"

"Oh tush, the woman's more barren than Halforn." He screwed up his face as she brushed past him and picked up her wine with shaking hands.

"You have no idea the lengths I have gone for you already. No idea of the sacrifices I have made. Do not ask this of me, Robert."

He came up behind her. "You need to decide where your loyalties lie, my dear. With me or with her. You cannot have both."

He left her standing there, quaking, no less shaken himself.

Christmas Day arrived and after insufferably lengthy church services, the feast had finally begun. William made way for this year's Lord of Misrule, Gregory, Duke of Duven, who had been rolled in atop a cartwheel-sized yule log. Duven would sit in William's chair throughout the near fortnight of festivities, in charge of all entertainments. Many court ladies had lobbied for Raleigh to be Misrule, but never had a foreigner taken the role. Besides, the more time William spent time with the man, all too fitting the title became. Raleigh hinted that the Spanish were content to help the French in their own internal wars, ignoring the Low Countries and England, which would put Troixden out of the Spaniards' minds as well, but Raleigh hadn't presented much evidence. He had this rambling way of conversing that led him far from the path of William's stated course. Whether or not it was intentional or a personality quirk remained to be seen. At present, Raleigh was seated at the far end of the long table, flirting with many a young lady of court.

Anna's father had returned to court as well, delighting both Anna and Cate. When the princess wasn't on William's lap, she was on her grandfather's, soberly telling him of her lessons. William still wondered about her visions and whether she'd had more. A few nights prior, he'd tucked her into bed, and having her to himself, he asked her about her brother.

"Have you seen him again?" William said, trying to be casual.

"He comes to visit me sometimes." She took up her hair, weaving it through her fingers. "He told me to be careful."

"When was this, sweetings?"

She frowned, counting on her fingers. "Five nights ago."

"How often do you see him?"

"Not often."

He smoothed her forehead. "And what does he call himself?"

She giggled. "Papa! He's William of course!"

He kissed both her cheeks and smiled. "Well, if you see him again, you tell him your papa and mama can't wait to meet him."

"Oh, he knows. That's why he said be careful." She said this so matter-of-factly, as if recalling a conversation with Countess Cariline. Then she wrapped her arms around his neck. "It will be well, Papa. Trust in the Lord."

He knew he shouldn't be indulging her or his delusions, but he couldn't help it. She was now four years old. Which meant four years without a whisper of another babe. Would Cate be his only issue?

All these thoughts swirled in his head as Duven's raucous and raunchy masque ended. The court hooted and hollered and raised their cups. Now it was time for dancing. He turned to Anna, her cheeks rosy and jolly, her eyes sparkling with delight. Taking her hand, he rose, calling the rest of the court to its feet. They would begin with a traditional line dance and at some point in the night break into games. Thankfully, all that was up to Duven.

William wished Anna's demeanor were contagious, but even as they danced, his mind buzzed in too many directions. Begging her apologies, he took his leave, Anna immediately claimed by Cate and Beaubourg.

"You look ponderous, cuz," Robert said, taking the queen's seat next to William.

"'Tis my lot in life it seems." He took a long swig of spiced wine and belched.

"Is it governance or marriage that makes your face look a horse this night?" Robert nodded his chin at a dancing Anna.

"Governance, of course." William studied Robert's profile. His friend looked gay enough, but he could tell there was something brewing beneath the surface, some wrestling Robert was trying to hide.

"That's good." Robert scratched his beard. "I just wondered as I've noticed you and the queen have not had as much time together as is your usual wont."

William sighed. "Robert, just tell me what you're getting at. I'm too tired to guess at your conjecture."

"I'm simply observing that you have both had your hands full with various duties and entertainments." Robert nodded toward court, and there, at the center, stood Raleigh in a low bow before the queen, her hands clasped in front of her, her face pure pleasure.

He watched as they took to the floor. Ever gallant, Raleigh bowed over Anna's hand and kissed her knuckles. As Raleigh rose, the picture of the two nearly stopped William's heart. They could be twins, with their dark hair and eyes, sculpted oval faces. Even the way they held their shoulders at the ready to dance. It was uncanny.

William sat mesmerized as the man twined and twirled about with his wife. She laughing here, tentative smile there, a flirtatious whisper from him with a quick glance to the king. Raleigh knew William was watching. And the man enjoyed it.

As the song ended, it appeared as though Raleigh was bold enough to ask for another, for Anna shook her head and gestured to the rest of the room. Raleigh again took her hand, pulling it to his heart, making fun of his own pleading. Thankfully, good old Halforn broke in, taking the privilege of rank to dance with the queen.

William expected Robert to make some quip about the whole thing, but he had vanished. Instead, Duven turned to him and started sharing his plans for the rest of the evening, and all William needed to do was nod and intermittently say, "Good, good."

Finally, William felt Anna flop down next to him, heard her contented sigh, and saw her lunge for a drink.

He excused himself from Duven with an "It all sounds devilishly good," and turned to the queen.

"Looks as though you were enjoying yourself."

She raised her glass to him, smile broad. "Only lessened by the fact that my dance partner quitted the floor much too early."

"Ah, but you'd no loss for suitors." His smile was placid.

She took a long gulp and plunked down an empty goblet. "You know I have always been surprised with how nimble and quick Halforn is."

"And our English visitor, he looks to be a fine dancer as well, yes?" He raised a brow.

"Oh he has skill, but I've had better partners to be sure." She gave him a wicked smile, obviously not catching his meaning. His false demeanor faded.

"But perhaps none that made you blush so."

She laughed. Laughed! "My liege, doth I detect a pinch of jealousy?"

William rolled his eyes, trying now to shrug it off as a jest. "Why would I be jealous of the likes of him? It sounds more as though I ought to watch my back with Halforn."

She ignored his parry. "Simply because I am besotted with, and married to, the most handsome and charming and witty of men, does not mean I am completely blind to such in others."

"Robert is handsome and charming. You've never blushed about him." William picked at a discarded crust of bread.

"That is because Robert is a self-proclaimed arse."

He looked back at her. "And Raleigh is not?"

"He certainly may be, but not as such in my presence to be sure. He's most likely too wily for that."

William harrumphed and went back to decimating bread crumbs.

Anna shook her head, crossing her arms across her pinked

bosom. "My king and my husband, would you like to retire at present so that I may prove my undying devotion to *your* skill?"

He looked sidelong at her. "Who said I needed convincing?"

"So you refuse the offer?" Her brows nearly hit her hairline.

He grabbed her hand, stood, and yanked her to him. Snaking his arm around her waist, he raked her with hungry eyes.

"My queen and my wife, have you ever known me to refuse such an offer?"

In one swoop he cradled her against his chest, her legs dangling over his forearm, her head thrown back in laughter. He strode to the throne room doors, but remembering his place, stopped and turned back to the pointing, cackling crowd. He caught Raleigh's eyes as he said, "Carry on. We shall see thee all well after breakfast."

With that, he nearly leapt into the darkened throne room, heading to his even darker chamber. He bent his head to nibble her earlobe. Skill. Ha. He'd show her art.

William pressed his fingers across the bridge of his nose. He felt woozy and dim. With all the drinking and the happy lack of sleep the prior evening, Council Table was the opposite of what he needed at the moment. Still, the grand master general stared at him, awaiting some sort of intelligible, and hopefully intelligent, response.

"How confident are you in this information, general?" William had to squint down the table at the man.

"If I may interject," Anna's father said, "two men from

Brussels are stewing in our Beaubourg jail as we speak. The letters they carried were, upon first glance, harmless. But surely they are a cipher of some sort."

"They were on their way to Laureland, sire," the general added. "They were captured, without official traveling documents in the eastern foothills of the Truss Mountains, just a stone's throw from the Laureland border."

"And they of course deny all this." William stood, started to pace.

"Laureland is incensed at Helena's execution," Daniel said. "The word I have is they've nearly sainted her."

"If they believed in saints," Robert said. William shot him a warning glare.

"And just what would they have had us do? Let her go on her merry way?" William pinched his nose again, head throbbing. "For God's sake her beheading was merciful—she got less than she deserved. When will they stop these suicidal plots of theirs and just be content with the freedoms they already enjoy? The French, the Spanish, no one else would be as lenient as we." He had rounded the table and now leaned his forearms on his chair back.

"If they're involving Brussels," the general said, "'tis not so suicidal anymore." Nods of agreement went about.

"Damnation." He shoved his chair, his council staring woefully up at him like aged hounds. "And what of the Spanish? Will they help us or do they want to roast us like a Christmas lamb?"

His only answer was eyes darting around, each man passing to the other. Finally, Daniel broke the silence.

"Spain is focused on fighting against the heretics in their Low Countries."

"Tell me something I don't already know!" He shoved his chair anew and was off to circle the table once more.

Daniel bowed his head, fingering the papers in front of him. "Perhaps if they hear men of Brussels are trying to aid Laureland, the Spanish will help us. Philip needs more allies in this region, not more enemies."

The general's chair creaked as he leaned back. "Seems to me, if Philip gained Troixden for himself, he'd be in even greater position to subdue the Lowlands, with clean access to England to boot."

"But can we not reach out first as his ally?" Daniel said. "Offer him unfettered access to our ports, offer him men to support the effort in the Low Countries, give him a reason to be indebted to us?"

"Or give him more ease to march in and swallow us up!" The general shook his head, his long, white beard lagging behind.

"Has our little English gift given us any intelligence?" Robert said.

"He claims we are not at the forefront of Philip's mind." William abandoned his pacing and slouched into his chair, staring out the window at the falling snow. "And the Spanish ambassador swears up and down that Philip holds us in the highest regard and would defend us unto death."

Robert let out a "ha!"

"Now the French," Robert said. "I am ready to believe the French are content to ignore us completely, for good or ill."

"God, the French." William rested his head in his hands. His chest started to convulse with an oncoming sneeze. He barely got a kerchief out in time.

"Majesty, are you ill?" Daniel was up and to him, hand on his shoulder. "Shall I order some honeyed lemon water?"

William waved him off with his kerchief. "Nay. 'Tis surely just this damp and too much celebration in the eve."

"Let us be content to ignore the French as well then, for the time be—" William cut himself off with another sneeze and the floodgates were opened. The day kept getting better and better.

"Majesty, let me order you some—"

"Cecile, I will be fine with a simple rest." William searched in his pocket for a fresh kerchief. "In the meantime, I need more reliable information on Spain, as well as on how far Laureland has plotted with these others. Have they come of their own accord? Or—" Mother of mercy another two sneezes. And the hammering in his skull . . . "Or did Laureland send for them? Also, who has taken the helm with the Earl, Helena, and Westerville now dead?"

He pushed himself up, dizzy, his head the weight of wild boar. "I will retire for a time, but will receive visitors once I wake."

"Or once your wife allows it," Robert said under his breath. But William didn't even have the energy to smack him for it. He made a vague gesture at them with his kerchief and stumbled toward his chamber and peace.

"I will not allow it," Anna said, perched next to a hardly moving William. She crossed her arms as if that ended the matter. She was already perturbed that it had taken two hours for someone to get word to her that the king was unwell. Poor Bernard had gotten an earful, though she knew it wasn't his fault.

"'Tis merely a cold," William said, sounding muffled, scratchy.

"And it will get worse if you don't stay in bed to rest and drink Mary's medicines."

"Having you so near does not exactly help in that regard." He made a sad attempt at a lewd grin.

She narrowed her eyes. "Then I shall sit outside your doors and personally shoo away all comers."

He grabbed playfully, albeit slowly, at her arm. "I'd rather you stay here and be my nurse."

She leaned over and stroked his errant cowlicks. "Wills, if you intend to go on as usual with this 'mere cold,' it could easily become something much worse. The country needs you in top form." She gave him a sly smile. "*I* need you in top form."

"Well, if you put it that way." He winked, then coughed, which turned into a long, loud nose blow.

"You sound like a herald trumpet." He began to laugh which launched him into another hacking fit. She rolled her eyes. "Mere cold." Getting up, she fetched the water pitcher being warmed by the fire and topped off his mug, adding more honey and a squeeze of lemon, just how he preferred it.

"Thank you, my love," he said, taking the proffered remedy. "You do take care of me."

"Well someone has to." She wrung out a warmed wet cloth and, before folding it on his forehead, kissed his creased brow. "We'll have you back on your feet in time enough to see what wonders Duven has wrought for us at Sunday's feast."

He nodded and nestled into his pillows with a light cough. Closing his eyes, he sighed. Anna cleared space on the bedside table for a pot of peppermint oil and crushed jasmine. Once he fell into a deep sleep, she would slip out to check on Cate, hoping she too had not succumbed.

Ah, my Wills. His eyes soon began the flutter of early slumber. As much as she wanted him well, she couldn't help wanting this time to last, no outside demands on the bedridden king. Just breath, just warmed drinks, just murmurs and love.

Anna was better than her word, for William was back on his feet by Sunday morning, though he did use the illness as an excuse to skip mass. He was no longer coughing, and while his head was still sore, his nose had stopped its carnage. He had decided to surprise her with his recovery, but knew he must meet with Daniel to receive any news and sign a surely leg-high stack of official papers.

Feeling pleased with himself, he was about to begin whistling, but noises round the corner of the hall stopped him. Normally, being king, he would have strode ahead, but something in the voices' tenor stopped him. He raised a hand to halt the groomsman who walked with him and craned his neck to listen.

It was a woman's voice, low, urgent. He couldn't make out her words. Then he heard Daniel's voice, soothing. It sounded like the woman was crying. William crept closer.

"—a hold of yourself." He heard Daniel say.

"Please, Your Grace," the woman responded.

William could stand the curiosity no more. "Someone's coming," she said as the king turned the corner. By the time his eyes adjusted, he caught a fleeing Lady Jane, wiping her cheeks and a pale-faced Daniel staring after her. William rubbed his hands together and called out to his friend.

"I hope I am not interrupting?"

"Just a trifle, Highness," Daniel said with a sudden bright smile. "How well it does me to see you back to health!"

William led Daniel inside. "I wish everyone would not fuss over me so. It really was nothing."

"Well, we would hate for it to have been anything other than it was." Daniel walked to his desk and waited for William to sit before taking his own chair. "'Tis lovely of the queen and Mistress Mary to take such care."

"And 'tis good of Lady Jane to take such care of you," William said, brows jumping. "Or am I mistaken?"

Daniel paled. "I . . . 'tis truly simply—"

"Cecile," William leaned onto Daniel's desk, "you mustn't need be so coy about it. Lady Jane is a fine woman. You could do much worse in a wife."

Daniel's eyes were only for the papers he was sorting. "I promise you, Majesty, 'tis only a business matter. We were discussing the nurse I hired for her last summer in Cecile. Lady Jane, bonny though she be, is merely worried about her boy. With your Highness ill, as well as a handful of others, she is desperate that her little John does not relapse."

William smirked. "Well, 'tis kind of you to show such concern."

"I've no new information on Spain," Daniel said, "especially as Raleigh has given me a wide berth and even *my* spies are allowed some time of leisure at Christmastide."

"Of course." William leaned back, realizing his prodding would get him nowhere. "But I assume business has continued, despite the Christ child and my own illness."

"Blessedly little." Daniel pushed the inkwell and quill to William's side of the desk. "But there are end of year leases to renew, alms to approve." He then slid twenty or so pages William's way. "Nothing new in the bunch."

William picked up the quill and started signing, shoving each back to Daniel to blot and drip with wax. Then each would be returned to the king to press his griffin signet, glistening next to his name.

"Should we not hand Laureland over to someone we trust?" William said, on to the fifth lease. "Wouldn't that quash all their plans and maneuvering?" He looked up at his friend, who frowned with consideration. "Make it a duchy, pulling all the lords together?"

"But who? We've already so many dukes and too few of true noble blood."

William stopped writing. "What about Robert?"

Daniel's eyes widened and then he laughed. Laughed like William had rarely heard from the man, somewhere between gasping and hissing.

"I'm serious!" William had to smile at Daniel's reaction.

"Whew!" Daniel took a gulp of his habitual chocolate. William couldn't stand the stuff—it was bitter, watery, and left an iron-like taste in his mouth. "Oh forgive me, sire. I just . . . Norwick?"

"His lands border Laureland, he craves more influence. Perhaps if we gift it to him he will see fit to leave his scheming."

"It would make him a larger landholder than the crown. His wealth would rival your own. He could almost instantaneously have you dethroned with a mere hint of the force and money behind him." Daniel was more animated than William had seen in quite some time. "I know you have faith in him, I know he's our cousin, but you cannot forget that he is your next in line."

"But would not the gesture be of service to us both?"

"It is more than mere gesture." Daniel folded his hands on his desk. "Do you know why Elizabeth has not yet married?"

"To keep France and Spain continually guessing at her loyalties."

"Surely that is part." Daniel nodded. "But that woman is smarter than most men put together. She will not bear a child or name a next in line so that her people, or her enemies, don't discard her for her heir."

"And what of Mary Stuart?" William continued scratching.

"It's precisely because of Mary Stuart. And from Elizabeth watching her father, constantly in fear of losing his throne."

"Don't tell me you too are turning on our Robert." He was nearly through the stack now, his mood deteriorating.

"William." The king met Daniel's eyes. "I will ever put you first in all obligations. Personal, political. Even amongst family. It is you I declared my fealty unto. And God help me, if you were to die, I do not think I could do so to Robert."

William nodded and pressed his seal, feeling the warm wax seeping around his ring, tugging at his skin. "Then who would you suggest?"

"Let me think on it." Daniel handed him the last of the pages to be sealed. "On a person and the logistics."

Daniel's tone irked him. As much as Daniel argued that Robert wanted more power, it seemed Daniel was becoming ever more comfortable with his own. In this conversation alone, he had deflected the king's questions, spoken in a way that somehow put his word, his judgment, above William's. And here was yet one more person aligning against Robert. Perhaps this was just the fuzzy effects of William's cold? Regardless, he left Daniel's presence with barely a "good day," hoping his wife could improve his humor.

Their Lord of Misrule had left the theme of the evening's feast a mystery, putting Anna at a loss for what to wear. She bit her forefinger as she surveyed the gowns strewn across her bed.

"Truly, none of you know the theme?" Stifled whispers were the only response. She turned, pinning Margaux. "Surely you know, Countess. For what entertainments would be complete without your involvement?"

Margaux curtsied, batted her eyelashes. "Sadly, Highness, I've been much too busy looking after my boys to be involved in the frivolity of masques."

Anna fought against rolling her eyes. "Yes, that is sad. For I so enjoy laughing at your performances." Margaux's face pinched up like a twitching mouse.

She was about to turn to Lady Jane for further interrogations, when a knock at the door interrupted her. Bernard scuttled in, looking uncharacteristically flustered.

"A Walter Raleigh to see you, Highness."

Bernard's eyes grew to bowls as Raleigh sauntered past him, jaunty smile on his lips.

"I do not believe I gave you leave to enter," Anna said, arching a brow at his penchant for disregarding etiquette when it suited him. He was handsome, witty, and charming to be sure, but he was young. He needed more disappointment in life to dampen his self-importance. Unfortunately, no one at this court—the ladies anyway—were wont to give him that lesson.

He leaned against the last column, crossing his feet, a rolled paper under his arm.

"Forgive me, Majesty, I was just so eager to tell you my news."

She waved a hand at him and smoothed back her mussed hair. "And what is it then?"

"Oh, it can wait," he said, fully entering her chamber, observing the mess of dresses. "I see you are otherwise embattled."

"Some might call it that. Perhaps you can tell me, Raleigh, what I shall wear to the feast, for my ladies will not spill Duven's secret. But my ladies forget that apparently what I wear has political importance beyond imagining."

Again unfettered by decorum, he strolled to her bed, fingering the skirts. He studied the gowns, walking around the bed to the far side.

"I would say . . . white." He peered at her through the bedposts. "For it matches the snow about us, and 'tis spotless, as thou art."

Anna smirked. "I would hate to steal your own queen's hallmark in wearing white."

Raleigh smiled broadly back. "Then pair it with silver and ermine, diamonds and pearls. For no one would mistake the jewel you are with mine own majesty, handsome as she be."

"What of red?" Yvette said, placing a pile of hoods neatly on the toilette.

"A touch brazen, don't you think?" Margaux, obviously done pouting, had managed to place herself on the bed's edge, giving Raleigh a perfect view of her milky bosom. "Much more the color a woman like you would wear."

Ignoring her, Yvette lifted up a blood-red damask kirtle, trimmed in matching velvet, gold, and beaver.

"Something like this."

It was beautiful, and she had only worn it once because of the stir it had caused. And as much as she hated to admit it, Margaux was correct. A queen in all red evoked a siren, not an angel.

"You could pair it with a green corset and sleeves, matching the holly and ivy." Yvette pulled out an evergreen velvet corset, and sleeves to match, with draping cuffs lined with the same beaver fur.

"Well now that does seem jolly," Anna said, warming to the idea. The green would temper the red. And it matched the palace trimmings. Thus, whatever Duven had in store, she would at least compliment the decor. "And with the king still in and out of his sick bed—"

"Still?" Raleigh said. "That is indeed a shame. The court just does not seem right without his noble presence. The festivities will surely suffer for his absence."

"I thank you for your concern, sir, but he is sure to be back to his noble self soon." Anna nodded to Yvette to put aside the red and green.

Raleigh clapped his hands, rubbing them together. "Now, Majesty, shall I tell you my news?"

"We are all on pins and needles, are we not ladies?" She need not turn around to know her retinue was ogling the Englishman. She even caught Mary, arms akimbo, studying the man like he had a queer malady she was trying to discern.

He came out from the bed and took Anna's hand.

"Please, Madam, make yourself comfortable, and ladies all." He led her to the chair she sewed in and situated himself on the window seat next to her—William's preferred spot, she noted with some ill ease.

"I have finished the poem," he said, retrieving the paper from the crook of his arm. She looked at him blankly. "The one about the garden?"

"Of course! How lovely." She gave him a genuine smile.

"I have dedicated it to you and your intoxicating court." She thought he winked at her, but she couldn't tell. He unrolled a sheet of fine vellum.

Anna placed her hands in her lap, but Raleigh took her right, gently squeezing her fingers. Her face felt hot, and she had to admit his touch was pleasing, as it had been on the dance floor. It would only seem prudish for her to snatch it away, as it was certainly tradition for men to make courtly love gestures to the queen. There were just few at her court who did so . . .

He cleared his throat and began.

Now Serena, be not coy;
Since we freely may enjoy
Sweet embraces: such delights,
As will shorten tedious nights.

If her cheeks didn't match those red skirts before, they certainly did now.

Think that beauty will not stay
With you always, but away,
So frail is all things as we see,
So subject unto conquering Time.
Then gather Flowers in their prime,
Let them not fall and perish so;
Nature her bounties did bestow
On us that we might use them.

It was indeed beautiful, the longing, mingling of sadness and loss, yet the twinkle of hope. Unconsciously, she leaned toward him.

Let's then meet
Often with amorous lips and greet
Each other till our wanton kisses
In number pass the days Ulysses
Consum'd in travail' and the stars
That look upon our peaceful Wars
With envious luster—

"I think we've heard enough."

At the sound of her husband's voice, Anna whipped her hand out of Raleigh's and jumped to her feet. He stood in the same place beside the bed as Raleigh had been moments before. He must have come through their passage. His hands were on his hips, broadening his shoulders, his eyes nailing Raleigh to his seat. Anna curtsied in haste.

"My dear, you are up and well! What glad tidings." She went to him, but the ice in his eyes froze her.

Raleigh too rose from his seat and fell into a bow. "Majesty, I was reciting a poem written in honor of your rose garden in winter. 'Tis an honor for me that you have both heard it."

"Perhaps next time you would offer it up at court," William said, "rather than in Her Majesty's private chambers."

Raleigh stepped around ladies on the floor. "Of course, how silly of me. I was simply so provoked by finishing the thing, I wanted to share it with the queen . . ." William continued to stare daggers at the man. "As she was there in the garden when I began it . . ." He stilled his gesturing hands.

William brought his hands behind his back and walked forward. "Since you seem so quick and adept at the pastime, perhaps you might pen us a poem for Twelfth Night, to be read at the feast."

Raleigh bowed again. "An honor, sire."

"That is all, Raleigh." William flicked his fingers at the Englishman.

"Of course." He bowed now to Anna. "Majesties."

All was quiet while Raleigh quitted the room.

"I was coming to surprise you," William said. "And here the surprise was mine."

Anna's stomach kinked. Why did she feel so guilty? Certainly the poem had been, well, brazen, the word Margaux had used, but the scene had been entirely innocent. By the strained smile on William's face, she could tell that wasn't what he'd observed.

"A bed full of half the court's dresses," he said, gesturing. "Why, wife, I have not known you to be so indecisive."

So they would be discussing this later. Somehow that was worse. The anticipation of the row would follow her all day. But she fastened a smile on her face.

"My ladies and I, being ignorant of Duven's theme, could not decide what to wear."

"And that is the second reason I came—to see what you had decided so I might dress accordingly."

The ladies had picked themselves up from the floor, curtsied, and stood at attention in a line. William strode to the place Raleigh had vacated and sprawled out.

"Well, what is it between?"

Anna flicked her eyes to Yvette, then Margaux. The latter was smirking, twirling a holly sprig between her fingers.

"A red and green ensemble was suggested," Anna said, "as was the white and silver. With the white fox trim."

"So refreshing, white," William leaned back on his hands. "Without blemish." She willed her heart to slow its bird-like beating. "Then I shall wear my gray silks with wolf."

"You'll both be a glorious sight t' be sure," Mary said, bustling between them to start putting gowns away. "Now that we've settled it, Madam, you've time to make sure His Highness is well recovered."

William tilted his head. "Why, Mistress Mary, you question the word of your king?" Anna's stomach unclenched at the sound of his gently mocking tone.

"I question the word o' any man whose eyes be puffed and his nose the color of a turnip."

William jumped up. "Oh-ho, and now you insult my robust good looks?"

Mary shook her head, tsking. "Majesty, you know I'd lay me very soul down for ye to trod upon if need be, but that don't mean I'm blind as a bat. Yer royal handsomeness could do with a wee more rest."

Thank God in heaven for Mary. The woman had sucked all the contentious air out of the room, replacing it with good humor.

"Off with both your majestic selves." Mary swatted them with a sleeve. "An' I don't want to see hide nor hair of ye until all's well with the world."

"You'll be waiting a long time for that, Mistress," William said, heading to the hall door.

"So much the pity, then. I'll miss thee."

William guffawed and held out his hand for Anna to take. Once he led her into the hall and shut the door, he dropped her hand, and with it, so went her insides. She could almost see the seething waft off him as he strode in front of her.

He pushed open his chamber door, not even bothering to ensure she followed. He went to his desk and poured himself a full glass of wine. With a small protest of hinges, Anna shut the door, hands held in front of her.

"Well," he said, after draining the glass, "at least one of us finds Elizabeth's gift *diverting*." He appraised her. "For my part, I shall have him out and off to his next shenanigans by January the sixth. He's given me no substance on Spain, nor England for that matter, and all he does is make eyes at the ladies of court." He poured another glass, offering it to her. "My wife most of all."

"Wills." She started toward him. "He is simply an overzealous youth. Were you not so at his age?"

"I knew better than to tangle with another man's wife. Especially a king's."

She accepted the glass from him, their fingers touching. His eyes were dull as they met hers. She could tell he was tamping down his anger. She bowed her head in thanks and took a grateful sip. He gestured to their leather chairs by the fire but didn't move to sit himself.

She sat on his chair arm, facing him. "I seem to remember a similar incident a handful of years ago, when one of us saw a pretty young thing presenting her art to the other. And someone, I won't say who, jumped to hasty conclusions."

He sighed, shook his head, and ambled over to her. Reaching down, he held her free hand.

"The way he looked at you, the words coming out of his mouth as he did . . ."

"'Tis exactly how I felt when Charity sang to you that day." She squeezed his hand.

He gazed down upon her, sadness in his eyes. "I know I'm no longer young, and I don't have a way with words—"

She kissed his hand to stop him. "William. There is no comparison. Nor will there ever be. He is like a new plaything for Cate. Intriguing for a time, but soon cast aside for her favorites."

"So you admit he's intriguing?"

"And you do not?" She yanked his arm, pulling him between her legs. "Come now, he's at least as striking as Robert, exceedingly more enchanting, and he has that sparkling, youthful exuberance about him. If you were not so prone to jealousy in this matter, you'd be sure to agree with me."

"I thought so at first. But then he started to prattle about my wife's amorous lips and wanton kisses."

"It was a poem about the fleetingness of youth, kissing time before it flies away with all beauty." Anna placed her unfinished wine on the low table.

"Surely you are not so naïve as to think he has not imagined these things of you."

"He can imagine them all he wants." She slid her hands up the sides of his thighs. "'Tis you, my liege, who needn't imagine a thing."

His eyes began to glow again, a smile tugging his lips. "Promise me you will not have audience with him again without my presence."

"If it will ease your mind," she rested her hands at his waist, "I shall not even dance with him again."

A full smile bloomed. "Enough with the petting of my bruised manhood."

"Then come sit by the fire with me, for Mary is right—you need more rest before you look yourself again."

He acquiesced, pulling her into his lap. He began to undo her hair, pearl by pearl, pin by pin.

"Speaking of amorous kisses . . ." he planted one on the nape of her neck. "Has Lady Jane made mention to you of a special liking about court?"

She scrunched up her face. "Lady Jane? Goodness no. The woman is loath to speak in general and I can verily say she has eyes only for her boy."

"You're quite sure?" His eyes twinkled.

"What have you heard?"

"I haven't *heard* a thing. I simply observed the aftermath of an encounter betwixt the lady and a certain half-brother of mine."

"Daniel? No." She laughed. "Why 'tis preposterous."

"That's what he tried to say, but I think I know a lady distressed in love when I see one."

"Out with it. The whole story." She crossed her arms.

"There's not much of one. I came upon them in the hall outside of Daniel's chambers a bit after mass. I heard them speaking in low tones. When I came round the corner, her normally neat as a pin appearance was disheveled and she'd clearly been crying. I think Daniel was ending their affair."

"Oh posh! She was probably upset about John for some reason."

"That's what he said! But has the boy has been ill?"

Anna frowned, thinking. Jane had seemed no different today than any other day and she knew the lady would tell her of fears about the boy's health.

"Well, no."

"Ah-ha!" He raised a finger as if that settled the matter.

"And since when have you seen Daniel in the presence of any woman, alone?"

"Exactly!" He waggled his forefinger again.

"No, I mean the man says he's celibate. The rumors of course are that he . . . prefers the company of men, but represses such desires for obvious reasons."

"Those are just the mutterings of ignorance." William frowned. "When we were in exile, Daniel was known to take a lady—well, I wouldn't call them ladies—to his rooms on occasion. Not that these encounters seemed to lighten his demeanor. That's part of the reason I always thought him truly celibate, someone disinterested in the act itself."

She took his chin, turning his face to her. "Then why do you think he's taken up a secret affair with Lady Jane, of all women?"

"She's a young widow, handsome in her way, devout, devoted, and living quite close to his quarters."

"That is my point. She is not some trollop. It would be a very respectable match and one that would not need be hidden in the shadows." She watched him ponder this, working his jaw.

He scratched his stubbled chin. "When we were young, I always suspected Daniel was in love with my sister. But being her half-brother, and a bastard to boot, this love was decidedly unrequited and unnatural. When she died . . . we were all torn asunder with grief, but his, his went deeper than say, Robert's, who loved Cate better than his own sister."

"So you think he has carried this flame his whole life, keeping celibate out of honor for your sister?"

He faced the fire, the dancing flames reflecting on his cheeks, in his eyes.

"And also for me. He has a loyalty to me that borders, at times, on obsession. He claims to have lived his life the way he has out of duty and gratitude for my mother's kind care and for how I saved him from my brother's wrath. That is why he guards my life, my crown, as his very own."

"He can at times be possessive of you." She looked at their twined hands. "And he seems uncomfortable in my presence. As if I'm an interloper. As if my place in your affections has somehow diminished his own place."

William chuckled. "Oh, I doubt that. He's nothing but the highest regard for you. I just think beautiful women make him uneasy. He doesn't quite know how to behave around them. Look at how he always gives Margaux wide berth, or Amelia, but talks very easily with Halforn's girls, or with Mary and Cariline."

Anna lifted her chin. "I don't like you disdaining the fairness of my ladies. They are all beautiful in God's eyes, and in mine."

"Alas, we men are not gods—or so charitable as you." He nipped the side of her jaw, drawing his hand up her bodice. She halted his progress.

"When I said you need to rest, 'twas not a euphemism."

He exaggerated a pout. "Why must you women terrorize me so?"

She patted his cheek. "All so that we may have you around to keep terrorizing." She extricated herself from his lap. "Come now, to bed."

"Under normal circumstances, that is a highly motivating phrase." He didn't move.

"You may also lounge here then." She marched over to Mary's medicines and mixed him another warm tincture. "Would you like me to bring you your furs as well?"

"I'd rather you keep me warm."

"You are nothing if not persistent." She came back, carrying a steaming mug, a fur over her arm. She handed him the drink and gestured for him to hold it above his head so she could spread the fur about him. Tucking him in up to his neck, she finished with a kiss to his forehead. "I don't want to hear word of you stirring until you come to escort me to the feast."

"Yes, Madam."

"I'm serious, Wills." But her smile was at odds with her stern words.

"No stirring." He held up a hand in oath. She gave another peck to the top of his head and made to leave. When she reached the hall door, he said, "Unless it's a drink. Surely I'm allowed to stir that?"

She made an exasperated noise. "You should have been a lawyer."

"Wouldn't want to disobey orders, Majesty."

"I'll give you something to stir," she said, shaking her head as she left.

"I'll be looking forward to that!"

The feast had the theme of tapestry creatures, and papier-mâché masks were doled out to each attendee. Robert surprisingly had little trouble telling who was who. Everyone had such specific quirks about their posture, their gestures, their clothing. He, of course, selected the fox mask. Apropos, and also matching his burnt orange and gold attire. He stalked through the crowd, looking for his victims. It didn't take long for him to find the first. Raleigh stood laughing with some of Duven's grooms, an elk mask shoved atop his head.

Robert entered the fray, with bows of deference from the other men. "Why, Raleigh, 'tis a shame you don't share in the celebrations. The elk would much improve you."

"As the fox does you, Your Grace." The other men had the good sense not to snigger.

"I hear there was a bit of a tête-è-tête with the queen this afternoon that caused quite a scandal." Robert pushed his mask up too, the better to see the man's reaction.

He laughed. "'Twas hardly private, what with the queen's entire entourage of ladies, two musicians, her head of chamber, and the king also present."

"Truly? Hmm." Robert looked about the room, feigning disinterest. "My sister tells it differently, but you know women. Always exaggerating these things into romances."

"Excuse me, gentlemen," Raleigh said with a little bow to his conversation partners. Recognizing their presence was unwanted, they melted into the crowd. "Just what did your sister say?"

"So it wasn't so innocent after all then?" Robert's face was impassive.

"It was entirely innocent," Raleigh bit out, "but I will not have anyone besmirching the queen's good name."

"Heavens, the conclusions you jump to, Raleigh." Robert

jutted his head to the side, cuing Raleigh to follow him. He led the man to the outskirts of the Great Hall, where fewer people mingled.

"'Tis not my conclusions," Raleigh said when they reached a windowed alcove. "This court is incredibly prudish, Your Grace. Why in England, 'tis near requirement to make courtly love to the queen, in the most ardent words possible. What I composed for the queen in honor of her garden was tame by comparison."

"Garden, was it?" Robert smirked. "Your queen is unmarried." Raleigh had easily taken the bait. Hopefully, in his youthful exuberance to correct the matter, he would stumble into more precarious encounters with the queen. "But I can't say I blame you. She is bonny, as you say across the water. And certainly keeps His Majesty content. Though he be aged, of course, and one can't blame the queen for seeking out the company of younger men."

"It was I who sought her company, not she mine." Raleigh jabbed a finger to his chest in noble defense of her honor.

"Well, I'm sure there's nothing to the way she smiles and titters upon you." Robert caught Raleigh glance to the head table, his cheeks coloring. "I'm surprised Philip allowed such behavior at his court, for I do believe he be just as devoted to his own Queen Anna."

"Let us just say, Philip's court was not as inviting as Troixden's." Raleigh's eyes kept returning to the royal pair, heads together in conversing.

"So you've nothing of import to convey then?" Robert concealed his surveil of Raleigh by searching the crowd, nodding at a few passersby.

"I'm at a loss for your meaning, Your Grace." Raleigh crossed his muscled arms, attempting aloofness.

"Oh come off it." Robert waved across the room at the English ambassador, Doemland. Doemland, as it turned out, didn't know Raleigh and was barely aware of his arrival. "You clearly implied you had knowledge of Philip's plans in regard to our borders and our lands. 'Tis the only reason you've been given leave." He faced Raleigh, sizing him up. He was young, yes, but there was metal there, honor, and a spark of fire. He could be looking at his former self.

Raleigh titled his head, scrutinizing Robert. "I can't say I comprehend your vehement dislike of me." Robert snorted. "I hear tell you and I have a common enemy. I would think, as such, we might become better acquainted. Come to some unofficial agreements on matters dear to us both."

Robert threw back his head and laughed. "Oh my dear, dear Raleigh. The queen may smile and demure at your performance and the king may look the other way, but can you really think I'd have any dealings with you? A spinner of tales, a bender of the truth, a pretender of a gentleman?"

Raleigh laughed as if they were sharing a delightful joke. "As they say, Your Grace, it takes a thief to catch one." He affected a dramatic bow. "And a Merry Christmas to you." He strode to the dance floor, taking the hand of tittering Brigitte, Margaux glaring after.

The cheek of the man. Robert didn't know whether to respect him or loathe him all the more. In any case, he felt the seed of the queen's affection was well planted. He went toward his own place at the head table, watching Annelore. She laid her slender hand on William's arm. William grabbed it, kissed it, then tucked it in the crook of his arm. Apparently all was forgiven. The queen's eye's strayed to the dance floor. They widened, then flicked away. He followed her gaze to find Raleigh struggling to keep a tipsy Brigitte upright. He smiled to himself. All Robert needed to do was water the seed and make it sprout.

Anna sat contently by William's side, all the court parading in splendor, and various stages of drunkenness, before her. Seeing her father resting against a far pillar, she begged leave of the king, taking Jane and Mary with her. In her haste, she nearly ran into the English ambassador's wife, Lady Katharine.

"Excuse me, milady," Anna said, hand to chest.

"'Tis I who shouldst be watching my way, Highness." She made a low curtsy, splaying her intricately woven green skirts. The gown depicted a tree, sewn in golden Celtic knots, its roots reaching down to the ground, leaves and branches twining around her torso. If Anna wasn't mistaken, a pair of gold-threaded eyes and a beard of leaves peeped out at the center of Katharine's bodice.

Anna hadn't taken much notice of the woman when she'd arrived at court, and Katharine kept mostly to herself. Doemland, the English ambassador, had asked to return to England for Christmastide, but Elizabeth had refused, instead sending Katharine to Troixden to ease the blow. Perhaps Elizabeth thought it better to have three pairs of English eyes in Troixden than one, flirtatious pair.

"Your attire is magnificent, Lady." Unconsciously, Anna touched a sleeve depicting a looping spider's web, as if a giant arachnid spun between the branches. Katharine didn't flinch when Anna rubbed the fine cloth between her fingers.

"Thankee, Majesty." Katharine bobbed again, but held Anna's eyes. "It took me some time. I am glad it pleases thee."

"You made this yourself, Lady?" Anna turned to Mary, shaking her head in disbelief. "You are gifted beyond measure."

"Spinning pleases me. 'Tis as if I can see the world in my hands, in the strings." She smiled with some hidden delight.

"You sew, embroider, *and* spin? I am amazed that your queen would part with such a treasure as you."

Katharine shrugged, the creature on her bodice winking. "I spun some things that displeased Her Majesty—hence I am sent here like an errant child for my husband to look after."

While she privately appreciated the woman's bluntness, Anna was unsure how to respond. "If it would please your Ladyship, bring your spinning to my chamber on the morrow. For I would like to see what the Queen of England so blithely turns away."

"As you wish it, Highness." Katharine curtsied and Anna passed with her ladies. But she felt the woman's eyes were still upon her. Or maybe some other mythical beast peered out from Katharine's back, watchful for knives.

Mary caught Anna's arm as they waded through the crowd toward her father. "Do y' think that was wise, dearie?"

"What exactly?" Anna weaved along, royal smile plastered to her face.

"You know nothing of this woman, and here the heretic queen has thrown her out of court."

"And so your advice is to follow the heretic queen and throw her out of ours?"

"Come now, think on it! You're letting the lion into the lamb's fold."

"I am the lamb in this scenario?" Anna kept moving, pushing away Mary's attempts to slow her. They reached her father before there could be further reply.

"My darling girl and my queen!" He bowed, then hugged her. She kissed his cheek, her own feeling his gray beard's downy tufts.

"I saw you standing alone and thought you in need of company." She roped her arm through his.

"I was simply taking in the grandeur of it all, lost in my own memories of Christmases past." She could tell by his eyes he'd been thinking of her mother.

"Well, enough ponderous thoughts for the night. What say you to a mug of hot honey-mead?" She pulled him toward the drink table, but her way was impeded by Mary, Jane hiding beside.

"Why, my dear Mary," her father said, "whatever has you in a lather? Surely not something the queen has got up to?" He winked at Anna.

"Your Grace knows her as well as I do." She pursed her lips and moved in, speaking to the duke in low tones. "Anna's invited the English ambassador's wife t' come spin for her in her chambers."

Her father gave Mary a meaningful look, cleared his throat, and patted Anna's arm. "Unfortunately, I can't tell my queen what to do, but I can tell my daughter, not to trust the Irish."

"So she's Irish then? I was wondering on the accent." The Celtic knots certainly made sense then, as did her skill. The best spinners were from Ireland and Scotland.

The duke stopped moving. "I'm quite serious, Anna. The woman was married for political convenience and is here at court against her will."

"Well then, we have much in common." Anna smiled as Mary scowled and her father sighed.

"Just promise me you will take heed in her presence," he said. "She is not a lady of this court and is loyal to no one."

"Is that something you know for a fact, or merely conjecture based on her origin? For if my feeble mind remembers aright, the Irish are devoutly Catholic, which would make them our allies." They had reached the table and Anna poured her father his drink.

"Anna, dear, let us not fight. It's Christmas." He took the mug from her, a tired look in his eyes.

"I will indeed drink to that, Papa." She kissed his cheek again, then, hoisting her mug, said, "May the season be bright."

"And calm," he added, with a pointed nod.

"Your Grace!" Halforn addressed her father. "I wanted to speak to you about my daughter's palfrey. Oh! Excuse me, Majesty." He bowed, taking Anna's hand to kiss.

"No apology needed, for we were just toasting the season." Anna lifted her glass to Halforn as well. "Father, do not forget the sleigh ride with me and the princess tomorrow."

"I would not miss it." He smiled at her, but his eyes were wary. She knew their conversation wasn't over.

Heading back to her seat, she and her ladies took to the hall's edges to encounter less obstruction or royal social duty. But she had barely gone twenty feet before she was stopped again.

"Majesty," said a breathless Raleigh, making a hurried bow. "I must speak with you privately in much haste." He motioned her to an alcove but she stayed planted to the stone.

"Master Raleigh, it is quite uncouth for you to ask this of me. And in such a bluster. Surely what you have to share may be said in front of my two ladies."

He glanced at Mary and Jane. "I simply do not wish more rumors to spread through the eavesdropping ears of courtiers."

"And you think pulling me aside will not add more grist to the rumor mill?" She shook her head, but pitied him nonetheless. He was earnest to be sure, well-meaning, if a bit naïve. His only answer was the pleading in his face. She stole a look across the hall to William. He was deep in conversation with Daniel and the grand master general. "All right, but only for a moment, and my ladies accompany me."

He held out his arm to lead the way to the nearest window alcove. It was smaller than the rest and buffered by a column, causing Anna and Raleigh to squeeze close to the panes and Jane and Mary to stand facing out as if shielding the two.

"It has come to my attention that there are those who believe I am paying court to you." He spoke quickly, as if spurting forth a practiced speech he had no wish to give.

She laughed, surprised by his formality and concern. "'Tis the work of foreign dignitaries to ply flirtations upon the queen. I do not take offense. But it is dear of you to be anxious."

"These rumors imply more than courtly love, Madam." He leaned closer. "They imply that I either have, or am planning to, proposition you."

Anna's breath caught. While she'd never admit it, a thrill shot through her at his words. This dashing, young, worldly Englishman, with lascivious intentions toward her? She swallowed the lump in her throat.

"And are you?"

He took her hand, encasing it in his own. His hands were warm and soft, not large and calloused like William's. "I would never do anything to tarnish your sterling reputation, Highness." He kissed her knuckles, lingering too long. "But if you were to wish it of me—"

She startled at his words, snatching her hand away. Fantasy was one thing, but the audacity . . . She had to stop herself from slapping him.

"Do not presume to be so informal with me. I am a queen and a happily married one at that. What would make you think I would risk all for the fleeting and trumped-up admiration of a heretic?"

She hadn't laid a finger on him, but his face looked as though she had. His eyes were wide, mouth open, cheeks crimson.

"'Tis neither false nor fleeting," he said. "I was lead to believe . . . but I see I have given even more offense. Please, Majesty, forgive me." At this, he clutched her hand again and fell to one knee, bringing her hand to his forehead. "Forgive my pompous presumption. It besmirches us both."

Anna's mind flipped through each time they had been together. What had she done, what had she said, to give him the impression she would be open to his advances? Raised away from court, she'd never been schooled in the etiquette of courtly love, unless one counted Bryan. But he'd intended more than flattery as well. Shame crept in her chest. Perhaps William was right to react how he did. Perhaps she was sending off some signal of which she was ignorant. Well, enough of it. Enough of her girlish thoughts, enough of her innocent smiles and clamoring for poems. Her eyes sought out William again and she found both him and Daniel frowning at them.

"You are forgiven, Raleigh," she said, anxious to get away. "But I beg of you, do not seek out my private audience, or truly any audience in which the king is not present, again."

"It shall be so," he said, still gripping her hand.

"Release me."

"Yes, of course." He rose, flustered, wiping his brow with a kerchief.

She broke through Jane and Mary, sending them fluttering after, and strode right to William.

He sat, eyes cold, chin on his hand, staring up at her.

"He only wished to apologize for the misunderstanding."

"It's not him I am concerned with." He didn't blink.

"Majesty." She went to both knees to be face to face with him.

"I specifically asked that you not be in his company without my presence. He is young and headstrong. You are a queen, and my wife. It is you who should refuse his suits."

She took his hand and kissed it. He closed his eyes. "Mary, Jane and I were already on the sides of the hall. He merely suggested we speak away from the crowd. It was very public and he was all remorse. I didn't think—"

"That's the very problem—you didn't think." He opened his eyes and now they blazed. "Not only do you fuel more rumors by such behavior, but you make me look a fool."

"Anyone with any sense would realize nothing at all was—"

"I'm not talking about people with sense." He drew his hand from hers, reached for a goblet, and slumped in his chair. "How many times must this lesson be learned, that 'tis not what's true, 'tis what people want to believe that counts?"

"If it makes any difference, I told him never to seek me out again." She got off the floor and slid into her own chair.

"Majesties!" Duven, not noticing their dour faces, popped between them. "The games shall begin shortly. Blind man's buff first. Who shall be the blind man?"

"I've no need of more foolishness this eve," William said.

Duven frowned, but his chipper mood was unaltered. "Right. I'll have it be Norwick then." And he bounded away.

William gulped his wine, sucking it through his teeth, looking out over the drunken horde of spectacularly festooned courtiers. "He was prostrate before you. Lips to your hand. No one cares what either of you said."

"With Mary and Jane right there to witness it? How stupid do you think I am?"

He pounded his fist on the table, stilling those around them. He smiled. "Just a fly," he said. "Please continue." He waited a moment for conversation to begin anew.

"Mary and Jane are your two most devoted ladies. They would do anything for you."

"Including help me plot to cuckold you?" She threw up her arms. "Is that what you think of me?"

"Dammit, Anna, it doesn't matter what I think!" He faced her, jaw clenched.

"It does to me!"

He opened his mouth, but then snapped it shut.

"I want you to tell me that you don't believe it," she spoke slowly to steady her voice. "I want you to tell me you would never believe I would stray from you."

He leaned within inches of her face. "And I want you to tell me that you have not considered it. That that *boy* does not set your heart a flutter. That if circumstances were different—"

"And what circumstances would those be? Hmm?" She sat back to study him. "If I were not forced to marry and were still skipping about in Beaubourg, when for truly no good earthly reason, this Raleigh appears and reads me poetry? Is that the circumstance you mean? Or if I had been married off to your tyrant of a brother instead of you?" He stared harder at her. "Because I cannot come up with a circumstance where *you* are involved in which I would turn to another. Ever. Even when you are being pigheaded and jealous and jumping to wild conclusions, I love you and there's nothing you or I or some English whelp can do about that."

"Mmph," was all he said.

Her chest heaved and she gaped at him. That was it? Mmph? She shook her head and gazed out over the crowd. By a far pillar she saw Daniel speaking with Lady Jane, a placid smile on his face. Jane didn't look up at him, but gestured delicately as she spoke. The conversation could merely be about her son and his new nurse, or it could be about more . . .

"I apologize." William said, avoiding her eyes. "But again, I must stress that it is not my opinion you need worry about. He is a heretic, a representative—no matter how minor—of Queen Elizabeth, and to show favor of any kind to him is to show favor to the Protestants."

"Then why did you invite him to court? Why not bid him on his way?" Since he wouldn't look at her, she continued to study Daniel and Jane. Was Jane blushing?

"If I send him away now, it makes the rumors appear even more valid."

She spied Duven, kerchief in hand, giving chase to Robert. She sighed, faced him. "I apologize for any part I have played, though unwittingly so. But may we please get past this misplaced jealousy? I do not know how many times I can prove myself true to you."

He reached for her hand, rubbed the side of her thumb. "I cannot help it, my dear. Men cannot help but desire your company, and I am jealous for it. All of it."

"But what will it take for you to believe you have it?"

As if driven by the devil himself, Raleigh appeared in front of their table in a low bow.

"Majesty," he addressed only William, "I apologize for my recent behavior. The English and Spanish courts differ in their deportment from here, and I should not have been so brash to assume any familiarity with those of higher rank than me. As a gesture of my sincerity, I am at liberty to share all you wouldst ask in regard to Spain."

William squeezed her hand, nodded to Raleigh, and rose. "Then let us retire with a select few to my council for refreshment."

The two left her presence, her stomach aching. They hadn't resolved their argument, and she didn't know if they ever would. Duven had lost Robert to the king's call, but found another victim in Margaux. That woman would use any excuse she could get to freely grope people.

Anna filled her glass, leaned against her chair back, and sighed. Let the games begin.

Monday morning dawned low and gray, threatening snow. All Anna wanted to do was wrap herself in furs by the fire and read, or go through lessons with Cate. But she pushed such selfish desires away along with her bed curtains and shuffled off to mass.

Upon returning to her chambers, she found a carved ebony spinning wheel set by the hearth, a stool and basket of wool at the ready. But Katharine was nowhere to be seen. Anna's mood brightened, as she'd forgotten her request of last eve. She asked Yvette to assemble a plate of food but only picked at some bread while waiting in her chair next to the fire.

She didn't wait long. Bernard, wary look upon his jowled face, escorted in Katharine, who today wore a simple olive-gown trimmed with darker velvet. She curtsied low and long as she had before.

"Lady Katharine, you are welcome," Anna said. "I am well pleased you've come and am eager to see more of your art. I wish my own hand were skilled at more than just herbs."

Katharine settled on the stool. "Begging your pardon, Majesty, but do not disparage the knowledge of herbs and healing. They too are an art, and of the highest order, for they have the power of life and death." Her eyes, one brown and one green, roved over Anna's face and hair. Anna could have sworn she winked. Bringing her attention to the basket, Katharine picked up a clump of near-glowing red fiber, she said, "Some spinners prefer using the distaff," she indicated a wooden pole at the wheel's opposite end, "but for this," she held it out for Anna to touch, "this I keep well held in mine own hands."

The fiber was soft as Cate's baby hair and had a spider web stickiness to it. "'Tis the softest wool I've ever felt," Anna said, stroking it.

Katharine guffawed, her casual manner reminding Anna of Mary. "'Tis no wool I bring to a queen! Mother Mary and all th' saints protect me. 'Tis silk. The finest to be had in these parts."

Anna had seen Beaubourg's spinners as a girl, Bryan's mother among them, but she hadn't given much thought to how thread and yarn were made, let alone fabric. Sometimes she'd sit for hours, entranced by the wheel's rotation, but never paying heed to what transpired, never watching the busy hands. She felt a twinge of embarrassment at her ignorance, and more than a twinge of guilt at how blithely she ordered new gowns to be made.

As if reading her mind, Katharine said, "Of course, most seamstresses use ready-made fabrics, but for me, to spin and weave and sew, to create from the very source to its end, that be the glory in it."

"Like an artist who mixes his own paint," Anna handed the raw silk back to Katharine.

"Or like a physic, who makes 'er own medicines." There was that wink again.

"My mother was a spinner." Margaux had quietly sidled up to them, staring at the wheel.

"She musta be a fine woman then. For true spinners are a rare breed." She laughed again, low and graveled.

"She's . . . she's dead." Margaux frowned, still staring at the wheel. She looked as though she was lost somewhere in a wood—cold, bedraggled, and without hope of ever finding shelter. In that moment, Anna glimpsed the young girl Margaux once was. The confusion and sadness of growing up without a mother, but worse than Anna's motherless childhood, for Anna had Mary and her father, and all of Beaubourg. Margaux had nothing but a cruel father and a selfish, spiteful brother. No wonder she clamored for more. Anna silently vowed to remember this when Margaux wheedled under her skin.

"D'na be silly, girl," Katharine said, almost scolding. "The dead are always with us. They never leave."

Anna shuddered and crossed herself. "I do not think the Scriptures would—"

"Flip the Scriptures," Katharine said. "All we anointed fly up t' heaven, but that doesn't mean the Lord don't allow us to watch o'er our loved ones, make sure they mind their ways."

"That's quite a presumption, Lady Katharine," Anna said, her voice lowered.

"My mother was burned as a witch." Margaux's voice was flat, and she now stared into the fire, as if seeing her mother writhing in the flames.

"Tush, then all the more reason." Katharine took Margaux's hand again, her strange eyes sparkling. "She be dancing with the Lord and coming back here to give y' kisses, with a tickle on your brow and the wind at your cheek."

Katharine released a pale Margaux and picked at the ball of silk, drawing a thin wisp away and twirling it to a bit of string protruding from the mechanics. A gentle tapping of her foot on the pedal sent the wheel spinning, the silk stretching and coiling. Her hands moved with the ease of oars through still water, the whole of this taking no more than a few seconds.

"Come closer, milady," Katharine said to Margaux, "and lend me a strand of your hair. We shall spin this thread for you and see what we find."

Margaux plucked a hair from her head, handed it to Katharine and watched wide eyed as the gold twined itself with red, disappearing in a blink on the flying bobbin.

Anna was unsure what to make of this scene. The bulk of her ladies now clustered, quietly shouldering to get a better view of the woman at her work, and Anna knew this tale would be soon spread. The woman presented herself as a Catholic, wore her rosary, and was Irish, for heaven's sake. But all her talk about the dead, and her spinning Margaux's hair . . . it smelled of witchcraft. Why hadn't Anna listened to her father and Mary?

Katharine gazed lovingly at her handiwork, as one would a child. "There." She swiftly unhooked the bobbin and unspooled the remaining thread, perhaps three feet in length, and handed Margaux the folded skein.

The lesson continued and two hours flew by while the

women drank, watched, listened, and learned. Anna felt like a child sitting at Bryan's mother's feet, nothing but the pleasure of methodical work on Anna's mind. It wasn't until the room darkened that she became aware of the time.

"My apologies in keeping you so long, Lady Katharine."

"No apology needed, Highness—'twas a joy. I feel I could keep here the night through without even a notice, so content am I at the wheel and in thy company." She began to gather her things, stowing the spinning wheel's free parts in her large woven basket. "If your master of chamber would not mind assisting . . ."

"Allow me," Margaux said. "For it's well time I check on my youngest, if it be Your Majesty's pleasure. He seemed a bit low this morning."

Anna nodded, unthinking. "I hope you will enjoy the rest of your stay here at court, milady, however long that be. And it would give me great pleasure to have you spin for me again."

"Whenever you wish it, I shall appear." Katharine curtsied and joined Margaux in leaving.

"Phew!" Mary exclaimed, plopping down and fanning herself. "I'll be glad when she's gone and that's no doubt."

"Mary," Anna said, "you've always told me to treat others all the same, as the Lord would do. Why now suddenly are you becoming a Pharisee?"

"Spinning hair int' thread? Seems like witchcraft to me," Mary muttered.

"That's a very serious accusation." Despite Anna's corrective tone, her own earlier thoughts on the matter convicted her. "And one that should not be bandied about. Especially in mine own chambers."

"We women must stick together on such matters," Yvette said. She sat curled on the window seat, nursing a warm mulled wine. "Besides, we certainly would not want our men to have more fuel for the fire of their warring ways."

"Enough of all this talk of witches and of war." Anna said, clapping her hands. "Let us have a game of cards before supper, shall we? Ruff and Honors?"

The ladies readily agreed and Anna hoped, though without much optimism, that the whole afternoon would be forgotten in the coming days' revelries.

"Your sister is up to something."

Yvette lay wrapped in a sheet, in Robert's arms before his fire. He leaned against the side of his leather chair, stroking her bare shoulder. It was well past midnight, but this comment shook him wide awake.

"I wondered as much. She's been avoiding me as of late, and since again her boy looks nothing like the king, she's out of trump cards." Robert shifted his weight to ease a leg cramp. "I have often wondered if she keeps the queen from child as she did before."

Yvette shook her head. "There's no way for her to do so, unless she has cast some spell upon Her Majesty. I never allow her alone near the food or drink."

"And she would certainly never turn to sorcery or spells. Not after what happened to our mother." Robert kissed her shoulder. "That sort of thing leaves quite an impression."

Yvette arched a brow at him. "And don't I know it. For you want to take an entire religion down for it."

Robert rolled his eyes and moved her off him. "It's not just that and you know it. Don't make me out to be a petty, spiteful child."

"I said nothing of the sort." She spread the sheet over her head, cloaking herself. "That's your own self-loathing talking."

"Ha!" Robert scratched his chest. "Self-loathing? I've not conscience enough for such navel-gazing as that." He rolled to his side, reaching for a goblet on the low table.

Yvette's dark eyes peered out at him from her shroud, the contrast of olive skin against pure white stopping his breath.

"So what now of my dear, sweet sister?"

"Lady Katharine, Doemland's wife. She visited the queen's chamber yesterday to spin. Your sister was quite taken with it." Readjusting the sheet against her chest, she crawled forward to steal a sip of Robert's wine. He took the opportunity to cup something of hers.

"Margaux has a new hobby. What of it?"

Yvette finished his drink, licking red moisture from her lips. Placing the empty goblet on the floor, she released the sheet to place both her palms on Robert's chest. Damnable woman, he wouldn't be able to concentrate for much longer.

"She spun Margaux's hair into thread, gifting her the end result." Her hands glided down to his stomach, his skin sparking in their wake. "Witchcraft was mentioned."

Before he could speak, Yvette took his lips, sucking and pulling. He dragged her the rest of the way onto his lap, straddling his hips. He could barely string a coherent thought together, but pulled away from her mouth.

"So you think she's seeking spells and potions to finally turn William's eyes to her?"

She frowned at him. "Margaux may be daft, but she's not stupid. She wouldn't actively seek out a witch . . . with your mother—"

Robert dragged his fingertips down her back, causing her to arch into him, her soft warmth blanketing his torso.

"But you said she was up to something." He now attacked the crook of her neck, salty and sweet. She let out a throaty sigh.

"Just don't be surprised if some drama unfolds before long."

"For now," he said between sucks, "I wish for drama to unfold right here." And in one deft move he had her on her back, wicked smile beckoning.

William was at his wits' end with this Raleigh character. After his bold pronouncements about Spain at Sunday's feast, when they had retired to William's chambers, the man remained coy and vague, sending William into such a fury, he had to refrain from physically tossing Raleigh out on his arse. Since then, Raleigh had avoided the king's presence. Well, he couldn't refuse an official summons. And if William had to endure the man's company, at least it could be while doing something the king enjoyed.

With snow pilling higher on the ground, a hunt was out of

the question, but a ride through the countryside would still enliven his lungs and refresh his spirit. Raleigh was ordered to ride out with him, along with any others who cared to join. Robert surprisingly begged off, claiming tiredness, and Daniel, never one for such exploits, stayed back as well. Thus it was a small party of Duven, Ridgeland, and Bolstad, one of Robert's loyal lords, whom the king had invited to Christmastide in thanks for his service the prior summer.

Unbothered by the cold, Raleigh proved a proficient rider, lending credence to his claims of fighting in France. Properly admiring the lands, with language a bit too flowery for William's taste, there finally came a time when William steered him away from the rest, so they might speak uninterrupted.

"As I'm sure you've been informed," William said, reining his horse to a clomping walk beside Raleigh's mount, "I've given the order for you to leave court in three days' time."

Raleigh nodded, gazing off at the snowcapped tree line. It was a shame, really. The man was so similar to Robert, but without the bitterness. William felt that at a different time, under different circumstances, he might befriend Raleigh. But such was not to be. Especially as the man couldn't keep his eyes off the queen.

"I fear my queen's gift was not received with the joy intended, and none to blame but myself." Raleigh patted the neck of his borrowed roan. "I apologize, most heartily, Majesty. But if I might have a few words of my own defense." William grunted in acquiescence. "I was put in a rather awkward situation, if truth be told. I am not an ambassador, thus unable to utilize official diplomacy, yet have heard things of statecraft that I cannot help but seize upon to best befit my country."

"I can understand the delicacy there," William said. "Yet you make your position more precarious by your advances upon my queen."

"Oh fie!" Raleigh squared himself to William. "Begging Your Majesty's pardon, but your court is the most squeamish I have yet to come across. Your queen was born to be adored by all men. If we fawn upon her, 'tis no fault of hers. I daresay she only has eyes for you." He frowned. "I shall henceforth avoid all women, be they even more comely than Helen of Troy."

William chuckled. He too was once a frustrated youth in search of love, or more to the point, lust. "I'm sure you shall find a lady fair who covets your affections. But a word to the wise—perhaps you should stay away from those already encumbered." Raleigh sighed. "And though I know your queen to enjoy such flirtations, she be not a wilting violet. The woman has the heart of a lion."

"You know her well then?" Raleigh said, forlorn look upon his handsome face.

"I couldn't say well," William said, "but Norwick, Cecile, and I did spend quite a summer at her court. She is enchanting, to say the least, but not one to suffer fools."

"I will heed the warning, sire."

They rode in companionable silence. As they neared the forest, William cleared his throat.

"I must bid you, once and for all, to speak of Spain. For your avoidance hints that, in the end, you've no intelligence to give." Just under the tree line, snow melted next to the trunks, exposing packed down, dying grasses. William let his horse forage for anything worthy of consumption.

Raleigh had no choice but to let his horse do the same. "Despite my unsteady welcome here, I have come to enjoy you and your court. My hesitations have only been in my mulling what would be best for your country and for mine. Spain and France vie for precedence as our enemy. And Troixden, being Catholic, would certainly lean toward these powerful allies over and against my Protestant England, no matter your personal opinion of my queen."

"Well said." Of course, all three of those countries, William knew, wished to play coy, only to reveal themselves as the devil if he could be lulled into compliance.

"But I can tell you this. And again, you must take it for what it is, the rumors about in Spanish court. Well-founded rumors, I'll have you."

"Spit it out, Raleigh," William said, his tone light.

"The Spanish indeed play you as friend. But they plan to overtake Troixden as their own."

William's heart dropped as his suspicions were confirmed. Sitting there, light snow falling from the branches above, surrounded by winter's hush, his kingdom's splendor splayed before him, he steeled himself to the knowledge that it might not be his much longer. For even if every man of Troixden, able bodied or not, armed themselves, he couldn't defeat a Spanish invasion. Better his countrymen be spared such bloodshed.

"I am sorry to be the bearer of such news," Raleigh said. "As you know, they are currently helping the French battle the Huguenots and are involved in major attacks in the Low Countries. It is from these strategic places they plan to surround Troixden, at which point they will offer you to surrender or to slaughter."

"Dear God." William threw back his head, images of war, of death, of his wife and child, of the gay faces of peasants across his land. Had it truly come to this? Unprovoked attack so Spain could better subdue the Low Countries, make the German states come to heel? For a closer port to conquer England?

"But all is not lost, sire."

William massaged his temples, eyes closed. "I suppose we now have a common enemy, is that it?"

Raleigh's horse nickered as if in agreement. "I have it from my queen, that if you deal lightly with your Laureland, if you give them, officially, the right to practice the Protestant religion, England will support you with men, arms, and coin in this war with Spain."

William laughed without feeling. "That would bring about civil war in my own lands. For my Catholic subjects are just a zealous. They tolerated Laureland, but no longer. Not after the bungled attempt to overthrow the crown—twice now."

"Would not civil war be better than no country left at all?"

"So my choice is between letting my own people slaughter each other or having the Spanish do it for them?" He yanked his horse from its rummaging, directing it back toward the palace.

"That is where the love your people bear you comes into play, Highness. You must simply explain it to them, not as a defeat, but as a defense."

William shook his head and sighed. "I will think on it, Raleigh. I will give you my answer before you leave."

His heart heavy with deeper sorrow than he'd ever felt, he kicked his horse into a full run, back to his palace.

William called a hasty Council Table that afternoon, barely taking time to remove his riding gear. The full council was present, all at court for the season, and they sat about the thick table, grim faced, some with red eyes. Even Bartmore was silent as William's news sunk in.

"'Tis grave indeed," the grand master general said. "And Your Majesty speaks true. We cannot hope to face the force of Spain and win. 'Twould be a death sentence."

"And yet we can't simply hand our realm over to them like some opulent Christmastide gift." William was pacing, as he was wont to do in these situations, as if physical exertion would force a solution to appear.

"I'm sorry, Majesty, but I'm truly stunned by this," Daniel said, brows furrowed at the papers before him. "For I have it from my intelligence that Spain makes no such move against us."

"Of course they wouldn't reveal their plans to us," Ridgeland scoffed.

"And they would reveal them to, for all intents and purposes, an English spy?" Robert tilted his chair back on two legs, affecting a relaxed demeanor despite his clenched jaw.

"What I mean," Daniel interjected, "is that by all accounts—and they are many—Spain is completely bankrupt. In fact, their men in the Low Countries have not been paid in months, their food supplies are running dry, and there are rumblings of insurrection amongst their very own soldiers. How on earth they would conceive of convincing these men to turn to another battle is preposterous."

"Then what is Raleigh on about?" William stormed back and forth in front of the giant window.

"English troops on our soil," the general said. "That's what he's on about. England wants access to France just as much as Spain wants access to England and all the rest."

"And so they would depend on rumors and fear, so that we might ally ourselves with England," Daniel said. "And it would be Elizabeth, and not Philip, asking for your crown in exchange for the lives of our people."

"Dammit!" William slammed his fist against the stone. "We cannot muster a fair fight against either!"

"Against England we may have a chance," Ridgeland said. "If we do not agree to these terms Raleigh has laid out, we can easily keep them at bay on shore."

"Our ships are many and strong," the general said, "and our shores mostly cliffs. It is why we've never been invaded by sea. I doubt the English would be so foolhardy."

"Apparently they are foolhardy enough to send a fop to spread known lies." William stalked back to his seat.

"It is possible they aren't willful lies," Halforn said. It was so like him to see no ill in anyone. Generally, he was good balance to have on council, but now, William wasn't in the mood for goodwill. "It is quite likely the plot was planned before the Spanish coffers ran dry. Certainly they have been planning something, what with the last war and that traitorous Valencia."

William had to concede the point. Raleigh might have heard true, but during his travels, Spain had whittled away their funds.

"Cecile," William said, "it does strike us that Halforn and Raleigh may be partly correct. Even knowing how costly wars are to the royal treasury, it baffles the mind that the Spanish would spend themselves into ruin. Especially in sending funds to the French."

"If it was in their hopes to take Troixden," Cecile said, "funding the French could be their means to two ends."

"They may have misjudged how long they would be at it," Halforn said.

"Though I must point out, I have heard nothing from ambassador Doemland like what Raleigh has put forth," Cecile said.

William didn't know what to think, what to believe. All he knew was that his realm's very existence hung in the balance, batted about by two countries as if they were cats and Troixden a half-dead rodent. And in the back of his mind, he could not help but worry for himself, for Anna, for Cate. What becomes of deposed royals? Nothing good.

"Norwick," William called to his cousin. "You have been too quiet. What think you?"

Robert sucked air through his teeth, making a high-pitched squeal of sorts. It grated on the king. Robert threw up his hands.

"Majesty, for once, I am at a loss."

William stared blankly at him. He knew if worse came to worst, Robert would have to support the English, as he desired a Protestant rule. But at the same time, Robert wouldn't want the crown further from his own head, or his sons'. In the end,

William was convinced Robert would fight for Troixden, no matter what religion reigned.

"I would be more inclined to trust in Cecile's theory than in Raleigh's." Robert scratched his goatee. "Even if Raleigh's information is not nefariously given—though why wouldn't it be?—it is sure to be old, as Halforn argues."

"But do you really believe Spain would spend so poorly, especially if they had grander ambitions?" William asked them.

Beaubourg spoke. "I don't wish to add more complexity to the situation, but we still have not discovered the truth behind the men from Brussels and why they were trespassing in Beaubourg without proper letters of travel."

"We fear there are bigger problems at the moment, Your Grace," William said, "for soon, they may have no crown to plot against."

"But if word reaches them of this English plan, that may embolden them further," Beaubourg said.

"Your point is well made. We want you in charge of the investigation, Beaubourg. Send all reports immediately to Cecile." William glanced at the dour men. "In the meantime, we want all of you to have your eyes and ears open. If you have men about the land, or in travels elsewhere, we want any information, no matter how insignificant it may seem, brought to Cecile, who will compile it all for us when we meet after Twelfth Night." He exhaled, tried to conjure a smile, but failed. "Until such time, be jolly in celebration. And if you can't be jolly in truth, for God's sake, pretend it."

It was the final privy court before Twelfth Night and William couldn't wait for his official duties to end. With the next day a Sunday, and Twelfth Night the following, his kingly office would be perfunctory. He hoped this brief respite would give him space to think—or perhaps not to think. He looked at his wife, enthroned at his side. She sat there, cheeks bright, face regal, clothed in his favorite blue velvet. As much as he wanted to spill forth all his worries to her, he didn't wish to steal her merriment of the season. There would be time enough to hear the whole of it come next week. He envied her ignorance. She must have felt his gaze, for she turned to him with a quizzical smile. He answered by bringing her hand to his lips.

The next case was brought before them, three farmers from Norwick's southern reaches. Bedraggled, they shuffled in, bowing again and again until William cleared his throat.

"And what cause brings you before us?" William said, still claiming Anna's hand.

"Majesty," said the leanest of the three, "we come fer compensation. Fer our crops 'ave been stolen and we 'aven't enough to feed our families through winter, let alone t' sell."

"Stolen, you say?" Anna sat forward.

"Yes, M'," the man said. "Stripped clean nice an' slow, all through summer. We's didn't notice at first, it being regular for folks to take a bit fer themselves given the chance, but this much . . ."

"By the time we realized the extent, there was nothing to be done," said the youngest, who was also better dressed. "All our neighboring farms had the same done to them."

"'Twas like ghosts came through," said the first, crossing himself. "Wee bit by wee bit wif near nothin' left fer us."

"Do you not check your crops daily?" William said, finding it hard to believe farmers wouldn't notice large quantities of their property being absconded with.

"'Tis just the thing, Majesty," the younger one replied, "we do check, perhaps not all corners every day, but the grain was taken, a foot here, a foot there, in different parts so as not to be noted until too late."

"An' animals too!" said the previously silent man, with scrabbled beard and few teeth to speak of. "I had one of me sheep taken. Then a fortnight later one of me cows. Same with the rest of me neighbors. Just a slow an' steady stealin' it were. I watched the markets fer my animals t' catch the thieves, but nary a one went fer sale."

"Norwick," William scratched his own chin, "why is this the first we are hearing of these raided crops?"

"I'm wondering the same," Robert said. "My good fellows, why did you not apply to me directly at harvest?"

"Beggin' pardon, Sir Duke," said the first, "but we've been a mite busy with th' harvest we did have, tryin' t' stretch it between us."

"Your Grace," William eyed his cousin, "We leave it to you to investigate this further. Perhaps a band of thieves have worked together and brought a surplus of grain to market."

"I'll also look to how many more farms have had such a fate, if any," Robert said, with a head bow.

"In the meantime," William addressed the men, "we will give you some restitution and more. You shall be our guests for Twelfth Night festivities. We simply ask you comply with His Grace's investigation into this matter with full and truthful disclosure."

"Yes, Majesty, thankee," the lean one said.

Cecile beckoned his secretary and scribbled some note as William shifted in his throne. Something struck him strange about this business, more than common thievery, but the answer eluded him. Alas, he had much bigger problems to worry about than a new crew of bandits.

He barely noticed when Robert delivered a note into his lap. Reading it, his heart raced.

Distracted, he nodded to the obeisance made as court ended. Before taking his own leave, he leaned over and whispered to Anna.

"Come to my chambers at half past. We've much to discuss."

His words weren't playful, were without innuendo. For Robert had written to him, in near gleeful terms, that the English ambassador's wife had been invited to the queen's chambers, without any mention to him. She was meddling again. No matter how innocent she made her actions seem, he could ill afford another scandal. She needed to be reminded, yet again, of her place. Though he was loath to do it.

Anna was shown into the king's official office, which he only used to speak privately with foreign dignitaries or to sign significant laws. He generally preferred to conduct business at the desk in his bedchambers. Anna had been in the room once, to watch him sign the declaration of war against Laureland. Only the fire and a small window provided light. William leaned against the sash, jaw in his hand, eyes glazed and to the floor. His jacket was unbuttoned, shirt laces loose. This was not at all what she'd expected. Certainly his words at court were stern, but often such discussions ended with peace, if not something more.

Holding a curtsy, she waited for their entourages to leave. With the door finally, shut she approached.

"Wills, why do we meet in this dreary place?"

He kept staring at a spot on the floor. "My bedchamber is too . . ." he flapped a hand, then flicked his eyes to hers, "distracting."

She crept closer. "It's never been before. Indeed, it has often been curative." She smiled, but his eyes, grayed in the darkened room, stilled her attempts at banter. She swallowed and folded her hands together. "My liege, please do not keep me in suspense."

He waved a hand again. "I'm still William."

"Not in this room." She shook her head. "And certainly not with that look upon your face."

William inhaled an attempt to calm himself, but when he faced her again, the flint remained in his eyes.

"I've been standing here wondering, for the past half-hour, why in God's name you would privately entertain Doemland's wife."

"That's all this is about?"

"You told me nothing of this visit, no matter how innocent. What were you thinking entertaining the wife of the *English* ambassador? It's bad enough you flounce around with Raleigh."

"Flounce?" This had to be a joke. Some strange game of misrule Duven and the king cooked up. "I have not *flounced* since I was Cate's age."

He arched himself off the wall, advancing on her in a slow march.

"And now, the mere fact that you even spoke to her, let alone invited her into your private chambers, will send all of court yet again whispering about how much the heretic English influence our queen."

He was upon her now, towering, breathing like a charging war-horse. Was this anger about Katharine, or Raleigh?

She stared up at him, the weight of her heart pulling down her shoulders. "I, who have been publically chastised by you for my 'international relations' would collude—"

"Why did you ask her in?"

"I admired her work. I had no desire to speak of anything but sewing—"

"It's the look of the thing, Anna! How many times must I tell you—" He threw up his hands and turned away from her.

"Do not speak to me as though I am a child."

"If you wouldn't act with such gullibility I wouldn't have to!"

"If you did not jump in such haste to creating rumor and scandal where there is none, we wouldn't have to keep repeating this argument."

He spread his hands wide on the desk and leaned on them, head hunched. She walked to him.

"But what's worse," she said, "is you would rely more heavily upon the trumped up rumors of court against mine own words."

He spun around and grabbed her forearms. "I don't believe a whit of what they say!" His face was inches from hers. "But that dreadful word 'heretic' was spoken in the same breath as your name, no matter who said it! It doesn't matter if you'd spent the entire day in prayer in the company of Bartmore himself—"

"This is not the king I know, not the man I married—jumping at shadows, allowing others to ply their lies!" His lips twitched, but he didn't speak. "You are king, Wills. *Your* word is final. When you make nothing of these things, the people will follow as they have always done." His breathing grew faster and shallow, his grasp on her arms loosening. "You are a better king, a better man, than any of them. You are strong, you are noble, you are just. Be those things again." His eyes roved her face. "I am not your enemy. I am your one, true, and unconditional ally."

In an instant, his fingers tangled in her hair, pulling her to him. His mouth slammed into hers, sucking, nipping, pushing her lips open. He backed her against the desk, the gilded wood digging her thighs. She tugged off his jacket, yanked at his shirt, freeing it from his trunks. His lips left hers and trailed down her neck, his hands fumbling with her skirts, shoving them up to her waist.

Bending her back, she heard the clank of his belt hit the floor. He raised up for a moment, her eyes fixed on his torso as he discarded his shirt. He didn't smile, but the hardness in his eyes was gone, replaced with a well-known hunger.

He slid his hands up her sides, her bodice feeling all the tighter, and bit her chin, dragging his lips up her jaw. He paused by her ear.

"I suppose this room is not so bad after all."

Apparently, she was forgiven. But no amount of pent-up lust would heal the sting of his accusations.

William appeared to be in a truly jolly mood this Twelfth Night. Anna hoped it was her little speech and its aftereffects that restored him to his good-humored self, but surely this last night of revelry played its part as well.

She and the king had already exchanged their gifts. She'd given him a book of psalms, the cover of which she'd embroidered herself, intertwining their initials, and he'd named a new ship after her, presenting her with a model of it made entirely of gold.

Cate sat on Anna's lap, fingering the model, squinting in the canon holes, careful not to touch the delicate ropes.

"It seems the princess is more taken with it than you," William said, grinning at his curious daughter.

"Oh, I think it delightful," Anna said, kissing his hand. "I never would have imagined anything named after me, let alone a ship. I will pray she always sails in peaceful waters and all the men upon her be blessed."

"You're a good woman," he said.

They had just finished the fourth course and everyone was full and happy, awaiting the next amusement. Raleigh, who had made himself curiously scarce the last few days, appeared before them in a low bow.

"Majesties." Upon standing he handed a perfect white rose

to Cate. "If you will indulge me, it is time I presented my promised gift to the princess royal."

Cate's face lit up, ship and rose forgotten. "Oh yes, please, sir!"

A smile tugged his lips. He clapped and the court hushed as twenty or so players filled the floor, all but one in white, looking for all the world like snowflakes. "It is my privilege and honor to present to you *The Shepherd's Praise of our Sacred Queen Catherine.*"

With nary a scroll, he began to recite, the players moving in practiced response.

> *Praised be Queen Cate's fair and harmless light;*
> *Praised be the dews wherewith she moists the ground;*
> *Praised be her beams, the glory of night;*
> *Praised be her power, by which all powers abound . . .*

Cate sat, stilled in awe as the elegant masque spun out before them, the richly dressed Queen Cate thwarting dragons, taming fairies, and winning the imagined realm's adulation. Even William laughed and clapped, seeming to have put all jealousy of Raleigh behind him.

When the poem ended, the whole hall erupted in applause, those seated rising to their feet and calling for more. Raleigh nodded and waved in acknowledgement. He then bowed to the royals.

"My joy comes with the delight it hath brought the princess." At this, Cate clambered down from Anna's lap, curtsied to the man, beckoned him to bend, and gave him a solemn kiss on his cheek. The people chuckled and Raleigh rose, eyes meeting

Anna's with something like wistful regret. She couldn't return the look, though she was sorry to see him go.

"I hate to leave this place, which has shown me such great courtesy, but I carry the memories of happy times and a benevolent court with me." He bowed again.

"And we wish you safety on wherever your learning takes you next," William said.

"And more happy times," Anna added, hoping he would leave knowing he still had friends in Troixden, regardless of politics.

"Thank ye, Majesties. And may your own Christmas be merry, may your love only grow, and may your realm be at peace."

William nodded in dismissal and Anna gave him a small smile. Servers bustled in with the beginnings of the fifth course and Raleigh disappeared, just as suddenly as he had appeared in the first place.

CHAPTER 8

Leap Year

No rest for the wicked, Robert thought, giving his name to the guard outside the royal chambers. He had woken early from a nightmare, him fighting in a fog. It took no sage to interpret: with his chief flirtation device in Walter Raleigh now gone, as well as utter confusion about England, Spain, and Laureland, Robert was lost in a brume, not knowing foe from friend, unable to see his way forward.

Finally escorted in, he found William only half dressed and Daniel already sitting in front of the desk, plunging through papers. The scent of lavender still hung in the air, signaling the queen's recent departure. At least the king would be in a good mood.

"Cousin!" William said, lopsided grin on his face. "How good of you to join us. As you can see, our fair Cecile has barely slept."

"Nor, daresay, have you, my liege." Robert winked and flopped into his customary chair, stretching his feet on the desk, hands behind his head, considering his surely well-used friend.

The king raised a brow. "Wouldn't you like to know?" A dresser placed a shirt over William's head, then helped thread his arms through the sleeves.

Robert made a face. "Thank God. I don't know how much longer I could stand looking at that chest of yours."

"Save your jealousy, cuz—it does not befit you." The king yawned and waved off the man offering him a jacket. "Cecile, whilst thou smack our fair duke's head for us, as we are indisposed?"

Daniel looked up from his papers, startled to be addressed. He blinked, owl-like, between the two, frowned, and went back to reading.

"I shall smack myself then," Robert said, and jerked his face left and right. The king chuckled. Heavens, it seemed Robert could ask for the world right now, William was in such good spirits. Maybe he should broach the subject of his Rob marrying Cate? But before he could say anything, Daniel cleared his throat.

"I wanted us all similarly apprized before full council this afternoon, and if there is no objection, I shall begin with the case of the men from Brussels."

Both Robert and William stared at Daniel. "Cecile, my

fellow," William said, chain of office being straightened on his shoulders, "why so serious?"

Daniel looked up at the king, unblinking. "We speak of serious matters."

Robert removed his feet from their perch, leaned forward, and patted Daniel's back. "Cecile, old boy, you certainly know how to kill a mood."

"Apologies." Daniel focused on Robert. "I didn't realize you now took accusations of treason so serenely."

Robert began to stand, but William stayed him. "Let's not fight, children." He eased himself into his calfskin chair. William hadn't soured, but Daniel was taunting a sleeping dragon in Robert.

"And what have you found, exactly?" the king asked.

"The queen had a letter from her father, and Lady Jane mentioned in passing—"

"Ah ha!" William raised a finger to the sky in triumph.

Robert's brow furrowed. Lady Jane? Since when did Daniel lower himself to speaking with women?

"So that's what this," William gestured at the whole of Daniel, "is all about. Trouble in love, friend?"

"As I've said before, my liege, we have no relationship save one of neighbors." Daniel fumbled with a quill in his hands. "When I give her payment for her nurse, I occasionally ask her observations on matters for which she was present to get a level-headed and unprejudiced opinion. Nothing more."

"So you say," William grinned.

"Huh," Robert said to himself. Lady Jane and Daniel . . . would wonders never cease.

"Norwick," Daniel said, turning bodily to avoid the king's grins, "what of the farmers' claims? The grain and absconded animals?"

This shook Robert out of amused contemplation of Daniel attempting lovers' exploits.

"Right." He found he couldn't look Daniel in the face. "For a mere fortnight's time, I've gathered that nearly every farm has had some amount stolen, with those hardest hit closest to Havenside—which is logical, more people, what have you." He tilted back in his chair. "I've not had word yet from anyone in the north of the duchy, but the one man's comment of ghosts seems to bear out. No one saw—or will admit to having seen, as the case may be—these thieves. And what's more, there was not any noticeable change in the Havenside markets. If anything, grain traded higher because there was less to be had. Hopefully this will help those hit most severely."

"'Tis strange indeed." William got up. "Where then has it gone?" This mumbled question seemed rhetorical. Suddenly he turned, snapping his fingers. "Did your men search barns for stockpiling? Perhaps the uprising right before harvest frightened people into hoarding."

"There's a thought," Robert said. "The men did look for stockpiles, but not farm by farm. And, like I said, they have not made it farther north. Perhaps some of those closer to Laureland itself would have reason for more fear." He leaned on the desk. "Another unusual fact, which may be more reason why I did not hear of this sooner—these thieves left the lands of my lords alone."

"They must have feared the recompense in stealing from gentry," Daniel said.

"Perhaps," William said, still walking about. "And perhaps it was the lords themselves who've gone astray. Send for Mounds and Bolstad. They may have some knowledge of the matter."

"That brings us to Spain." Daniel straightened the papers in his lap. William groaned and rammed his head against the bedpost. "'Tis not actually that bad, Highness. For all reports point to the Spanish being well and truly without funds. Though they make a good show of it."

"Is this true?" William spun around, face alight.

"With the celebrations of Christmastide, word traveled slowly, but the Spanish, despite Philip's continued threats and bargaining, have declared bankruptcy. They've no funds to pay soldiers anywhere, let alone the Low Countries. And as for helping France, all those funds were borrowed in the first place."

William whooped and Daniel finally allowed himself a smile.

"Why didn't you bring this to me immediately?" The king brought his hands to his face. "So many sleepless nights could have been averted."

"I didn't wish to bring incomplete information, sire. I wanted to be entirely—" Daniel was cut off by a wallop on his back, William beaming down at him.

"I could kiss you, Cecile!"

"Please." Robert held up his hands as if to shield his eyes, but grinned too. For the Spanish were certainly no friend to Robert's plans. Besides which, blast himself, he reveled in his cousin's joy.

William poured three goblets of wine so full the liquid sloshed over the sides. He hoisted his high, not minding the red mess he made.

"A toast, my friends!" Robert and Daniel duly stood and raised their goblets. "To peace, to Troixden, and to poor, poor King Philip. May he remain so!"

The men clanked glasses and drank their fill, until Daniel, per the usual, brought them back to business. "So that makes dealings with England simple as well."

"It appears our English *diversion* did just that," William plunked down his goblet. "Flirted with our women, plied us with lies and false bargains, then went on his merry way."

"Good thing we've added more ships to the fleet then. We'll send more men to keep an eye on the sea." Daniel made a note. "I'll speak to the grand master general before council."

"I must say I'm amazed at our good fortune." William rested his elbows on the desk. "A bit too amazed."

"You think there's still some plotting afoot?" Robert asked.

The king tapped his fingers against his cheek. "There is always some plotting afoot."

"Our foreign friends do keep reminding us of how diminutive we are," Daniel said, "and now we may rejoice in it rather than our pride be offended. We are too small for them to give notice just now."

"And you don't think England will see an opportunity with Spain unable to aide us and France refusing to?" William poured another drink.

"Hence more ships." Daniel gave a perfunctory smile.

"Where did Raleigh get himself off to anyhow?" William sat back again, tracing his goblet rim.

"He caught a ship at Owen in north Ridgeland. The manifest said it was headed to Scotland," Daniel said.

"And we believe this?" William said.

"The man's a rat." Robert brought down his chair's front legs with a thud. "As long as he's out of our country, that's all I care about." He refilled his drink, took a long drag, and wiped his mouth on his sleeve.

"With this relative calm, I wonder if now might the time to strengthen alliances." Daniel fingered through his papers. "By soliciting a marriage contract for the princess."

Robert nearly spit out his wine. William frowned. They both started talking at once.

"I really don't think—"

"I had been thinking—" Robert stopped then bowed his head in acknowledgment of William's precedence to speak.

"Must I really think of marrying off my girl now?" William winced.

"Most royals do secure such an alliance at an early age," Daniel said, still not speaking directly to the king.

"Who would there even be? There's a dearth of royal sons about." William shook his head.

"Ferdinand or Diego of Spain are candidates," Daniel said.

"Absurd!" Robert couldn't contain himself. "Why would we marry Catherine into a bankrupt state that has hinted at overthrowing us?"

"What he said." William was up again. "If we marry her to

Ferdinand, when he becomes king, what's to stop him from proclaiming himself king here as well?"

"Presumably we will have our own king to defend us in such an event," Daniel said, his eyes following William's progress around the chamber. "On the other hand, if we marry her to Diego, the second son, he would have no such claim."

"But what does that gain us?" Robert said. "Spain is already supposedly our ally. We only embolden them further by presenting this marriage." He folded his arms and shook his head. "We should keep our princess close to home. She should, like her father, marry within the realm."

"To one of your boys, I assume?" Daniel scoffed. "And what does *that* gain us?"

Robert was up now too, glaring at Daniel, the dragon fully awakened. "You were the one to argue the king marry in our borders—now suddenly the idea is ridiculous? Certainly it gains Rob, as it does the princess. For if the queen continues without male issue, Rob will be king, making Catherine queen in her own right of her own country."

"You both realize I'm in the room, correct?" William glowered at them. "Thank you, cuz, for pointing out yet again my and my queen's greatest failure."

Robert strode to him, undaunted. "But don't you see? 'Tis not a failure if she marries Rob. 'Tis a victory for her, 'Our Sacred Queen Catherine.' And if the queen bears a son—"

"When," William interjected.

"*When* the queen bears a son, Catherine is no worse off and in fact of higher rank than her husband."

"There would have to be dispensation from His Holiness,"

Daniel said. "And even then, the whole purpose of royal daughters is to marry them to foreign princes to strengthen alliances."

"'Tis easy for you to say, Cecile, for she's not your daughter." William brushed past Robert and motioned for someone to bring him his boots. "There is no need to make any decisions now, nor anytime soon. She's barely past four. We've plenty of time."

"But if we seize this moment of peace—" Daniel started.

"If I am forced to play my daughter like a pawn I shall do so under threat of war to bring about peace. Not the other way around." The king stamped a foot, jamming on his boot. "Are we finished here? For I certainly am."

"I have nothing more, Majesty," Daniel said.

William stormed out of his chambers without another word. Robert waited until the king was out of earshot, then turned on Daniel.

"How could you be so imbecilic as to broach Cate's marriage? He was in such a pleasant manner and you've skunked it with your endless, copious items of business!"

Daniel huffed. "I care not for his moods, but for intelligence in his policy decisions. Besides, I'm not the one trying to push my son on a throne that is not his."

"Dammit, Daniel, you stick your nose where it doesn't belong." Robert grabbed his discarded jacket from the chair.

"If it's anything to do with the king, it is my business." Daniel folded his hands in front of him and looked mildly at Robert.

"He is not allowed his own private thoughts? Not allowed to make any move, no matter how minor, without your thorough approval, is that it? Or is that just your dearest wish?" He slunk on his jacket, yanking it closed, not even bothering with the buttons.

"Again, Norwick," Daniel curled his lip as if Robert's name disgusted him. "I do not appreciate your insinuations about my relationship with the king. Being such, as he has often said himself, means there is no such thing as privacy in his life." Daniel gathered his papers and rose. "He depends on me and I am here for him. Not off scheming how to better myself and my position, using whomever and whatever I may to gain my desires."

"Not scheming, eh?" Robert drew near so none could overhear, threat obvious in his voice. "So what do you call making sure the king depends on you alone? It may not be fleshly as you claim, but you delude yourself as to your place in his conscience. Indeed, you should get in line. Behind his council, behind his daughter, and certainly behind the queen, for that woman will never let you be first in his heart, no matter how smart and kind and devoted she thinks you are, and no matter how much you desire it." Daniel stared ice at him. Robert jabbed a finger into Daniel's chest. "And know this, Half-cuz. If the choice ever comes between his bastard brother and his cousin, he will always choose true blood. So you'd better get behind me as well."

Daniel stepped back and straightened to his full height, which was still inches below Robert. "It seems I am not the only one who is delusional, *cuz.*" He turned. "If you'll excuse me, I have very real business to attend to."

Robert let him leave. Walking past Daniel's seat, he noticed a paper scrap on the floor. He bent to pick it up:

Jane: John fine. See nurse.
Doemland. ~~Witch?~~

Queen: courses by week's end?
With Will 3x - ~~Raleigh~~? Other?

Robert chuckled. So Daniel was keeping even closer tabs on the queen than Robert was. He folded the note, shoved it in his pocket, and left the chambers, whistling.

Anna's heart warmed at the scene before her. Her father crouched next to Cate on the nursery floor, giving her a mathematics lesson with blocks.

"So if I take these two . . ." he reached out, hiding two blue cubes beneath his robe. "What is left?"

"You must give them back," Cate said, stoic. "For they belong to me."

The duke chuckled, ending with a cough. "No, my dearest. You are to tell me how many blocks are now on the table."

"But you've taken them." She frowned up at him, cheeks puffed out in consternation.

"'Tis no use, Father," Anna said, bringing him a cup of warm wine, "for she is a royal born. All she surveys is hers."

She helped him up from the floor and handed him the cup. He thanked her and took a sip.

"I remember you at such an age. Not nearly as loquacious, but just as obstinate."

"And I wonder where I came by that?" She took his arm and led him to the window seat. Settling in beside him, her eyes fell to Cate, concentrating on the tower she was building. "I wish you didn't have to go to Beaubourg. We've had you two full months and more, yet I still find I'm jealous for your presence."

He smiled at her, eyes twinkling. "And I wish nothing more than to pass the rest of the time God gives me on this earth flitting around my two ladies."

"What dour words for such a young man." She laughed outwardly, but was inwardly stricken. As though someone had plucked a string inside her, a low, dirge-like hum reverberated in her core. It hadn't passed her notice that his beard was almost white, that his eyes were more crinkled, his knuckles starting to knob.

"You are good to say it, but we both know I'm no longer in my summer years." He took her hand. "Have I told you how proud you have made me, my dear?"

She smiled into his face, rolling her eyes in jest. "Yes, Papa, a thousand times and more. I do not wish to hear you try and give me your last will and testament. You may not be in summer, but you are certainly not in winter."

"Hush now and give your papa what he wants without argument for once." He flicked his eyes to Cate. "I am proud of you yes, as a queen. But I've never told you how very much of your mother I see in you. Especially around Catey . . ." Words caught in his throat. He wiped his eyes and blew on his wine. "How you are gentle yet firm, allowing her curiosity to be fed, but teaching her propriety. I don't know if you remember, but she was a wonderful woman, your mother."

Tears gathered in Anna's eyes. She engulfed his hand in hers. "Of course I do. I remember her every day. And 'tis an honor to think you see any part of her in me."

He brought her hand to his lips, trembling. He sniffed, then chuckled. "I also see her when you keep that husband of yours on his toes."

"I don't know about that. Seems I've been stepping on them more than anything else."

"To be sure, but that's all part of it." He released her and leaned against the sash.

"If only I could give him an heir, I feel things could go smoother between us."

Her father near hooted at this and wiped his eyes again. "Excuse me dearest, for I do not wish to belittle your desire. An heir is the hope of us all to be sure, but the two of you . . . well, you've two thick skulls and yet you love each other to distraction. Smooth be not your destiny."

She frowned, not wishing to be mocked, even gently, where sons were involved.

"Oh, Anna, you have the love of a man who would lay his country down for you. Worry not about sons. They will come. And if they do not, you've already had better luck than most. I don't need a soothsayer to tell me that much."

"Where is all this sentiment coming from today?"

"Can't a man be loath to leave his child and granddaughter?" He hoisted himself up and smiled down on her. "For I know you shan't visit until April at the earliest, nor I to court unless the king calls full council. That is two long, lonely months for me to bumble about Beaubourg, boring our citizens with tales of how delightful my progeny are."

"Granpapa!" Cate exclaimed. "I built it!"

Both Anna and the duke walked over to admire Cate's block

tower. "It looks like Stone Yard," Cate said. "But happy because of the colors."

Anna shivered. It had always bothered her that the view from her chambers took in the whole of it, a blight against rolling hills and fair skies. She didn't know whether Stone Yard or the palace was built first, but knowing the legacy of Troixden's past kings, it didn't surprise her that their queens were placed within daily sight of the prison, reminding them of where they might end if they dared go against their husband and sovereign.

That Cate, so young, would know of its purpose . . . how quickly the innocence of youth flew.

"Why, there's my girl!" William bounded into the room, arms wide.

"Papa!" Cate scrambled to her feet and charged her father. He picked her up and twirled her, peppering her with kisses amid her giggles. Finally setting her down, he strode to Anna and embraced her.

"I've wonderful news," he said. "I'm glad you shall hear it in person, Beaubourg. We send you off with glad tidings to keep you warm for the coming months." Taking Anna's face in his hands, he gave her a quick kiss. "The Spanish are bankrupt!" He clapped his hands and did a little jig, to Cate's delight.

"So it is true!" Beaubourg whooped.

"They are no threat to us—to anyone. In fact, their own men in the Low Countries have not been paid in months and are liable to revolt."

"Then we are truly safe." Beaubourg beamed. "I shall return home well satisfied and relieved."

"God be praised," Anna said. "'Tis glorious indeed." She took William's hands. "And what of Laureland—are they finally content as well?"

William met her father's eyes across the room, some unspoken sign given and received.

"Just their normal grumblings, my dear," William said.

She knew he was evading her, but for now she didn't care. For now she would revel in the fact that her husband wouldn't be in harm's way, that her country wasn't under immediate threat of destruction, that they could finally breathe a bit easier.

"Well then," she took Cate's slip of a hand in her own, "this calls for a celebration. We shall fete you off, Father. Shall we dine together in chambers tonight, just the four of us?"

"The perfect cap to end Council Table," William said. "Now, one more kiss from both my ladies, and grandfather and I shall be off. And with any luck, the meeting will be a short one."

Cate broke from Anna and clung to William's leg. He lifted her into his arms and gave her lips a delicate kiss. "Be good to your mama, Catey dear." She wrapped her arms around his neck and kissed his cheek. Setting her down with a pat on her curls, he sauntered over to Anna. Snaking his arms around her waist, he pulled her close and kissed her softly.

"And after we sup, you and I shall have a celebration of our own." He winked and left the room, her father in his wake.

"I love Papa," Cate said, with a little sigh.

"I do too, dearest. I do too."

William slowed, allowing Beaubourg to match his pace. "I take it you've more to reveal in regard to Laureland. What have you discovered from these men of Brussels?" the king asked.

"Unfortunately, we had to release them. If we had detained them much longer, we would have had diplomatic issues at hand." Beaubourg lowered his voice. "However, we did discover they were on their way to Laureland. They claimed to just be passing through our lands, as it is a shorter journey to Luxembourg."

"Which is ridiculous. 'Tis a good five-hundred-mile longer journey." William strode on, nodding at various palace workers, scribes, guards.

"Of course we found nothing amongst their papers to accuse them, though we took the lot. They've been translated and we assume they are ciphered. We've the best men attempting to crack them as we speak."

"And you say they were found traveling east."

"Yes, Highness."

"With any luck then, we've thwarted whatever message they intended to deliver to Laureland." They'd reached the doors to Council Table, but William paused with his father-in-law before heading in. "We will pray no more comes of this. But we will watch our borders all the more. Once you are in Beaubourg, I expect you will send your best men to the northern border and to the foothills of the Truss. Any movement—even peasant woman selling baskets—is to be reported through Cecile's people. Anyone from outside Troixden or from Laureland is to be held at Castle Beaubourg."

"My men are already on their way and some have already set camp in the Truss."

William clasped the duke's arm. "I'd expected no less. And I've already seen the grand master general about an increase in ships, though if anyone wishes to port, they would probably do so farther south in Ridgeland."

Beaubourg nodded. "Is there anything else you need from me, my liege, before I depart on the morrow?"

William thought for a moment, then smiled. "I need you to stay safe and whole. For the queen's sake, as well as mine own."

"I intend nothing less." He gave a small bow and the two men entered council to share the good news.

Robert and Yvette had just finished supper. It was the leap day, the bissextus of February, the day of oddities. A day when anything might happen. When he was a child, Robert used to think that if he looked out his window at midnight, he might see strange and magical creatures, unicorns butting through the gardens or dragon-tailed owls swooping down on unsuspecting, frog-faced mice. His mother used to hang cedar and peppermint at the thresholds to ward off evil spirits and bad luck. To this day, Robert always carried a sprig of peppermint on the bissextus, for Lord knew he needed all the good luck he could get.

Finishing the last bite of boar, he wiped his mouth and reached for his beer. "Has Lady Jane spilled her deepest thoughts to you yet?"

Yvette glowed like a jewel in the candlelight, dressed in deep plum, her black eyes catching the dancing flames. She shook her head. "Lady Jane is a very private, quiet woman. The only thing she speaks openly and long about is her son."

He sat back with soft eyes anticipating dessert of a carnal kind. "And what of him?"

She scrunched her eyes, thinking. "He has been well for quite some time now. At least since the summer. It seems being at the palace, with the constant doting of his mother and nurses, has him as robust as any young lad. He's not even caught cold this winter, which I believe is a first for him."

"Nothing of Daniel?"

"As I said, she speaks only of her son." She pushed away from the table and ambled to him, dragging a finger along the wood as she approached. He watched it, anticipated its sensation on his own skin.

"Anytime I even hint at the queen's dealings with the king, she turns wine red and scurries away. I think she'd faint dead if I mentioned any love betwixt her and our fair Daniel." Reaching Robert, she placed delicate hands on his shoulders and began to knead. He groaned. "Why are you convinced everyone is jumping into bed together?"

He laughed. "Because that is the way of court, Madam, as well you know." She jabbed her thumb under his shoulder blade. "Ouch!" He half-heartedly swatted at her. "Must I count them all for you? Starting with my sister . . ."

"Let's not talk about your sister." She moved her thumbs up the spine of his neck sending quivers through his body. "Unless, of course, you'd wish to soon be cold and alone."

"Let us speak of pleasantness then." Removing one of her hands from his neck, he sucked her knuckles. She bent over him, kissing his forehead.

"Your Grace! Your Grace, make haste!" Pounding on his door startled them both. He didn't recognize the voice, but recognized terror behind it.

He sprang to the door, thrusting it open. "Is it the king?"

One of Daniel's secretaries stared up at him, bleary eyed, face mottled from exertion. "His Majesty has called full council. We are under attack."

He barely registered hearing Yvette gasp behind him. He was halfway out the door before he turned. "Make sure the princess is with the queen. Stay with them both in her chambers. You are all safest there." She nodded and he flew down the hall, not bothering to return for his jacket, let alone his chain of office.

"Are they at the palace gates?"

"My Grace, they are far off, though no doubt Havenside is their destination." The little man scurried, mouse-like, before Robert, his livery swishing almost to spark.

"Where, man? Where the devil are they? Who are they?"

The man kept going, not even bothering to turn to answer. "They are to the Laureland side of the Truss, even into the northern lands of your own Norwick."

Robert stopped, grabbed the man by his coat, swinging him about. "Who, dammit?"

The secretary gaped at Robert, his lower lip trembling. "The whole of Europe."

Robert left the stupefied man behind and ran.

He reached the council doors the same time as Halforn,

sleep-rumpled but with a look of shocked wonder identical to the secretary's.

"'Tis treachery about, there's no doubt," Halforn said, eyes glazed. Robert gave a brief nod and pushed into the room to find the full council, save Beaubourg, all standing, whispering among themselves. The king stood at the giant windows, facing the utter darkness.

"How did we not hear of this?" William said, his booming voice silencing all conversation. "What good are spies and loyal lords and messengers—what good is an army if we hear not a whisper of advance until they've eaten nearly a quarter of our land?" The king wheeled around and Robert instinctively jumped back. In the night, in the dim light, face contorted with the devil's wrath, he was the spitting image of King James. "What use are any of you? My wise council!"

"Majesty," Daniel said, even he not daring to get within ten feet. "Some of council are still not informed of the full—"

"That's the damned problem! None of you—not even you, Norwick," he pointed at Robert, advancing upon him, "whose lands are even now being pillaged, your wife and son tucked ignorant in their beds—not even you knew. Or if you did you would not speak it. I will have your head if it be so!"

"My liege, do not break open my heart with images of my family and accusations I've no knowledge of! If any armed foot hath tread on Norwick soil, they shall surely pay with their lives. Mounds and Bolstad—"

"Mounds and Bolstad we've heard nothing of!" William stalked closer, the men of council backing up as he came. Robert, trapped by the thick wooden door, could retreat no farther.

Daniel stepped once more into the breach. "Majesty, your anger is justified, but these gathered need the full details, so they may be dispatched to their best purpose."

Robert could have sworn William growled, but his stance relaxed a hair, eyes still tracked on his cousin. Robert was too stunned to know what to do. Invaders in Norwick? His family threatened? The whole of Europe? And the king accusing him of being involved with it all?

Daniel slid to his chair, pulled it out from the table, and sat with folded hands.

"Within the past hour, riders from four directions reached the castle, each speaking of men—hundreds if not thousands of men—flying Laureland flags, marching unheeded. Scouts from Beaubourg estimated a camp of at least one thousand at the base of the Truss on Laureland's side. More have poured through from Luxembourg, pushing into eastern Norwick through Laureland and Luxembourg itself. Our reports tell us that so far, the masses of troops are at the northwest and southwest ends of Laureland's border." Daniel unrolled a map, tracing two lines, one bulging into Robert's lands, thankfully south and east of Cheval. All the men, except the king, hovered around. Drawing his finger across the middle border of Robert's duchy and of Laureland, Daniel continued, "There has been no movement spotted here in the central border. As you can see, it appears they wish to take the path of least resistance, least notice, to get to Havenside."

"They'll have another thing coming if they reach Duven!" Gregory said, striking a chair back.

"But we've no men amassed!" William's cry came as if from a wounded beast. A bissextus beast. Unconsciously, Robert crushed the peppermint in his pocket between two fingers. "We've sent all home, fat and merry, to be with their women, retiring until spring."

"Those riders who reached me were calling to arms along the way. Even as we speak, men are preparing to move the realm over," Daniel said.

"They're off their heads attacking in the winter," the grand master general said. "Their men'll die of starvation and the elements more than arrows and swords."

"Now we know who's been stealing crops and animals, and why." William said, almost to himself. "They've been stockpiling all summer for this very attack. Dammit, how did I not see?"

"So was seizing the castle a ruse to distract us from their thieving?" Halforn said.

Robert shook his head. "That was just gravy, their second plan. They well and truly hoped to take the throne this summer. Westerville revealed as much."

"Yes, but who?" Bartmore said, his face more sallow than usual. "Laureland does not have this many men, this much organization."

Daniel lifted his hands from the map. The paper curled, rolling Troixden in on itself like a pill bug.

"They have help," he said. "In the form of William of Orange."

"So this is not the Spanish?" Halforn said.

"In a way, they are partly to blame," Daniel said. "With the Spanish forces unpaid and unhappy, the Protestants have become bold. And with pleas from Laureland for help, knowing the Spanish can't aid us and the French refuse to, the Protestants see Troixden as an easy target to gain more influence against the Spanish and the Emperor."

"Enough with the speculations of who and why." William said, striding to the table and gripping its edge. "We need to arm. Now."

"We'll have one thousand men at the palace ready to march on the morrow," the grand master general said. "If we send out swift riders ahead, we'll pick up men as we go."

"What of papal troops?" William addressed Bartmore.

"Surely His Holiness would be eager to remedy the misunderstanding of our last engagement." Bartmore sniffed, looking down his nose at the rest of them. How he somehow felt above all this was beyond Robert. Didn't he realize his own position—his own neck—was at stake?

"We should make Cheval our headquarters," Robert said, spreading the map and jabbing his finger where his house lay. "It gives us the advantage of being between both fronts and at the ready if they decide to push through the middle."

"Our knights and Havenside men will head straight to Cheval." William bent over the map as well. "Norwick, split your men in thirds: one east, one northwest, and the rest at Cheval." He pointed to Ridgeland on the map. "Halforn and Ridgeland, your men will surge to meet Beaubourg's and Norwick's at the southern tip of the Truss. Duven and Cecile, yours will push to the east until they encounter rebel forces." The king took a deep, steadying breath. Robert could see his mind working out the strategy, the battlefields, all thoughts of anguish and anger pushed aside at the scent of battle. "Tonight, every one of you send your fastest riders, be they stableboy, page, or lord, with the call to arms. I want every able-bodied man in this realm ready to fight by week's end."

"Of what service may I be, Your Majesty?" Bartmore said, for once assuming an acquiescent posture.

"You shall fight the war of public opinion, Eminence," William answered, heading for the door. "Call a special mass for our men. Order the priests to sermonize against these unprovoked attacks upon our realm and our faith. I want all of Troixden up in arms, literally and figuratively. For we do not fight merely to quiet some unruly upstarts. We fight for our very existence." Pulling open the doors, he stopped at the threshold. "For God and country, my lords. And now to work."

"Long live the king!" they proclaimed en masse as William quit the room.

Ridgeland and Duven descended on Robert, explaining who they would send and where, suggesting various courses of immediate action, but Robert couldn't focus on what they said. He felt as though his mind were being drawn and quartered. To his very bones he wanted Troixden to be Protestant, but not if that meant foreign conquest. Could he somehow, some way, convince William to change course and declare with the Lutherans, or even the stoic Calvinists? It could end the bloodshed in an instant, something he knew William desired above all else. But would that satisfy Orange? Would he not wish to have a conquered Catholic country under his belt, to thumb his nose at the Spanish and finally gain the independence he and his countrymen so craved?

Robert gave Ridgeland and Duven a noncommittal nod, hurrying from council to escape all other voices but his own. It didn't help. Until there was more information, Robert would have to follow his king, even into certain hell.

The farther William got from council, the more focused became his purpose. Thoughts of blood and death, trudging armies through the winds and wet of winter, popes and Protestants, flew from him like ravens taking wing to roost miles away. His chambermen and others would take care of necessities. All that was left for him, all that he needed, was Anna.

Her chamber was locked, eight men standing guard. They parted at his approach, opening the doors wide. Entering, he heard the faint rustle of fabric, gasps of startled ladies.

"Papa!" Cate ran to him, arms ready for embrace. He knelt, enveloping her, clasping her to him as if her youthful sparkle could keep him whole.

"My sweet princess." He kissed her curls. "You have a very special job to do for me, for I am to be away." She nodded, chin at his shoulder. "You must strive to make your Mama smile, every day. And every day you shall give a kiss upon her cheek and tell her 'tis from Papa."

Cate released him with all seriousness.

"I will, Papa. And you shall hug yourself each day for me."

His breath caught, tears fighting to gain purchase. "Indeed I shall, my girl." He held her to him once more, conscious of her silken hair, her plump cheeks, her small frame.

"I will come home to you, Catey." He didn't know if he believed it, but it gave him some small courage.

Reluctantly, he let her go, her hand nestling into his. Coming fully inside Anna's chambers, he spied his wife, back straight, eyes quick, surrounded by hushed ladies in full curtsy. He knew at a glance she was in full knowledge of the news. She stood, slow, smoothed her skirts, then curtsied.

"My liege lord."

"Come," was all he said, striding to their private passage. He felt her follow, felt her eyes watching him. Barely inside his own empty chamber, lit only by hearth fire, he turned, pinning her to the door. He took in each feature: soft brown eyes; high, pink cheeks; wet, bow lips; slight upturn of a button nose; dark, arching brows stark against porcelain skin—treasuring them up in his mind's eye to recall in weeks, months from now, in the cold and mud and blood.

"My Anna." His knees nearly buckled at the thought of leaving her—perhaps permanently. She cupped his cheek, her thumb stroking. He turned his face to kiss her palm, breathing her in, willing time to halt. "I fear this parting over all others."

She shook her head. "You've promised the princess. You must return to us."

Her mettle, her belief in him, if he could bottle it up, or if he could somehow consume her, make her part of himself so her resolve could guide him . . .

Their lips crashed together. Her hands curled in his hair, pulling him deeper, his mind fading to only the hum of his veins, the throb in his chest, his body.

"Wills," she said, breaking from him to breathe. "When—"

"Let right now be you and me, not king and queen. Just man and wife, too soon to be parted."

A tear sparkled at the corner of her eye. He kissed it away. She held his gaze, unmoving, then slipped her hands under his jacket, sweeping down his arms to undress him. She fumbled at his trunks and he inhaled, urgency racing through him. Yet he stilled her and backed away.

"Slowly," he said.

She nodded and slid her fingers through her shoulder ties, unlacing her sleeves, eyes never leaving his. Reaching around her back, she pulled her lower lip between her teeth as she worked her stays. His body thrummed, his desire to cherish warring with more wanton instincts.

Pushing down her skirts, she stepped out of them, petite feet bare. Unable to resist any longer, he tore at his shirt laces, but she raised a hand for him to stop, shaking her head, melancholy smile on her face. She drew her hands to her hair, loosing each pearl and pin, locks tumbling down, framing her shoulders, her back, him feeling each tendril as if they hit his chest. At last she stood in nothing but gossamer silk and the ruby necklace he'd given her.

In two steps he was upon her, stooping, pooling her chemise up her body, gliding his hands over her thighs, her hips, her torso, up and over her head. Her arms came down around his shoulders and he lifted her, bearing her to the bed.

He lay her down, reverent, and observed her watching him undress. He didn't have her patience and was done in moments, roving her body.

"I love you, Anna."

"I know you do, Wills." Her smile could topple mountains.

He took his time, prowling over her, mouthing a knee here, a hip there, the inside of a wrist, finally hovering inches from her lips. Snaking her hand to the nape of his neck, the other to the low curve of his spine, she brought him to her. And he spent his last hours at Havenside in the grip of her grace.

Morning broke with no mercy. The blade-steel sky clung to the ground, fog wisps swirling in the wake of horses and men, the air hanging on William like a second set of mail. He could barely make out the queen and court, huddled in their furs at the palace gates. When all was ready for departure, soldiers mounted, stallions stamping the ground, the Troixden standard, hoisted yet limp on its pole, William strode to Anna, taking a knee before her.

She removed her glove so he could kiss her skin.

"Bless us, my queen."

As was tradition, she held her free hand above his head and said, "Go in the name of God, His hand to keep thee, the love of Christ in thy veins, the strong Spirit bathing thee, all three to shield and aid thee, behind, in front, below and above, and bring thee back victorious."

There were no cheers this day, no cries of assured triumph, just the shifting weight of a thousand men anticipating their grim task. She reached into her wolf-lined cloak and brought forth her favor, balling it up in his hand. He closed his fist around the favor but felt something hard. Unwrapping the small bundle, he found a thick chain with a square gold pendant, a ruby set in its center. He narrowed his brow in question, and with deft fingers, she popped the clasp, revealing a miniature of her and Cate.

"I know it's not practical for battle," she whispered, "but I thought you might wear it and know we are with you, as you are with us."

He stood and looped the chain around his neck, tucking it under his livery. "I shant take it off."

Cupping her face, he gazed upon her.

Her jaw trembled. He could tell she was trying to be strong, queenly, holding back tears. Unable to stand the formality, he folded her under his cloak as though his arms were wings. He kissed the top of her head, feeling her shake in his arms.

"Oh God, Wills." She pushed away from him, wiping her face. "If you don't leave now, I'll never let you go."

Whatever happened, whether he came home in victory, as a vanquished king, or in a casket, he knew this war would change them. He wanted this last moment of them as they were. He wanted to look at her with eyes that had yet to stare again into those of dying countrymen, of ravaged women, of starved children. He wanted her to see him, undarkened by this war and all that it would take from him.

He hesitated, desperate to kiss her once more, but it would undo them both. Swallowing his own emotion, he bowed to her.

"For Troixden and for victory, my queen."

CHAPTER 9

Once More to Battle

nna wasn't content to sit idle during this war, no matter how Daniel hemmed and hawed and worried his hands, commenting about queenly duties. As if a queen must only throw feasts, give alms, and wave at crowds. As if a queen couldn't lead. Couldn't rule. William had put them both in charge of diplomacy and domestic policy in his absence, and she was determined to take on that charge with all she had. She wasn't pregnant this time. Daniel had no excuse to tuck her away "for the heir's sake."

She bustled into the council room, a stack of curled maps in her arms, steadying the teetering pile with her chin. Dumping them on the illustrious table, she rubbed her hands together. "I think that's all of them." She smiled up at an equally smiling Halforn. "Shall we get started then?"

Halforn set his beer mug on the table, spilling a bit of foam down the side. "I am at your service, Madam." He unrolled the first map, an enlarged Norwick. Various pages stood at the ready, paperweights in their hands. "Shall we put this one in the middle? As far as we know, most of the battles will be fought in Norwick."

Anna unfolded others, stretching over the table, looking for either Beaubourg or Laureland. "And we can line up the rest around it, with the larger map of all Troixden at the end, or perhaps hung up to see it better?"

Bartmore, who had strolled in to see what all the commotion was about, scoffed. "Surely this is completely unnecessary." He waved a hand at the table and the puzzle of Troixden's duchies she was piecing together. "Any information we receive will be after the fact."

Anna stood, hands on hips. "Begging your pardon, Eminence, but if you are not here to help us, I daresay there are better things you might do to further the war efforts."

"But that is my point, dear lady." Anna tried not to bristle over his flouting of royal address. "What you two are doing has no impact or help on the war either. Your, ah, talents, are better used dressing richly and walking about the city, not closed up in here staring at maps of battles well finished."

"You mean I'm better off leaving the hallowed ground of manly thought here in council to flit about like a pretty bird, sitting content on my perch until one of you has need of my . . . talents?" She found the map of Duven and wondered if she should stake it down yet. There was no notion that the rebels had made it that far, but Duven was moving his men . . .

Bartmore huffed. "I would not put it so indelicately. But in essence, yes."

"I am merely ornamental, then?" She smiled at him, savoring his squirming.

"A queen's role is to dote upon her people, not politics."

She searched for the map of western Luxembourg. "Tell that to Elizabeth. Or Catherine de' Medici."

"And these treacherous women you use as example?" Bartmore laughed humorlessly. He came around behind her, surveying her work. "Of course, the true role of a queen is to give the country an heir." Despite herself she reddened, stomach clenching. "Perhaps if you spent less time attempting to prove your intelligence and theological superiority, sparking these rumors of heresy, there wouldn't be a war to be watching in the first place."

"That is not only uncalled for, Bartmore," Halforn said, "it is beneath a man of the cloth."

Bartmore looked down his nose at the man. "It makes it no less true. And it is what everyone is thinking."

She steadied her breath, but her eyes still blazed as they met Bartmore's.

"Seeing as the king be not here for such blessed circumstances to occur, I am performing my foremost queenly duty in keeping the rest of the country safe and making sure our king comes home quickly and alive. And if these are not your most urgent duties at present, perhaps you might flit off to Rome again and see if the pope will send his troops this time around."

She turned from him and plunked a gold weight, emblazoned with a griffin, on the corner of Duven. She knew he recognized the dismissal, but instead of leaving he sniffed and snarled his lips at her bustling about.

"Fine," he said with another flick of his hand. "Play at your puzzle making. I have urgent appointments."

Her insides uncurled at his departure. She was proud of herself. Years ago, she would have left the room in tears after an impassioned diatribe, defending herself and the king. Now she could take the impact of such arrows, no less stinging, but not unduly wounding.

"Your Grace," she said to Halforn, "have you found Laureland yet?"

He sighed. "I have not. And I fear they have not found themselves, either."

"That is why we fight," she said, meeting his saddened face. "To help them find themselves."

He nodded and held up his mug to her in toast, a grin creeping back across his face. "As I said, Majesty, I am at your service."

The maps were spread, the battle lines drawn. Much to Cate's chagrin, Anna had used her colored blocks to represent the different groups of men, William's blue, Norwick's red, Duven's green, and so on. The rebels were colorless, white, like ghosts both haunting and unreal to her.

She now sat across from Daniel at his desk as he made the final touches to yet another plea to France for support. They both knew it would go unheeded, but in the peculiar etiquette of war, one needed to reach out to one's allies, at the very least to acknowledge that they were such, and that any skirmishes near the borders wouldn't bleed onto their lands.

"If they be so concerned about their borders, perhaps they should send us men to help defend them," she said, watching the quick movements of Daniel's quill.

"Wouldn't that be nice?" Daniel said in the same vague way she responded to Cate when she wasn't listening. He fluttered a paper under her nose. "Do you wish to sign it?"

"'Tis from us both, is it not?" He nodded and she took it from him. Reaching the end, she saw Daniel had signed right beneath the valediction.

"You've not left space, Your Grace."

"Truly?" He scrunched his face. She showed him the bottom of the page. "My apologies. Habit, I suppose. Would you like me to rewrite it?"

She sighed, placing the letter on his desk to sign. "Nay. The French aren't worth all that paper." She signed neatly above Daniel, to the right of the close.

She handed it off to his secretary to prepare it for travel. "Might I make a suggestion?"

Daniel had already returned his attention to a stack of correspondence collected at his right elbow. He looked up at her, brows raised. "I wish to avoid the, well, misunderstandings we had during the previous war when we were left to run the country jointly."

"By all means." He spread his hands wide.

"I believe a start would be a new location for our meetings. Me coming here . . . it does not seem neutral ground."

He chuckled. "We are both on the same side, Highness. Of course this ground is neutral."

"Come now, Cecile—you are more discerning than that." She smiled at him to take the bite out of her words. "This is your chamber, we are surrounded by your things, your pages and secretaries. It is a room designed to intimidate."

"I wouldn't think you intimidated by anything, let alone a room." He folded his hands in front of him, leaning in.

"I simply believe it would be more prudent to meet in a place of equality. Halforn and I have conveniently set up council with maps. We could meet there."

"To be quite honest, it is more convenient to meet here, as I've all the correspondence, writing materials, and records at hand."

"You also have a fleet of men to carry such to council," she said.

He had that look he sometimes got when trying to placate an underling.

"That's quite a disruption for mere appearances." He chuckled again. "Not exactly helpful to productivity when my men could be about their regular duties, which obviously have greatly increased."

"There was a time, Your Grace, when you simply would have made such arrangements in the first place. It seems you have become comfortable in your high position. Forgetting to whom you speak so casually."

He had the decency to blush. "By all means, Highness, if it makes you more comfortable."

She nodded, taking his measure as his pale eyes met hers. "Then it is settled. Unless there is some emergent need, we shall have our daily meetings in council. In the meantime," she withdrew two letters from her skirt pockets. "These are to be sent with the next post to the front. I need not tell you they are of a personal nature, for the king's eyes alone."

He nodded, taking the sealed letters. "Of course, Highness."

She rose. "Well then, thank you, Your Grace. Shall I see you this eve at supper?"

He rose as well, giving her a slight bow. "I look forward to it."

"As do I." She left him with his various papers, but the conversation had done nothing to soothe her anxious stomach. Everyone assumed Daniel was morally and intellectually superior, that nothing occupied his mind other than how to serve his king and country better. But Anna had glimpsed behind that diplomatic mask, and what she saw made her wonder whose best interests were truly in his heart.

Anna didn't feel like eating. Daniel had sent a note informing her that the accounts he was working on were taking longer than usual, and Halforn wished only a light supper in his rooms. There was no way she would dine alone with Bartmore, so she ate with her ladies in her privy dining chamber, wishing she were in William's, feasting with him and Cate.

"I could eat an entire pig!" Margaux exclaimed, digging into another portion of pigeon pie.

"Storing up for the winter, are we, Countess?" Yvette said.

Margaux glowered back. "By all means, laugh. For you've never known the hunger of a woman with child."

All at the table stilled. It beggared belief. But if Anna thought about it, Margaux's boy Henry was about six months old and since Margaux, like many noblewomen, didn't breastfeed, there was every possibility she was with child. The thought of it lessened Anna's appetite all the more.

"And what does your fair husband have to say?" Yvette said. "For by my count, you have not been in his company for quite some time."

"You, of all people, should have nothing to say on that account!" Margaux said, falsely aghast.

"Ladies, enough," Anna said, calculating in her own head how long Mohrlang had been from court. He'd been there at Christmastide. But so were many other fetching gentlemen, including Raleigh. "Surely the Countess had much to celebrate with her husband at the holidays." Margaux pursed her lips, self-satisfied.

The women ate again, slowly and quietly at first, but soon murmured conversation swelled about the table. Lady Jane sat to Anna's right and the queen reached out to squeeze her wrist.

"Lady Jane," Anna said, conjuring a smile she did not feel, "tell me of Lord John and how he fares."

"Wonderfully, Majesty, thanks to your kind care and provision." Her eyes lit as they always did when John was mentioned. "He's not had a fit in months, and he excels at his studies. The tutors say he is far ahead of the others in Latin and mathematics."

"I'm delighted to hear it." She leaned in with a whisper. "And none have guessed at your . . . private beliefs."

Jane dropped her eyes to the table and gave a quick shake of her head. "We've been very careful, Highness."

Anna released Jane with a gentle pat, relaxed back in her chair, and picked at a few grapes.

"And what is this I hear of His Grace of Cecile?"

Jane's face paled. "I-I don't—"

Anna laughed. "Goodness, Jane, 'tis nothing to be embarrassed about. He is a good man, would be a fine match for you. And you for him."

"A match, Highness?" Jane looked at Anna, shock hollowing out her features.

"Come now, Jane, you can tell me. 'Tis no crime to seek another husband."

Her brows crept up her forehead. "Husband? Oh no, milady." She knifed her hand back and forth as if to wipe away the very idea. "He is merely my neighbor. And doles out the payment for John's nurses. Nothing more."

"The king said he thought you two were in a lovers' spat of some sort a while ago." Anna watched Jane carefully.

"I assure you, Highness, 'twas nothing of the sort." Her eyes were pleading. "I would surely tell you of any suitors, or even hoped-for suitors."

"I relent, dear Jane. I should not have teased as it distresses you so." She smiled in genuine regret. Yet one more conversation she had mucked up this day.

Anna pushed back her chair, rising. "I fear I've a headache. I think I shall take some rest."

Mary jumped up, waving at the others to sit. "I'll see to ye, Majesty."

Anna smiled in thanks, taking Mary's proffered arm. They strolled to Anna's bedchamber.

"I admit ye've looked quite peaked of late, dearie," Mary said, frowning with concern. "And your hand's clammy."

"With the king gone and all this courtly infighting . . . It tires me in body and spirit." Gaining her chamber, Mary helped her remove her outer clothes.

"And I suppose that nasty Margaux and her blessed announcement did nothin' to help ye." Mary heaved off Anna's boots. She'd been on a ride after meeting with Daniel, hoping to bring her some serenity. It hadn't worked.

"Oh, Margaux's goings on are the least of my worries at present." Anna took a grateful seat on the side of her bed.

Mary stood, hands on her hips, blinking. "Y' need to eat something, dearie."

Anna's stomach roiled at the thought. "Please don't mention food."

Mary pressed one hand to Anna's forehead and one to the back of her neck. "Y' don't feel hot." She pooched out her lips, considering the queen.

"I just need to rest." Anna tucked her legs under the covers, scooted back, and propped her back up with pillows. "And some peace and quiet. Mary, would you allow all but my night maid and you the evening off?"

"I'm sorry to say 'tis the shrew's night to stay with ye."

Anna shielded her eyes with her forearm and groaned. "And I can't make an excuse to replace her without sounding petty."

"How about I say, 'due to the countess's condition, Her Majesty is requesting a volunteer to replace her,' something of that sort."

"Perfect, Mary, thank you." Mary made a little curtsy and turned to go. "Wait." Her nurse turned, quizzical. "I just . . ." Anna sighed. "I am missing just we two. I'm missing our carefree days of Beaubourg."

Mary harrumphed but smiled, pulling up a tuffet to sit next to Anna. "They were hardly carefree. They just seem that way in yer head because now you're full of woe and worry."

Anna reached for Mary's hand. "Perhaps. But can we just remember them so? Just for this evening? Can we remember the first time I bested Bryan in a race? The times father took me out riding? How you taught me about herbs. Mother's laughter . . ."

"The time you came home, muddied from head to toe to find yer father entertaining dignitaries?" Mary's whole body shook when she laughed.

"I'd forgotten!" Anna laughed too. "Oh, the look on Papa's face. He couldn't decide whether to beam with pride or beat the tar out of me."

"Oh, yer father would never have lifted a finger to ye." Mary wiped her eyes.

"He said something like, 'Begging pardon, but my daughter is indisposed.'" She saw his face in her mind's eye, smile fighting with a frown. "And he sent me to bed without supper."

"Ah, but I snuck you sweet rolls and cheese." Mary held up a finger in her defense.

"You've always been my salvation, Mary." An empty glass at

her bedside caught her eye. "You know, I think I will have just a bit of something, now that you mention sweet rolls."

"As you wish, Majesty," Mary gave a robust curtsy and left. But Anna never ate the roll, for she quickly fell into a deep sleep.

William could take it no longer. And he could tell Robert was antsy too. They'd been over a fortnight at Cheval, with no sign of the Laurelanders or anyone else coming from Norwick's central border. Riders charged back and forth from the two fronts throughout each day, in hails of sweat and mud and breathless reports. Two horses had already died from exhaustion. And among them all, he'd no letter from the queen, no note of love or encouragement. He'd received one on the road, but nothing since. He feared something was wrong, that she was hiding some terrible news, trying to shield him from more worry. Yet Daniel had said all was well, and he'd even heard from blasted Bartmore: the pope would muster papal troops. Though they weren't currently en route. Nor mustered, most likely.

He had commandeered Robert's study, tables now covered with maps and correspondence, half-drunk glasses of wine and stiff bread crusts among wizening grapes scattered about. He frowned out the cracked-open window at the darkening hills beyond Robert's precisely manicured shrubs. He was unsure where to go, but he knew he couldn't stay put.

"By all accounts, we should head east," Robert said, lounging upon a chaise. "That front is longer and in need of more direction, more centralized decision making. And if we were on the ground, we could decide upon actions directly instead of all this damned waiting around."

"But that is why the grand master general is in the east," William said, turning back to the desk, searching for a clean cup. "If we head to the Truss, we could make quick work of them. A decisive victory gives us more men to move east, as well as the momentum we need to push these bastards back where they came from."

The rebels were skirting the eastern edge of the Truss Mountains, heading to the valley where Laureland, Beaubourg, and Ridgeland met. At worst, the Troixden army could wait out the rebels, hemming them in until their supplies ran dry.

"If we are waiting in the Hedgewood Valley with our fresh men, we're sure to easily overtake them." William gave up on finding a clean glass, picked another, threw the stale contents out the window, and filled it again.

"But that may be so without troops from here." Robert sat up, resting his arms on his knees. "'Tis Duven and the rest who need fresh men, as they are stretched the thinnest. What would we add at Hedgewood than more men lolling about in wait for the enemy to appear?"

"We are closer to Hedgewood, can take it easily, then head to Duven in renewed vigor." William couldn't admit it to Robert, but he needed to be close to Beaubourg, as if being close to Anna's home would bring him closer to her. It was ridiculous, but there it was. And in the end, both directions needed help.

"We are heading west. As soon as the sun is up."

"The real battle to be won is in the east!"

"The decision is made, Robert." William leveled his eyes at his cousin. "No more arguments."

Now Robert was up, all insouciance gone. "I will argue when the decision is foolish and risks me and my men."

William rounded the desk, bearing down. "That's where you are wrong. They're not your men. They are my men. And I will do with them what *I* will."

"This isn't some duel, Wills—I'm in earnest. We will be of no use in the west!"

"And I am not your friend in this scenario—I am your king and your commander. We leave at sunrise for Hedgewood."

Robert stood, nostrils flaring, jaw twitching. It was the look he used to get when they were boys, right before Robert would tackle William. But he never won those wrestling matches. And he wouldn't win this either.

He finally lifted a dark brow. "As you wish, *my liege.*" He strung the last word out as he made an exaggerated bow. "I will ready my—excuse me, *your* men—posthaste." With that, Robert stalked out of his own study without a backward glance.

William sank into the nearest chair, head in hands.

God help us all if Robert proves right.

Robert could admit it. He was self-righteously sulking. Since they'd arrived at Hedgewood and set up camp, they'd had nothing but bad news. William had been right about one thing: Beaubourg's men were thin, in numbers and in body. Not feeble by any means, these men of the north were made of sturdier stuff than most, which made it all the more shocking to see them in such diminished form. They hadn't been able to push back the rebel forces, and had, as William predicted, retreated to the valley in wait, to rest, recover. The king's arrival buoyed them, but that shine diminished as the waiting continued, despite signs the rebels would be to the valley in two days' time.

Adding to this, upon the king's arrival, word came from the grand master general that he, Duven, and Norwick's men were still unable to push back the rebels. At least their line held. There had been no word since. And of course, there was still no movement from the pope, other than his agreement to send men.

William was disagreeable too. He stomped about his tent, biting the heads off half his staff. The king never yelled at his staff. And Robert was in no mood to cheer him, for what was there to be cheerful about?

Certainly Robert could poke about to find the gold in all this manure, some way to further his agenda, but he wasn't so bent on revenge that he wanted William of Orange—or "the Silent" as some called him—on Troixden's throne.

"Your Grace." One of William's trembling servants appeared at Robert's tent door. "His Majesty wishes an audience."

Robert left his desk, approaching the man. "I doubt he said it so politely." The man's eyes grew round with terror. "Don't worry, I won't tell."

He made the short trip through the drizzle to the king's tent. Already he could hear William hollering.

"I need numbers! Why would he send you without numbers?"

Robert entered to see William slam his fist on the desk, the exhausted rider startling.

"Highness," Robert said, with a swift bow.

"They say multitudes of Duven's men have either died from, or come down with, dysentery!" William jabbed his arm at the messenger, as if the man were the disease bearer. "Dysentery!"

"'Tis common enough in war, especially in the damp." Robert nodded to the rider.

"I don't care if it's common," William spat. "I care to know how many men it hath put down!"

The messenger looked to Robert, perhaps hoping for better reception. "I would estimate a good third, Your Grace."

"Estimates will not do, you fool!"

Robert knew better than to say something as condescending as "calm down," to the king, but he'd had never seen William so wound up. Not even after his sister died. Or his mother. Not even when he was banished by his brother James. The king was making illogical decisions, barking cruel commands, upbraiding people he normally praised. Robert had to do something to get the king under control and quickly.

"Might I have a word, Majesty?" Robert said in his most humble voice. "Alone?"

William's steel eyes flashed to him, but he nodded. The tent cleared like rats off a sinking ship.

"Be honest with me, my liege," Robert said. "What has you in such foulness? 'Tis not the king I know before me."

"Perhaps because we sit like geese awaiting slaughter, perhaps because I've just lost nearly two thousand men to a damned disease, perhaps because we've made no movement on any fronts!"

Undaunted, Robert advanced. "All this is true, but the king I know, the king I serve with my body and soul, does not berate his lessers. The king I know looks at such setbacks with determination in his eyes and a sword in his hand. The king I know greets each blow as a challenge, with a smile on his face and a lion's heart. The king I know is better than . . ." Robert gestured at the whole of his friend, "than this."

"The king you know has been routed by another." William sank into a chair. "Oh God, Robert, my nightmare has come true. I'm finally my vainglorious, tyrant of a brother."

"I beg to differ." Robert swiped an apple from the sideboard and sat as well. "For if you were your brother, you would not think yourself a vainglorious tyrant."

The king sat silent, squinting at his desk. He swallowed hard.

Robert leaned forward. "Wills?"

"I've two letters. Two. In an entire month."

"She probably does not want to use up scarce resources of riders and horses—"

"I receive word from Daniel. Twice a week his letters come." William shook his head. "There would be no more resources utilized were the same rider to also carry word from the queen."

"Is that truly why you are in such a state?" Robert shook his head. "Lord, man, she probably knows you need to concentrate on other things at present."

"That's what worries me. I fear she's hiding something dreadful. Perhaps Cate is ill again, or she herself is."

Observing his friend, Robert took a big bite of the apple, but it was mealy, crumbling in his mouth.

"Yet you've never been one to take such out on your men."

William rubbed his neck and winced. "You asked for honesty, friend, and I will give it." He looked up to the tent roof, heavy laden with pools of rain. "Something in my bones tells me no matter what we do, we will lose this war. And when we do, I do not fear for my life, but for my wife and child. For you and for Daniel. And for all the other good people who hath served me well and long."

Robert swallowed his tasteless bite. "If you look at it on the whole, Wills, we're not so bad off. The rebels have made no progress, our lines have held, even with weak, tired, and sick men."

"But we don't have access to reinforcements as they do. Men from the Low Countries, fed up with the emperor's rule and hungry for freedom, will stream across our borders, replacing their fallen. We've no such help. Spain and France have turned their faces, the pope sits on his troops. For all we know Elizabeth is launching ships to fight us as well."

"What did your mother always say when your brother would pick on you and you'd best him? 'You may be small, but you be mighty.'" Robert smiled, remembering.

"And that I must use my might for good, not violence." William sighed, collapsing down into his chair.

"Well we've no choice in that last, but think on it. We may be a small country, but we are mighty in heart, in fealty, in bravery. Our people will not so easily be defeated." Robert was rousing himself with his own words. They would prevail, because they had men of spirit, fighting for their homes, their families, their way of life, not fighting for some vague cause or to fill their purse. "Think of the Israelites!"

William laughed. "*You're* bringing up the Scriptures?"

"They were small and mighty too. And yet they faced constant threat." Robert jumped up as if rallying his troops. "They were afflicted, but not crushed; perplexed, but not despairing; struck down, but not destroyed."

"That verse is from Paul, friend, but I take your meaning." William drummed his fingers on the desk. "Still, the Israelites had God on their side."

"And we do not?"

"Our cause be just, but I have not seen any pillars of fire come down, have you?" William sat back with a sigh. "But there sure have been a multitude of plagues."

Robert frowned. At least William was now more aware of his strange behavior. Perhaps that's all Robert could do in one day.

"Cheer up, cuz. For we've a battle to win tomorrow." Nothing put a spring in Robert's step like wielding a sword. He winked at the king, who gave a halfhearted smile back.

"I'll just have to let your enthusiasm be enough for the both of us." He nodded in dismissal, but as Robert bent to go through the door, William called out, "Norwick? Thank you."

Robert nodded and left the king to his own solace.

Another fortnight passed with sparse news from William. It was well into March, and apparently they had made it to Cheval, with all quiet there. Robert's wife and boys had stayed, fearing to travel and be attacked, though Daniel reckoned they would soon be sent to court for safekeeping. By all accounts the others were yet to reach the invaders, but it would be any day now, if they hadn't already. Much to Anna's chagrin, Bartmore had been correct. Her maps would be sorely out of date with how slowly word was reaching them.

William made no mention of her letters. She'd received only one from him, brief, but loving. She was desperate to know each detail. How were they coping with the late snow—was it making the mud worse or freezing it, how were their supplies holding, what of the people, the farms, were they safe as well, how were the men's spirits holding?

"I wish I had more, or better news, Highness," Daniel said, hunching over the maps, moving the blocks into different formations and back again.

"As do I." Anna sat in William's chair, chin resting on steepled fingers as she stared out the tall window. "Once this snow finally passes, I was thinking of how we might interact with the people, drum up support and spirits. Since traveling may be dangerous, I thought we might invite the folk of Havenside in. From peasant to mayor."

Daniel nodded. "We could show them our confidence by treating them to some joviality and succor."

"And word would spread, that not only are we unruffled by this incursion, we also have enough money to fight a war and please our people. Unlike Spain."

"What if we did something involving the princess and the children?" Daniel picked up a quill and started scratching away. He often did this when he had a burst of inspiration, as if he must see his thoughts written before he could speak them. "Certainly there is some feast day soon that would be appropriate?"

"The feast of St. Patrick is little over a week away—the

children would adore it." Anna sat up straight, brightening for the first time in days. "Why Daniel, 'tis perfect! Not only will we show our people our strength and our commitment to the True Faith, but Doemland can share with his queen how we held high this Irish saint, showing support for Ireland's continued fight against England and heresy. In fact, I shall visit his wife, see if she can enlighten us any further on how our Irish brothers and sisters celebrate Patrick."

"I am not sure if that is wise," Daniel said, still making notes. "For there have been whispers—"

"Oh tush, she's not a witch and we all know it." Though a shudder swept through her as she spoke.

"You and I may know that, Highness, but the gossip about court is that Lady Katharine is partly responsible for the countess's new pregnancy." Anna's blood raced. She hated how quickly people assumed witchery when babies were involved. "Everything from a potion to a spell, to calling forth a demon has been bandied about." He caught her eye with a weak smile. "It looks like your rival may soon have a downfall."

"The countess would never be part of such dealings." Anna stood and tried to pace off her frustration at the pigheadedness of slanderers. Didn't they realize the power of their pens, how people could be slain with just a whisper? "As much as the countess irks me, I've no wish to see her vilified. If she is to have a downfall, it should be of her own making, and we, as Christians, should mourn it."

Daniel crossed his arms. "I thought you would be, if not gladdened, at least justified by it all."

"The countess has never been a serious threat to me," Anna said. "She merely plays at sabotage, whilst I know William would never stray from me."

"Come now, you do not delude yourself into thinking she is only aiming to be the king's mistress?"

"What are you implying, Your Grace?"

"There is more than one way to turn a king's eye. More than one way to make a queen unfit to wear the crown." He met her eyes, trying to impart something. Daniel moved his eyes to her belly then back to her face. My God. Did he think Margaux was keeping her barren? And more to the point, was she? If she was, how?

Anna's head pounded and she took the nearest seat. The countess couldn't be that cruel. Anna had seen the pure, guileless love Margaux had for her own children, even for Cate. She often caught Margaux grinning at the princess's antics, like a doting auntie, not a conniving weasel. The woman, despite it all, was a mother at heart. Anna couldn't fathom, no matter how deep Margaux's jealousy and indignation, that she would keep Anna from bearing a child.

But she was so haughty about her boys . . . always hinting around, like a dog sniffing a bush before marking its territory, how her boys had royal blood. They were not simply gentry; they were nobility.

Daniel had gone back to writing. "I know nothing other than the fact that desperate women do desperate things."

"She does not strike me as desperate anymore," Anna said, voice flat. "She's gloating about her swelling belly."

"As I say," he didn't look up from his work, "the rest of court does not share her high opinion of herself at present."

There was a firm, quick knock at the council door. "Majesty!" It was Bernard. Anna nodded to a guard to allow entry. His face was blotched, hair untidy, and he was kneading his flat cap. "The countess. She's . . . we don't know. Feverish, in pain. Mistress Mary is with her now, but she worsens." It was as if his words weren't sinking in, as if all her inner turmoil about Margaux had conjured Bernard, standing here. "She is rambling. Asking for a priest. Asking for you, Majesty."

"Excuse me, Your Grace." Anna leapt to her feet, something like guilt ripping through her.

"Begging pardon, Highness," Daniel said with a small frown, "but given our conversation, do you think it wise to attend upon her?"

"And refuse a possibly dying woman?" She made her way around the great table to Bernard.

Daniel waved this away. "I doubt she's dying, Highness, and if she is, there will only be more speculation."

"How can you be so callous?"

Daniel stood, coming to within inches of her to whisper, "I am only trying to follow the king's orders in protecting you. That includes gossip as well as physical harm. If she be ill, all the worse that you catch it, even without the further implications of whatever services the countess has employed to get herself with child." Anna shook her head, ready to retort. He grabbed her arm, his thin fingers pinching. "You must listen. It was only through much effort—quite a bit on my part as it happens—that your name was kept far from this whole witch business. If you go to her now, that work will be in vain. You will be embroiled in this at a time in which the country can ill afford it. Think of our fighting men. Think of the king."

"That is all I do, every minute of the day." She twisted out of his grip, rage at new heights. "I think of the king, of this war, of our people. And one of our people is crying out to her queen in mercy. I will not disdain her."

"You dig your own grave." He stepped back, eyes mere slits.

"And you forget to whom you speak, Your Grace."

She turned, leaving him there, his hands clenched as tight as his jaw. Something about the way he watched her go agitated her. Surely he would continue to follow the king's orders regardless of her actions, for Daniel would die a thousand deaths for William. Whether he would lift a finger for her unless directed by the king, she no longer knew. And it frightened her.

Concerns about Daniel slipped away as she neared Margaux's chamber. She could hear moaning, crying out in unintelligible sobs. Entering, the stench of sickness assailed her. Someone, probably Bernard or Mary, had seen fit to bring Anna a wide apron and she donned it, heading straight for the bed.

Margaux reached out with grasping hands and wild eyes. "Highness, you saved my Frederick, you must save this boy too." Anna looked down the length of Margaux, saw the blood pooling between her thighs. Her heart froze. Margaux's hands were hot and clammy, her face wet, colored a greenish hue. She may have already had blood rot.

"We will do what we can. Just try to breathe." She patted Margaux's hand.

"Where is the priest? Oh God—" She sobbed again. "I am wasted!"

Doing away with formality, Anna took Margaux's jaw in her free hand, pulling her face to focus on Anna's. "Margaux, you are not going to die. Not now. The priest is on his way—"

"Not Bartmore—"

"Heavens no." Anna's face curled. "But he will not be needed, for we will have no last rites today." She took a glass of what she recognized as Mary's sleeping draught and helped the countess drink. Taking a fresh wet cloth, Anna wiped Margaux's lovely blonde hair, now soaked with sweat, away from her face, pressing the cloth to her forehead. Anna nodded, with all the firmness of a determined nurse, and joined Mary at the foot of the bed.

"Have the court physician's been called?" Anna asked, looking from Mary to Yvette, both grim faced.

"They've been sent for," Yvette said from a nearby table. She was crushing cramp bark berries and clove together in a pestle.

"I've steeped the raspberry leaves in wine." Mary gestured to the table. "When milady's finished, we'll give her some of the mixture as tea and some we'll make to a paste and insert."

"When will it be ready?" Anna said, unlacing the sleeve at her shoulder. Margaux was considerably more still, but kept craning her neck about in seemingly both physical and moral pain.

"I'm about to do the mixing." Mary dipped her hands in a bowl of rose water, then took the pestle from Yvette. Pouring a slow stream of the wine-tea into the berries, she simultaneously stirred it together until it was the consistency of mud pies. She handed the curative to Anna. "Here. Try the paste on her. Though with this much blood, I can only send up me prayers."

Anna went to the bed, calculating from the end of Christmas. A little more than two months. She sucked her lips into her mouth, biting to keep the emotion from overtaking her. She wanted to vomit, felt faint. But she must press on and help Margaux.

She got on her knees at the end of the bed and lifted the sheet. A bright red a stain, about the size of a trencher, spread beneath Margaux, though it was by no means saturated. More akin to blood from a cut.

"Countess, I'm going to check you now and give you a poultice." She folded the sheet farther up Margaux's belly. "It may feel cold." Margaux only grimaced in response, mumbled something incoherent. Dipping two fingers in the paste, Anna carefully inserted them inside Margaux, rubbing her vaginal walls. She knew she must check the cervix. If it felt like the tip of a nose, the baby would most likely be fine. For some women around this time, did bleed, then carried the child to full term. But if the cervix were soft, like lips . . . Anna stretched her middle finger forward, searching. Margaux rocked her hips off the bed with a yowl, Anna's fingers slipping back. The queen swore under her breath.

"Relax, Countess, I'm simply making sure the babe is secure."

"Ungh . . ." Margaux's thigh's tightened, her vaginal walls clamping down on Anna's fingers. It looked and felt everything like a contraction. It ebbed, and Margaux slumped back on the bed. Anna readjusted herself, took a steadying breath, and felt again. She grit her teeth to stifle a cry. They were too late.

She caught Mary's eye over her shoulder and shook her head once. Mary nodded then bent to her medicine kit, pulling out new herbs and oils, tools to hasten the birth, to draw down fever, to put Margaux in a deep sleep.

The countess hoisted herself up on her elbows. "What's happening?" She looked like a frightened little girl, all her typically sharp angles melting into anxious hope and fear.

"You need to rest, Countess." Anna wiped her hands and wrung out a fresh cloth, tenderly stroking Margaux's hands, cheeks, and forehead. "Your body knows what to do, but it can only do so if you rest."

"Rest?" And there was the Margaux Anna knew, face contorted into disdain. "Well, that's very well and easy for you to say!"

Anna tamped down the urge to bite back, her emotions roiling.

"Here, take some more." She handed Margaux the draught and the countess drank greedily. Another spasm hit.

"This isn't right," Margaux said. "She told me I would have another babe soon."

"Who told you what?" Anna sat forward.

Margaux became very still. "I—nothing. I had a dream." She sank down, closing her eyes. "My mother came to me in a dream."

"I'm surprised you stake belief in dreams." Anna knew Margaux had to be talking about Katharine.

"You and the king do." Margaux licked her dry lips. "At least in your daughterrrrrr—" Her sentence ended in a howl. Anna stood abruptly. Damn it all. And poor Cate. She didn't understand why these "visits" from her brother and her grandmothers were anyone's concern. She'd been having more of them and Anna tried to hush her, tried to steer her away from such talk. But, stubborn like her parents, she continued to speak, plain and blunt. As if she'd just had a chat in the garden with Matilda. Of course, in Cate's mind, she *had* just had a chat in the garden with Matilda. Whatever Anna did, she mustn't mention any of this to William. It would only bring him more worry.

She snatched Mary's carafe of sleeping draught and carried it back to the bedside, filling Margaux's mug to near spilling. The next few hours would be delicate and painful. It was true what Anna said: the body did know what to do and the more rest Margaux had, the easier it would go. Despite all her jumbled feelings about her rival, she didn't want the woman to have to see her dead baby, didn't want her to also die. Maybe if Anna concentrated on that, prayed with all her heart for forgiveness, patience, kindness, maybe Anna could end this day without the weight of both guilt and mourning on her shoulders.

Hours later, Margaux was in a heavy sleep, her breath so slow that at times, it seemed as though her chest wouldn't expand again. Sometimes her body jolted, but her face remained a serene mask. Anna moved from her seat by the window to the end of the bed, simply for something to do. The priest had come, and finding Margaux sleeping and no baby yet born, he left with instructions for them to send for him if needed.

Anna carefully folded up the sheet over Margaux's legs and

frowned down at the now significant stain. In the crook of Margaux's thigh was a small, gray sack, no more than an inch long and covered in wine-dark blood. She wanted to cradle it in her hands. She beckoned to Mary, who came, saw the bundle, and scooped it up tenderly.

"Poor wee thing," she said, clucking her tongue. Mary had surely seen a hundred miscarriages, but she still shed a tear over every one. She gently punctured the sack with a fingernail, a squirt of fluid soaking her palm. Anna stared with horrified wonder. The babe was curled in on itself, arms across its chest, as if giving itself a hug. It had distinguishable fingers and toes, the cord, thick and strong, extending from its belly, its skin gossamer pink. She could even see tiny eyes and ears, but where the back of its head should have been, there was nothing but a hollow, as if someone had taken a miniature spoon and depressed it above the baby's spine.

"My God," Anna whispered, her hand covering her mouth. She couldn't help the first thought that came to her mind, no matter how irrational: witchcraft.

Robert was right. They would fight that day and the next. And the next. The rebels flowed through the cracks in the valley, filling it like a lake with all manner of men, from peasants with farm implements to fully armored and mounted knights. Despite their incongruous appearance, they were well organized and fierce.

Robert had convinced William to stay at camp, a vantage point that gave him full view of the field. William begrudgingly agreed that his person would not sway the fighting either way. Still, he didn't like having to stand there, powerless, and watch.

Neither side had gained ground in all the days of fighting. William thought his men had sufficiently surrounded the valley, but fog had thwarted them the first day, their position of offense lost. Now it was a scrimmage in the mud, each side losing multitudes. If it didn't end soon, it seemed no one would get out of this pit alive. He could watch no longer, so he strode about camp, a small train of guards and pages following, his mind turning over the various scenarios, unable to see a solution. If they couldn't even win this battle, how could they expect to win in the east?

He had burned an hour with his walking and turmoil, coming back to stand in the same mud-molded footprints he had left. But for the first time in weeks, what met his eyes brought a glimmer of hope.

Robert's men had surged forward, pushing the rebels up against the mountains' base. Their line had thinned, Norwick fighters surging on. Then, the rebels raised the white flag. He heard shouts of "surrender" echo and he almost danced with joy. He saw Robert ride up to the man holding the flag. After a few moments the man rode off, returning with another. Then all three headed toward William.

He met the men in his tent, Bolstad and Ridgeland already at his side. Robert bounded in as if he'd been on a ride in the country rather than in the center of a fierce, hours-long battle.

"Majesty, our countrymen of Laureland wish to concede."

Two grim-faced, burly men shuffled forward with slight bows. "Highness," they mumbled.

"Their supply chain is broken and they've nowhere to go but up the mountains. Now the only question is what to do with them."

"Now wait just a minute," one of the men said. He had large, globule eyes that stuck out of his skull like a fish's. "We only said we surrender the day."

"That is not how war works," William said. "'Tis not like a tournament. We shan't allow you to regroup and refresh to attack anew when we clearly have bested you."

"But His Grace said—"

"We care not a whit what His Grace said. You stand before your king now." William leaned forward in his makeshift throne. "And whether you wish it or not, your sovereign decides your fate." The fish-eyed man blinked, mouth clamped shut. "Now, you can either return to living in the peace that We have so graciously and continually provided you and the rest of Laureland, or you may all march in chains to Havenside to be dealt with like the treasonous wretches you are."

"Majesty," Bolstad said, "might there be a third option?"

William was irritated to be contradicted, but his curious part won out. "And what is it you suggest, Bolstad?"

"With so much sickness in Duven's ranks, perhaps we send these men to serve the ill so that others might be available to fight."

"That's a death sentence!" fish-eyes said.

"Not necessarily," William said, considering. He looked the men up and down, tapping his forefinger on the throne arm. "An interesting suggestion for traitors indeed, Bolstad, but unfortunately unfeasible for two main reasons. First, there is a problem of food and supplies. We would have to feed these here, taking needed stores away from loyal subjects. And second," William sat back, head resting against the wood, "we would sooner trust the devil than a Laurelander."

"We only wish to be left in peace!" This from the thickly beard, knob-nosed man.

William pushed out of his throne, gladness at the victory quickly fading. "As do We! We have let you worship undisturbed throughout our reign, not something to be tolerated by any other king, in Troixden or any land. But you are not content with this. You want control, you want the rest of your countrymen and your king to sink to their knees and spout your heresy. It will not happen. No matter whom you seek help from."

"But you burned that mason, you killed Lady Helena!" Spittle landed in the man's beard as he spoke.

"How dare you speak to your sovereign so, wretch," Ridgeland said, moving forward, flexing his sword hilt. William held up a hand to stay him. He glanced at Robert who was still bouncing slightly, biting his lips to hide a smile. And what had he to smile about? It seemed to William any mention of Helena's death would call to mind how Robert botched it all. If Westerville were still alive, would they have been informed the minute foreigners crossed the border—or even before? The look William gave his cousin turned Robert dour, his feet firm on the ground.

When William spoke, his voice was soft, but with no less steel. "We never burned the mason, and Helena earned her fate in ways you know nothing of. A taste of Stone Yard will perhaps give you a taste of what your slander and treason deserve. Perhaps then you will realize the precious nature of the freedom you so blithely turn from in your heedless grasping for that which is well above you."

He turned to his lords. "Ridgeland, send your men east now to help with the efforts there. Tell all along the way of our swift victory here."

"An honor, sire." Ridgeland bowed.

"Bolstad, take your men and those we can spare from Halforn's men and round up these criminals. Those who beg mercy will be spared and sent back to their homes. Pay no heed to deserters, for they'll be help or hindrance to no one."

"Highness," Robert said, "begging pardon, but methinks you show much mercy. Too much."

"And what would you have us do, Your Grace? Slaughter them all in the grass? Mayhap mercy will prove yet again they've need to fight no longer."

"If this were their first treasonous act, mercy might do such as Your Majesty says." Robert bowed his head, showing a remarkable sense of decorum. "But this be the third time these Laureland bastards have taken to arms against thy person and thy throne. They have not proved themselves worthy of mercy."

Robert befuddled the king. His cousin was a proponent of what these men ostensibly fought for, so why was he wishing to kill them wholesale? Wouldn't he want Laureland helping to press his own case against the Catholics, want them as allies rather than further enraged?

"We appreciate Your Grace's logic," William said, "but our orders still stand. Of course, those who resist will pay with their lives."

"Then you may start with me!" The bearded man puffed out his chest, jabbing it with his thumb.

William shook his head. "'Tis a pity to lose such bravery."

"Stupidity is more like it," Robert said.

The man's chest heaved, eyes wide, unblinking.

His companion backed away. "Don't do it, Oskar."

"You may make your sniveling way back home, a traitor to the cause, but I shall die here like a man." He spat at his friend.

"Now don't go soiling His Majesty's carpets," Robert said, clucking his tongue.

"They're about to have worse than that," Ridgeland said, unsheathing his broadsword.

"Hold, Ridgeland," William said. Despite his royal demeanor, his insides recoiled at the thought of shedding any man's blood outside of battle. He had barely clawed his way out of James's bloodthirsty shadow, and now he must be party to this. And yet, the man insisted. He would be nothing but trouble on the long walk back to Havenside. They were better off rid of him. William sighed. "Outside, if you must and if the man still insists."

"I'd rather die now than live one more day in tyranny."

It struck William with grim finality: these Laurelanders would never stop. They would never stop because they only saw what they wished to see, believed lies that fit with their pre-conceived notions. Anything short of William separating from Rome wouldn't stop them and, looking at this bravely deluded man, the king wasn't sure even that would solve it.

"Then die you shall." William nodded at Ridgeland. Two guards held the man, shoving him after Ridgeland, who strode from the tent in solemn dignity. Another took the first man, his eyes bulging even more than before. William was sure those eyes would haunt his dreams.

Robert and Bolstad bowed and made to follow. "Will you not join us, Majesty?" Robert said, stopping at the tent opening.

"I have seen enough blood these past three days. I've no wish to witness more." He sank back into his throne, waving Robert out.

It was over in minutes. William heard grunting, surely guards getting this Oskar in place, the swish of Ridgeland's sword, the abrupt, moist ripping of flesh, like the dressing of a buck, the horrified gasp of Oskar's companion. Then Robert's almost bored voice. "Spike it. Put it there, overlooking the valley so they all can see it."

More grunting, another sound of juicy flesh. Then, from far below, cheers.

William closed his eyes and prayed for deliverance.

At that point, there was nothing left for them but to head southeast in the wake of Ridgeland's men. With one last wistful look at Beaubourg's border, and a touch of the pendant Anna gave him, William and his diminished army crossed Norwick, uncertain as to what they would find. With any luck, this war would end before April did.

Anna was glad to be outdoors, the early spring sun cutting through the chill to warm her face. She hadn't been outside the palace walls since Margaux's miscarriage a week past, due not only to nursing the countess, but the constant sheets of rain.

Margaux was mending in body, if not in spirit. Certainly she was grieved for the babe, but she also flinched any time someone came to her rooms, and she only spoke in whispers, eyes darting about. Anna surmised Margaux had heard the rumors, heightened because of her mangled baby. No one would outright accuse the countess, but Margaux was the most seasoned court gossip. She knew how this worked. No one would have to accuse her publicly for her to be condemned in the court of opinion. Anna also noted that Margaux had become sickly sweet to the queen, perhaps hoping to find refuge if this dragon of accusation started to breathe fire. The countess had insisted on accompanying the queen on this stroll, declaring she'd been in bed long enough. Despite herself, Anna felt protective of the countess.

Anna had been so tossed about in mind that the world, even with the cheerful sun, struck her as morose, painful. As if William had swept away joy in his leaving. But she always felt this way when he was gone, even more so when he was in daily danger. What was so different now?

Daniel joined her walk as well. Anna had done her best to smooth over their conflict about helping the countess, talking of plans for the Feast of St. Patrick celebrations. Daniel soon softened. He guided her around the last of the tall hedgerows. Raised voices met them and Daniel's arm became rigid, his placid smile turning to a grim line.

Anna saw a small fleet of guards, unyielding, and a flash of blonde hair. Mary was there too, arms crossed, frowning at the gesticulating man. A small, feminine gasp came from behind.

Flicking her eyes to her periphery, she found Margaux, posy of wildflowers crushed in her hand.

Releasing Daniel's arm, Anna took up her skirts, hastening her pace to the commotion. Voices roses and fell, then all turned silent as she reached the small group. It was Bryan, facing off with her guards, his face bent in a bow, chest heaving. Bryan's presence could only bode bad news. Her mind flew. How could he know of William before her, before Daniel? With his permanently injured arm, he was home at Beaubourg raising his family . . .

"Majesty," he called, relief flooding his features. "I've urgent news."

"Gentlemen," Anna said, waving away the guards, "you may leave Sir Bryan and his business to me." She met Mary's red puffed eyes, and though Anna's face remained stern, her heart hitched.

"Highness," Daniel said with a slight bow. "I will leave you to your . . . private concerns." He looked Bryan over, face unreadable, and turned to leave. It must not be Wills, or Daniel would have stayed. Anna grasped Daniel's forearm.

"No, Your Grace, please stay," Anna said, eyes roving from Bryan and Mary. "For I fear this audience." Daniel's brows raised, but he remained, saying nothing. She came to Bryan, desperate to embrace him, desperate to stop his words.

He fell to a knee, grasped her hand, holding it to his mouth, lips trembling. He wouldn't look at her.

"Majesty, I came as fast as I could, for I knew you'd wish to hear this news in person. From a friend . . ."

"Please, sir, say what you will, and quickly." She cupped his chin, forcing his face up. His skin, which she remembered as both soft and taut, was now rough, weathered. Aged. Unshed tears gathered in the corners of his clear-sky eyes.

"Your father—the duke—you must come now or it will be too late."

Bryan rose and continued in a hurried stream about her father's condition, but Anna didn't hear him. It was as though he spoke through a feather pillow, blocking the sound. Her legs quaked. She glanced at Mary, who stared back at her, forehead crinkled.

"We must away," she heard herself say. She turned to Lady Jane on her right, and something about the single tear winding down that sweet woman's rosy cheek brought Anna back to reality. "Ladies, make haste—Your Grace, I—can you . . ."

Daniel took her forearms, bracing her, and looked straight into her eyes. "Madam, I know this is news you wish not to hear, and your grieving heart bids you hasten, but I must object to your leaving."

Bryan spoke Anna's own outrage. "How can you dare to detain the queen?"

Daniel turned on Bryan, eyes ice. "You, who so care for Her Majesty, should be in support of me in this. Or has everyone forgotten the war that is raging, even now possibly on Beaubourgian soil?"

"Our castle is on the coast, Your Grace, well far from the fighting," Anna said, struggling to keep her voice even.

"With all due respect, Highness, we do not know that."

"But Sir Bryan does. He would not be here if there were danger in taking me to my father." Anna shook loose from Daniel and lifted her skirts again, making to leave.

"And what of the English? Have you forgotten them? That damnable Raleigh sailed out, surely eager to put us in our place." Daniel's face remained impassive. "He would know of our present trouble and Elizabeth would not miss this chance. Ships may be arriving on the coast any day for all we know."

"I will not let conjecture keep me from my father's final days, Cecile."

He startled when she used his name as casually as a man would. "I can see this is a battle I shall not win."

She nodded, ignoring his fluster. "I will take Jane and Mary with me." She paused, her eyes settling on a panic-stricken Margaux. Did she still fear the vultures of court? There was no room in Anna's heart for vengeance. "And Margaux as well. Send Countess Cariline with the princess and of course her nurses along tomorrow."

"And now you risk the health of the princess. You've no clue what illness strikes your father and yet—"

She jutted a finger in Daniel's face, patience long flown. "Do not ever imply that I would risk my daughter, that you would know better the care of my child."

His cheeks twitched, but otherwise he went still. They both breathed for a moment in that posture. Then, with a formal bow of his head he said, "I shall follow tomorrow as well with anyone else from court whose presence is necessary or a comfort to your person."

She nodded. And with shaking limbs, turned and hugged Bryan. Throwing her arms about his neck and pulling him to her chest.

"Thank you, Bryan. Thank you for coming," she managed. She released him, wiped her cheek, and seeing Daniel, regretted her inelegance. But her father lay dying, and whatever the politic Daniel or the nattering Margaux thought of her was of no consequence.

The two-day drip was excruciating. Her mind concocted images of her father dying in pain, alone, cold, calling out her name, her mother's. How she wished she could have ridden on horseback. It would have been faster and occupied her mind. But the carriage was a necessary trapping, carrying her, her three ladies, and their hastily packed trunks, Bryan riding gallant and silent by its side, occasionally glancing upon them, grief writ on his face. The duke had been a father of sorts to Bryan, as his own father, drunk and cruel, had died when Bryan was thirteen. And with all the time Anna and Bryan spent together, he couldn't help but come under the duke's tutelage and care.

When they stopped at a Kilburn inn for the night, Anna heard the whispering voices of Margaux and Bryan late into the night, but Margaux returned to the queen's rooms with clothes and hair undisturbed. At least Margaux wasn't using this as an opportunity to bring her own brand of comfort to Bryan. Anna fell into a fitful sleep, images of Bryan and Margaux, her laughing father and the fighting king all floating in her mind.

They finally reached Beaubourg in the early evening to find the town in solemn wait. A soft rain fell from the low sky, candles lit every window, hay roofs dripped their own tears to the ground. No one was about.

Once they reached the castle yard, Anna discovered where everyone had gone. The yard was filled to the walls with villagers, each with one hand raised to the carriage, the other holding a candle. Anna's breath caught. It was just like when her mother died. Her memories of that time were blurry, as she'd only been a child, but this picture was frozen in her mind, rearing up within her with the force of years. Suddenly she was five again, staring with awe out her window, grief and fear coursing through her in equal parts. She fought that child's desperate need to be with her parents, as the carriage door opened and that same smell of wax mingled with dirt and horses swept over her. She was the queen now. The fate that girl had feared would be bleak was sealed. She wasn't abandoned. She would send her father back to her mother and to God in cheer, not in shouts and wails.

Bryan took her hand as she stepped from the carriage, giving it an extra squeeze when her feet touched the ground.

Together, the crowd cried out. "God save the queen!" They knelt, steadying their candle flames, but paying their skirts and breeches no heed. Anna placed her hand over her heart, blinking back tears. After all the hatred, the slander, the accusations from court and beyond, her people still stood with her, still knew her for who she was. Their own. If only William could see this. Could know the support he had from his countrymen.

"Good people, rise," she said, Mary, Margaux, and Jane taking their places beside her. "To see you here, honoring my father, honoring your king, it means more than . . . Bless you, one and all. I will tell His Grace and His Majesty of your devotion. It gives me strength to face the days ahead."

The villagers climbed to their feet, some wiping away tears. Then, a single soprano voice began, clear as any bell. "*Pie Jesu, pie Jesu . . .*" It was Charity, her freckled face glowing, its roundness diminished into that of a woman. "*Domine dona eis requiem . . .*" Anna could wait no longer. She left the villagers aglow in candle flame and the music of angels, to the cold, silent darkness of the castle.

Anna crept to her father's room, not bothering to change out of her traveling clothes, discarding her cloak and gloves on his reading chair.

"Papa?"

He lay in his bed, a log-lump, barely creasing the sheets, his head sunk into his pillow like a cannonball. Velvet damasked curtains, closed against the fading day, cast the room in an eerie green glow, making his face all the more sickly. She sat in a little wooden chair at his bedside, candles providing the only warmth in the room. His chest rose in a rattling tremble, his keen, twinkling eyes remaining closed.

She took his hand in hers and laid it in her lap. She squeezed and he squeezed back.

"Anna, my darling girl." He coughed, struggling for a clear breath.

"No, Papa." She leaned over him, smoothing back his thinning, brittle hair and kissed his sun-spotted forehead. "Don't exert yourself. I'm here. I will not leave you."

"I will rest forever soon enough." He managed a smile, rolling his head to the side. His cheeks were hollows, bones jutting, proclaiming their prominence, their permanence beyond the flesh. She couldn't believe his transformation in barely a month's time. His eyes flickered open and he squinted at her. "I would look at your loveliness or die trying, my dear."

She reminded herself that she'd promised not to cry in front of him. Did not want to send him off with the heaviness of her sorrow.

"I've been talking to all who've gone before us." His smile was mischievous. "And that little brother of yours is a talker."

"And what do they say?" She smiled back. She'd been at enough deathbeds to know that many of the dying thought they saw those who had already passed, perhaps helping to make them ready for heaven. Some people thought it sorcery or the devil, but what she wouldn't give to see her mother, even if it were the concoction of her own mind.

He gave a soft chuckle. "That's not for you to hear. But know that where I go I will be happy and at peace and finally with my love again." The length of his words made him cough and wince. She handed him the syrupy mixture at his bedside. It smelled of poppy, honey, lemon, and mead. "My only regret is to leave you, my dearest girl." Tears glistened in his gray eyes.

"But you leave me well." She kissed his hand and laid his palm against her cheek. "For you leave me loved."

"I fear I leave you surrounded in treachery. Your court is ready to boil over . . ."

"Rumors and plotting and ill-humor may bend me, but they shall never break me. For I am a daughter of Beaubourg." She kissed his palm again and brought it back to her lap, cradling it like a newborn pup. "And with the king by my side, well, we can withstand anything they throw at us."

He nodded as best he could and looked up at the ceiling. "You just keep that babe of yours safe and all will be well."

"Babe?" Her free hand leapt to her belly.

He chuckled again. "I suppose some of the things your mother told me I *can* tell you."

She looked down at herself, full of wonder. Could it be true? She had been due to bleed a week ago, but this wasn't the first time stress had put her off her cycle.

"I would not tease you so," her father said, looking sidelong at her. "You'll be convinced soon enough."

Her heart couldn't stand much more. Her father dying in front of her, her love over the hills in harm's way, and a baby—a boy? But these were the imaginings of a man at death's door, seeing a future he hoped for his only living child. They were the same false dreams of her daughter, seeing her parents at odds and wishing to make things right by foretelling an heir.

"Your mother and I will be right there with you when you celebrate his birth," he said. "For you know how I love a royal baptism."

She laughed through her withheld tears, recalling how her father had met her mother, their eyes locking across the sanctuary at the baptism of William's brother, James. Let her father believe anything that might comfort him. She wouldn't be foolish enough to think a son was soon to be hers.

"You rest now, Papa," she said, laying his hand at his side. "I will go and change. Shall I bring a book to read to you?"

He closed his eyes and smiled. "Whatever would please you, my child."

She leaned forward and kissed his clammy cheek, tasting a salty tear and realizing it was hers.

"Papa . . ."

He brought his hand to rest upon his heart. "I know, my darling girl. I know."

Three days later, the only other man in the world beside William who loved her without reservation, without reason, without judgment, was gone.

She couldn't bear to leave his rooms, but she also couldn't bear to look upon the human shell that was no longer her papa. So she sat in his outer chamber, setting up court in miniature, allowing only her ladies, the princess, and Daniel in her presence. Last word from the king was that they were headed to the Truss at Hedgewood. No doubt they were climbing the foothills, whipped by wind and sleet. No place for anyone, let alone a king.

She wondered, yet again, how long it would feel as though a crow had pecked out some vital organ from her insides. She knew the scar tissue would never heal. There would always be a lump there, fibrous tissue, stubborn and rough to the touch. And if prodded in just the right way, unexpectedly and out of nowhere, it would bring her to tears.

The sun shone on his funeral day, as if mocking her grief.

"Tush," Mary had said. "Your father ordered it up special himself to be sure. He's with your mum, free from pain. He'll let ye have your grief, but then he'll want that strong face set to running the realm again."

Anna had nodded. Mary was right. Her father's brightest attribute was joy in whatever he faced.

The sad little party consisted of her ladies, Cate, Daniel, Bryan, along with his wife, siblings, and mother, the castle servants, and dear Moltmann, who'd made the trip at her request. A single, riderless stallion, her father's favorite, stood sentinel. Her mother was buried overlooking the coast, not far from Anna's meadow, and her father wished the same. Anna stood, wind whipping her skirts, lashing escaped hair across her face. She had no tears left to shed.

Moltmann performed a beautiful graveside mass, unconventional and frowned upon for a nobleman, but she wouldn't refuse her father's last request. A collective cry from the household went up as the first shovel of dirt hit the coffin. Anna trembled. She felt a rough but warm hand close around hers. Bryan. Unable to watch her father commended forever to the earth, she turned into her faithful friend, his arm encircling her shoulders, drawing her to his chest. He rocked side to side like a mother with a babe. "Shhh, shhh," he whispered as she gasped into his thick jacket. She heard Daniel clear his throat. Damn him and his decorum. If he'd had his way, she wouldn't be here, wouldn't have shared her father's final moments.

Bryan kissed the top of her head. "'Tis all over now, Anna."

She nodded, wiped her face and nose with one of her mother's kerchiefs. She patted his chest once. "Thank you, dear friend." He nodded back with a wistful smile.

"Come," he said, "let's retire to the castle and recall warm memories of His Grace."

She broke his embrace and slung her arm through Mary's, who lay her head upon Anna's shoulder, face puffy and red.

"That's right," Mary said. "His Grace'll want us to drink a toast."

"Or many, if memory serves," Bryan added. Chuckles and sniffles followed this as the train returned to the castle, the stallion plodding ahead alone, instinctively going home.

Anna reached out her free hand to clasp Bryan's and caught Daniel's eyes flick away, lips pursed.

"We shall drink and feast as to make my father proud," she said, head high, face set to her vacant, lifeless home.

It was late when Anna readied herself for bed, but sleep was far off. She released her ladies and settled herself at her old desk under the window that faced east. Somewhere, beyond the hills and snowy peaks, William battled for his country and his life. She stared at the moon, in and out of view behind clouds, thinking if she concentrated hard enough, prayed hard enough, William would feel her love and be buoyed.

Personal letters from him were sparse, though she wrote thrice a week. She hadn't dared write since her father's illness, as William would be grieved. She knew the king loved her father, had adopted him as his own. Yet she couldn't help pouring her heart out to the only person she knew wouldn't judge or scold or tell her to shut up her grief in a locked drawer. So she wrote her husband. Letter after letter that she would never send, tears marring the ink.

Finally putting down her quill, her eyes rested on the stable. A soft glow spilled from the door onto the yard. Her father and his beloved horses. She would take them to the royal stables, but what would she do with the castle itself? Being queen, she had no need for her rank as duchess and would bestow the duchy to Cate. Regardless of what her father hinted and her daughter proclaimed, she wasn't convinced she would have sons. And even if she did, Cate deserved her own castle. But until Cate came of age, what then? Maybe she should have Bryan and his family be the castle's custodians, keep the servants in employment, provide him extra income, a place to raise his children. The legitimate ones.

Her vision blurred in ruminating, but movement in the stables' shadows caught her eyes. Horse thieves? Who would dare, with her father's grave freshly laid? She saw a cloaked figure move from the shadow to the light. Turning as if looking for someone or something, she recognized none other than Margaux. A sick knowing grew inside her. Margaux ducked into the stable and out of the light.

Anna watched and waited. About five minutes later she saw a light growing brighter from the stable loft window. Five more minutes and another figure appeared. Her heart sank as she watched Bryan go inside the stable. Margaux she would expect this from, but she had thought better of Bryan. He was married with two children, and here she had been pondering letting him live in her castle. If this was how he would behave in it, she wanted no part.

She thought she saw another figure in the shadows and leaned closer. This person was cloaked in black, hands gloved. She couldn't make out if it was a man or a woman. The figure looked up at the stable loft as a giggle floated to Anna, then he or she pressed against the stable and glanced at Anna's window. She shuddered and blew out her candle. Just as quickly, the figure disappeared. Had she imagined it? She wouldn't put it past her presently addled mind.

Calming, she shook her head and climbed in bed, unable to help the jealousy that sparked in her heart. Not over Bryan— all her childish yearnings for him had long passed—but over what Bryan and Margaux were up to. It would be weeks, if not months, before Anna would enjoy the delights of her husband. She huffed, turned on her side, clamped her eyes shut, and tried to sleep, willing the day to end.

CHAPTER 10

Last Battle

*I*t was worse than they'd expected. Duven's men were nearly decimated, with fewer than eight hundred battle ready. Duven had been holding the southern tip of the Luxembourg border, where his men, until the dysentery, held a firm line a mere hundred yards inside Norwick. Thankfully, the disease had wiped out some of the Laurelanders along with their Luxembourg friends, but since there was concern of spread further down the front lines, the grand master general had separated Duven's men from the rest, deciding that Laureland's ground gain was worth keeping the rest of the men healthy.

It was a fatal decision. Word soon spread and the rebels flooded Duven's weak defensive line, pushing miles farther into Norwick, both armies drawn together in a giant, tangled swarm.

Robert was incensed. It was all fine and good to battle in Laureland for they'd brought it on themselves, but for the bastards to be mucking up his lands, pillaging his crops, terrorizing his towns—it would not be borne. And sitting there, in the royal tent, going round about whether or not the king should go into battle the next day was only increasing Robert's agitation.

"We cannot risk you, Highness," the general said, as if repeating the same thing would convince the king.

"What we cannot risk is more land lost." William said, pacing. "We cannot risk middlemen with skewed information. We cannot risk making decisions based on what others think they see. How am I to command the army if mine own eyes do not witness the battle firsthand?"

"But if something were to happen to you—"

"By all accounts we are losing this war." The king snared the general with heated eyes. "If our strategy, or fighting, is not changed, our conquerors will expend me anyway."

"You know very well His Majesty is one of our best at arms," Robert said, unable to stop bouncing his knee. "Let us just be done with this so we might make ready for the morrow."

"Here, here, Norwick," William said. "Let us stop arguing and plan."

Reluctantly, the general bent over the map, pointing. "In the past week at least two thousand men have pushed through our lines, keeping us at bay. Even with Duven's losses, we almost match their numbers, but many of them are fresh. They seem to be cycling men through in droves." With his finger he drew a circle on top of the wide plain they camped upon. "To push them back, we need to break their lines, cut them up into smaller units, here, here, and here."

"Halforn's men are only a few days behind us. That should bring our numbers over three thousand," the king said. "And surely, once the rebels get wind of the other five His Holiness is sending, they'll have no choice but to turn tail."

"Are the pope's troops truly coming?" Robert raised a doubting brow.

"Aye," said the grand master. "Received official word three days past and confirmation through Cecile's channels that a force is gathering in southern France as we speak."

"So all is not lost," said Ridgeland, who leaned against a tent pole. "I can command my and Halforn's men, Norwick his, and split the rest between Your Highness and the general. At the very least we can hold our positions until the papal forces arrive."

"I want them out of Norwick, now," Robert said. "I say we funnel them all into Luxembourg—it's just as close as Laureland. They want to be free from Troixden's rule? Fine. Let them live elsewhere."

"But Luxembourg is where the troops are coming *from*," Ridgeland said. "And wouldn't we risk angering the Emperor?"

"The Emperor is angered already, at least publicly," the king said. "But he is powerless to do anything about it. He has his own battles to quash and no money to do it with."

"But should he then not be held responsible for the acts of his people?" Ridgeland put his hands on his hips, making him look like a giant, angry heron.

"Are you suggesting we declare war against the Emperor?" Robert said, incredulous.

"Of course not, Norwick," Ridgeland said, thick with disdain. "I merely point out the international effects of your ill-advised plan."

"Ill advised?" Robert sat up, eyes blazing.

"Enough!" The king raised a hand to stop the two men. "We can't win a war if we can't even keep peace in our own ranks." Ridgeland had one last sneer for Robert, but then returned to his tent pole position. William sighed, closed his eyes, pinched the bridge of his nose. "I see your point, Norwick, but with fewer numbers and the men already worn, I think it wiser to follow the grand master general's proposal." Robert made to object, but William stayed him. "If by weeks' end we've lost ground, I'll consider all options again." The gathered men shifted their stances while Robert fumed. "That is all. Prepare your men."

William dismissed them with a wave. Robert considered staying to have it out with the king, but he knew that as in war, he must chose his battles carefully.

At least Robert wasn't gloating. Of course, even William's vainglorious cousin would find nothing to crow about after a long, bloody week of defeat. William suffered bruised ribs, a thick gash on his right forearm, and three brushes with death, though he'd made up for it in scores of slaughtered rebels.

The grand master general's plan was doomed to failure when William of Orange joined the battlefield with two thousand more men. The king halted the butchering by noon, asking Orange for potential terms. Not quite the white flag, but time to rest his men, wait for the damned papal reinforcements, and come up with something, anything, to save his country from these foreigners.

Rain lashed against his tent, candles burned low, while his mind pondered the problem. Robert, unusually taciturn, sat composing letters to his family and Yvette, answering other correspondence of now seemingly little importance. He'd told the king it helped clear his mind.

William had finally received two letters from Anna, one describing how Cate insisted on standing as still as possible in the garden to see if a sparrow might land on her. He could picture her there, in some pastel pink silk, frown of concentration on her face, her cheeks and nose turning red from the crispness of early spring, Anna trying not to giggle at their serious princess. Much to Cate's chagrin, the birds landed everywhere but on her outstretched hands, on benches and branches, on the thick fountain lip mere inches away. The other letter was also blithe and loving, a little too blithe. He could tell she was trying to distract him, to take him away from the grimness before his eyes, and he was grateful for it, even if it only helped for a moment. For each time he saw his wife and child, his home, in his mind, defeat's crushing blow would then slam his heart. What would become of them?

"I know you're going to think this is another ploy of mine, Wills," Robert said, "but hear me through."

"Seeing as I've no ideas, I will readily hear yours, even it be flowing with self-interest." William winced at the sharp pain in his chest as he sat.

"You may be able to appease all sides and still maintain your rule if you follow the example of the English court."

William rolled his eyes, the only part of his body not aching. "I don't want Elizabeth anywhere near this—she'll just use us to get to France."

"I don't mean Elizabeth, I mean her father. When he declared himself head of the church in England, he did not technically declare against Catholicism. Indeed, nearly all of the trappings of the church still existed. In a way, he was the steward of Catholicism on English soil, without recognizing the pope—a foreign prince, in Henry's words—as his ruler."

"Come now, Robert, not even his own people saw it that way. It was a clear declaration against the Catholics."

"I would argue that if it weren't for Anne Boleyn, a true Protestant, Henry might have continued on being, for all intents and purposes but in name, quite Catholic," Robert said. "His more Protestant-leaning countrymen would have been satisfied, and the average peasant headed to mass would have seen no difference."

"If it weren't for Anne Boleyn, he would never have left the church in the first place." William shook his head. "This smacks of desperate maneuverings, a spinning of words."

"Even Luther declared himself Catholic to the grave." Robert gesticulated, as he always did when trying to hide excitement. "He saw himself as a reformer within the church, not wishing to spark a movement outside of it."

"Let's pretend I do such a ludicrous thing. What earthly reason would Orange have to forgo his winnings?" William gingerly leaned back. "Why would he not march into Havenside, declare himself king of not merely Troixden, but the whole of the Low Countries, and engage with the Spanish and the Emperor from a new seat of legitimate power?"

Robert shrugged. "If you declared yourself head of the church—"

"And were summarily excommunicated, turning our largest allies against us—"

"If you were head of the church, Orange would be fighting against his own purpose to try and take your throne. He would lose an ally."

"But he's besting us, Robert." William closed his eyes, inhaled. "This crazed idea may have stayed him weeks ago, but now, when he is on the brink of victory, there is no reason for him to take such terms."

"And yet, you are speculating on what he would demand."

"As are you."

A guard outside announced a messenger, who, after genuflecting, presented those terms. The king scanned them, then carefully read through. There was no surprise, though the words still stung, giving him a renewed headache.

"He wants all the land he's won," William said, "all of Laureland and parts of Norwick. He cedes Hedgewood."

"He cannot have it." Robert wiped his hands together as if his pronouncement made it so. "Proclaim yourself, Highness." Robert glanced to the listening messenger.

William considered the messenger too. "Tell your leader we do not accept his terms. That is all." The man nodded and tore out of the tent, as if fearing William would set him on fire.

"This mayhap be a poor decision, but we shall fight." William called in a page. Robert's face betrayed nothing. "Gather the men. I shall speak to them." The page left as quickly as the messenger had.

"Wills . . ."

"I know what you're going to say. You're going to say I should listen to you, this is suicide . . ."

Robert shook his head. "I was going to say, I am proud to fight with you another day."

William nodded, then pushed himself out of his chair. "Help me dress, will you?"

Robert helped William into his official armor, draping velvet cape and chain of kingly office across his shoulders, pressing the crown onto his aching head.

"You make even me tremble in all that garb," Robert said.

"'Tis about time." William pulled on his gloves, took one last look in the mirror, and headed out to greet his troops, Robert following.

He shook the men's hands, listening to those who would speak to him. He stopped in the middle of them and raised his hands.

"Good men of Troixden!" At this call, all bent to one knee, not only out of respect to the king, but also so his voice would carry to those at the rear. Though he'd witnessed it many times before, William was overcome by the gesture of these proud, brave, and loyal subjects. He wouldn't disappoint their faith, their fealty. Damn Orange and Laureland to hell—he would reclaim every inch of Troixden soil.

"Our enemies claim parts of our realm—your homes, your farms, your towns—as their own." Grunts and boos erupted.

"But it shall take more than a man, despised by his own liege lord, bent on his own lust for power, to win our fair lands. For we may be weary, but we shall not waver. And like the Israelites of old, we shall overcome. When the sun doth rise, we shall fight anew for what is ours by rights and by God. These heretics shall behold true fealty and faith and fierceness at the ends of our swords and arrows. And we shall send them home, be it Luxembourg or hell, for we are the sons of Troixden!"

Deafening hurrahs broke over the crowd, coupled with shouts of "long live the king!" He waved again and made slow progress through the men, back to his tent. Once inside, he wanted to collapse on his bed, but held his dignity while his dressers unhooked his armor and removed his finery. *Such fine words, wee Wills.* The voice in his head sounded like his brother. A brother who never went to combat, but William, weakened by exhaustion, had no defenses. *And how exactly do you plan on accomplishing them, when a mere speech has you flat on your back? Mighty indeed.*

His dressers left him and he strode to his sideboard, guzzling whatever tonic he found there, hoping to drown out the condemnation and the pain. He would ride with his men in the morrow, come what may.

Invoking the Israelites must have produced this miracle. William could see no other explanation. Of course his men had been inspired, not simply by his words, but by an intrinsic desire to protect their people, their land. But that still couldn't explain how, in two days' time, they had pushed back Orange and his followers. They remained squarely in Norwick territory, but Laureland's border wasn't far off. William and his men planned to create two long flanks, hinging at the center to clamp down on the enemies like a jaw, forcing them out of Norwick and Laureland, herding them into the horn of Luxembourg.

William could feel the tide turning. *And that, dear brother James, is how a king keeps a country.*

Anna woke, the smell of her breakfast of fresh bread and cheese churning her stomach, for the sixth day in a row.

Margaux had pulled out the king's favorite blue and gold silk gown for the day, as Anna planned to ride into Havenside proper and visit the people. She wanted to appear carefree and regal at the same time, a queen of the people, but a queen nonetheless. As her stays were tugged she wasn't the only one to notice that her bodice laces were not as tight as normal. As her ladies murmured and tittered she knew there was no question any longer. She was with child.

She must tell Daniel, especially before anyone else did, but her heart sank with the knowledge that it would be him and not William to be the first to know. For William could not, under any circumstances, be told. It would only distract him, worry him, make him want to be by her side even more than he proclaimed in his intermittent letters.

Calling for Bernard, she caught Mary's eye, and the nurse

winked. "Bernard, please inform Cecile I wish an audience this afternoon after I return from town."

"Yes, Majesty," he performed his jig. "Will there be anything else?"

"Please take the letter there on the table—'tis for the king—and deliver it straight to Cecile's outgoing messenger." Anna fingered the tucked curls in her hair. Margaux and Brigitte had done another impeccable job.

"As you wish it, Majesty." He took the letter and left in a swirl of green and cardamom.

The day was bright, with spring warmth in the air, fresh buds poking verdant from branches, people about their business with merry smiles and hale greetings. She returned to the palace buoyed by their welcome, strengthened by their faith in William's cause. And for a few hours, her unsettled stomach was forgotten.

Heading straight for council, she found Daniel stretched over the map, orange block in his hand.

"Ah, Majesty." He bowed efficiently. "I am just resetting our lines."

Eagerly, she approached the table. "So you've more word?"

He tossed the block in the air, catching it effortlessly. "Unfortunately yes." He was thoughtful. "I hate to even mention it, Majesty, but such is war. You may wish to sit."

His words didn't help her nausea. "I feel better on my feet. Please do continue."

"Your father's death left a brief hole in our defenses. Especially as Sir Bryan was occupied," he eyed her, brows hitching, "with other things."

Anna kept a straight face. It must have been one of Daniel's lookouts who'd witnessed Margaux and Bryan's rendezvous. She silently blessed Daniel for being discrete.

"Indeed, while we were attending upon his funeral, armed men from Brussels skirted through the border of Beaubourg and into Laureland." He plunked the orange block in the center of northwest Laureland. "There are only about five hundred men, but from what we hear at the front, any surge in our enemies' numbers is a blow."

"We must warn His Majesty." Anna studied the map, placing her finger atop the chess piece king they used to represent William.

There was a hint of condescension in Daniel's chuckle. "If we know of it, he surely does. I merely wish to keep our little map up to date."

"Should we not ensure he knows? It certainly is no extra hindrance on our part to rest our minds."

"My mind is at rest, Majesty, and if my mind be, yours can be also."

Why did it always have to be such a struggle between them? Why would he not realize her only desire was for William's safety and victory? She wasn't trying to win some contest of wits or smarts or devotion. She simply wanted her husband back.

"My mind, Your Grace, is erratic these days, I must admit." She paused, suddenly nervous, for the last time she'd been pregnant, he'd treated her like a prized piece of porcelain, and she had no wish for that. She took a deep breath and forged ahead. "Your Grace, it has become necessary that I tell you I am with child."

Daniel's face didn't change other than a hint of a smile. She didn't know what she'd expected, but she thought he'd have more of a reaction than this.

"Congratulations, Majesty." He inclined his head. "The king will be overjoyed, as will the realm."

"As I'm sure you know, I wish to keep this as quiet as possible. When I begin to show in earnest, I shall quit my public appearances, unless there be an urgent need." She folded her hands together, feeling oddly exposed. "I do not wish to be coddled merely because of my state. I wish, from the very start, for you to trust that my singular goal at this time is the protection of my children and the safe return of my king."

"I understand your concern." He crossed his arms over his chest. "And I would beg that you remember I too have the same call. And that an outside observer such as me may notice things effecting thy person which Your Highness may not. Especially in one as tenacious as your royal self."

"'Tis duly noted." She smiled, even though inside she felt hackles. He wouldn't mind her wishes in this. She'd have to figure out a way around him. And if he did suspect something and confront her . . . well, playing dumb always seemed to work for Margaux.

The king and his soldiers finally reached Laureland. Robert and his men, with the king on his left flank, relentlessly pushed Orange back over successive days, and now, even amid swords flying about, Robert breathed relief when they crossed the shallow start of the Orlea River, the divide between Norwick and Laureland.

As Orange's men were mostly mercenaries, the more ground they lost the more men deserted, valuing their lives over coin. But Robert's men, the king's army, they knew their lives—and possibly their families—were forfeit if they lost. This was a key component of the war that Orange misjudged. He was used to men rallied to the cause in his own lands, mistakenly relying on that fervor to carry over into another land, and forgetting that his enemies possessed the same zeal. Robert, still mounted, slashed his way through the throng in search of the very man, hoping to cleave off his head. He saw the king, a hundred yards off, charging behind a shield of riding archers. They would surely win the day—even if it meant losing, for a time, Robert's hope of eradicating the Holy Church from Troixden.

Then he saw the men the king charged: they were fresh, on mounts, with a flag he didn't recognize whipping above. Discarding his hopes of filleting Orange, Robert rode hard back to his men to face this new challenge. Arrows tore through the air, spearing horses, gouging appendages. Robert's own horse took an arrow to his brave chest, buckling to the ground. Blood spread fast, discoloring the white coat, his eyes rolling with fear. Robert couldn't let his loyal beast die like this, but neither did he have time for gentleness. Hastily, he covered the horror-shocked eye, bringing as much calm as possible. With the other hand, he nudged the armor off his horse's brow. Taking short sword in hand he stabbed, below the ear and behind the eye, underneath the connection of the jaw, straight into the brain.

The horse shook violently then stilled. But Robert did not have the luxury to grieve.

Quickly, he took stock of his surroundings. His men, mostly on foot now, were surging forward, up and around him, Bolstad leading the charge. With a deafening sound of metal clashing, his men plunged into hand to hand. He followed suit, clambering over the fallen, shoring up the rear. He could hear Orange's men coming up behind, their battle cries growing louder as they neared.

Robert had yet to meet one of the fresh men as he fought his way toward the strange flag so to place its lord. Most of the enemy was easily picking off Robert's men from above. What moments before had been a sure victory was turning into wholesale slaughter.

Using a dead man's shield to block an incoming blow, Robert sliced a rebel's tendon, as the man rode by. Robert heard a satisfying howl then a thump. He was almost to the flag bearer. Making quick work of two men on foot, he pivoted, only to find another horseman bearing down. He deflected a blow, but the man seemed uninterested in fighting and rode on.

"Raleigh!" Robert heard another call. The man reined his horse, circling back. It took Robert's mind a while to reconcile what he'd heard. Surely, somewhere, there was another Raleigh. This couldn't be the knave who'd so recently departed court. But the way the man sat and rode, so cocky and sure, so full of youthful exuberance, it could be no other. Robert cursed. English soldiers might not be far behind.

How had they not caught wind of this? How did a regiment

of hundreds make its way undetected through the realm? Were Beaubourg and Halforn conquered as well, Englishmen even now pouring across their shores, raping and pillaging their way toward Calais? He must find the king. Or die trying.

William sat in his makeshift throne, forehead resting on his fingertips. They had fought until well past sunset for the third day in a row, finally calling halt when clouds socked over the moon. He, and the bedraggled, disillusioned remnants of his men, trudged back to camp in the gloom. It was over. His forces were down to a trifling fifteen hundred. No match for the combined armies of Raleigh and Orange.

Raleigh had crossed into Troixden with an army from Brussels, Daniel's scouts arriving a day too late to inform them of the attack. Thankfully, he wasn't backed by English troops— he was only volunteering his services as he had to the French Huguenots, though in light of the mess before William, that brought little comfort.

At least their line had, for the most part, held. Even with the heavy losses on William's side, the rebels were unable to retake Norwickian ground. Still, with the papal troops held up by skirmishes in France, it would be weeks before any relief might come, and his men, though they had Troixden pride and fervor in their veins, couldn't hold for that long. Every day, young men barely out of boyhood, and farmers, grim and determined, came to camp wishing to fight, though they'd no training and meager weapons. He had to turn them away. He didn't want to see more of his people bloodied, didn't want to look into the glassy, dead eyes of laboring men and their children. And the remedy was spread across his thighs. Conditions of a cease fire. Demands, really.

Ridgeland, an injured Duven, leg bound and bleeding, the general, Robert, and a handful of servants and pages all gathered in silence, watching the king, waiting for him to speak. The words wouldn't come. Either he sent his countrymen to their deaths or into the arms of his enemies.

He took one more breath, wishing with all he had this was a dream, a nightmare he would soon wake from, Anna curled in his arms by a warm fire in his chambers. Lifting his head, he looked each man in the eye before he spoke.

"They offer armistice, but with steep terms." William stood, holding the page aloft. "They claim Laureland for themselves, to be annexed into the Luxembourg duchy." The men held their silence, faces stoic. "And with it, they promise no more incursions or interference with our realm or governance."

"How can they make such promises?" Ridgeland said, riled. "They are self-led men, not the Hapsburgs."

"Surely Spain will claim Laureland as its own," Duven said, struggling not to wince.

"And, at that point, it would not be our worry," William said. Part of him was relieved by the idea of Laureland becoming someone else's thorn, but his pride bristled at any part of his kingdom being conquered, no matter how belligerent that part had become. "And you are correct, Ridgeland—they be self-proclaimed, though they will also have every last one of our men dead by week's end if we do not stop this war."

"Better to die with honor, sire," the grand master general said, nodding sagely.

"If there is glory in death on the field, it has not been my privilege to witness." William handed the terms to a page and resettled himself in his throne. "And thus, as king, and as councilors, we must decide how we wish to respond. Not with vain glory in our hearts, but with practicality and the safety of our people highest in our minds."

"Begging pardon, Majesty," Ridgeland said, reaching to read the terms himself, "but I still do not understand how we, a sovereign nation, would be forced to come to terms with, well, no better than armed marauders. They are not sanctioned by any government."

"Thousands of armed marauders," William said. "'Tis how the Vikings conquered, and the Saxons. We were conquered by both, our ancestors coming from their stock. They come and they steal and then become nations unto themselves."

"And we shall help them along?" the general said.

William tore out of his chair, stopping inches from the man. "And what wouldst you have us do? Let them tear through the rest of our land, killing innocents, raping women in front of their children, beheading the lot of you, ascending our throne? Is that a better end in your mind, general? For that is the other recourse. Which will you have?" He could see the general seething, but the man smartly remained silent. "Do the rest of you wish the same? For we would love to hear more alternatives."

He raised his arms, surveying the rest of his men.

"We could think of it as a true truce, not a surrender." Robert took the paper from Ridgeland's hand. "Since, as His Lordship indicates, these men are not a sovereign nation, there is nothing to stop us from regaining Laureland in the future." He passed the terms to Duven. "When they're thoroughly distracted by Spain and our numbers rebound, we can reclaim what is rightfully ours."

"I say good riddance." Duven handed the terms back to the page. "They've been nothing but a nuisance, whining about religion when they've basked in Your Majesty's generous freedoms. Let them see how it feels to be ruled by Hapsburgs."

With each vote for agreement, William's heart sank. "And Ridgeland, what of you?"

"If those damnable papal troops—"

"Indeed," Robert muttered.

"You know they will not be here in near enough time," William said.

Ridgeland's face fell. "It seems there be no other recourse."

William nodded and strode to his desk. "Bring me wax."

"I will not be a party to this!" The general stormed from the tent, out into the deepening night. William wished he too could flee this fateful moment.

Despising his own words, he wrote, *We accept said terms of armistice. William II, Rex.* His secretary pooled hot blue wax, then red below for Robert and green for Duven as witnesses. William pressed his ring, still on his finger, into the blue, the initial heat stinging, wax oozing up the sides of his finger, but he didn't flinch.

The deed complete, the men filed out of his tent in solemn silence, three pages surrounded by guards sent to Orange with the surrender. Robert stayed behind, giving William space, but hovering just in case. In case of what, William didn't know. It felt as though part of him had blackened and died. It wasn't grief he felt, but a lacking, as if he'd lost a foot in battle, forever to forget its loss, only to stumble about, determined to put on two boots each morning.

"I should have just let you have it," William said, taking up a glass of lukewarm wine.

"What do you mean?"

"A while back, I'd suggested to Daniel that we simply give you Laureland. For it sorely needed a strong hand and a strong leader."

Robert's eyes grew wide, his jaw clenched. "Beg pardon?"

"I thought it a brilliant idea actually." William folded his hands in front of him, eyeing his friend. "But Daniel dismissed it. Said with you holding most of the land, and with your penchant for the Protestants, we might be fighting a civil war against our own cousin."

Robert gripped a chair back, pressing so hard his fingers turned white. "And you agreed?"

"I was content at the moment to bring it up at another time if need be." William could see Robert tremble. "But another time never came. War came instead."

"You say it so casually—as if we'd all had a fine joke!"

"Robert, this is hardly—"

"Do you know what you've done? Daniel doesn't trust me, so you've handed our lands on a gold platter to the likes of Orange and Raleigh! How is that for loyalty?"

William pushed up, chair crashing to the floor behind him.

"Do not deem to speak to me thus, not after what I've been forced to this day."

"Which never would have happened if for once in your life you'd listened to your own counsel instead of perfect, blameless Daniel!"

"Don't drag him into this." They were nose to nose across the desk.

"You're quite the pair, aren't you?"

"Meaning?"

Robert shook his head slowly and William swore he heard a growl. Whether it came from him or Robert wasn't entirely clear.

"You just count yourself lucky I didn't throw in with the rebels." Robert pulled away, eyes boring through William. "For if I did, I certainly wouldn't have stopped at Laureland."

CHAPTER 11

Home Fires

April had come and gone and all Anna could do was wait yet again. Each morning she woke, nausea was replaced by ferocious hunger, and then she was hit by the reality that William was heading home, defeat weighing heavy on his shoulders.

She had known something was afoot when Daniel avoided her on that fateful day. Finally, she cornered him outside his chambers, demanding to know what news he'd received. He blinked at her three times, as if he didn't recognize her. His face, already so pale, was ghostly, his eyes red rimmed.

Blood rushed away from her head, her knees weakened. It had to be William. He was gone. She thrust a steadying hand to the wall, focusing on Daniel's chest as all in her vision blackened, save the emerald set in gold at the center of his chain of office. It was a beacon, keeping her aloft.

"'Tis not the king," he said quickly. She regained her sight, but not her legs, remaining propped by the stone. "But we are defeated."

"Defeated? But would not that mean . . ." She couldn't bear to finish the sentence.

"Please join me, Highness, and I will tell you all there is to tell."

She followed him, but everything he said was a blur. Something about Raleigh and William of Orange, Laureland's annexation. The next day she had to ask him to repeat the whole, for she couldn't take it in at the first. Knowing Raleigh had snuck through Beaubourg, as her father was dying, drove the wound deeper. He'd written her poetry, delighted her daughter. She'd defended him to the king.

Adding to this forest of emotion was her daily wrestling with the decision not to send word of her pregnancy. She and Daniel had agreed it was best not to sway William's mind during battle, but now, in the drudgery of the long journey home, surely the news would cheer him. Yet selfishly, she wanted to see the look on his face when he found out. Ultimately, each time she wrote letters of encouragement, she couldn't bring herself to share the news.

Besides, the king would be home in a fortnight. So she wouldn't fret like last time, she convinced herself he would arrive on the first of June rather than the expected middle of May. After a cold meat breakfast and short mass, she headed to council, finally able to return the maps to storage. She had left them where they lay after Daniel told her of their defeat. She couldn't bring herself to see with her own eyes the land that was gone. And now, standing above battle maps, marking each orange and blue block, each knight, pawn, and her beloved king, the loss overwhelmed her and she wept, salty tears falling on the maps she rolled. She didn't care that Margaux saw, or Bernard, or the smattering of other attendants. A queen should grieve for her land, or what kind of queen was she?

Picking up the full map of Troixden, she paused. Her fingers moved, obeying some outer force. At the upper right-hand corner she tore, ripping off that beastly land, now forsaken to the Low Countries. She ripped Laureland away and threw it in the fire, the room silent but for the crackle of swiftly burning vellum.

She wiped the tears from her eyes, straightened herself, and kept on. But when she reached the detailed map of Laureland, she paused. Picking it up, she handed it to Bernard. "Keep this safe. For somehow I think we shall have use of it again."

"You could hang it in your privy," Margaux said.

Anna hid her smile. "A quaint notion, Countess, though I would not wish to daily contemplate our loss."

She didn't have to wait until June. May twenty-sixth, three months from whence he left, the king and his men came home. Anna stood in the courtyard, holding Cate by the shoulders, surrounded by those who lived and worked in the palace, from the kitchen maids to the gentry. She marked William's progress by the subdued applause traveling through Havenside's streets.

The first riders clomped across stone, griffin of Troixden still bravely rippling above. Then he came, flanked by Robert and Ridgeland, head held high, but face worn, grim, plain gold crown glinting in the shining sun. Even in defeat, he was stunning. Dismounting without ceremony, he strode to them. Anna, distracted, felt Cate leave her hands.

"Papa!" Auburn curls danced, blue silks trailing behind as she ran with abandon into the arms of her crouching father. He clamped her to his chest, her head to his shoulder as though she were a missing part of his body. Anna saw his lips move, whispering to his girl. And her own bittersweet tears fell, hot and full on her cheeks. She wiped at them, not wishing him to see her weep, even if it be in gratitude at his safe return.

When he was within three yards of the queen, he placed Cate gently on the ground, taking her hand in his, swinging it as if the two were on a jaunty spring stroll. His eyes raked Anna from head to toe and back again, pausing at the mound in her skirts. His brow creased, then he fell to a knee, taking her hand, his tight beard rough, lips soft.

"My queen," he said, barely audible. Then his arms were about her waist, his head to her belly. "My blessed queen."

She placed her hands on his head, the texture of his hair strange in its sticky uncleanliness, but she didn't care if he'd swam in the polluted Orlea all the way from Laureland. Releasing her, he stood, taking her face in his hands.

"What will become of us, my Anna?"

She smiled, remembering that horrid, soaking day on the balcony before the first war. "You are home, we are safe. What hell may come, we shall face it together."

He nodded, calloused thumbs caressing her cheeks. He kissed her, long and soft, but still decorous. She couldn't help the disappointment that rippled through her when he broke away to acknowledge Daniel and the others gathered, but she accompanied him, smiling at those that paid him homage. Even the cooks had baked him three of his favorite sweet loaves, still warm with butter and cinnamon from the oven, the women blushing under his adulations.

While they made their way about the crowd, the rest of the men, only about one hundred, saw to their horses and made their way into the castle. She caught Robert's black eyes following her. She met them and was taken aback by their intensity, their scorn. Looking to her left, he found Yvette, who stared back, impassive. He jutted his chin and she nodded, unspoken command received. Following was none other than Bryan. Her breath caught again, praying he hadn't told William about her father. Though if he'd met up with the king without being called into service, he would've had to give an explanation.

Now there were two things she'd kept from him. He must be wondering, even surrounded by all the smiles at his return, why his queen had left him ignorant of so much. They'd finally come to the entrance of the Great Hall. He took her hand and kissed it.

"I must meet with the council, for there is much to tell and to hear." She wanted to protest, wanted to be present as well, for she as much as anyone had kept other domestic issues running smoothly in his absence, but something in the glint of his eye told her to keep her peace. "Will you do me the honor of waiting in my chamber for my return?"

"I've waited these many weeks, what are a few more hours?" She went to curtsy, but he stopped her decent, taking her fully in his arms as he'd done Cate, his strength enveloping her. He brushed her lips then left without a backward glance, heading to council with purpose.

It would be two hours if not longer. Enough time for her to change, let her hair down loose as he preferred. She motioned to her ladies and they retired to their business. For with the men returned, she must needs return to being a bauble.

It was four hours, but Anna didn't mind. She puttered around William's chamber, handling his things, reading bits of his books, be they poetry or tomes on diplomacy, even fell asleep in his stuffed leather chair. She opened the windows at his desk, letting in the fresh spring air. His bed was changed even without her order, down to the feathers and straw. Platters of meats, fruits, cheeses, pies, and pitchers of his favored spring wine sat at the ready, and she in her blue silks.

She heard his approach, for he wasn't alone. Metal against stone marched closer, voices all speaking at once. His doors burst open to reveal a veritable gaggle of men, William at the center, Daniel and Robert flanking him. They all stopped, mid-sentence and en masse, struck dumb it seemed, by her presence. The king surely couldn't have forgotten what he'd asked of her. But he too stared at her blankly. He held some letter in his hands, thick with wax seals. Without a word and eyes never leaving her, William handed the letter to Daniel, who observed the queen with what felt like mild censure. With a flick of the king's hand, the entry cleared as quickly as it had filled, the doors closing with deafening force.

He didn't move. "I wish to have you. Here. Now. On the very rug if I must." Involuntarily her hand leapt to her throat, breath escaping her. "But I fear, before I can be free with you, before I can shut out all else, I must hear what you have to tell. For it seems you have kept much from me these months." He prowled forward. "The babe, your father, disputes with Daniel . . ."

So that's why Daniel had looked so stricken. With an inward wince, she nodded.

"But that be all, Wills. And all so that your mind might be kept on the war."

"Am I so weak as all that?" His eyes were sad when he reached her.

"You are stronger than all of us put together, my liege."

He shook his head. "Nay, 'tis you who are strongest, my Anna." He smoothed his hands down her shoulders, squeezing her upper arms in tenderness. "But it does remain that I can hold more than one piece of information in my mind at a time."

"I didn't want you worrying over me."

He laughed, throwing his head back, and she thrilled at the sound. Her Wills, home at last.

"I worried about you every moment of the day and night. At least the news of the babe would have cheered me." He grew serious again, searching her face. "I would have fought harder to keep this country in one piece for my heir."

"But you did keep it. Your actions were not defeat, they were saving our realm from complete destruction."

"What kind of inheritance is a country torn asunder?" He threw up his hands, turning from her.

"And what kind of an inheritance is no country at all?" she said as he gave a woeful smile over his shoulder and then poured a glass of wine. "We are proud of what you have done. A lesser king would have sent himself and his men to destruction, trying to prove some manly purpose only to leave the rest of his lands in the hands of his enemies. I know you think signing that armistice was weak, a defeat, but it was victory for the rest of us. Mayhap now we will have much deserved peace in our lands."

Her speech elicited only a shrug. She went to him, spreading her hands across and down his back.

"Wills. Don't listen to those who would bring you down to the dirt. They are ignorant of true statecraft, they disdain the hopes of the people. You acted as a king your mother would be proud of."

He nodded and took a long drag of his wine. "And you are avoiding my questions."

"Must we have it all out now? I wish to forget it all for a time."

He faced her, smirk on his lips. "You may out with it whilst I bathe."

Setting down his goblet, he stripped without further ado, and she had to steady herself with his desk seeing him bare, bruised, slashed, and covered in sinewy muscle. He climbed in the bath, teasing her with his jumping brows. "Sit, my dear, and spill."

"I shall leave my father for another time, for I do not wish to relive that sorrow when I am so happy to have you home." She made her way to the tub's edge, took soap and sponge in hand and rubbed them together.

William pointed to his back. She smiled, taking his meaning, and knelt behind him, lost in the feel of the sponge gliding over his skin.

"So then speak of joy. Speak of our son."

"You say it with such confidence," she said, watching oil-slicked water waft from his body. "We'll be changing this water before we've even finished with your top half."

"Anna!" He slapped the water. "Stop distracting me."

She laughed. "But of course, my liege." Wringing water out over his shoulder, she traced its track down his bicep. "Surely you remember the evening we spent before you took your leave."

"Every night for three months."

"It seems that was a more fateful night than we thought."

"You were with child this time entire?"

"I was not certain until late March. There were signs, but I either did not see them, or refused to believe them, refused to hope." She came to his front. "Come now, dunk so I might wash thy royal coif."

He obliged, breaking the surface with a sputter, rubbing his face. "Heaven above, what water and soap do for a man's countenance."

"And for a wife's nose."

He gave her a lopsided grin. "Watch yourself, Madam, else I have you plunged in here with me."

She shoved the sponge into his chest. "Here then, wash thyself. For I've no more tales to tell."

"Oh no? None of our fair Daniel?"

She made a face. "He simply dislikes a woman speaking her mind."

Chuckling, he took the sponge and fished about for the soap. "He be not alone in that regard."

She clucked her tongue.

"I can see it shall indeed put thee out of sorts to pour through the past weeks." He scrubbed under his arms with vigor.

"Very observant," she said. "It seems you can indeed hold two diverse thoughts in your head at a time."

He wagged a finger at her. "I warned you." She jumped up with a yelp as he lunged for her. He cleared the side of the tub with ease. "I've been chasing bastards across the country for weeks, my dear. A wily pregnant woman will be no match."

"You wouldn't, Wills." She ran behind his desk, him stopping at the other side, water streaking down his body like tears. She never thought she could be jealous of water.

"Oh, I shan't throw you in that filth. For I've other ideas on what to do with you." That grin of his . . . But she stood her shaky ground.

"And what if I object?"

He ambled around the desk, dragging a finger along the thick, dark wood. He stopped inches from her, using the same finger to tip her chin. "You shan't be able to object, my love. For my lips shall long occupy yours."

With that pledge, he proved true to his word.

William met Daniel in the hedge maze before going to council. While there was much business to conduct, he wished to be out of the castle's cold confines. Perhaps the months out of doors had ruined him for palace life.

They reviewed various agenda items and came around to Robert.

"And he's still not speaking to you?" Daniel said, eyes to the pebbled path.

"Oh he'll speak to me in public, simply to answer orders or other official duties, but no, we haven't spoken more than a dozen words since the armistice."

"If I would have known how he would react, I would not—"

"Daniel, you cannot blame yourself for this. I am just as much at fault." William kicked a stone. "And he has a point. This whole war might have been avoided if I had put my personal concerns about Robert aside. If I hadn't listened to so many voices speaking ill of him."

"And I apologize that I was one of those voices." Daniel nodded, grave.

"You are not the only one of whom I speak." While his initial thoughts were of Anna's constant, biting words against his cousin, he also remembered Daniel's doubt, during Havenside's capture especially, and William had to admit those doubts spoke to him more strongly than Anna's. "Regardless, I should have pushed harder, sought out if he were up to the task of ruling Laureland and Norwick—could've found a way to make his holdings less, so as not to compete with the crown."

"I beg you to stop this conjecture, my liege." Daniel stopped their progress. "You did everything in your power, with all the information you had, to save this realm. And you did save this realm, Laureland be damned."

Why did everyone feel the need to stroke his pride? William strode onward, knowing Daniel would follow. Perhaps he needed time with Cate to soothe him. He picked up his pace, hoping for even a brief visit with his daughter before council.

"A king cannot help but question his actions," William said, "especially those past, to mayhap change the future."

"Indeed, but to wallow in it does not help the present." Daniel almost had to jog to keep up.

"I am not wallowing. I simply should have trusted my instincts more. Shouldn't have been so merciful with proven enemies of the crown." They were in the courtyard, headed straight for the wide open doors of the Great Hall.

"I hate to say this—"

"Then don't." William grit his teeth, trying to stem his illogical temper.

"But that sounds much more like your father than you."

William whirled around, catching a startled Daniel by the jacket. "At least he kept his country whole." Without waiting for a response, without waiting for his own regret, he stormed into his castle, heading straight for the nursery.

Passing bowing and scraping courtiers, he arrived at Cate's room and breathed relief. He entered without knocking, startling Cariline and a bevy of nurses and maids.

"Papa!" If the word didn't thaw his heart, her boundless smile did. She leapt into his arms and he swung her about, short legs flying out behind, giggles smothering him.

"Oh, my princess, how well it does me to see you." He cradled her to him as best he could with all her skirts and plumage, her arms pressed around his neck.

"Thank you for your audience, Your Majesty."

"Oh-ho, aren't we quite prim and proper today?" She smiled, her cheeks blooming a pleasant pink. "You've grown into a young lady in my absence."

She nodded, eyes big, trying her best to be regal. Wiggling out of his arms, he put her down and she made a perfect curtsy. He laughed and clapped, mood truly lightened. She slipped her hand into his and drew him toward the window seat.

"I wish to speak with you, Papa."

"For you, Catey, anything." He let her drag him to the tufted pillows bedecking the wide sash and sat without ceremony, hoping she would climb into his lap. Instead, she settled next to him and smiled, just like her mother, save her dimpled cheek.

"I saw grandmama last night." William found it hard to keep a straight face when she spoke so solemnly. She was too adorable.

"You're having your dreams again? You know Mama dislikes you to speak of them."

She crinkled her nose, ignoring his interjecting. "And she said you did right."

A half-smile froze on his face. He cleared his throat. "Catey, dear heart, you know you shouldn't speak such things."

"That's why we went away from them." She gestured at her nurses.

He couldn't argue with that, but still, her decisive pronouncement caught him off guard. "That was thoughtful, but—"

She patted his knee. "Don't be scared, Papa. She just wants you to be happy now. So my brother can come."

There it was again, her insistence at a brother. With Anna's pregnancy, his mind had returned to Cate's fevered prediction, but seeing her again, hearing her speak so matter-of-fact, made him tremble with both excitement and fear. Anna was right. Especially if the babe she carried was a boy, they would have to stop Cate from repeating these dreams or visions or whatever in God's name they were.

He took both her hands in his. "Darling, thank you for telling me, but you truly do need to keep these . . . conversations to yourself."

"But grandmama said it was important."

"Well you can tell her thank you. And . . . and I love and miss her." He gave what he hoped was a convincing smile.

Cate shrugged. "She knows. She says whenever you smell lavender in strange places, that's her saying she is proud of you."

William stilled, stared into his daughter's eyes. How could she know those were the very words he longed to hear? And how could she know that he often did smell lavender where it shouldn't be? In the stables. At council. In the tent when he signed the armistice. He'd always thought his mind was tricking him into conjuring Anna, for she smelled of lavender too. In fact, he smelled it now, all around him. Or was it more mind tricks?

"I understand." He smoothed a loose curl behind her ear. "But again, my princess, I must ask you to obey your mother, and me, in this. Please treasure these messages in your heart. Will you do that for me?"

She eyed him, wary, pursed her cherubic lips. Then a devilish smile to mirror her mother's spread across her face and she hopped off the window seat.

"Let's play pony now, Papa!"

And before he knew it, his jacket was off and he was plodding on all fours, Cate lightly kicking his ribs as she demanded he go faster. And while their conversation wasn't forgotten, it was swept away in the simple, overwhelming joy of being home.

It had been over a month since Robert had spoken more than ten words to the king. Even at his weekly meetings with only Daniel and William, he managed, for the most part, to nod, grunt, or to speak only to Daniel. He hated to admit it, but this self-imposed censure was wearing on him.

And today, there would be no avoiding his cousin. William had made sure of it. To celebrate the royal's seventh wedding anniversary, and to restore some joviality to the palace after the Laureland defeat, William had ordered a week-long festival, complete with a games, feasts, a tournament, and even a fair on palace grounds. Today's game was tennis. William facing Robert. So, they would have it out on the court. Though a joust better suited his temperament, Robert would have to tromp the king in sport.

He arrived first, giving Daniel, as scorekeeper, a slight bow. Scooping up a practice ball he said, "Does he really think a tennis match will make me talk?"

"Seems to me he's just as content to keep this silence as you." Daniel could be so smug.

"And you're content too I take it, back at the king's side. Alone."

Daniel arched a thin blonde brow. "I daresay being a lout to the scorekeeper is not the best strategy."

Robert bounced the ball, caught it. "You're right. You're all I've got now."

"Just play the game," Daniel said.

He felt more than saw the crowd flow to the ground in curtsies and bows as William approached. Robert moved away from Daniel, to the far corner, bowing low so he wouldn't have to look at the king.

"Cousin," William said, passing to the other side of the net. "You'll have to face me sometime."

Robert grunted, rose from his obeisance. "Isn't it quite the other way around?" Robert hit his ball against the wall, using the warm-up to avoid eye contact.

"The tennis court is hardly the place for you to air your perceived grievances." William cracked a shoulder, stretched his neck.

"Give 'im hell, Majesty!" Someone shouted from the crowd, stifled laughter following.

"He gives us enough of it, does he not, good fellow?" William called to the heckler.

"You've not glimpsed hell, cuz," Robert said, quiet enough for only William's ears. "Not even close."

William came to the net. "Is that some sort of threat?"

Finally, Robert looked in William's face, held his stare for a long moment. "It's whatever you make it to be. Isn't that what being king is all about?"

Robert stepped back to his baseline, readying for play.

"The king's service," Daniel called.

William lobbed, heavy handed as expected, and Robert returned, making the king run the court. Back and forth they went, sweat gathering on Robert's brow until William hit right on the line.

"Fifteen-love, king's service."

"That was out, Cecile." Robert spun, hands on hips, glaring Daniel down. "It was on the other side of the line."

"I am the one sitting on the line, Norwick." Daniel made an infinitesimal shake of his head, as if to say *don't push this*. "I can understand from your vantage point it may have appeared—"

"Damn my vantage point, it was an out!" He flicked his eyes to his sister, who stood with chest pressed into the viewer's netting. She had taken this whole fight between him and the king in stride, trying to use it to her advantage. She probably thought if William were bereft of one Norwick, surely he would enjoy the company of the other.

"We can reset," William said. "We hate for anyone to think we won this match falsely."

"There's no need for that." Robert stomped back to place, even more annoyed to be made to look like a petulant child with the king's magnanimous remarks.

William served again and Robert managed a point to tie. Polite clapping followed. Robert served, the ball whipping through the air, hitting just inside William's baseline, the king unable to get purchase behind it. The crowd gasped as one.

"Twenty-fifteen, His Grace's service."

Robert allowed himself a superior grin at the king, who, much to Robert's surprise, laughed back. Robert felt his face reflexively relax in light of his friend's good humor. Was William throwing the game to get Robert's guard down? He tossed the ball in the air to serve, distracted by his thoughts. The second his racket made contact, he knew he'd lose the point. The hit was too high, too hard, would soar out of bounds. But Robert, it seemed, wasn't the only one distracted. William was focused on someone in the crowd. Robert watched, in slow, creeping horror, as the ball, faster than a galloping horse, slammed into the middle of the king's chest.

William stumbled, falling against the back wall, barely keeping his legs beneath him, his face contorted in pain. Both Daniel and Robert ran to him, Robert pulling the king's arm over his shoulders, to keeping William standing. The crowd was too loud, pushing in, people were everywhere, but all Robert saw were William's eyes, clamped shut, hand to his heart where the ball hit.

"Lay him down!" Someone called, but Robert ignored this.

"Wills, can you hear me?" Robert searched his friend's face. "Are you all right? Where does it hurt?"

"Ahhh—" the king curled into his chest.

"Get Norwick away!" Someone called. "He's trying to finish the job!"

"Wills! Wills, Goddammit talk to me!"

"My neck . . ."

"What?" Robert felt hands pulling on his free arm. "Wills, open your eyes!"

"Rob—ahhhh!" William hunched over as if he were going to vomit. Robert's attackers hauled him back.

"Don't you touch him." It was the queen, elbowing past him, kneeling beside the keening king.

Still stunned, Robert let the crowd edge him back, watching as chambermen fought to keep the people at bay, guards ordering people from the court. He looked down at his hands, dispassionately noting their tremble. He staggered as if drunk to the court entrance, still in a ghostly state, when Yvette took his arm in hers.

"Come with me," she said. He obeyed.

Anna had no shame about tearing William's shirt open and plastering her ear to his chest in the middle of the tennis court. His breath was shallow and quick with a slight wheeze. Ever-present Daniel was by her side.

"He needs air," she said, not bothering to address the duke properly. "These people need to back away. We need to get him to his chambers on a litter."

Daniel bid the guards to do as she ordered while she fingered William's neck, checking his pulse.

"Try to breathe slowly."

"I can-can't bre—"

"Shhh, don't talk, just slow breaths. Try, my love." She hated that the courtiers saw him this way, gasping, weak, their king laid low by a mere ball. "Get these people out of here, Cecile." Daniel's face colored at the snap in her voice, but nevertheless, the court was cleared of all save the litter and guards.

"We're taking you to your chambers," Anna said, smoothing her thumbs over his stubbled cheeks. "Can you manage onto the litter?"

"I . . . walk . . ."

"You can barely breathe and your heart is racing. You shall not walk."

The look he gave her sent cold shivers down her legs.

"I understand 'tis beneath your dignity to be carried through court on a litter, but what of the king hobbling? We must get you to your chamber and get your clothes off."

A shadow of a smile came to his lips. "Don't . . . tease." His breathing was deeper, but his heart was still erratic.

"We will take you through the back halls so few people see you." He glowered and she glowered back. "This is not up for debate."

Without waiting for his response, she stepped aside so the men could settle him on the litter. Within moments they were headed to his rooms, his wheezing more pronounced now that he lay prone. She masked herself in stern royal calm, resisting the urge to hold his hand as she didn't want him to appear even feebler. But all that fell away when they transferred him to his bed.

"More pillows." She was queen no longer, focused only on his health, not on dignity, and certainly not on the judgments of those around her. If she barked like a general, so be it. "And open the windows—all of them."

She finished the work she'd begun on the court, ripping his shirt clean off, revealing an angry red and purple welt, the size of her palm, in the center of his sternum. He was squinting at her in the bright light.

"I've got to check for fractures, Wills. It won't hurt any more than it already does."

He shook his head and winced.

"Fetch a chamber pot," she called to no one in particular, "and someone find Mistress Mary."

"I'm right here," Mary said, appearing as if by magic at the foot of William's bed, her kit tucked at her hip.

"We've got to check his ribs," Anna said, while Mary rolled up her sleeves and came to Anna's side.

"May I touch ye, Yer Majesty?" Mary took his grunt for assent. She ran her fingers over his ribs, gently pressing each bone. "You feel his pulse, dearie." Anna cupped his chin, finding both arteries in his neck. "Now, when I ask ye t' breathe, I wan' ye t' take as big a breath as ye can manage." William nodded. "Now, please."

His whole chest shuddered as he drew air into his lungs, his face clenched in pain. Mary splayed her hand over his sternum, fingers nestling between his ribs. "Again." Anna felt his pulse speed with each inhale, but it didn't jump or stop or flutter, a good sign. Mary readjusted her hands. "And last breath, Majesty." He let out a hiss at his exhale.

Mary nodded. "No breaks. Just going t' have a nice bruise and some pain for a wee bit."

"Are you sure?" Anna let go of his chin, fingering his chest. "What about this lump here?" Next to the welt there was a knob of bone, often sign of a fracture that hadn't broken the skin. William hissed again as she pressed.

"Feel his other ribs. Same thing," Mary said, confident. "That one's got swelling 'round it 'cause it was hit. 'Tisn't broken."

"And his heart?"

"I'm right here." It came out as a wheezed whisper.

"Of course, I'm sorry." Anna caught his eyes and saw annoyance masking worry. Or perhaps those were her own feelings.

"Yer heart be still beating, Majesty," Mary said with a teasing smile. "You shall live another day t' dazzle us all with your handsome smile an' fine teeth."

"Don't make me laugh," he whispered, "it hurts."

"Well, I've got something with me will take that right away and send y' off t' the best dreams y' ever did see." She patted her pocket, a clink of glass responding.

"Then cheers." He wasn't too sore to wink.

Mary handed him the elixir, heavy with poppy, and he gulped it, despite his obvious pain of swallowing. Within ten minutes' time, he was in deep sleep. Anna sighed with relief.

"I should be givin' you some as well, my dear." Mary clucked her tongue, surveying Anna's dishevelment.

"I want to be here when he wakes." Anna pressed her hand to her hair.

"Which won't be for quite some time." Mary filled another bottle, shook it, placed it on William's bedside table.

"Still . . ." Anna watched him breathe, his chest moving, sometimes shaking, sometimes shallow, his mouth open to get all the air he could. "Send in Margaux and Brigitte to at least fix my hair. I can manage the rest to make myself presentable."

"I don't care two spoons about presentable." Mary gathered her kit. "You and the babe need rest, not all this commotion."

"I will be of better mind if I am at his side, and if I tire, I will lie beside him."

"Suit yourself." Mary shook her head. "Do y' still want the pair of hens?"

Anna sighed. "Send them. The least I can do is give the king a turned out wife to wake up to."

Mary clucked again and left. Anna moved to William's desk and sat in his chair, waiting for her ladies. A handful of chambermen went about their mysterious duties in the shadows, quiet as dust. Soon the appropriately grim-faced Margaux and Brigitte were allowed entry, carrying a tray of Anna's combs, brushes, and pins. They started in on Anna's hair without comment, though she could tell Margaux was bursting to speak.

She finally succumbed. "I cannot believe the audacity of my brother." She pulled a curl around her finger with a huff. "First he thinks he can just turn up his nose at the king and now whacks him in the—"

Anna held up a hand. "Enough, Countess. We were all there. We know what he did."

"You don't think he did it on purpose do you?" Margaux said with false horror. "I mean, he's certainly a scoundrel . . ."

"Whatever I think of your brother's motivations are certainly none of your business." Anna fiddled with a quill.

"I of all people know his darker side. Why I've barely said a word to him myself with how he's snubbed the king—"

"I said enough, Countess." Anna spoke barely above a whisper so as not to wake the king. "You are here only to fix my hair and be away. I do not require your opinions."

"As you say, Highness," she said with a sigh. Brigitte stifled a giggle, causing Anna to wonder what face Margaux had pulled.

A low, long creak heralded a visitor's arrival, and unless it was the court physician, she would send this intruder away. Hair half pinned and dangling, she shot out of the chair and charged at none other than Robert.

"What mad lapse of reason convinced you to come here?" She couldn't unfurl her full wrath upon him, having to settle for accusing fingers and shout-whispers.

He bowed low. "I have come to see to His Majesty's health in person, as I am the sorry cause."

"Sorry cause?" Anna chortled. "Indeed you are a sorry cause, and will be more so if you do not leave this instant."

He brushed past her into the room. "I hate to bring up technicalities at a time like this, but I do outrank you, Madam."

"I am queen." She followed him to the edge of the bed dais.

"Queen consort. Begging your pardon of course." Was he hiding a smirk?

"I don't care for your technicalities, Norwick, nor your tone." She strode to him, inches from his face. "I am in charge of the king's care and as such, I will not have the man who tried to harm him anywhere near his person."

Robert balked. "Try to harm him? You can't be serious."

"Oh, I am quite serious, *Your Grace*." She backed him toward the desk and his shocked sister. "Do not play me a fool. You have long, long planned to take the throne and when you could not get it through manipulation and war—"

"Those are grave, and I add ridiculous, accusations. I only came to see that he is on the mend as is reported about court."

"Or perhaps slip something in his drink?"

"Your Majesty!" Margaux cut in, face flush. "You cannot accuse him so! I've certainly no love for my brother, but he would never purposefully—"

Anna turned on the countess. "And why should I trust your word, ever? A woman who disdains her husband's bed." Margaux's blue eyes clouded. Brigitte gasped. "A woman who, for her life entire, has tried to claim *my* husband's. God knows what lengths you've gone to."

"Keep my sister out of this," Robert said, his voice crackling. "Your grievance is with me."

"The business I have with your sister is none of yours." Anna whirled back to face him.

"It is very much my business." He leaned in, black eyes boring into her. "When you accuse me of attempted regicide, my sister of adultery and trickery, it is all very much my business. I have put up with your spiteful words against me and mine own, the poison you fill the king's ears with, and still, who does he remain loyal to?" His eyes narrowed, as if he could see the knife twisting in her heart. "If you and Daniel hadn't filled the king's head with lies about me, perhaps we would still have Laureland."

"That has nothing to do—"

"Didn't he tell you? His one true confidant? Or perhaps he only tells you bits and pieces because he knows how feeble—"

She opened her mouth to speak, but he spoke over her.

"He was going to give me Laureland, before the war. He thought they needed a strong, loyal hand, but your poison against me held him back."

"He makes his own mind—"

He advanced on her. "I warned you on your wedding night. You continue such disdain of me at your own peril."

Before she could strike back, he strode out the door, his sister scurrying behind. Brigitte stood there, confused face contorted, twisting a comb in her hands. Anna cleared her throat and sat.

"Continue," she said. Brigitte tentatively began anew, curling and tucking Anna's hair back into place.

She looked to the bed, William still deep in slumber. Thank God he hadn't heard that row. Yes, he had asked her to trust his own belief in Robert, but that was before the war, before Robert had taken to making himself out to be a victim, before he had deliberately hammered a ball at William's chest. Surely, the king must be wavering on Robert's so-called fealty if he didn't give him Laureland. But as she watched William there, she couldn't erase Robert's confident, derisive words. *You continue at your own peril.*

CHAPTER 12

Broken, Not Bent

Two weeks had passed since the accident and Robert, it seemed, had buried whatever injustice he held against William. The king was well aware that something had transpired between Anna and Robert while he was recovering, something he didn't wish to further dig into and unsettle the tentative, though perhaps false, peace that follows grave injury.

William kept this foremost in mind as Daniel and Robert met in his chambers for their weekly briefing.

"And finally," Daniel said, sitting even straighter than normal, "we must do something about Beaubourg. Shore up the borders there with a strong presence."

William sighed. "I'll need to talk to the queen about it. I know she wants to give it to the princess . . ."

"Begging her pardon, but 'tis yours to do with as you will, Majesty." Daniel folded his hands in his lap. "As her father had no male heir, the duchy reverts to the crown."

"'Tis a little more delicate than you make it sound," William said, checking Robert's reaction. His face was unmoved. "The queen has some ideas on the matter. Besides which, there is precedent for a female to inherit."

"However, it still stands that we need to defend not just the northern border, but now the Truss."

"Thank you for pointing out the obvious." William didn't mean to sound so acidic. Daniel was only doing his job. But he knew Anna would be incensed if there was even a hint that Cate wouldn't have Beaubourg outright. And he didn't wish to further their bickering.

"I may have a solution, if I'm allowed such boldness." Robert thrust to the edge of his chair. The king, surprised by this sudden engagement, nodded. "I have long felt, as you know, the princess should be betrothed to my Rob." Daniel opened his mouth, but Robert held up a finger. "If you give Beaubourg to the princess and betroth her to Rob, then set me as regent over Beaubourg until they are of age, you have the power of the crown and my men behind Beaubourg. Hell, you could even have Sir Bryan man the castle, have him be the regional eyes and ears of the place. But this way, you keep it with the crown, the queen gets what she wants, and we put a strong face to the Low Countries."

"And you get what you want," Daniel said, almost under his breath.

"It seems you've given this much thought," William said, easing against his calfskin chair, steepling his fingers.

"We've seen what happens when lands have no central force of control," Robert said. "Without a duke for the lords to answer to, all is chaos."

"And yet it gives an avowed Protestant the whole of the north of the realm," Daniel said.

Robert's dark eyes became slits. "As I recall, that argument of yours just lost us a quarter of our country."

"The war would have happened anyway," Daniel said, "the wheels were already—"

"Enough." William pushed out of his chair to pace as the men watched him. "'Tis quite a bit to consider, but I will consider it."

"The crown would still hold the land, but I would oversee the lords, keep tabs on the markets—"

"But then why the betrothal?" Daniel said. "It doesn't add—"

"Because it's the least I deserve!" Robert sprang from his chair, breathing heavy. He caught William's eyes. "And you know it, Wills. After all I've done for you, after all I've done for this realm, this is the very least you can do to repay me."

"A king does not need to repay," Daniel said.

William walked to his cousin, surveying him from foot to crown of his head. He knew he must lay to rest their battle of wills. And with Anna pregnant, what harm would there be—especially if the land was still under the crown's control and the betrothal contract made clear that Catherine was ruling duchess?

"You're right." William shrugged.

"So you'll do it?" Robert's eye's widened in disbelief.

"I'll speak to the queen about it."

Robert snorted. "She'll dismiss it out of hand."

"'Tis true she dislikes you, but she cares more for our country than she cares for personal umbrage. Something you ought to remember." William went back to pacing, not entirely sure if he believed his own words. "We are finished, then, for today."

"Beg pardon, sire, but Beaubourg, in the interim?" Daniel said.

"Send Sir Bryan to the castle," William said. "I believe the queen was thinking of doing something of the sort anyway. A gesture of kindness for his service at her father's death."

"Are you quite sure that's appropriate?" Daniel said.

"Why ever not?"

Daniel cleared his throat, not meeting William's gaze. "Just, he tends to swing in and out of favor . . ."

"It's been six years since he's been out of favor," Robert said, "unless something happened during the war."

Daniel, concentrating on gathering his papers, gave the desk a weak smile. "Shall I send word to him?"

"I will speak to the queen about that also," William said. "And tomorrow we will send word as needed. Until then, nothing of any of this until she and I have hammered it out together." This addressed straight to Robert.

Both men nodded and took their leave. It wasn't until the room was empty that the full weight of what he agreed to set in. Hopefully Anna could see the larger picture, see the benefit for Cate, the benefit for the country.

"Have you gone well and truly mad, Wills?"

Apparently his wife wasn't ready to see any larger picture. William eyed Anna, wary, as she ripped indiscriminately through overgrowth in her garden. William had sent her ladies farther off so he could speak to her in private, believing the location and the beautiful day might set her in a right mind. He was mistaken.

"His Rob is a pleasant fellow," William said, rousing positivity, "raised by his demure and gentle mother, far from court and its intrigues."

"There is absolutely no reason on this earth to simply hand Norwick *my* lands—" She ripped out some spindly looking grass from the roots.

"You know the lands are ultimately the crown's . . ."

"Whatever happened to 'my worldly goods I give thee'?" She brandished a weed at him.

"That is why I am making plans to keep them perpetually in our daughter's hands." He took two steps closer, careful to avoid flying debris.

"And why do you need blasted Norwick to do so?" She tossed the plant into a growing pile of verdant refuse. "Cate is a princess royal, well above any son of a . . . duke."

"And as such, would you not rather have her here, instead of Spain or France, or God save us, Scotland?"

She directed her attention back to the pockmarked ground. "I wish you would use your own authority. You don't need Norwick, you don't need any of them. *Your* word is law. They should jump when you flick a wrist. Instead 'tis you who jump."

Her words stabbed like her shears.

"Dammit, you have to stop this!" He was to her in two strides, looming. "We owe him, Anna. I owe him—my life thrice over and more." He hit his chest, ignoring the soreness. "I am alive because of him. You should be kissing his feet, not digging his grave."

"Shall you take all that is dear and give it away?" Sun and exertion had pinked her skin, but it was fury that colored her face.

He took her shoulders, his own frustration and pride and some long and deep-held loyalty boiling up in him.

"I asked you once to trust me when it came to Robert. You agreed. Do you now take back that pledge? Now is the time you choose to turn from me?" He searched the brown bowls of her eyes. She closed them.

"I will never let our child be subject to him or his sons. You doom her to the fate I so feared." She opened her eyes. They were wet, but tears neither gathered nor fell.

"Yet fear has not been your fate." He felt her falter beneath his hands.

"Before this moment, this moment when you auction off my home and my child to the highest bidder, I would have agreed."

She twisted away, faced the stone wall, her entire body rigid, while his felt as though it could soak into the very ground. His rational mind told him to give her time, let her cool, that she often said things she didn't mean in a passion. But his heart, his heart could take no more.

"And so this is what breaks us?" He shook his head. "Norwick?"

"'Tis not Norwick, but your placement of his desires over mine, over our child's." She brought a hand to her belly.

"I do this to protect our realm, not to please Norwick. It is you who put your feelings above our country, and that is what wounds me most. I never thought you so facile. But now I see truth."

He didn't know if she turned to him, didn't know if she picked up her skirts to follow, for he strode from her garden, blinded, with only a faint "Wills!" bidding him farewell.

Anna knew she needed to slow her breath if she wanted to keep from fainting. Standing there amid her weeding, bees and bugs and worms all carrying on their work, oblivious to the devastation William had just wreaked on her heart. Give Robert control over Beaubourg? Marry Cate to Rob? He knew—he *knew* this would devastate her. She barely noted her ladies hurrying back, Mary's concerned words, Yvette trying to take her arm. She ripped off her apron, leaving it in the dirt, and walked, trance-like, to the palace, her ladies a mere thrum behind. She didn't recall how she made it to her chambers, but she climbed in bed, closing the curtains womb-like around her. Her sobs were silent, tearless, and soon sent her to a restless sleep, until her babe's hiccups brought her back into wakefulness.

Candlelight danced through the curtain gaps. She must have missed supper, not that William would have minded. Her mouth tasted like her heart felt. Wrung out, dry, swollen. When she felt this way, she'd always sought solace with the one person who was now the cause. But there was one more person . . .

"Mary?"

Her nurse poked her head through the curtains. "Dearie, you've got to tell me what has happened."

"Has the king visited? Messengers?"

Mary's face told Anna the answer before her words. "Nothing but a message from His Grace Cecile."

"Cecile?" Anna snuffed. "What on earth could he want?"

"I've no notion, but he seemed insistent."

She asked for wine and took stock. Thinking logically, a strong northern force was needed to shore up the borders, both new and old. But why not give the privilege to Duven or Ridgeland, who certainly behaved with valor and loyalty? After all, Ridgeland's lands were to the south of Beaubourg and his attentions wouldn't be divided. And to throw Cate into the fray . . .

She startled when Margaux parted the curtains and curtsied. "Will Your Majesty need her toilette before her audience with His Grace?" The look Anna shot her sent Margaux faltering back.

"Your wine, Majesty," Lady Jane said, avoiding eye contact.

Anna drained the glass. *Get a hold of yourself, he has a country to think of, not just your wishes.*

"Will you see His Grace?" Mary asked, face apprehensive.

"Yes." The answer surprised even her. "I will see him at his first convenience."

Mary passed Anna a damp cloth. "Let us get you changed and presentable and I'll send Bernard with word."

"Thank you, Mary." She felt a knot hovering at her collar-bone, as if deciding whether to become a sob or to be swallowed away beneath a mask of dignity. She cleared her throat and stood, head high. She was queen, after all, and about to bear a prince. What had she to weep over?

She allowed her ladies to primp and preen, changing her into a thicker gown for evening, and soon she was on her way to Daniel's rooms, trying to keep from wishing she would see the king.

Daniel's door was open wide, dozens of candelabras giving his chamber a merry glow.

"Majesty!" He bowed, held his hands out to take hers. She allowed it, and he kissed her ring.

"Your Grace is happy this eve." Anna tried to manifest a smile, but failed.

"I believe I have a solution to all of our ills, and wished to bring it to you before the king." Daniel led her not to his desk as was his custom, but to his window seat.

"And why come to me, when you know the king and I are out of sorts?"

"Because I know the king would not act upon it without your approval, regardless of any current upset between you." Daniel didn't sit, but stood before her, as if he were a suitor about to recite a sonnet.

"You certainly have my attention." She folded her hands in her lap to keep them from trembling. If Daniel thought her and William's fight a mere spat, perhaps she was blowing things out of proportion. Perhaps William wasn't as upset as she was.

"Beaubourg is at risk," Daniel said, "as we both know. With Brussels and Laureland at its borders, there is no reason why Orange or the Emperor or any other might try to pick it off." He paused to make sure she was following him. "We need a

show of continued strength there, and as intelligent as the princess is, she is no replacement for sheer force."

"The issue is not the princess," Anna said. "Obviously, I
don't think a child could bring the protections we need."

"I understand Norwick's full proposal upset you." He pulled
up his desk chair and sat before her. "So I suggest a smaller one.
Let him have Beaubourg and leave the princess to marry whom
is best fit."

She balled her hand tighter, nails digging into her flesh.
"He would control nearly half the realm!" She stood, staring
indignation upon him. "What is to keep him from rallying our
enemies to take the very crown?"

"He would not permit a foreign king on our throne."

"He would want himself there."

The child kicked within her and she knew she must calm
herself. Daniel was the last person at court she wanted to see
her unhinged.

"Why do you think I keep such a close eye on the king, on
Norwick?" This surprised her. As smart as Daniel was, she
thought he too was blinded by some ill-founded loyalty to
Robert. "But I know this also: he will not usurp the king to do
so. He will not take arms against him."

Anna gave him withering look. "What of Ridgeland? It
makes much more sense geographically, and Ridgeland too is
renowned as a fierce fighter." She crossed her arms. "Besides,
there is no question of his loyalty."

"Norwick has earned—"

"Norwick has earned nothing!" She was so sick of them saying Robert somehow deserved more than he already had, as if

he must be appeased. "He has performed the duty of a subject and noble, as all the rest have done."

"I am trying to fix the mistake that lost us Laureland in the first place." Daniel stood, his patience with this doting farce clearly over. "I was the one who advised the king not to give Norwick control of Laureland. If we had just done so . . ."

"If you had done so, nothing." She stared at him. "Nothing would have changed!"

He squared himself to her, grabbing her hands.. "I am trying to keep this realm from further degradation, trying to protect the very people you so boldly claim to love, yet due to your groundless grudge against a man, you would leave them to the wiles of our enemies."

"Release me now, or Norwick isn't the only man at this court I will have a grudge against." He let her go as if burned. "You may think me easily threatened, as I am a woman, but never forget, it is my word above even yours, dear Daniel, that the king heeds."

He laughed without mirth. "He may love you, but he will not sacrifice the safety of his people for you, especially now, when you've wounded his pride." He strode to his desk, picked up a parchment. "I had dearly hoped you would be amenable to this, but now I fear Norwick shall have all, and you shall be left with nothing."

"What are you implying?"

"Take it as you will, Madam." He nodded as if dismissing her.

She couldn't believe his gall, his self-righteousness. But she knew that if William would cleave to Robert even at the expense of his marriage, nothing she could do would dissuade him from

Daniel. She must find a way to make up with William, and quickly.

"You forget, Cecile, all will change when this babe is born. This is not over, not by a mile."

She left him to his schemes, hurrying to see to her own.

She sent William a note, for he wouldn't see her.

> *I'm disheartened we've fought so, Wills. You must know how much it grieves me. Might we start again? I shall be in the royal gardens by the fountain if you see fit to join me.*
> *All of my heart, your,*
> *˜A*

So she idled, circumventing the gardens, waiting for him to appear, spaniels lapping happily at her heels, none the wiser to her anxious heart. She knew he had council, and no doubt it would be a long one. Still, with each passing minute, her worry intensified.

The high, hot August sun bore down as she lumbered once more around the fountain, her legs bowed by the girth of her growing child.

"Let us find you some shade, dearie," Mary said. But there was none to be had, unless one stood directly next to the towering boxwood hedge.

"I will be fine if I sit." She gave another furtive glance to the palace doors, but they were still as gravestones.

She sat on the fountain lip in just the right spot, the shade cast by the bubbling tiers covering at least part of her thighs, the gurgling waters producing some coolness. How she longed to plunge into the shallows and soak away her sweat. Mary plopped beside her, Lady Jane settling herself on Anna's other side. Yvette and Margaux were having some earnest argument by the hedges, and the rest of her ladies floated through the aisles of curated shrubs and blooms.

"Highness," Jane said, holding up a hand to shield her eyes yet still squinting, "'tis certainly none of my business, but you have often been a boon to me in listening to my worries over Lord John . . ."

"Is he ill again?" Relieved to have something else to worry on, Anna immediately chastised herself. It was exactly what William was talking about with her selfishness—how could one be relieved a child was sick?

Jane shook her head and looked down at her fidgeting fingers. "I thought you might feel the need to unburden yourself. To me . . . or to anyone."

"That is dear of you, milady." Anna dragged her fingers in the water. "As is obviously no surprise, for not a lick of my doings are ever private, the king and I have had it out. And I fear this time, 'tis not just a harmless squabble." Since she hadn't been facing him, she could only judge by his voice, but the edge that was in it, the flat way he dismissed her concerns . . . she'd broken something and she hadn't the first clue how to fix it.

"Oh but he loves you, Highness. Surely time will ease his umbrage." Jane lay a hand on Anna's leg then quickly withdrew it. "Beg your pardon, I shouldn't assume to—"

But Anna drew up Jane's hand and kissed it. "You have always been a true friend to me, Jane."

"'Tis my honor to serve you," she said, voice cracking.

Out of the corner of her eye, Anna saw the doors swing open. She jumped up, nearly knocking over Mary in the process, smoothed her skirts, and willed herself to calm, with little success.

Sure enough, it was the king, striding out of the palace shadow, a veritable army of councilmen and courtiers following. He was in earnest discussion with Daniel and Ridgeland, brow furrowed, hands flying to make some point. Anna's ladies hurried to gather round her, and when the king's party met her own, the women curtsied en masse. William broke off his conversation, silently surveying the ladies. It was as if an imaginary fence kept both sides at bay. His gaze finally fell on Anna, his eyes both firm and sad. She swallowed.

"Majesty," she said, deepening her curtsy. She had spent so long fretting over the fact they were fighting she'd forgotten to be angry. But seeing him flanked by Norwick and the recently cruel Daniel, she remembered that he too had much to apologize for. This wasn't some embarrassing scrape she'd gotten herself into. He was as much at fault as she was, if not more so.

William's only response was a grunt.

"Shall we take the air?" She rose, head high.

He nodded, then strode off, hands clasped behind his back. She scrambled to follow, the men and women mingling by the fountain.

"You walk too quickly—you must remember my pregnant body." She said it lightly, hoping to start things off with good humor.

"Our heir is always and forever at the forefront of my mind, Madam." He bit the word off, like rough, dried meat.

"I was not implying otherwise." At least he slowed his pace, though he didn't take her hand. They walked in silence, the thin space between them tense.

"You'll be pleased to know council is still debating the options for protecting the Beaubourgian border."

"As a matter of fact, it does not please me." She watched a bird circling high above, wings stretched full, soaring. "For I wish our country well and safe as quickly as possible."

"With exception." He held up a finger, but still didn't look at her. They reached the garden edge and were forced to turn, the sun now at their backs.

"I wouldn't put it that way." She glanced sidelong at him. "No matter Norwick's loyalties to you as king, he—

"I know you are wrong."

"How do you know it?" She stopped, facing him.

He considered her a long while. "I know his heart." With that, he kept walking.

She followed on his heels. "And can you not be wrong about someone's heart?"

"As of yesterday, I wouldn't have thought so, for I thought I knew yours so thoroughly as to stake my very life upon it."

"And I you!" She didn't mean for her voice to shrill. "I thought you had more regard for our daughter, more regard for my feelings."

He shook his head. "It doesn't matter what I feel. What matters is the safety of our realm!"

They'd circled back to the fountain, courtiers gathered on

the far side trying to appear indifferent, yet stilling their conversation.

"Stop trying to make this about duty to our country." She climbed up on the wide lip of the fountain so she could see him eye to eye. "Why can you not acknowledge that you hurt me?" She lowered her voice. "Why can't you recognize the fear I would have as a mother, knowing our sweet child was under the wing of that hateful family? There is not a Norwick alive who has an ounce of pity for me and you expect me to clap my hands and say 'as you wish' while they turn my own child against me?"

"And why can you not trust me?" He got right in her face. "Why can you not recognize that I don't have the luxury of acting upon my own whims and desires, that I am constantly taking all into consideration—yes, even your opinions? And all I get from you are shrieks and rebuttals and debasement." He narrowed his eyes, but she stood her ground. "You tell me to trust my gut, to stop letting these men influence my own mind, and yet what do you do but second guess my conclusions?"

Her heart crumbled with the truth of it. The baby kicked her kidney, but she refused to grimace. *Who's side are you on anyway, little one?*

Adjusting her stance, she sighed. "You've no idea what it's like, being made to sit mute while men carve apart all I have known and hand it out like Christmastide presents."

He guffawed, throwing his head to the sky. "And what do you think I feel about Laureland?"

She frowned. Another kick, or perhaps an elbow. This time she winced, curling to her left side.

William's face grew wide with concern. "The babe? Are you

all right?" He reached for her, but she swatted him away with both frustration and pain. He ignored her rebuff and grabbed for her. She stepped back, forgetting she was standing on the lip of the fountain. Before she could scream she was in water up to her shoulders, her bottom sore, wrists strained, and palms scratched from the impact. She was only vaguely aware of shouts coming from the other side of the fountain. All she saw was William's face, mouth an O, brows to his hairline, struggling not to laugh.

She scowled at his extended hand and managed to get to her knees. "I can't reach you."

William knelt on the edge, thrusting his arms farther out. She bent to meet him, registering his barely concealed smirk. Gripping both his hands, and with all her might, she yanked him. He fell with a splash like a breaching whale, soaking her hair and face, but her satisfaction wasn't dampened.

He sputtered to the surface, face crazed as courtiers scrambled. She slid her eyes to him and bit her lower lip to stifle laughter. He got up, dripping like laundry, hitting away his servants' hands. She'd done it now. Here she was trying to convince him he had dignity and what did she do but make him look a right fool? Ah, but she couldn't help it. That smug look of his . . .

Still in the fountain, he bent with his knees and scooped his arms around her.

"Don't exert yourself," she mumbled, but he ignored her, hoisting her in his arms as if she weighed no more than Cate. His mouth was set in a hard line as he climbed out, both of them raining upon the dry ground.

"The queen has rightly pointed out our need for a bath," he said. His head chamberman bowed and scurried off to the castle to ready one.

"Majesty?" Daniel said, taking in the two of them, trying to ignore the circumstances. "About Beaubourg . . ." He flicked his eyes to Anna.

"Later, Cecile," William said, then marched through the parting spectators, all silent in their horror or delight, Anna squirming all the while.

As they crossed the threshold, Anna dared to look at him. He looked down his nose, holding her eyes. And burst out laughing.

"Do I smell as bad as all that?" he said, after his hoots subsided.

"You certainly do now," she said, relieved to join in his mirth. "Ugh, the swans have been prolific in excrement this season."

"Ah but, my dear, you still smell like the finest wildflowers." He tucked his head to hers, then reared back. "I take it back. You smell like a butcher."

"Well then, aren't we the pair?" She patted his cheek, her sopping cuff leaking against his neck. He took the back halls to the stairway to their chambers. She relaxed in his arms and realized, for once, she must relent. She couldn't tell him to trust himself then storm at him for doing so.

"Will you join me then, so we may talk peace?" The sadness in his eyes still shone behind his present merriness.

"You know it's all because I love you, that I fret so, that I rage so."

He mounted the stairs, readjusting her in his arms. "And it's out of that love that you need to trust me."

She tightened her arms around his neck. "I can live with that."

August had turned to September's Michaelmas, and Anna and William's tentative peace still held. Though, if truth be told, she had been extra careful, extra cheerful, extra accommodating. For the first time in her marriage, she fabricated her feelings. She rationalized that every now and again one needed to put in additional effort to get along and that there was no harm in putting on a happy face for the king. But deep down, she knew he could tell. Because he knew her too well. For the time being, both were content to live the ruse. Besides, it would all sort out once the babe was born, and if her cravings for meat and ale were any indication, she was definitely having a boy. She caressed the top of her belly as she made her way to the king's chambers. Barely two months until her seclusion. Then everything would be truly well again.

When she entered, she found Daniel furtively whispering to William. She and Cecile had been cool but cordial since their argument about Beaubourg, and with council still unable to come to a conclusion, she felt justified.

Daniel stopped speaking and merely nodded his head at her, instead of his usual blush and bow. Then he began again, leaning closer to the king so that she wouldn't overhear. He put a hand on William's shoulder and squeezed. William smiled. Anna's gut twisted, remember Cecile's words, wishing it were her whispering in the king's ear instead.

"Always watching out for me," William said, patting Daniel's hand. Then he opened his arms to Anna. "Ah, dearest, let me make you comfortable." He led her to her favorite chair by the hearth and settled her into a throne of pillows. "Would you like to prop your feet?" He too was being overly doting.

"Thank you no, my liege." She smiled, kissed the hand that had so recently clasped Daniel's. "It seems you are buttering me up for something."

William smiled with humorless eyes. "You are too perceptive." He sighed and sat on the arm of his own stuffed chair. "I have come to a decision about the protection of Beaubourg."

She gazed into her lap. She must not react. She must speak her peace logically and pleasantly . . .

"I've decided Norwick should act as agent over Beaubourg."

She swallowed, not looking up. "And what prevailing argument convinced you?"

"It was my plan," Daniel said. "The one I spoke to you about, Madam."

She whipped up her head, narrowing her eyes at Daniel. "I was speaking to His Majesty."

"There's no need to take it out on Cecile," William said. "Norwick will only take care of the logistical operations of Beaubourg and its safety, and you will be in charge of any domestic areas that you see fit, such as harvest and markets. He is only there to provide military strength, not to run the place."

"Isn't that worse?" She wanted to stand, to match these men eye to eye, but she was stymied by her belly and the feathered pillows. "He can run a wool market for all I care. His military strength is what worries me."

"Dammit, why must we retread this weary road?" William rose, shaking his head.

"Because you throw my concerns to the wind, twisting them to sound like accusations against you." She struggled out of her down cocoon. "I'm not against you. I continue to be the only person who has no agenda other than truth and your happiness, though you refuse to see it."

"I too only look for Your Majesties' happiness," Cecile said.

"For once, will you stay out of this, Cecile?" She slashed her eyes to him. "Please, if you've any of the love you claim to bear us, stay out of our marriage!"

Daniel's lips formed a thin, pale line, but he was the least of her worries at present.

"And now Cecile is your enemy too?" William wheeled on her. "Will you leave me no one but yourself? No one's words but yours? You say you're truthful?" He gave a humorless laugh. "You've been prancing around for a month batting your eyes like Margaux, pretending all's well with the world."

"And what of you? Plying me with jewels, ponies for Cate, laughing too heartily at my mild jokes." Daniel cleared his throat, reminding her of his presence. "Should he really be here for this?"

"As I've told you before, nothing about your private life is private," Daniel said, eyes boring into her.

"Is that some sort of threat?" Anna said.

"Stop! Both of you!" William's shout rang in the rafters. "I want both of you gone from my sight."

"But, Will—"

"Highness, there's no need—"

"Out!" His roar even startled the baby, who jabbed and kicked her as if rudely awoken. She made a quick curtsy and left through their passage, not knowing whether to cry or scream.

Upon arriving at her chambers, she found her women gathered around and laughing. Seated at the center of this adoration was Bryan. He'd been recalled to advise on Beaubourg, but she hadn't seen him during the handful of days he'd been at court.

"Majesty," he said, striding to her side, his sky-blue eyes sparkling. He knelt and kissed her hands. "I finally behold divinity."

She blushed despite herself and let him take her arm. "You look peaked. Perhaps some refreshment?"

"Thank you, friend. I am indeed in want of refreshment and good company."

"And I am always at your service." He led her to her chair, grabbing a stool for her feet. "You seem troubled." He poured her wine while her ladies flitted about, trying to make themselves appear busy. All but Margaux. She sat in the window seat, bouncing her eyes between Bryan and the queen.

Anna waved a hand. "'Tis nothing. Or rather, 'tis nothing I wish to speak on." She took the proffered wine. "Tell me of home. What news of your wife and children? What of your mother and siblings?"

He sat on the opposite side of the sill from Margaux and regaled Anna with stories of his healthy boys, and all the men seeking Charity's hand. She let the tales bleed together into a pleasant hum, nodding occasionally and reminiscing about his earnest face and the sweet, simple life they'd had all those years ago. At some point, Lady Jane and Margaux excused themselves to make ready for the Michaelmas feast, and Bryan too said his goodbyes.

"If it be not too bold," he said, bowing again over her hand, "but may I have a dance this eve?"

She laughed at his formality. "You may have as many as please you, Sir Bryan." For heaven knew the king wouldn't wish to be at her side.

The king had to admit she looked stunning. Even though that afternoon left William steaming, he could still be struck dumb by not only her beauty, but by her essence, her soul, shining brighter than the crown on her head. How he longed to find a way back to their tranquil, laughter-filled times. They'd had struggles to surmount then too, but they tackled challenges together, smothering their hurts with love, tenderness, grace. What had changed?

He had no chance to ponder further, for Cate flung herself about his knees. "Isn't it splendid, Papa?"

He hoisted her up, resting her on his hip. "It has been quite a while since the last feast, hasn't it?" He looked about the Great Hall, trying to see all the puffed-up courtiers through his daughter's eyes. They really did put on a show. He kissed her temple.

"And Mama's like an angel." Her eyes were big as she observed the queen across the room. Anna wore a new dress of ivory and gold and sure enough, all she needed were wings to look the part. He set Cate down and pulled a blooming white rose from a bouquet on the table.

"Why don't you go give this to your Mama, with both our compliments?"

Cate stuck her face in the flower, giving it a big sniff before scampering to Anna's side. He watched as Anna leaned down to better hear, and Cate pointed across the floor to him. He didn't need to be standing there to know Anna had admonished Cate not to point, for their daughter flushed and her arm fled to her skirts. But Anna still smiled and accepted the rose, burying her face in it as Cate had done. She looked to William, who raised a glass in toast to her. Her return smile was genuine. Relief swept over him. Maybe he was forgiven. And maybe he'd forgiven her.

They were to have dancing before the main courses and the music began, a galliard of some sort, though only a smattering of people went to the floor. Perhaps now would be the time to make things up between them. He set his glass down and headed around the pillars to where Anna had been standing. But she was no longer there. It took him no time to find her, for there she was, in the center of the floor, dancing with Sir Bryan. On the opposite pillar stood Margaux, eyes aflame as she watched the couple, though her face held a courtly smile. He might as well put the woman out of her misery.

He strode to her and bowed, offering his hand, which she took with relish. He hoped he could deposit her with Bryan and sweep away the queen at the end of the dance.

"Majesty, I've always remarked at how lithe you are in the dance." She batted blue eyes at him. He refrained from rolling his.

"And you, Countess. Tell me, how do your boys fare?" And that was all it took for her to prattle the rest of the song. He ended the dance on the far side of the floor from Anna and made to lead Margaux to Bryan, but Halforn, blast him, had taken up the queen's hand. The king had right to the queen of course, but William didn't wish to be boorish. He turned Margaux back around and ran smack into Bryan. The knight nearly fell to the ground in obeisance.

"M-majesty, Countess!"

Margaux worked her fan so fast even William felt the breeze. "Rise, sir, and enjoy the rest of the festivities." William tried to hand over Margaux to Bryan, but the man only gave another stiff bow.

"'Tis a pleasure as always, but I must beg your pardon as I am on an errand of ale for the queen."

"Ah, well then, let us not keep her waiting."

Bryan hurried off and Margaux sighed. William patted her arm. "He'll be back, Cousin."

"Thank you for being so good," she purred, then tilted up on tiptoes and kissed his cheek—at the exact moment Anna glanced at him. Her eyes flicked away, but not before he saw her brows knit.

"I must release you to better hands," William said, making as hasty an exit as Bryan had, Margaux stunned. He again swam toward his wife, but this time was intercepted by Daniel. William shook his head and pushed past him. "Not now, Cecile. I'm in no mood."

"No mood for my abject and humiliating apology?"

William sighed and stopped. If he hoped for forgiveness, the least he could do was give it himself.

"I was entirely and completely out of line this afternoon. I've no right to speak to the queen, or to you, in that manner, especially of something so delicate. She is absolutely correct. I have no business interfering, or even knowing about what passes between you—even when it involves statecraft. I trust you to inform me of anything you feel important, and otherwise, I will keep my pointy nose and my sharp tongue out of it."

William shook his head. "She has a way of getting under a man's skin. But I wouldn't have her any other way."

"She does speak her mind. Boldly. And that is not new to me. Even more reason I should not have been so biting and superior."

William nodded and glanced to the dance floor. Now where had she gone? His eyes found her drinking by the sweets and laughing at something Bryan had said, her hand on his forearm.

"Think on it no longer, friend."

He let Daniel steer him back to the head table. Cecile talked of how and when to inform Norwick of the formal decision, but the king barely listened. He took up his wine and surveyed the dancing while Cecile droned. Like a fairy flitting to and fro, there Anna was, back on Bryan's arm in a pavane, him leaning in to hear her speak.

"He was such a comfort to her at her father's passing," Daniel said.

William startled and faced Daniel. "How was he a comfort?" William turned back to watch his wife.

"With you away and her needing to be strong for the princess,

I think it was good for her to have a friendly face. Someone who knew her. Knew her father. He barely left the castle or her side the entire time."

"Quite devoted." Bryan's and the queen's smiles were broad.

"We are lucky to have him back at court." With that benediction, Daniel bowed and left.

The song ended, Bryan bowed, and Anna raised a hand to her chest. William thought at last she would seek him out, but as the music began, she didn't even look in William's direction, just kept laughing and talking with her old beau.

The longer he watched them, the more he felt a childish jealousy fill him. A picture flashed in his mind, of his father raging at his mother during just such a feast. He was drunk and she'd been dancing with Halforn, who had more hair and less flesh then.

Thankfully, the main courses were brought, and along with them an end to the dances. Bryan deposited the queen next to William with a formal bow. Anna sighed with contentment then turned to William.

"Why did you not wish to dance?" she said. "Every time I looked your way you were either talking with Cecile or frowning into your cup."

He harrumphed.

"So I am still *persona non grata*. I had thought the rose an olive branch—"

"You'll excuse me, my queen. I seem to have lost my appetite." He stood without looking at her and stalked off in search of anyone or anything that could bring him back to his right mind.

What on earth was the matter with the king? What had she said? He was all smiles and flowers and toasts, then suddenly storming out of a formal feast. Certainly they'd fought like wolves earlier and she'd been afraid to even show her face this night, but when she saw Cate in his arms, his smile soft, kissing her round cheek, the tightness in her chest melted away. Then he danced with Margaux, eschewing Anna, and then avoided her altogether.

Crestfallen, she picked at her meat, even though her growing heir demanded she eat the entire boar. Thankfully, both Robert and Daniel were occupied elsewhere and didn't sit in their usual seats next to her and the king. She worried she'd strangle one and knife the other if they came too close. So she nibbled and made small talk with Duven and Halforn, counting the minutes until she could justify retiring.

No sooner had the plates been cleared than Daniel appeared at her elbow.

"Majesty, I beg your apology." He spat it out, like Cate when she knew she was in trouble. "I have forgotten my station, my place, forgotten my own mind. I have behaved foolishly, and worse, unkindly, when I know we both, as you have oft reminded me, desire the same thing. I cannot say what came over me, but I can say whatever disease of the mind it was, 'tis well and truly done."

"Oh, Your Grace." Her smile was tired. "I'm sure Mary has something for that."

He laughed and took Duven's vacated seat at her side. "Truly, Highness, I've been dreadful with it all day, nay, for weeks since we fought before. I—" He shook his head. "I've been so afraid for him, for the country, and I thought I could do it all on my own, that I was smart enough to outsmart all the other foxes. And look where my pomposity got us."

"Your Grace, you are the least to be sorry for the lot we're in."

"Ah, but I see not all is mended, for the king is left and surely it is because of my grievous behavior."

She collapsed in her chair. "'Tis something I have done. Again."

He chuckled. "Let us not fight over who the king is most angered at."

She shook her head. "You're right. But these days, I can't help but think—" He appeared so earnest, so guileless. She remembered how, for so long, he had been nothing but confidant and friend. It was only these ugly wars that had made them squabble. And perhaps he might have some insight into the king that she did not. "To be truthful, I fear his affection wanes."

Daniel pulled back his chin in astonishment, making him look like a long-necked heron. "Don't think it, Majesty. He would not be so pained when you disagree if his affection were decreased."

"Come now, he loathed his brother with much passion and no love."

"But his brother was a horrid man. Responsible for both his sister's and mother's deaths by negligence at the very least, if not outright duplicity."

"My point exactly." She lolled her head away from him. "He can be angered by those he does not love."

"Yet do you not think there was some . . . disappointment there? That his brother should have been a better man, and that undergirded his anger?"

"So, you would argue if he were not so committed to family honor, his brother and father would no longer haunt him?"

Daniel shrugged contemplated his nails. "I think things that may appear to be hateful on the outside are often done out of love." He looked at her, his smile beatific, but his eyes—something in them made Anna wish to weep.

"Ah, Norwick." William sat at his desk in his chambers, before council. His cousin stormed in, red to the tip of his ears, sword jangling in its sheath, snorting like a boar. William knew he'd heard the news, though William had wanted to be the one to tell it. "And here I thought you would be pleased. You now have control of nearly half the country in all but name."

"You still think I'll betray you." Robert didn't move, just watched William as if he could smite him with his eyes. "You believe the poison your wife pours out about me."

William jolted. "Leave her out of this, cuz."

"Why should I when she won't leave me out of this?" Robert grunted. "I suppose she convinced you too that my Rob was Satan's spawn and unfit for her daughter?"

"A betrothal between the princess and Rob gains nothing for the crown," William said, matching Robert's stance. "The state of our international affairs are too precarious to promise her—"

"So I get the privilege of spreading my already strained men thin to flank the border, with no bonus in it for me, for my son? What of his inheritance?"

"*His* inheritance? And what of Cate's? She is to be completely disregarded because she is female?"

"That smacks of the queen's defense." Robert rolled his eyes.

"I told you to leave her *out of it!*" William slammed his fist on the desk. "Here I hand you near complete control over the whole of the north and you are whining to me that your son did not get a princess to boot? Will you never be satisfied?"

"Not when you don't listen to reason, not when you allow others to manipulate you to their own ends."

"You mean against *your* ends." William came around the desk, stopping at the edge of the short stairs, towering above his cousin. "As much as you are loath to believe it, I came to these conclusions of my own accord, Robert—not the queen, not Cecile—me! When will you recognize that it's my word and no one else's that is law?"

Robert jutted his chin. "When you start acting like your own man and not their shill."

"Leave my sight." William nodded to the doors, his voice frighteningly steady. "And be glad if I do not rescind Beaubourg for your thanklessness."

Robert opened his mouth then shut it. He raked William with his eyes then flicked his thumb under his front teeth and left.

William paced, mentally reviewing the conversation. Why was Robert so angry? It was his damned suggestion in the first place. Certainly, the king had allowed only agency and not regency, but that was semantics when it came to actual implementation. And William still hadn't seen the queen since leaving the table like a child the previous evening, wishing to avoid swallowing his pride yet again. What was the matter with all of his most beloved? The September winds blew bluster with them to be sure.

The only fix for this was seeing Catherine. Her smiles and pets would soothe. He made for his jacket and the door, but upon hearing a creak from his private hall, he stopped.

"Majesty," Anna said with a curtsy.

"Have you come to lambast me as well?"

She screwed up her face in confusion. "No, I—I just wanted to thank you."

He sighed, sinking in his leather chair. "Well, now those are words I haven't heard from anyone in quite some time."

She approached cautiously. "I want to thank you for not allowing the betrothal."

"Well, a fat lot of good it's done me." He scratched his stubble.

"I know you didn't do it for me, but I'm grateful regardless."

He beheld her, copious belly, simple day dress, hair pulled back in a gold threaded net. She'd come to end their feuds and he was being peevish. He patted his chair arm, beckoning her. She settled herself carefully, back straight, no part of her touching him. He brought his hand to her waist.

"'Tis not true, really." He smiled ruefully. "I did do it for you. Besides, deciding Cate's destiny so early, and just to appease Norwick, was not an intelligent or strategic decision. And I knew it would wound you. It seems I've been doing too much of that lately."

She scrutinized him. "And I too." She rested her hand on his shoulder. "Whatever happened last night?"

"I was being ridiculous is what happened last night."

"About?"

"Honestly?"

"'Tis generally the best course."

He couldn't look at her. "You and Sir Bryan. So glad in each other's company."

She chortled. "Surely you're well past any jealousy over *him?*"

He took her hand and kissed it, finally daring to meet her eyes. "It was more jealousy for the easy way you had together. I long for that for us again."

"We can have it back, Wills. We just need to . . ." She shook her head, undecided.

"We need to return to the sanctuary we created together. The time when you and I are Anna and Wills, not queen and king—what did you call me? King William the Sound?"

Her smile was wide. "King William the Just. As you still are, my liege." She cupped his chin. "I admit Bryan does stir up memories of uncomplicated times. He's an uncomplicated man."

"And I'm complicated?" He peered at her, almost sheepish.

She laughed. "Oh, you're singular. And engrossing and witty and . . . mature."

"You mean I'm old?"

"Good heavens, man, I'm complimenting you." She laughed. "I mean Bryan is boyish, like a loyal pup bounding about, desperate to play. You—you're . . ." She swung her arm over him as if presenting him to court. "You're captivating, assured. Almost fearsome in your regality, like a stag or a lion."

"So I make you tremble?" He was grinning now, sliding the backs of his fingers up her torso.

She bit her lip, nodded, but then halted his caresses. "Despite my desire for you, you know we must fix this." She fanned her hand between them. "And not just with bed sport."

"It's a damn—"

"Good place to start, I know." She smiled back at him. "But if we ignore the hurt in our hearts after lust is fulfilled, even our lovemaking will be soured."

He stroked her arm. "True enough. So how do we heal the wounds we've dealt each other?"

She climbed into his lap and kissed him softly. "With faith, hope, and love."

CHAPTER 13

Haunted Man

Despite their efforts to start anew, as September slipped into October, William still felt a barrier between him and Anna. The war had changed them both, made them more cautious, more prone to pessimism. It used to be that when one of them was in a foul mood, the other would uplift the first. Now they seemed to sink into foulness together. They hadn't fought since Michaelmas, but neither had they returned to their easy ways. William couldn't help but think she was keeping something from him. Something that niggled at her, distracted her, kept her from truly relaxing with him.

Or maybe he was the culprit. Maybe it was his constant worry that with the loss of Laureland, his court and his country had lost confidence in him. Maybe he was the one unable to let loose because he feared being caught off guard again.

He stood on the balcony overlooking the gardens, watching her on this rare sunny day. The air was crisp with an occasional stiff breeze, but with her lying in only weeks away, he knew she couldn't resist such a day of freedom. Sir Bryan was still at court, staying until after All Hallows, and he ambled along, flirting with the ladies, Margaux sulking behind. Anna had one arm tucked through Mary's, the other swinging Cate's hand. The queen and her nurse shared some private joy, faces reddened by the wind, smiles visible even at this distance. Suddenly, Anna stopped and put her hand to her belly. She grabbed Cate's hand and plastered it to her navel. Cate's brow furrowed, then startled as Mary and Anna laughed. Cate bounced on her heels, gesticulating excitedly. Anna placed the princess's hand again. Cate waited, then put her whole cheek to Anna's belly. With a jolt, she pulled away and giggled.

William chuckled to himself, wistful. He and the queen hadn't been able to soak in this pregnancy. The distance between them meant little time to laze about in bed and feel for baby kicks.

Cate said something to her mother then kissed Anna's belly, giving it a pat. All the ladies clapped and the stroll continued. Bryan ran up behind Cate and swung her in the air. He could tell by the tilt of Anna's head she was gently scolding her friend. Bryan set the princess down and took Cate's other hand. William frowned at the domestic scene. It should be him out there swinging his daughter, laughing with his wife, but here he

was stuck with mounds of paperwork and interminable meetings. He made sure his guards weren't watching and blew his
oblivious ladies a kiss.

He dragged back to his chambers, counting again the number of days before Anna's seclusion. Twenty-three. He would
carve out some time for them to treasure being together.

William, still pondering, found Daniel waiting by his desk,
hands behind his back, sun from the window brightening his
hair all the more.

"Why, you're nearly an hour early, Cecile." William strode to
the desk, but the look on Daniel's face stilled him. Not since his
sister's death had he seen his friend this grim. William grabbed
Daniel's arms.

Daniel blinked twice. "I am afraid I have troubling news."

William widened his stance, ready for the blow, whatever it
was. "More invasion?"

Daniel shook his head again. "I—I beg your pardon, sire. I've
been standing here trying to think how best to say it, yet I still
don't know how."

William willed himself to breathe slowly. He wouldn't lose
his temper, he would listen to what his friend had to say and
make a decision. He would be calm.

"'Tis the queen."

"What about her?" Calm.

Daniel winced, turning bodily from William, addressing the
far wall. "The queen, she . . . of course, one cannot be one-
hundred percent certain, but everything does indicate—"

"Spit it out!"

"It is possible the babe she carries is Sir Bryan of Beaubourg's."

He let out a mirthless guffaw, barely comprehending Daniel's statement. "Is this some sort of twisted joke?"

"Dear God how I wish it were, Wills." Daniel turned back to the king, face contorted. "But I've been investigating through my channels quietly for some time now, ever since the ill-advised flirtations of Raleigh and—"

"This is complete and utter nonsense, do you hear me?" William rounded the desk, fisted Daniel's jacket. "You are better than to believe court gossip. Every time Margaux is pregnant, I am the father, and every time the queen is, Bryan is the father. Since when did you start lowering yourself to such vermin?"

"From what I gather, it was not deliberate, Majesty." Daniel spoke quickly, as if the king would lob off his head before he could finish. "She was surely wounded in spirit at the loss of her father, you were far away at war, possibly dead as well. He took advantage of the situation—"

"What are you even talking about? All this bizarre conjecture!" He released his friend and laughed again, a worm of doubt burrowing into his mind. *Bryan was such a comfort to her at her father's passing . . .* "I'm sorry, Daniel, I just don't believe it. She would never betray me thus."

"I'm—I'm so sorry. I would never have believed it myself if it weren't for Raleigh and—"

"Don't speak his name to me."

"Majesty—"

"Someone is setting this up—Robert, his sister." William unconsciously jiggled his leg, staring flint at his friend. "Westerville from the very grave."

"I wish—"

"You must have some *proof*, surely. Not just your imaginings. If such a feat were even possible there would be witnesses."

"It was actually me, sire. I was witness."

William felt this punch to his guts. "Good God, Cecile," he sat again, head in his hands. "Why would you wait so long to, even . . .?"

"I could not finally confirm it until after the knight returned to court. But what I saw after the duke's funeral . . ." The king moaned. After her father's funeral? She had more dignity than that. "I was walking the grounds, unable to sleep, and I heard the queen in the stable—"

"In a Goddamned stable?" He chortled. It was as if he were hearing about someone else, in some other place, not his wife. "And how do you know it was the queen and not some rutting stable hand?"

"I saw her. There and later, cloaked and entering her chamber."

"She could have been visiting the princess, wandering the grounds as you were, or any number of other things."

"I thought this as well." Daniel walked to the edge of the stairs, meeting the king's gaze. "But I heard them beforehand, outside the stable, laughing and sharing tales . . . and later, I saw Sir Bryan on the upper floors, outside the queen's chambers."

"Surely you have misinterpreted things. Filling in blanks with poison from Norwick. He's twisted this all in your mind— he excels at that. He's threatened by my heir, angry about Beaubourg, the betrothal. He's trying to harm me the only way he thinks he can."

"I don't think—"

"I don't give a damn what you think." William pushed out of his seat. "Guards! The Duke of Norwick. Make haste."

William observed Daniel while they waited, but the man didn't seem agitated, only sad. Soon Robert came bouncing in, jaunty grin on his face wiped clean as he saw the scene.

"What's happened?"

William was upon him in three strides, hand on his neck, shoving him to the wall. "What have I ever done that you would treat me thus?"

Robert's eyes were wild, hands grabbing at the king's.

"Sire, he had nothing to do with it." Daniel's voice was unnaturally high. William's hand grew tighter, Roberts face redder. "You don't know that, Cecile. Somehow this is his doing, him or his devil of a sister."

Robert's look of fear and confusion had William releasing his cousin without a word.

"If I may," Robert said after a cough. "What exactly am I being accused of now?"

William spun around. "Cecile claims the queen has been unfaithful." Robert's face turned the color of stone, hands stilled in straightening his jacket. "He believes the child she carries may be none other than Sir Bryan of Beaubourg's."

Robert laughed. "She'd never be so bold—"

"So you claim you know nothing of this, this foolery?" William got back in Robert's face.

"How could I? 'Tis no secret I've never taken to the queen, but that I would partake of dealing you ill . . ." They were inches apart. "Wills . . ."

William turned from him, face flush.

"Besides, what would it gain me?"

"The throne for one. Oh, scoff not, next in line. You know very well what rides on this pregnancy."

"Your wife, sire, may or may not be loyal, but do not throw me to the dogs so you don't have to accuse her."

The king turned to Daniel. "I want you to question Countess Mohrlang. Rigorously."

"My sister is not so idiotic as to—" The look on William's face stopped Robert.

"And then Lady Yvette. And the rest of the queen's ladies as well. And keep them separate from each other while these interviews are conducted."

Daniel nodded. "I planned to, but I felt I needed to bring this to your attention before things . . . went too far."

"Too far? Do you accuse her of continuing this farce?"

"I only meant, if the babe . . ."

"Were blonde," Robert finished. William could have sworn he saw his cousin's brow twitch upwards.

William charged him again. "You little—"

"Sire?" Daniel raised his voice. "Unfortunately, there is the matter of the law."

William stood feet from Robert, seething. "What law?" He bit off the words, drilling his eyes into his cousin.

"The one about pregnant queens," Robert said, squinting back ire. "The one James passed after Minerva birthed him a bastard."

William snorted. "The one where-in if a pregnant queen is accused of infidelity she's sent to the Yard immediately so as not to hinder further investigation? It's ludicrous."

"It was made for the protection of both parties," Daniel said, eyes to the ground.

"I'm not going to jail my wife on such feeble—"

"I'm so sorry, William," Daniel said, voice cracking in true concern. "But we must."

He shook his head, pacing again, chin in hand. She couldn't pretend, put on an act, lie to his face like this . . . But hadn't he thought she'd been keeping something from him? Hadn't they struggled to find further connection since Bryan returned to court? And Bryan, finding reasons to be in the queen's presence . . . their sniggering at the feast, was it at William's expense?

No. It simply couldn't be. Not Anna. He pulled at his hair, anguish marring his face his intestines like coiling snakes. He must see her, look her in the eyes. Then he would know. And he would feel a fool for doubting her for even one second. Without a word, he walked down their private hall, fully expecting her to be back in her rooms. Shooting out the other side, he found her bedchamber empty. Catching movement out the south window, he opened it to holler for her, dignity be damned. But the picture he saw stopped his voice.

She was walking, Mary and Bryan flanking her, the knave looking at the grass as she spoke to him. He threw something for a dog to chase. Mary and Anna laughed at something. William squinted his eyes to better see, heart pounding, nerves alert.

The group stopped, Anna smiled and said something to Bryan. Then, with blushing smile still on her face, Bryan reached out his bold, wide hand to spread over her belly. She gazed at the man with such fondness. Then Bryan startled and laughed as Cate had earlier. William felt he would vomit.

Why would Anna allow any man, let alone Bryan, to touch her so intimately, and in public view? Unless he had some claim . . . the whole of William went cold, as if plunged into the north Orlea, frozen, watching them, his faith withering away like autumn leaves. Daniel would not lightly accuse. Robert would, but not Daniel. And until this moment, William would have sworn on his life Anna wouldn't betray him thus.

She glanced up and saw him. Her face lit like the sun and she waved with both arms.

"My love!" she called. "Come join us!" Bryan looked smug as a cat that had swallowed a mouse. As she came closer, the joy on her face turned to concern. "My liege? Whatever is the matter?"

He could take no more. He slammed the window and stalked back to his rooms.

"Take her and Bryan to Stone Yard," he said. "You can question them there as befits the law."

"I am so very sorry, Highness," Daniel hung his head.

"Leave me."

His voice was surprisingly steady considering his whole body felt ripped asunder. When the last person had left, he fell to his knees, an animal sound escaping from deep within, sobs overtaking him.

"My Anna," he whispered. "How could you?"

Anna returned to her rooms immediately, William's face haunting her steps. She knew it had nothing to do with Cate, thankfully, but perhaps there was more talk of war, perhaps he had to ride out again in haste. She couldn't bear to think of birth-ing their child with him in harm's way. She entrusted Cate to Cariline and hurried with the rest of her ladies. Robert met them in the hall, whispered something to Yvette, then uncer-emoniously grabbed his sister's arm. He hustled the two women away without even an attempt at permission. Dear Lord in heaven, was he taking them to some safe shelter? Was it plague? She picked up her skirts with one hand and the other held her belly, moving as quickly as her ballooning body would allow.

Rounding the corner to her chambers a fleet of guards stood in front of her closed doors. It must be sickness. She must get to William. She made to turn, but the head of the royal guard called to her.

"Begging your pardon, Highness, but you must come with me."

"What is this? Why? Is it the king? Is he ill?"

The guard stared above her head. "'Tis His Majesty's wish that you come with me."

She turned wide eyes to Mary, who frowned at the men. "Of course, if His Majesty believes it to be the best course of action. Let me first get—"

"My apologies, Highness, but you may not enter your cham-bers."

"Why ever not? Are they contaminated in some way?"

"Please." There was sadness in his eyes, pleading, anxiety. "Please come with me now, Madam."

Anna nodded, heart in her throat. She clung to Mary, the rest of her ladies as well looking flustered and frightened. They huddled, allowing the well-armed men to surround them.

"Where are we going, sir?" Anna asked as the guard led them through the throne room.

"I am under orders, Madam." They were taking back ways, skirting the Great Hall.

"That does not answer my question."

"I know."

"Since when is it your right to refuse a question of your queen?" They were out in the stable yard now, heading east.

"Since the king commands it."

"Stubborn man," she muttered. "When will the king realize that keeping me ignorant only makes me the more nervous?"

"He doesn't like t' scare ye," Mary said, nestling closer to Anna. "'Specially in light of the babe."

They stopped in front of the great wooden door of Stone Yard, the wizened and knobby jailer standing, arms crossed, to the side. The guard nodded and the jailer unlocked the door, swinging it on screeching hinges.

"Here?" Anna said, bemused. "The king wants us to shelter in the Yard?"

None of the guards nor the jailer would meet her gaze.

"If you would follow me, Highness," the jailer said, polite as you please. He scuttled to the stairs and hoisted himself onto the first step, using the rope strapped to the wall as a railing. The stairwell was only wide enough for one, so the confused and disgusted line of ladies trundled up behind him, two of the king's guards following.

"If it's the plague, or any other such, being holed up in this dank, dripping place will only hasten the disease." Anna used a hand on the curving wall to steady herself. She touched something slimy. Brigitte gave a scream that echoed up and down the tower, scaring birds roosting in the eaves.

Anna's hand flew to her heart. "My Lady, what is it?"

"A-a spider! Big as my hand!"

Anna couldn't tell if it was a trick of the dim light that made Brigitte's face look green. Who could blame her after that nasty bite some years back?

"Carry on," Anna called to the jailer.

They had to pause and rest multiple times, the spiraling stairs seeming to extend to the stars, but at last they reached a door at the top.

"I apologize for the climb," the jailer said, "but we couldn't very well keep you with the riffraff."

"I suppose so." Anna frowned as he opened the door. The cell was larger than she thought it would be, fitting a bed, desk, even a settee. Faded tapestries hung on the walls and a merry fire crackled in the sizable hearth. There were two fresh pallets on the floor, and the small bed was unmade.

"We hadn't time t' change out the mattresses, Highness, begging your pardon, but someone should be here soon." He gestured to the room at large. "At least we got the fire a-going."

"Thank you, sir—I'm sure all will be well in this trying time." Anna nodded. "But I only see two pallets. Where are the rest of my ladies to bed? Surely not in some other . . . cell." She shivered despite the warmth.

"Begging your pardon again, Highness, but I was told three ladies were to attend thee."

"Three?" Anna felt sick. Surely the king wouldn't be so

callous as to allow her ladies exposure to whatever evil befell the palace. The jailer nodded. "But how are they to be kept safe?"

"Safe, Highness?" He peered at her from under his bushy white brows.

"Yes, from the sickness or attack or whatever is happening at the palace?" Her ladies drew closer to her, as if in a mass they couldn't be taken away.

"There's no sickness, no attack." He gave her a blank look.

"Then why ever are we here?"

The jailer looked incredulously at the king's guards, then scoured the face of each lady, finally landing on the queen.

"Why, don't My Lady know why she's here?"

"I was simply told I must follow these guards, as the king wished it." Her heart pounded. "And if there is something unsafe at the palace, where is the princess?"

The man shook his head, slowly. He parted his hands, keys jangling on a ring. "I suppose it be my duty to tell ye this, Highness . . ." He didn't look at her.

"Tell me what."

"You're accused of treason."

A shriek was all she remembered before she fainted.

"Did you have anything to do with this?" Robert eyed his sister across his desk, noting every blink, every flick, every swallow. "Tell me truthfully now, for 'tis not just *your* neck on the line."

"I am just as surprised as you pretend to be," Margaux said, examining him back.

"That didn't answer my question." Robert sat forward.

"I am not the one bringing about this end." Margaux frowned at him.

"It's not at an end, not nearly so." He leaned back, still watching her.

"What I don't understand," Margaux said, "is why the king's perfect pet would accuse her. That certainly makes it sound as though it's true."

Yvette uncurled herself from a chair by the fire and walked to the sideboard, refilling her wine.

"You have been more taciturn than usual, my dear," he said to her.

"I don't believe any of it," Yvette said, her voice ice.

"It doesn't really matter if we believe it, it just matters if the accusation holds," Margaux said.

"You're a wicked woman." Yvette narrowed her eyes at Margaux.

"You know I didn't mean it like that—"

"Do I? By all accounts you've done nothing but try to damage the queen with your devious and vile schemes."

"Are you going to let her speak to me like that?" Margaux put her hands on her hips, scowling at Robert.

Robert laughed. "Yes, for she is being all too kind."

"You can both go to hell." Margaux rose, pressing back her hood.

"Right along with you, Sister."

She harrumphed and left his chambers. Robert sighed. He pushed out of his chair and sauntered to Yvette, who sat staring into the fire. He drew a finger up her cheek and twined it in her hair.

"And what did Grand Inquisitor Daniel ask of you?"

"What I'd seen, heard, where I was." She jerked her head around, peering up at him. "I was with her the entire time. If anyone was sleeping with anyone it was Margaux with Bryan."

"And is that what you told Daniel?"

She looked back into the fire. "Robert, it's a lie. And I told him as much."

"But is it really so terrible?" She stiffened beneath his touch. "With the queen out of the way and the heir declared a bastard, the throne is within our grasp, without harming a hair on William's body."

"You say without harm?" She shook off his hands and left her perch. "Your friend, as you call him, will be devastated, never to be the same again, never to trust again. And what becomes of the queen and babe? Dead like Minerva?"

"He wouldn't kill her, he'd send her to a convent." Robert didn't understand where all this anger of hers was coming from.

"Did you set this up, Robert?" Her deep, dark eyes filled with a sorrow he'd rarely seen there. "She's kept you from ruling Beaubourg outright, kept Rob from marrying the princess . . . you've every right to be sore, but this? I know you loathe her, but she is a good person. And the king loves her."

He stared at her, unmoving. "How could I have set it up? I was at war, by the king's side if you remember."

Her smile was melancholy. "That didn't answer my question."

"I didn't do this! And it pains me to think you would think it of me."

"You were the one wanting me to get her in bed with Raleigh." She followed him back to his desk.

He waved a dismissing hand. "That's not what pains me. I'm the devil clean through. What pains me is you think I'd execute a scheme—especially involving the queen—without your involvement and knowledge, or consent."

She laughed, hollow. "That's all that pains you?"

He gave her a rueful smile. "Well, my dear, if even you paint me as the guilty party, though you know I am not, yes, that would pain me above anyone else's accusations, for I am a selfish man."

"And that's what pains me," she said, and left him even more confused and shaken than he'd been in the king's chambers.

"Treason!" Anna paced the small room like a stalking tiger. Mary, Amelia, and Brigitte were all that were left to her, though the jailer had said the ladies would be allowed rotation. Just what she wanted, to be imprisoned on a rotating basis with Margaux. "Adultery? Me? Me!"

Mary shook her head for the thousandth time. "This is all just a misunderstanding. The king's just got t' follow the law. It'll all be swept away by the morn, mark my words."

After Anna had come to, the jailer had explained King James's law.

"But the king *is* the law! If he believes the claims to be absurd—as he surely does and as they are—he can simply change the law."

"What if he doesn't think they're absurd?" Brigitte said from the settee, looking innocent as a butterfly.

"Oh be quiet, Brigitte!" Anna wanted to strangle her. "This is probably something you and your detestable countess cooked up. And I'll see you both hang for it!"

"Dearie, don't be taking it out on the girl," Mary said, lower lip sticking out in a deep frown.

"I've been accused of cuckolding the king, Mary, with whom God only knows and by whom, the devil—and I know it's a Norwick! And you wish me to be kind and retiring?" Mary clucked her tongue but otherwise stayed quiet. "If I could speak to him, this would all be put to rest. And yet here I stand, while Margaux goes flitting about, crowing of her triumph, probably trying to wheedle her way into his bed as we speak!"

"Don't make it worse than it is," Mary said.

Anna went to the tiny window and spied a sliver of her own darkened chambers. How many times had she watched a candle flickering in this very window, wondering about Bryan, about Helena? Anna stared at the palace, willing the king to appear, sending him her heartbreak, her bewilderment. He couldn't possibly believe such nonsense.

"How anyone could take such accusations seriously is ludicrous."

"I heartily agree," Mary said. "And so, surely, does the king."

"You're right, Mary." She tried to shake away the fear coiling at the base of her spine. She strode to the desk and grabbed a fresh quill. "And I shall write to him now so I may be back in my chambers by breakfast."

Daniel interrupted the king at breakfast, which was no matter, for William couldn't eat. Or sleep. Since Anna had been taken he felt nauseated. Yes, the law demanded she be held, but his temper had cooled by nightfall and it all seemed wrong. Daniel must be mistaken in his observations. And certainly this law could be changed. William would get to the bottom of all of by noon. That belief was the only thing keeping him functioning.

Daniel bowed and William took a letter Daniel wordlessly offered, willing his hands not to tremble.

> *It is beyond belief, husband, that you would countenance such vile accusations against me. Even if it be the law, why must it be followed when you know the claims to be false? Undoubtedly the slippery intrigues of crafty tongues who would have me and my opinions kept from your good graces demand my captivity. Who says these despicable things of me? How and when would I have achieved such illicitness? I do not know how such a bad opinion has been formed of me. A thousand eyes see all I do, from even the walls themselves. How you could hold to even a thimble of it as truth shatters my heart. Tell me you've thrown these scoundrels to the dust,*

*that we may return together in peace. Damn the laws. You
are the king. You know the truth in your heart.*

Your constant wife,

~A

"I'm sorry, Majesty." Daniel hung his head, glum. "I wish it
were better news."

"Better news?" A smile tugged at William's mouth, his heart
lightening. "Why, this letter shows me she's innocent. She's
incensed, appalled." He could almost see her, big brown eyes
wild with indignation. "Whatever you thought you saw and
heard, Daniel, it's been misconstrued. After all, it may have been
another woman you saw." He clapped a hand on Daniel's shoulder, relief blazing through his body like warmed wine. How had
he mistrusted her? Even in a moment of raging? The doggedly
diligent Daniel could slip up once in a while. She would be back
in his bed this night and, while it would certainly not be forgotten, at least they could put this behind them.

Daniel shifted his feet and glanced at William's happy face.
He didn't return William's smile.

"Begging pardon, Majesty—may I read the letter once more?"

"Of course." William handed it over. "This calls for a drink.
Robert? Mead or wine my friend?"

"Wine. Red." Robert stood studying Daniel, one black brow
raised.

"Majesty," Daniel said, "I fear . . . how do I put this?" He was
almost musing to himself.

"You haven't had much trouble putting it out, lately," Robert said.

Daniel looked to Robert, as if it were easier to speak to him than to William.

"She doesn't deny it. Nowhere does she say it is false."

William grabbed the letter. He scanned it again with hungry eyes.

"Of course she does! She's, she's outraged even at the thought!"

"Majesty." Daniel had that insufferable patient tone in his voice. "Of course she's outraged. She has been caught red-handed."

"Give it here," Robert said, snatching the letter from the king and reading it. "I would say she's implying her innocence by being so, well, counter accusatory."

"Exactly," William said, taking the letter from Robert and pointing at the evidential sentence. "Even if it be the law, why must it be followed when *you know the claims to be false?* You see—there, right there!"

"She says *you* know the claims to be false." Daniel pursed his lips, voice growing quieter, as if he feared the harm his words would render. "She does not say 'these claims are false.'"

"Pshaw." William's heart beat as if to leap from his chest. "I will go to her myself. I will look in her eyes and put this all to rest." He headed straight for his wardrobe and almost tore the door off in search of his cloak.

"Majesty, that is unadvisable, she's sure to—"

William turned and had Daniel by the collar before anyone took another breath.

"You're talking about my wife—the mother of my children, the queen of our people. I will not jail her on hearsay and conjecture, or the clever bending of words and intentions. You must give me proof, *real* proof Daniel, not your extrapolations, or I go this minute and release her. And you from your duties."

Daniel's eyes grew, their blue nearly startled to white. His mouth hung open like a fish. The man swallowed, his Adam's apple bobbing down then up in his ghostly pale throat. William could snap Daniel's neck right here. Right now. And make all of this stop. . . William loosened his grip, Daniel slumped against the wall.

"I didn't want to have to do this," Daniel said to the floor. "I have proof. Incontrovertible proof. But I . . ."

"Well produce it!" William waved his arm as if this proof would magically appear.

"It involves a dear soul, who fears for her safety and that of her child."

"She should fear her safety should she not come forward." William clenched his jaw, barely able to stand the fraying of his nerves. "Fetch her. Now."

"Yes, Majesty." Daniel bowed and shuffled out.

"Shall I attend with—"

"You stay, cuz," William said, throwing Robert a look of death. "I wouldn't want you meddling with our so-called proof."

"So you don't believe it?" Robert sank into William's desk chair, brows furrowed. William considered him, saw a man deep in thought, a man just as flummoxed as he was, and William's temper melted slightly.

"Honestly?" William sighed. He picked up Anna's discarded

letter. "I would never believe it of her, but Daniel seems so convinced, so sure. He wouldn't tell me something so preposterous if it he didn't think it true. I think . . . I think Daniel misread something . . . somehow."

"Why don't you just go to her?"

He sighed again, heart aching, mind's eye seeing her laughing in the garden, Bryan's hand on her belly. He ran his own hand over his face.

"I will." He picked up a glass of wine. "After Daniel gets back with this bribed washerwoman or what have you."

William paced before the fire as the two men fell into tense silence. They didn't wait long. Daniel was soon back, a guard announcing him with a quietly weeping woman on his arm. But this was no washerwoman, no kitchen wench. It was Lady Jane. Anna's favorite.

William moved to them, worry etched in his brows.

"My lady, why are you not with the queen?"

Jane shook her head, avoiding William's face.

"Majesty," Daniel said, "you asked me for proof. The Lady Jane will furnish you with it."

William could do nothing but blink down at the cowering lady in her court finery.

"Tell him," Daniel said, pleasant, "tell His Majesty."

"Please, Your Grace . . ." She trembled, but Daniel squeezed her hand.

"I will keep you safe," he said, cloyingly sweet.

She took in a shaky breath. "I-I saw them, Highness," she mumbled to the floor. "The queen and Sir Bryan. Together in Beaubourg."

William felt the room keen to the left. He thrust out a hand to steady himself, but gained no purchase.

"Together *how*." Daniel was smiling encouragement, but his eyes were focused, certain.

"M-m-must I?" Jane managed.

Daniel put an arm around her shoulder. "Take your time, milady. No harm will come to you for speaking the truth."

Lady Jane stopped weeping and gave Daniel a look of horror. She shrank out of his arms and fell to the king's feet.

"Have mercy on me, Highness," she said, pleading at William's own unsteady knees, "I saw them . . . intimate."

"How many times, milady?" Daniel prompted, impatient despite his soothing tone.

"T-twice. Two times." She looked up as if remembering. "Once in the stable. Once in the closet room next to her chamber." She shuddered and looked to the floor again.

The same places Daniel had spoken of. All blood surely left William's body.

"Who's paying you?" William grabbed her arms, his wrath spitting in her face. "Hmm? Who? Why! Because these are damn lies." Her face contorted, she looked to Daniel for help. "Don't look at him, look at me. Who's telling you to say these things?" She shook her head then looked at Robert with desperate eyes.

"Majesty," Daniel said, gesturing to Jane, "she's no reason to lie. She is one of the queen's most trusted ladies."

"I'm aware of that." William released her and frowned down at her crumpled form. "And as such, she is all the more in danger of being exploited."

"That may be," Daniel said, calm, "but she came to me of her own volition. And as it matches with my own observations, I cannot see how someone could manipulate her."

William glanced at Robert, who stood scowling at the whole scene.

"Who else did you tell?" William rounded on the quivering Jane.

"No one, sire."

"You're positive?" He crouched in front of her, trying to sound kind. "It didn't slip to a servant, to another lady-in-waiting?"

She gave Daniel a furtive glance.

"I was too afraid, Majesty."

"Then why did you tell Cecile?" She remained silent, eyes to the ground. "Lady Jane, if someone is controlling you, that person will be dealt with. But surely you do not wish your queen to be punished."

She jerked up her head and caught his eyes for an instant before breaking into fresh sobs.

"Highness," Daniel said, "she came to me because she could not stand to live with the knowledge any longer. She feared she would somehow be punished—she was afraid for her son. But as the queen's womb grew, she could no longer stay silent. She is loyal to you, to Troixden, despite her fear of the queen. I told her we would protect her. Protect her son."

William swallowed, only partly absorbing what Daniel said. "Fear the queen? When has anyone had cause to fear the queen?"

Daniel shrugged.

"Is this true, Lady Jane? The queen, Sir Bryan? All of it?" He couldn't help the choking sound in his voice.

Her only reply was a nod.

It took Robert a few stunned moments to follow the raging king out of his chambers, catching up to him halfway across the throne room.

"Wills, where are you going?" He grabbed at the king's shoulder to slow him down. The last time he'd seen William this angry was when William's sister had died. He had torn into the throne room, hurling vitriol and violence at his brother, then the freshly crowned king. It landed William in the dungeon for a week and caused his banishment until James died. Wherever William was headed, whatever he wanted to do, Robert knew no good could come of it.

The king shook Robert off his shoulder and kept moving.

"I've no need of company, cuz."

"You can't see her like this. You'll regret—"

William stopped abruptly, seizing Robert's arms.

"I'm not the one who should sow regret."

As much as Robert loathed the queen, he felt pity for the woman on the receiving end of those eyes.

The king turned again, hustling down the enclosed hall that ran along the outer rim of the palace, leading to the side entrance by the stables. He threw open the doors, startling languid guards, and proceeded across the keep, heading straight for Stone Yard.

Robert looked up at the tower through the whipping rain and saw light flickering above. He would be surprised if its occupant was still alive by morning.

William yelled at the guards to open the doors and they jumped to do his bidding, hands fumbling in the slick cold. William barged in, grabbed the first torch he saw, and turned to the bug-eyed men.

"Where is he?" The king's voice echoed off the narrow walls, making him sound like God in the whirlwind.

The jailer nodded then beckoned the king to follow, keys clanging with his leisurely pace. William's shoulders were set like a mountain ridge, tense, huge, ready to crush. The party came to the main staircase and instead of heading up, the jailer led them down. Only one thing happened below ground at Stone Yard, and that thing kept young boys wide-eyed at night. It didn't matter how brave you were in battle, how many kills you had in war—every man shuddered at the chambers that slept beneath this prison.

As they went down the spiral steps, a low keening met Robert's ears, like a fox caught in a claw trap. The whimpering intensified as they descended, calling through the staircase like a sorrowful ghost. They halted outside a curved wooden door, light streaming through a barred window only a hand's-breadth wide. The noises inside ceased when the jailer lifted his keys. The king was almost on top of the man, chomping to get inside.

The door swung and William strode inside, Robert and the jailer tumbling after. The ceilings were surprisingly high and arched, like a cathedral's crypt. The main room was a good twenty yards wide with smaller chambers off to the sides on all corners, giving it the feel of an eight-pointed star. In the center of this main room was a large wooden table placed over a drain in the floor. Iron manacles strapped a man's ankles to the table, his feet so bruised and beaten they looked more like clubs.

Robert's eyes trailed to the head of the table to find the contorted face of Sir Bryan, an angry red welt across his cheek, one eye swollen shut, his shirt torn open, revealing whip-like lashes across his muscled chest. There was an acidic smell of urine mingled with blood, sweat, and something sweetly sickening. Like hundreds of daisies slowly molding. Bile rose in Robert's throat.

"High-ness," Bryan managed. He looked relieved to see the king. He started to cough, struggling to bring a chained hand to his mouth. He turned from the king, spitting a mixture of blood and phlegm to the floor.

Robert came closer, staying well behind his enraged friend.

"After all I have done for you." William's voice was dangerously low. "Letting you live in the first place, sending you home a war hero. And how do you repay me?" Bryan's open eye grew wide. William grabbed the lad's hand, twisting at the wrist. Bryan's fingers were puffed and seeping, lacking the fingernails he always maintained so well . Bryan winced but made no sound.

"All lies, my liege!" Bryan moaned. "I would never dishonor her so, never betray your trust. How could you even think it?" He turned his one good eye up to the king.

The king shook his head. "Why do you not simply confess your treachery?" William's shoulders tensed even further, his grip making Bryan's wrist joints crack. "It may give you a swifter death."

"You and your henchmen can threaten until God returns, but I will not confess to the vileness I'm accused of." Bryan coughed again, curling away from the king as best he could.

"This is no idle threat." Robert could hear William's sneer. He closed his eyes. He didn't want to watch this. "Your lack of confession will not save her."

Another moan brought Robert's eyes open. William had released Bryan's hand and was now bending over him, looking every bit the predator over its dying prey. Robert moved toward them. This must stop. Guilty or not, Robert knew William wouldn't be able to live with himself in the morning.

"My liege, if the rack, the cage, and whatever else they've done to him has not loosed his tongue—"

William flicked his eyes to Robert, boiling hatred darkening them. Robert took a step back. This was not his friend. This was a fiend.

"He will confess to me," William said, turning the dominance of those eyes upon his victim. "He will tell me of his sin. Of hers."

Bryan's face wrenched as if William's words had burned him. He opened that one sad, drooping eye and rolled it to meet William's, unafraid.

"If you believe it of her, you do not deserve her."

He spat, bloody spittle missing its mark and landing instead on William's sleeve.

William swung, his knuckles crunching against bone, blood spewing from Bryan's mouth and nose. Robert dodged the deluge. The knave's jaw was undoubtedly broken.

William withdrew a kerchief—a lacy one with A & W entwined

upon it—cleaned the back of his hand, and threw the bloodied
fabric on Bryan's shaking chest.

"That's all you have left of her now," the king said. He turned
to the jailer.

"Bring him close to death. If he does not confess, we draw
and quarter him at week's end."

With that, William left the torture chambers, not bothering
to see if Robert followed.

Something had changed. Anna could feel it in the air. Could
smell it in the wind-whipped hail pelting her cell, pinging against
the metal bars of the glassless windows. Why were there bars this
high up to begin with? The windows weren't wide enough to fit
through, and even if they were, she'd fall to her death. Perhaps
they were there to make a point. To remind those within of
their impending doom.

She sat on the edge of her small bed and looked at her retinue of women, hovering in the far corner, straining their eyes in
the faint light of the few candles they had been allowed, hands
at their needlework, pretending all wasn't ill. She felt the baby
roll inside her, a slow rotation of shoulder or knee.

William hadn't responded to her letter. How absurd this all
was! Obviously someone was taking this slander seriously, as she
could hear the wails of a tortured man floating up through her
windows, up through her very cell floor. But William knew her
better than this. Of all the treachery she might foist upon him,
adultery wasn't even logistically possible, let alone something

she would think to do. When was she alone? Who among her ladies could she trust with such a secret? Even if she paid handsomely? Seeing her fall would be more reward than any gold for the likes of Margaux.

She glanced at her ladies. Only Mary was there to bring her solace. Lady Jane was not among them, nor was Duchess Stefania or even the happy Countess Amelia. She was left with the taciturn Countess Cariline and the giggling Brigitte. Margaux and Yvette were glaringly absent, leading Anna to speculate about who planted the seeds of this unfounded rumor. She would have Robert's head on a platter before this was all over.

She clutched the ruby necklace at her breast. *Wills, use your sense!* She would write another letter. Perhaps he didn't receive the first. Perhaps Robert or Margaux had gotten ahold of it. She strode to the rickety, worm-holed desk, but a thunderous knock on the door stopped her. Thank God he'd come! She pinched her cheeks and smoothed her gown, ready to fall into the king's arms.

Her jailer, a kind man, with soft hazel eyes and white tufts of hair sticking out at all ends, announced her visitor.

"The Duke of Norwick to see Your Highness."

Her heart fell to the floor. Where was her husband? She took a deep breath. Well, at least she could twist Robert's lies in on themselves. With witnesses. The cat comes to the mouse. And discovers the mouse a lion.

"Thank you, good sir. He may enter."

The door swung to a red-faced Robert, dark curls askew, hands twitching at his sides. He hesitated, sized her up, then strode in, black eyes glinting in the candlelight.

"Highness." He gave a curt nod.

It took everything within her not to slap that superior look off his perfect face.

"So, Norwick, you've come to gloat over your temporary success?"

"You too then? I'm the favored scapegoat. But you can't escape this, oh queen."

"Whatever trap you have laid for me, I will not fall into it. I am of clean conscious. The king will believe me above all others." Her eyes matched his fire. "Even above your lies."

He glanced at her silent ladies, their eyes on their work, ears most certainly alert to the man standing in their midst. He took a step toward Anna. She could see his chest rise and fall. His voice was almost a growl.

"It is *your* lies, your treachery that will bring you to your knees. Or has Sir Bryan already done that? Coaxed you to your knees?"

She couldn't stop herself this time. Her hand moved as if of its own will, straight to his face. But Robert was quicker. He had her wrist, stopping it an inch from his cheek.

"Unhand me, you bastard." She was ready to spit. He pulled her closer, her extended belly hitting his trunks, their chests inches apart.

"I'm not the bastard here." He flicked his eyes to her womb.

She wrested her hand free and took another steadying breath. She turned her back on him, heading to her desk. So they thought she'd been with Bryan? *Bryan*, for the love of all that was holy. This got more convoluted as time wore on.

Her gut clenched. "So 'tis Sir Bryan I hear screaming at all hours?"

"You recognize the wails, do you?"

She felt the blood drain from her face, dripping down through her like tar. She finally, fully, understood. They all thought her growing baby was Bryan's bastard. This wasn't some obnoxious rumor that would clear up with a few conversations, a laugh, and end with Robert stripped of his lands. This was about the succession. This was about the fate of the kingdom. This was about William's deepest fears realized.

She spun around to face him, eyes deep with fury.

"He has done nothing! *I* have done nothing!" She pounded her finger into her chest. "And you know it! Why you have come up with this ruse, poisoned the king with these wild and unfounded allegations, I do not know, but you will pay for them. Pay for them with your life."

"Slander me all you like, Madam." He leered at her. She could have sworn he licked his lips. "But no one will be looking to hang me when that babe of yours comes out with blonde hair."

"And if it does, wouldn't that please you?" She knew she shouldn't have said it once it left her mouth. Robert's jaw clenched, his hands fisted. He shook his head, moving closer to her, his breath hot on her face.

"How could you do this to him? How could you betray him thus?"

"I have not betrayed him in any way. Ever!" Her heart pounded, cheeks flushed, ready to scream, to hit, to harm. "If there are any blonde babies to explain, they are your sisters. For she is the one to oft warm Bryan's bed."

Robert's hand flinched, as though he wanted to strike her. She locked eyes with him, trying to find a crack in his demeanor.

"Throwing accusations at my sister will do nothing, Madam. Especially when we all know the truth."

She squeezed her palms against her temples and screamed, causing her ladies to jump and Mary to rise. This couldn't be happening. William could never, never believe this of her. She had to see him, had to set this to rights. She turned from Robert and went to the desk again. She would write William—demand his presence. There was no way he could see her, hear her, and believe any of this.

"The truth is your sister has tumbled with Bryan many a time, and I have been faithful to my husband—even before I knew of his existence." She yanked a quill free of its inkpot, spotting the page. "No other man has touched me and nothing any of you hounds of hell say can change that fact." She scribbled on the page. "The king knows this. He will not believe it of me. There is no one on earth who could convince him."

"Oh, but there is one." A smile tugged at the corner of Robert's mouth. "And he has witnesses."

Anna stopped, mouth in mid-retort. Her belly contracted, the giant, bulbous muscle crushing down on her and the baby. She braced herself on the chair back and breathed through her nose.

"How—how is that possible?"

"I never question Cecile's ways," Robert shook his head, smiling fully at his triumph. "But even you must know he has eyes everywhere and always."

"You've managed to convince Cecile?" Their relationship had become rockier these past months, but Daniel knew how devious Robert was. He would wave all this off . . . unless . . . "What witnesses?"

"Why, one of your very own ladies."

Margaux. Damn that woman to all the horrors of hell. She pointed fingers at the queen to wheedle out of her own misdeeds.

Another contraction hit. They were just the normal late-pregnancy spasms, but they gripped her in the same way pain gripped her heart. She was trapped by lies, cut off from the king, her accusers running free. Nevertheless, her heart told her William couldn't possibly believe it. He knew her. And he knew the damnable Norwicks.

"When this is over—and it will be in short order," she pointed a condemning finger at him, "I will have both you and your sister in chains."

And then Robert dared to laugh. A long, hard roar of a laugh.

"My sister's certainly wily, but she's not your accuser. 'Tis your favorite, sweet Lady Jane."

Anna sank to the cold stone floor. This—infidelity of a queen, a pregnant queen—was high treason. Anna would lose her head. Jane would know this. Jane would never betray her so. Robert must have discovered she was Lutheran. He must be blackmailing her.

Anna let out a guttural moan and Mary rushed to her side.

To save her own neck, Anna must betray the trust of her lady, her friend, who had proved to be no such thing. But was Robert lying to her? Saying the one name he knew would most wound her?

And who would William now believe, Anna or the "innocent" Lady Jane? She must believe in the love, the vow, the bond she shared with him. She must continue to hope, or she would be lost. She rolled her brown eyes up to Robert, towering over her like a vulture.

"Get out of my sight, Robert."

"There's nothing more for me to see here anyway." He wiped his hands like Pontius Pilate, stern satisfaction on his face, turned from her, and left, the resounding clang of door and lock following after.

Anna loosed her sobs. Great, heaving waves poured out of her as she clung to Mary's chest.

"Tush, tush, Anna dear," Mary said, a soothing hand rubbing Anna's back. "The king'll come to sense. We'll all make sure of it."

The ladies all voiced their agreement, gathering around her. She breathed in Mary's scent of spiced bread and roses, a flood of happy childhood days filling her mind in welcomed comfort. But there were no wildflower fields for her to run in now. No rabbits to chase, no herbs to macerate into healing balms.

Her womb clamped like a vise, snatching all air from her lungs. *No. No, please, God. It's too early.* A trickle of fluid ran down her thigh, then a gush. She widened her eyes at Mary, terrified.

"Get the queen out of these clothes and on the bed. And send for all her ladies," Mary said. "We've an heir to receive."

Robert left the king's presence the next afternoon, whistling. While he thought something fishy was going on, he didn't mind that the ends gave him more influence with king, even if his friend was transforming into a tyrant. The queen would never have agreed to the match between the princess and Rob, but now their betrothal was signed and sealed. His son would one day be king, no matter what sex Annelore's babe turned out to be. He smiled to himself.

Muffled voices floated to him from the queen's corridor. He kept pace quietly, wondering if he might glimpse the intrigue that had imprisoned Her Majesty. In the dark hallway only a few torches blazed, one hapless guard standing watch by the queen's chamber. Through the dim Robert saw two women clinging to each other. As he came closer, they ripped apart. He couldn't believe his eyes. It was Yvette and Margaux.

"Well, well, as I live and breathe." He chuckled, sauntering up to them. "What are you two up to?" Margaux sniffed. He could see her eyes were puffy and red rimmed. She flicked a tear from her cheek.

"All this time," she said, shaking her head, blonde tendrils tapping her cheeks as she looked to the shadowed ceiling, "you've said *I'm* the evil one. I'm the one who plots gruesome and Godforsaken plans. Yet 'tis you, Robert." She leveled the blue intensity of her eyes at him. "You are the devil himself."

Robert screwed up his face and looked to Yvette, whose own eyes were cold.

"What are you on about? What is so Godforsaken about the princess marrying my son?"

"You can't be serious." Disdain molted Margaux's face. "The queen, you dullard! You had to go and antagonize her and now this!"

"And since when have you ever defended, or even liked, the queen?" He laughed. "She's finally out of your way. You can go try your hand with the king now, free and clear, once you rid yourself of your husband. Best of luck, sis." He reached out to pat her arm but she recoiled.

"The queen went into labor," Yvette said, staring past. Margaux hiccupped and covered her face with her hands.

"It's early," Robert said, almost to himself.

"Yes. Quite." Yvette set her lips in a line, eyes still hard.

"I don't see how this makes me Satan—"

Margaux tore her face from her hands, her delicate features twisted in pain and rage. "He's dead! The little prince is dead! Just like my child!"

"He's not the prince, Margaux." Anger from out of nowhere stirred him as he looked at his trembling, blotch-faced sister.

"He looks every bit the king—his eyes, his hair, even the shape of his chin." She spat the words like daggers.

"And you should know what a son of Sir Bryan looks like from your Frederick." Robert curled his lips. "They're going to kill him you know. At week's end."

She slapped him. Hard. His cheek stung and he tasted the metal of blood in his mouth.

He grabbed his sister's shoulders and shoved her to the wall.

"Robert!" Yvette yelled behind him.

"You dare raise a hand to me?" He spoke through gritted teeth, tiny spittle bubbles hitting her cheeks. "I didn't put her in the Yard, she put herself there. And the last thing I need is my little sister suddenly having pity on a bastard child and coming to the treasonous queen's aide."

For the first time, Margaux didn't wilt beneath his strength, didn't flinch at his rage. It was almost as if it made her stronger, bolder.

"It's true I hated the queen since before I met her. I still want her place, her husband, but this has gone too far. I held the prince in my arms, Robert. So tiny. So helpless. So beautiful. You men are content to throw them away like moldy bread. I would not wish it on my worst enemy."

He dropped her shoulders, staring in amazement.

"And he was no bastard, that much I know." She straightened her sleeves and skirts without looking away from his face. "And even if he was, how dare you be so callous? How dare you and the king, and the ever-so-honorable Daniel—who I'd think would have a little compassion—how dare you discard a child?"

"I—I didn't know she labored. How could I have stopped it?"

She sneered at him. "You're so damned smart, Robert. You figure it out." She turned and headed into the queen's chambers. He watched her, too stunned to move.

Yvette took his hand. "Come away," she said, pulling at him. "Let her be."

He glanced at Yvette and saw that she too held unshed tears.

"You as well?" He rolled his eyes, trying to come back to himself.

"You're not a woman. You can never understand." She sniffed, straightened. He let her escort him away, to the stairs leading to the throne room.

"And that makes you hug my sister as if she is your bosom friend?" His head felt muddled. He wanted to chalk it up to women's silliness, but he couldn't. His sister and his lover were many things, but neither was silly.

"It brings some kinship, yes."

Robert stopped when they reached the throne room and looked into her dark, almond eyes.

"It just seems the entire court has gone insane," he said.

"If you'd seen . . . if you'd seen that babe, that miniature William, struggling to breathe. How the queen cradled him in her arms, how she sang to him and kissed his tiny hands and feet . . ." The words caught in her throat and she looked away toward the wall of windows, up and out to Stone Yard's tower.

He swallowed and reached for her chin, pulling her gently to face him. A solitary tear drifted down her cheek, hanging off her jawline. He wasn't used to this frailty. He had no idea how to comfort her. He felt tenderness and revulsion all at the same time.

"She won't let the prince go, Robert." She cleared her throat. "He's dead, he's blue, and she won't let him go. She sent everyone, even Mary, away. We all left the Yard to the echo of her voice, singing to her dead prince."

Robert's breath left him.

"My God."

"God has nothing to do with this."

She wiped her cheek and left him there in the darkened throne room.

Anna stood alone in her cell, tiny Justinian wrapped in Catey's old ermine blanket, which Margaux, of all people, had brought from the nursery. The queen cradled her long-awaited son to her chest, her face inches from his, his bulbous sea-blue eyes closed forever to the world. She kissed his soft forehead and sang again.

> "Lully, lullay, thou little tiny child, bye, bye, lully, lullay.
> O sisters too, how may we do, for to preserve this day.
> This poor youngling for whom we do sing,
> Bye, bye, lully, lullay."

Her voice cracked as she sang through tears she thought could no longer come.

> "Herod, the king, in his raging,
> Charged he hath this day
> His men of might, in his own sight,
> All young children to slay."

She kissed him again. "I'm so sorry, my boy. Your father turned out to be the monster I feared. And he slay us both as if we were dragons. But Mama is here. Mama will always be here." She swallowed hard and finished the carol.

> "That woe is me, poor child for thee.
> And ever mourn and sigh,
> For thy parting neither say nor sing,
> Bye, bye, lully, lullay."

Her breasts throbbed against her corset like two beating hearts, hard as the stones that encased her. She could feel the milk streaming forth, could see it staining her silk. She held him closer.

She remembered resenting that the windows in the cell didn't provide a better view of the palace. She thought seeing the goings-on could somehow help her, somehow make her understand what had gone wrong, who had said what, how her husband was so easily and without merit turned against her. But now, she couldn't care less if she ever laid eyes on Palace Havenside, and all who dwelled there, again. She stared into the night, the hills slightly darker than the sky. She could see the stars and wondered if her mother and father were looking down from one, sending her light and strength. If they were, she couldn't feel it. "So much for that baptism you promised, Papa."

She thought of her mother and how many babes she'd lost, how many children died before they could walk or talk, how many dreams died with them. She thought of her own brother, who'd died along with their mother, and wished she had shared the same fate . . . no, not that. Despite it all, she wouldn't trade the world for Cate. The princess was the only thing that kept her from complete despair. From striving to take her own life.

What had they told her Catey? That Anna was visiting some far-flung township? She was smarter than that and William knew it . . . He probably had already secured his next queen. Was probably feeding Cate lies, telling her how much better her "new Mama" would be. She let out a guttural yell to the hills.

A knock on the door interrupted her lament.

"Leave me!" her voice strained.

"Majesty, I've come about the boy." She went rigid, jaw clenched so tight her teeth hurt.

"You are not worthy of his presence. Or mine, Robert."

"For the hundredth time, I had nothing to do with this. I just came to tell you . . ." She heard him sigh. "I'm sorry for the little prince."

She exhaled and sat in the wooden chair by the window. She tucked the ermine tighter around the prince's gray face. Taking a lock of his chestnut hair between her fingers, she curled it around her thumb.

"If you mean that, Robert," she said, "I thank you for it, but please go."

She heard the sound of coins and Robert's low voice speaking to the jailer.

"When the queen sees fit, find Moltmann and have the child buried in the royal mausoleum with the full rights of a prince of Troixden. This is for your pains." The coins shifted. "And for your silence." More chiming. "For I was never here."

William stared unseeing at the star-sprinkled sky outside his window. Daniel had left him various documents to review and sign, but he couldn't rouse himself to concentrate on issues of squabbling lords. His mind was dull, his head ached. He took a long drag of spiced wine, trying to focus on its numbing feel on his tongue, its warmth as it hit his belly, the aftertaste of clove, but all it did was recall the many nights he'd spent drinking it, a beaming Anna at his side, her chocolate eyes dancing in the firelight.

It couldn't be true. Yet Daniel's evidence was so precise, so tight. Daniel had never steered him wrong, would never willingly hurt William so deeply. He reviewed it all in his head for the millionth time. What did Lady Jane have to gain? Nothing. And everything to lose, as Daniel said. And what did Daniel have to gain? A hollowed-out, distracted king? An angry, bitter friend? The shame of admitting the queen he had lobbied for turned traitor of the highest order?

But William's heart, his heart screamed that she was innocent. Yes, she'd been distant, irritable—anguished by her father's death, lonely . . . but with Bryan? She couldn't wound William more grievously and she knew it. He couldn't reconcile the image he had of her in his soul with the facts in his head. But that had always been his failing, using his gut instinct instead of his mind. It was what had gotten him exiled, what perpetuated the wars, what lost him Laureland. Indeed, it was his mercy toward Sir Bryan that led directly to this present circumstance.

He knew he should go to her and have it out, but he feared the outcome, feared any hint in her eyes that she had strayed.

"The Lady Yvette of Havenside," his guard called, over the pound of his staff.

"I'll allow it," he called. While he eschewed all other visitors, he could use some womanly advice, for he was sick to death of men's.

She entered, dressed head to toe in black silks, a flash of red revealing itself at her feet. She wore a veil of mourning and, as she paid her obeisance, she lifted it above her headdress revealing a gaunt, pale face. She clutched a plain ebony box in her hands. Leveling her eyes at him, she spoke.

"Majesty, I have come with grave news of the queen."

Bile rose in his throat. She couldn't be ill, could she? He nodded for her to continue.

"The mental anguish and physical strain of her imprisonment sent her to early labor."

He took two steps forward, wanting to seize her, shake the information from her stoic form.

"Is she—are they . . .?"

"The queen lives. Your son breathed for less time than our interview here."

"Son?" He stared at her, dumb. He was going to be sick. He wanted to tear his hair and run screaming from the place like a banshee. He took rapid breaths, focusing. Swallowing, he remembered himself, remembered the queen's crime. "He was not my son."

"Is your heart so blackened, Highness?" Her raven eyes flashed. "That boy was more like you than any painted miniature could be."

A son—his son—dead? No. Damn all these women and their lies! He had to contain himself, had to squelch the anger, the grief, the fear, the guilt. He balled his hands into fists and released them. Ball, release, ball, release, fingernails cutting grooves in his palms.

"You may not speak to me so casually, lady."

She marched up to him, right up to his chest as if he hadn't spoken at all.

"I may and I shall." Her forehead only reached to his nose, but her fury loomed above him. "Because someone must."

He turned from her and strode back to the window, staving off the flood. He grit his teeth.

"If he was my son," he bit out each word, "I am grieved, but it does not negate the facts of her treason."

"You know these are falsehoods. You must know it." She followed him to the window, speaking to his back. "You must take a hard look at yourself, at those who counsel you." He could hear her silks rustle as she shifted her weight, the box she held clacking against her rings.

He turned, glaring at her. "You think I have not done that? You think I have not looked for the worms under each stone? "

"Sometimes we may see a worm as an industrious helper, rather than a plague on our crops."

He brushed past her. He needed to get away from this contrary woman.

"Please, enough. The evidence against her mounts, and no one is more aggrieved than I."

"I do believe 'tis Her Majesty who is the most aggrieved."

"And you may join her ranks if you do not watch your tongue." He lorded over her. "I have warned you twice now."

She set the box she carried down on the desk, opening it as she spoke. "But you have not seen evidence of the queen's innocence." She held out a bundle of letters to him. "The queen wrote these letters to you when she was in Beaubourg at her father's death, but never sent them." His eyes bore into the papers. He didn't know if he wanted to read them or burn them.

He shook his head. "Her own words cannot defend her. They wouldn't be trustworthy."

"Trustworthy?" Her voice hitched, cheeks blazing. "You trust the words of others over her own private ones? Words she wrote thinking no one, ever, would read them? You have truly gone mad then."

"I will not be mocked, lady." He ground his teeth together, his jaw popping. She was Robert's mistress, and he must be careful, even if her welcome was worn well past thin. "State more than feeble female sentiments or leave me."

"I am not the only person at court who believes your unquestioning devotion to the Duke of Cecile is mislaid."

Cecile now? Would this witch-hunt never end?

"Yes, the man is a bastard. Yes, if his mother were not a whore he would be king in my stead. But he has never—not once—tried to secure a higher place. It took convincing to bring him on to council after James's death."

"Yes, King James." She pursed her lips, seeming to consider something. "Is it not strange to you that Cecile's appearance at court coincided with King James's failing health shortly after? That Cecile often requested private audiences with the king— the man who had publicly called him no better than a dog? The man who Cecile saw firsthand destroying our realm, exiling you and shunning your mother—"

"Out. Out out out!" He gripped the table so he wouldn't harm her. "I am sick to death of those I trust with my life being accused of treachery!"

"Rail at me all you want, Majesty." She took her leave slowly, eyes accusing arrows. "Throw me in the Yard, chop off my head—but someone must speak the truth to you, even if you don't wish to hear it."

She tossed the letters at his feet and left without so much as a curtsy.

He picked up his glass to take a long, trembling pull, but finding it empty, he threw it at the closing door, the metal making a dull clang as it hit the floor.

Head in his hands, he crumpled to the ground, mind spinning. What the hell was this about Daniel? Was Yvette trying to say Daniel slowly poisoned James? It was absurd. Besides, what would that have to do with the queen now?

He gulped air. Opening his eyes, he saw Anna's letters scattered at his feet. Her lovely curled script on sheet upon sheet of yellowed paper.

> *My darling, where are you? I'm desperate for your voice, your arms, your lips. I'm wretched without you . . .*

He picked up a letter at random.

> *Dearest Wills,*
>
> *I am gutted. My father lies dead and for all I know you also. How I loathe this war! I am consumed by grief, but if I am honest with myself 'tis not fully for the loss of Papa, 'tis that I must bear his loss without your embrace to calm me, without your smile to soothe me, and I ache . . . You would tell me to put on a brave face, you would tell me to be the queen . . . I will be again, I promise you, I just need these*

hours of solitude. And yet I revolt against them, for I am drowning in my sorrow, the sorrow of your absence . . .

He picked up another.

My love,

I'm looking at the moon. 'Tis full and bright—so bright I don't need a candle to write by. I see it and imagine you see it too, off somewhere east of me. Perhaps you've wrapped yourself in furs and have taken a midnight stroll to ponder its glow. It gives me comfort to imagine we are gazing at the same heavenly object. That if I send all my love into the moon you will feel it rain down upon you in silver light. Would you laugh if you knew I held such childish wishes? What I wouldn't give to hear that sound . . .

And another.

W-
You walk in my dreams. The ecstasy you brought to me this night shocked me awake, only to find the wretchedness of an empty place beside me. This yearning . . . fly home to me, love.

He flushed, his own yearning for her rising. He riffled through the pile.

King of my heart,

Our son grows strong—and yes, I'm convinced of a prince, for this pregnancy is so different than Catey's. All I crave is meat, ale, and, of all things, to watch the boys of the village in their hand-to-hand practices. And I crave you. Always you. I'm beginning to understand what it may be like to be a man, heightened like this, constantly desirous of our night-time dealings. I've taken to carrying one of your shirts about just so I may smell you at will. Sadly, it loses its scent.

Catey misses you but assures me, in the strange way she has, that you are hale. I wish I had her confidence. Daniel keeps telling me no news is better than ill news. And yet, with no news my mind is a whirlwind of wild tragedies. Why can I not assume you have crushed them in a day and gained some of their land to boot? Why must my mind always find the route to fear? This is why I don't send you these letters. You do not need my worry to add to yours, you do not need my lament to send you to distracting thoughts of home. You need our strength and that's what I shall send you. But these letters—it feels in my heart as if you've heard them, read them, and it helps me to muddle through . . .

There were at least three dozen, as if she'd written three times a day. All signed with the same phrase, *Come back to me whole and hale, my beloved, my king, for my heart beats outside my body until you return it to its place.*

A moan escaped his throat as he cradled his head in his hands and wept.

Margaux stamped snow from her shoes on the white marble of the Great Hall and shivered. An early cold snap had sent blankets of snow to hush the castle, robing it in a white glow. She didn't remove her cloak hood for she was content to do the queen's bidding in secret. There was a box of letters she must fetch, hidden behind the thick books of the queen's library. The queen wanted them burned. Immediately. Margaux contemplated whether or not she herself would read them first. She may pity the woman, but it didn't mean she was cured of intrigue.

Small clusters of courtiers dotted the hall, whispering in the evening gloom. She wondered, fleetingly, if rumor spread of the child's burial. The king had barely left his chamber, and as she hurried past she heard someone say, "the bastard had hair gold as straw."

She caught her tongue before it lashed out, intent on her mission. How strange it was to feel defensive for this woman she had so long loathed, how strange to want to soothe her, help her, when all Margaux had wanted was for exactly this. The queen shamed, removed. Margaux with another chance for the crown.

Perhaps it was the thought of Bryan, chained, tortured, his screams echoing up to the queen's cell, punctuating the sorrow, the fear that hung around them. After all, she cared for him, deeply, would weep when he died, this father of her first son. This man who'd never loved any woman but the one he couldn't have.

She drew her cloak closer about her and sped her pace. Arriving at the queen's chamber she found no guard and the door ajar. She pushed it farther open and crept down the arched hallway to the sound of whispering and quiet sobs. Coming fully into the chamber, she saw Bernard crouched over a crumpled Lady Jane. Jane's face was puffy and twisted, she held her stomach and rocked back and forth on her knees, oblivious to Bernard or Margaux.

"Take me to Norwick, I must see Norwick," Jane moaned between sobs. She clutched a stack of letters to her chest. Where these the same Margaux sought?

"What is the meaning of all this?" Margaux hastened to Bernard's side and glared down at Jane. "What could you want with my brother?"

Jane's eye's widened and she crawled to Margaux, grabbing her skirts.

"I can stand it no longer—not after the babe . . . I must see him!"

"I found her like this only moments ago," Bernard said, face aghast. "She only repeats your brother's name."

Jane's wail cut through them. "I must tell him this is over. I am done! I don't care what they do to me."

Margaux's blood ran cold. She crouched down to Jane, grabbed her shoulders and shook.

"Why must you see him?" She tried unsuccessfully to make eye contact.

"Please, I can only speak to him . . . please, don't let him hurt me."

So it *was* Robert. He was manipulating Jane. He'd made her give evidence against the queen to Daniel. *Clever. Very clever, brother.*

"Obviously she's mad," Bernard said. "We must give her a draught and let her sleep it off."

"No!" Jane wailed, keeling away from Margaux, burying the letters in the crook of her arm. "You cannot make me! I demand to see His Grace!"

"Countess," Bernard said, stern eyes appraising them both, "I've tried to offer her rest and relief to no avail. We've nothing left to do but bring her to the duke."

Margaux turned back to Jane, twisting her arm, trying to shut her up, hoping to snatch the letters.

"Why can you not walk there yourself?" Margaux sneered at the lady.

"The heart is willing, but the flesh is weak." She turned her cow eyes to Margaux. "Please, you must help me. You have sons. You know you would do anything to protect them—"

Robert was threatening Jane's son? She couldn't abide any more of this. The way these men treated their women, their children, like they were toys to be discarded when broken or bored with. She was still of royal blood, by God. To watch her brother fall, after all he'd done to her, it would be worth it.

She stood, pulling an unsteady Jane with her.

"Help me, Bernard." She put an arm around Jane's waist, attempting to straighten her. "We go to my lord brother. He can clean up this mess he has made."

The first snow always sent Robert into contemplation. Something about its serene beauty coupled with its wildness, its ability to kill plant, animal, and man alike. The fact that it couldn't touch him here in his warm rooms unless he wanted it to. It made him feel like the gods of myth.

He stole a glance to Yvette seated across from him by the fire. She finally returned to him after the quiet burial of the prince that morning. She was still unconvinced of the queen's guilt, even more so now, and spent her time away from Annelore trying to ferret out what she saw as the truth.

A scuffle outside his doors brought his attention to the present. Sobbing, protests, his sister's bark. He sighed. Not another go-round with Margaux. Not now. Not when he'd finally nestled into a bit of peace.

But the doors flew open before he could forbid it, revealing a grim-faced Bernard, his jacket and sleeves askew, gripping the armpit of a limp and disheveled Lady Jane. Next to her was Margaux, her blue velvet gown impeccable, her stare frostier than the iced-over moat. Without preamble she strode in, mouth twisted.

"You."

He rose from his chair to meet the battle head on.

"Here I am, Margaux. What is it now?"

"It was you all along. I was right, and you didn't even have the decency to admit it!"

"You are rarely right about anything." He chuckled. "Do pray tell, sis."

"Bernard and I found your accomplice blubbering in the queen's chamber. She wants you to stop harassing her—to stop threatening her son!"

He frowned and scrutinized Lady Jane, who was now nothing

more than a pile of velvet on his crimson rug. He shook his head at Margaux.

"What in the hell are you on about?"

Yvette, watching the whole scene in silence, rose and went to Jane's side, caressing her back, whispering to her.

"You claim you have nothing to do with her?" Margaux sneered.

"I have seen neither hide nor hair of Lady Jane since she gave her testimony to the king."

"Ha!"

Robert snorted. "Margaux, I am tired, and through with your, and everyone else's, histrionics."

Yvette caught his eyes, her face pale. She held a pile of letters.

"Robert. This lady must speak with you."

"No one's stopping her." The look in Yvette's eyes prevented a more biting retort. "Bring her here."

Margaux helped Yvette lift Jane from the floor. They placed her on the chair in front of his desk and stood sentinel beside her. His sister looked as though she would bite him. Lady Jane attempted to speak twice but dissolved into shaking sobs.

He cleared his throat and sat behind his desk. "Bernard," he called. The man came forward as well, his attire righted. "Tell me what happened."

"Your Grace, I came to the queen's chamber as I do every day, to make sure all is still in order. I found Lady Jane on the floor by the bed." A low keen from Jane interrupted his narration. He coughed and continued. "She kept saying over and over 'I'm sorry' and 'I'll make it right.' When she saw me she burst into tears and would not be comforted."

"Was she at the birth? Did she mishandle the prince?"

Margaux pounced. "So you call him prince now?"

He raised a warning hand at his sister. "Margaux—"

"Stop! Stop it!" It was Jane. She lifted her red and swollen face from her hands. "Your Grace, you must hear my confession."

"I am not a priest, milady." He saw her eyes, full of sorrow, determination.

"A priest cannot help me. No one can, for my actions have sealed my fate. I am here because you, Your Grace, can help the queen. For she is innocent of the charges I agreed to convey."

His mind reeled. The sweet, demurring, if somewhat cloying, Lady Jane had lied? Why was he always in the middle of these messes, through no fault of his own?

"If you've come to confess to a crime, 'tis the Duke of Cecile you should prostrate yourself before." She shook her head with vigor, terror creeping into her eyes. "I assure you, he would be more merciful than I."

"I-I can't—I . . ."

"Lady Jane, my patience wears thin. If your conscience—"

"Robert, just listen to her." Yvette's glare pinned him to his chair.

"Begging your pardon, Your Grace," Jane said, "but it is of the Duke of Cecile's treason, and mine, that I speak of."

William glanced at his cards, then across his desk at Daniel. His friend's face glowed even whiter in the candlelight.

Daniel discarded. "I know this is not the sort of comfort

you've come to expect," the corners of Daniel's mouth tugged up, "and the circumstances are not what they should be, but I enjoy our nightly time together, William. It reminds me of our youth. It feels like we're in this together again."

William smiled back, but he couldn't mimic his friend's warmth. The hole in his heart, in his gut, would not be filled.

"Have we not always been in this together?" William picked up an ace of spades.

"I didn't mean—just . . . solitude can breed self-pity."

"Of course, my friend. I enjoy your company as well." William was rewarded with a quick smile. "Except you always beat me at cards." He took a swig of cider, his mind up in a tower with his wife, mourning her—their?—dead child. The lines of her letters swirled in his head. *My heart beats outside my body until you return it to its place . . .*

Daniel met William's eyes and pursed his lips. "I'm so very sorry, William. About the queen."

William tried to shake the nightmares from his head. "And yet there are those who say you have no pity for her."

There was an uproar outside his doors. The men gave each other a look of concern, but before either could speak, in charged Robert, followed by a trail of armed guards, one gripping Lady Jane's arm. Behind them came Bernard, Yvette, and Margaux, each looking various shades of grim.

William and Daniel stood, Daniel backing away from the desk. Robert plowed forward, head shaking, eyes blazing. But he wasn't headed for William. He strode to Daniel. Daniel yelped and tripped over his chair, only to be caught by Robert, who punched him square in the face.

"Norwick!" William roared and ran to Daniel, helping him sit up. Blood ran through Daniel's fingers as he dabbed at his nose.

"Get away from him, Majesty," Robert said, anger pulsing off him in waves. "He wishes you ill."

William got to his feet and shoved Robert's shoulders, sending him back a few steps. "What in God's name is going on here?"

"Our precious, ever innocent, ever *dutiful* Daniel has been playing you for a fool, Majesty. Lady Jane has just confessed to me. Cecile has been blackmailing her for years, gaining any information on the queen that might be useful to him. And trying to lay the blame with me!"

William looked down at his bleeding half-brother. Daniel didn't look up.

"And that information has done us well," William said, narrowing his eyes at Robert. "'Tis hardly treachery to use spies. And you are one to talk about spies in the queen's chambers." He pointed at Margaux and Yvette.

"But that is just it," Robert said. "He never *has* obtained any useful information. And when he could not get what he wanted, he threatened the life of this lady's child and forced her to confess crimes the queen did not commit."

"Good Lord, Robert—"

"Ask him!" Robert yelled. "He claimed the queen took the knave as a lover. Accused your son of being a bastard. Hid the queen's letters to you and yours to her during *both* wars." He gestured back to Jane.

Daniel had righted himself and was watching Robert, face rigid. "Where did you come up with these falsehoods, and what use are they to you?"

In one swoop Robert was in Daniel's face again. "My false-hoods? It seems you've been torturing this woman so you can get your precious William back. Was I next? How did you think to eliminate me, hmm?"

"Stay away from him, Robert." William pushed Robert back, but his cousin wouldn't relent. William's mind was full of disparate accusations, flooding together, clouding each other.

"Are you happy now?" Robert's spat. "Did you think you could somehow take her place? In his life, in his bed?"

"Robert!" William's breathing grew shallow.

"He speaks nonsense, Majesty." Daniel mumbled, sending disdainful looks in Robert's direction. "I don't know why Lady Jane would tell this tale. Perhaps it's Norwick who pays her to falsify her testimony, afraid of his own place at court."

"Unlike you," Robert said, "I've never doubted my place with the king. We have an understanding, we two." Robert's eyes flashed to William's.

"Enough!" William looked at each person present.

"Just ask the lady," Robert said, with that all-too-familiar cock of a brow.

"But she is obviously lying," Daniel said, kerchief to his nose. "She tells tales to me and now she tells tales—"

"I want all of you out," William said, his head throbbing. "You've turned my chambers into—"

"It was me!" Margaux's voice cut through William's. She had broken free from Yvette and was standing at the edge of the dais stairs, cheeks pink, chest heaving, tears brimming in her eyes. "It was me with Sir Bryan in that stable. And the queen saw it, saw me enter. I remember her squinting down at me. Scowling. Heaven knows she saw Bryan too."

It seemed even the walls held their breath.

"And you are just telling us this now?" Anger and relief flooded him in equal parts, for all knew that Margaux would never lie to protect Anna. He didn't know why she divulged her role, but he could almost kiss her. He called to his guards. "Take the countess to the dungeon."

"But, Majesty—"

"But nothing, cousin. You will be dealt with later. Now, we get to the bottom of this whole tangled business."

"Robert!" Margaux's yelp was like that of a pup.

"She's a witness, you cannot simply drag her—"

"I can do whatever I will!" William's temples threatened to explode.

Daniel shuffled forward, head bowed. "Majesty, I could have sworn I saw the queen that night, but if the countess claims it was her . . ." He looked at Margaux with pity.

"Because they look so similar," Robert said.

William considered Daniel. He was flush but calm, the only one in the room not riled. His voice was even when he said, "I weep for the babe, no matter whose son he is, but the queen's treasonous acts still—"

"'Tis your treason," came Jane's rasping voice from the floor. "Yours, and mine. And I shall burn for it, but I will conceal it no longer."

"Still yourself, milady—this state befits you not." Daniel was almost gentle in his scolding.

"Tell him why," Robert strode to Jane, knelt beside her, "tell the king why you accused the queen."

Her mouth trembled as she looked to Robert, pleading in her eyes. He nodded.

"I—I'm a Lutheran. The queen knew it. The Duke of Cecile found out. He said he would have me and my boy burned if I did not do as he said. Said the queen would not be harmed, only sent to a convent. But then the prince . . ." She broke down, face to the floor, heaving sobs into the stone.

William looked at Daniel, who, for the first time, appeared shaken. "She's—she's obviously overwrought, spilling non-sense—"

"What, precisely, is nonsense?" William said, closing in on his friend.

"All of it." Daniel gestured to the forsaken woman.

William nodded, keeping a cool demeanor though his insides rioted. "And what possible reason would she have for her claims?"

"Norwick surely fed her this, this script." Daniel attempted a look of offense.

"And what would be in this for me?" Robert snorted and stood. "I'm the one who dislikes the queen. I'm the one who just got my son nearer to the throne. Why would I want her alive, let alone out of prison?"

"To take my place!" William startled at Daniel's shout. "You've always been jealous that I am first in the king's heart. You see an opening to take me down and the queen too, so you trump up some bizarre—"

"There you are wrong," Robert countered. "You aren't first

in the king's heart. You never have been. First it was Matilda, then it was his sister, now the queen and the princess—"

"Just stop this, Norwick," Daniel said, chin high. "Can't you see how your schemes are harming him?"

"I am not a child." The quiet strength in William's voice silenced them both. He'd been listening to their squabbling, stunned at their juvenile accusations, as if he were a toy to be fought over and won. "I do not need coddling, and I do not need advisors who puff themselves above their stations." He turned to Jane, who still faced the floor. "Lady Jane, speak your peace."

Pressing her hands to the floor, she held herself up, face mottled. "On the life of my son, I swear it to you, my liege. His Grace Cecile promised my and my son's lives if I said I'd seen the queen with Sir Bryan—nothing less would have provoked me to do such a thing. I stole the war letters betwixt you and the queen that His Grace hid to prove he has been manipulating you both. You must know the love I bear the queen, that only the life of my child—"

She grasped after him as he stood, backing away from her as if she were a rabid mutt.

"Yet your love for her only goes so far." His disdain grew the more she shook before him. "Did you not think she would protect you? As she obviously has been?"

"His Grace is so powerful, he said he'd harm my son—" William turned from her. "Please, Your Majesty, have mercy."

"You had no mercy for me. No mercy for the queen. And none for my own son." She wailed again. "Guards." Jane was hoisted and dragged next to Margaux, whose frown deepened.

William went slowly to his sideboard. He filled a goblet in silence and drained it. Placing the empty cup down, he crossed to his desk and leaned on his fingers. All eyes followed him, but his were fixed on Daniel.

"Why, Daniel?"

Daniel's shoulders slumped, face gray as the walls. "You can't truly believe—"

"You asked me to believe the impossible mere days ago, why shouldn't I do so now?"

Daniel met the king's eyes, sorrow, regret, and longing mingled together.

"She was destroying the realm, Wills, destroying you. Her advice to you in statecraft, from the very beginning, has been wrongheaded, and yet more often than not, you listened to her, cosseted her." His voice took on the lawyerly, patronizing tone he used in council. "First it was taxation, then it was Moltmann, then the war, even little things like when or when not to host tournaments. We became such a laughingstock, our enemies conspired against us and have now taken our lands. And what does she counsel now? A child and woman to rule our northernmost border." He spread his hands, shook his head as if that settled things.

William felt as if he'd been punched, the soreness in his chest from the tennis accident blooming anew.

"If any of this—any of it—had been such a concern, why did you not bring it to me?"

"I tried," Daniel searched William's face, finding no grace, no mercy. "But you wouldn't listen, you stopped listening to me—only, always, to her!" His voice increased in pitch and volume. "I watched her manipulate you daily with her batted eyes and pouted lips, taking you to bed when she couldn't get her way. And it drove me to distraction. How she thought she could run this realm, run you."

"You've no right to speak of her this way, not after what you've done." William came around the desk.

The dried blood on Daniel's lip cracked as he smiled. "I've no right?" He cackled. "You're the one with no rights, my liege. If it weren't for me, you wouldn't even be king." William stalked closer. Daniel's eyes were wild. "You, so gallant, off nursing your wounded pride while your brother left your mother to die in a cold, ruined castle by the coast, but I was there." He hit his chest, as if the madness of their shared father had finally won out. "She was not even my mother, yet I was more devoted than all of her children."

William crossed his arms to keep from wrapping his fingers around Daniel's neck.

"You were the one who pleaded with me to stay away—"

"And so I did tell you to stay away, for I knew you couldn't stomach what would come next, no matter how much you loathed James. Even though I did it all for you. All of it!"

"I never asked you to do any of this!"

"But our people needed it. We all needed you to be king. I needed you to . . ." Daniel seemed far away, as if thrust back in time. "My liege and my brother, do you not see? I've sacrificed my life entire for your family, this realm. I've never asked a thing in return. Was I supposed to throw all of that work, all of my life, my heart, away for a misguided, usurping woman? To let her take my rightful place—"

William held out a hand. "Your chain of office, Cecile."

Daniel started to shake. "You can't, this isn't—"

"I will hear no more from you!" William massaged his head, a sickness welling up inside. How could he have utterly misjudged this man for so long? Then an image sprung to his mind: Anna, alone, cold, afraid. Their child, gone. And a rage to rival all burned in his chest.

He yanked Daniel's chain to a close around his pale neck.

"My liege!" Daniel gargled.

William tightened his grip. "You think I can't stomach killing?" Daniel's face went red, eyes popping. When it looked as though he would faint, William released, yanking the chain over his blonde head.

Daniel keeled over, gagging.

"Guards!" William dropped the chain of office to the desk with a thud. Armed men surrounded Daniel, Margaux and Jane left huddled together.

The king strode to his wardrobe and pulled out his cloak. "Norwick, deal with the prisoners."

Then he stalked out of his chambers, pace accelerating the farther he went, tears of regret splashing his cheeks, desperate to hold his Anna again.

Anna heard commotion floating up the stairs, echoing in her cell, but paid no heed. Surely Norwick had come to taunt her again. Or the executioner. She didn't care, for the life she knew had ceased the moment she was shut in, her heart ceasing to beat the moment her son took gasping breaths, shuddering as his spirit fled his tiny body. She now awaited her own death with something like anticipation.

Thus, even when her cell door flung open, she remained in the little wooden chair, staring out at the melting snow, watching drips from the roof fall to the earth.

"Anna, my love." She didn't stir her from her meditation. "All is sorted, the perpetrators put away. You may come with me now, finally."

She spoke to the barred landscape. "Why would I come with a man who imprisons me without question?"

"Anna, look at me please."

"And yet you gave me no such grace."

"You've got to understand—"

"I understand completely, for court gossip reaches even here. This was no mere nod to the law of the land. You *believed* I would betray you thus."

"I never truly did, not in my heart of hearts. Anna, come home. You've got to come home."

"Home?" She guffawed. "I've no home. You've given my lands to Norwick, you've cast me out of my chambers—but worse, out of your heart. I've no home left to return to."

"It was Daniel," William's face twisted. "I still don't understand why, but he concocted the whole of it. He threatened the lives of Jane and her son . . .You can see why, when it was his word . . ."

She turned and stared coolly at her husband. As numb as

she felt, there was still something in her that urged her to fling her arms around him, to sob into his chest, to let him comfort and soothe her. But that man, the man of open arms and sweet words, was in her imagination.

"Do you not think I am in torment about this?" He made to come closer, but she stood and backed away. "To hear such vile things spoken about you by those I trusted—"

"You speak of torment?" It was his turn to back away as she advanced. "You know nothing of it until you've lain upon the birthing bed, only to have your perfect son, the heir the whole country has been praying for, the one justification of your own existence, die at your breast, his startled eyes—the same eyes as your once beloved—closing forever. That is a torment I shall never heal from."

"Let us grieve together, Anna." He knelt and held out his hands in supplication. "I cannot take away what has happened, but together we can walk through this trial."

"You've killed our son!" she yelled. "And my soul with him." Reflexively she fingered the chain about her neck. She frowned, pulling it free from her bodice, the ruby glinting dull in the fading light. She drew the chain over her neck, transfixed by the blood-red stone.

"I know you are hurt, angry, and rightfully so, but please do not forsake us." His voice was thick with desperation. "You're all I have."

"Then you've nothing." She tossed the necklace to his feet and turned back to the window. "Just as I have."

Her cell door was left open, but she ignored it. Did not want to give the king the satisfaction of her return. But eventually, the thought of her ladies in such close and discomfiting quarters sent her back. She went in the night, so few would see and she would have less chance of running into the king. She was relieved to make it to her chambers without incident. Dear Bernard had kept her rooms cheerful and warm, obviously convinced of her imminent return. She hugged the startled man, who, after a few breaths, returned her embrace.

"Your Majesty, I am relieved to find you back where you belong." He whispered to her like a confidant. "Not one of us believed such tripe about you."

"Thank you, Bernard. If only my husband had your faith." She released him with a sad smile.

"Don't say it, Majesty. For even the stoutest of hearts can be led astray."

"But yours was not. Even in light of the same evidence."

He led her into her bedchamber, ever the gentleman. "Begging your pardon, Majesty, but it seems to me the king never quite believed in his own happiness."

"It seems to *me* he lacks faith in those he should believe."

"In a way, yes, he lacks faith. Faith that his life will be a pleasant one, a blessed one. Despite his general jolly demeanor, his life has been one of pain, of reacting to the evils of men and the world." He settled her in her favorite chair, offered her a cup of warm wine. "It's as if, in finding you, he had never fully trusted his luck."

"He has never fully trusted me." She pulled a fur blanket up to her chin.

"Truthfully, Majesty, I think he has not ever fully trusted he could have such constant good as you in his life. So when Cecile, someone who, to the king's knowledge, has never bent a truth, tells him this good and beautiful thing is not so good and beautiful, it is like he was expecting it all along."

"That's no reason for him to behave as he has."

He bowed his head. "'Tis no excuse, but perhaps a way of understanding how the man you so care for could come to such a low place." She frowned at Bernard, wondering at his speech, the most words he'd ever said to her at one time. "I see I have spoken out of turn and I beg your pardon, Majesty."

"Not out of turn, but I do not wish to hear more. He must make his own defenses if he is ever to sway me. And even then, I do not know how much good it will do him." Bernard did a shortened version of his jig-bow and retired to his regular place by the door.

Mary came next, Cariline with her. "The princess has been asking for ye, dearie." Mary kneaded her knobbed hands. "She be awake even now, waiting for you."

"What have they been telling her?" Anna asked Cariline.

Cariline looked to Mary who nodded. "She knows the truth, at least some of it. She's been so sad about her brother."

"Who told her? What did they say?" Anna leapt from her chair, ready to storm the nursery.

A strange look passed between the two nurses again. "She said her brother told her," Mary said.

Anna stopped in her tracks. "Who heard her speak thus?"

"Thankfully just us two," Mary said. "But she's awfully

heartsick about it. Doesn't understand why her father didn't listen to her."

Papa needs to believe in Mama . . .Why had she not remembered it before? And here William was so quick to believe their daughter's odd prophesies about a son, but forgot the more imperative part. And in his zeal, what was he left with but an estranged family?

"Bring her to me. We shall sleep together this eve."

Cariline curtsied and left to fetch the princess while Mary, Amelia, and Brigitte helped Anna into her nightgown. She wondered fleetingly where Yvette and Margaux were. Their behavior had been so strange at the prince's birth and she hadn't seen either of them since his burial. Margaux, all trace of conceitedness gone, even wiping Anna's brow with the tenderness of a mother, whispering encouragement, the devastation on her face when Justinian closed his eyes forever. How she'd determined to fulfill Anna's wish to have her private letters destroyed, but then never returned.

Yvette too, was more impassioned than Anna had seen her. Battling alongside Mary to ease the queen's pain, to bring forth a living son. Wordless as she left a strong sleeping draught at the queen's side.

Where were these women now, especially if Daniel were to blame for it all? She sat waiting for Cate as Mary brushed out her hair. Daniel. No wonder it was hard for William to shake such accusations. Still . . . didn't William know her better? She saw Mary's earnest face reflected in the mirror. If Mary had come to Anna with similar news, would she believe Mary outright? She sighed. Of course she would. But the first thing she would do, the very first thing, would be to confront William. She would assume Mary had gotten it wrong somehow. And that was the crux of it. That he'd not even given Anna the chance to defend herself. If he had, they might be laughing in bed together right then, William feeling the kicks of their unborn son.

The doors opened and Cate ran to her mother, leaping into Anna's lap. Anna curled herself around her girl like a mother cat, rocking her, kissing her curls.

"My dearest love," she whispered, feeling Cate shake in her arms. "Mama's here now."

"Why didn't Papa heed me?" Cate sat up, arms still tight around Anna's neck. "He promised he believed me, but he didn't listen."

"Sometimes men do not heed the truth, even when it stares them in the face." Anna smoothed Cate's hair. "But let us speak no more of this tonight." She hoisted Cate off her lap and took her hand. "Let us nestle in bed together like two bunnies and sleep as long as we want."

Cate's eyes widened. "Even skip mass?"

Anna laughed, helping Cate into the great feathered bed.

"You may even skip mass if you should sleep so late."

Anna climbed in behind, wrapped her arms around her child, and lay her chin on top of Cate's head. The princess gave a contented sigh and soon both succumbed to their dreams.

William, again, couldn't sleep. He lay awake in his giant, empty bed, in his dark, cooling room, listening to the muffled activity coming down the hall. Anna must be back. It took all he had to keep from running to her, lying prostrate before her, begging her forgiveness. *Just give her time. She just needs time.*

But neither of them were known for their patience. He worried she had come to pack and move to one of the other royal holdings, perhaps into Castle Beaubourg, taking the princess with her. He wouldn't stop her, not after what he'd done. That one rash moment of him watching her with Bryan in the garden . . . his gut wrenched . . . but the law said any claim against her, no matter how small, must have her put in the Yard for safekeeping. It was not his fault she went into labor, it was Daniel's. His deceit . . .

Who in the hell was he kidding? Anna didn't care what Daniel said or believed, she only cared that William doubted her, even for that fleeting moment. But it was more than a moment and he knew it. Daniel had truly and thoroughly convinced him . . . no, not thoroughly, for he had still held out some hope, buried deep. And when Yvette came with those letters . . . how he wanted to free Anna, fold her in his arms, to hell with what evidence Daniel and Jane put forth. And his son . . . he couldn't even think on it.

Dammit! He knew! From the very beginning he said Jane must have been corrupted somehow—why didn't he listen to his instincts, his heart? Jealousy was a wicked master. He was haunted by Bryan's swollen, unrecognizable face, the knight now lying in chambers next to Robert's, being mended by the king's own physicians. No one knew if he would survive the night.

All these sins, piling up at his feet. Would he add more in executing Jane and Daniel, or did their sins deserve even worse? Anna would know how to talk it through with him, what questions to ask, what notions of theology and politics might come into play. But would she ever speak to him again? He wouldn't, if he were in her place.

A soft knock on the door had him bolting upright. Could he dare hope it was her? He couldn't stop his disappointment at seeing Robert, carrying a candelabra and a large, sloshing pitcher.

"I thought you could use some company, my liege." He headed straight to the dwindling fire and stoked it, adding a log for good measure. He wasted no time in filling two cups to the brim and toasting the king in silent salute.

William pulled on a long shirt and joined him, drinking gulps of dark, oaky wine. "I'm not much company, cuz." He slouched into Anna's chair as Robert took his.

"I didn't expect you would be, but if we're both to stew the night away, we might as well stew together."

William nodded and gazed at the fire. Neither spoke for some time.

"Why did he do it, Robert?"

Robert shrugged. "He's in love with you."

"He's not in love with me. Not like you always imply."

"I'll rephrase. He lives through you, through your pleasure, your confidence in him. He has always been the rug you wipe your feet on, and glad to be. He is of use to you, of more use than anyone. But the queen, she left him in the dust." Robert took a gulp. "Oh, for a time it was fine. He was delighted to be the one who had brought such delight to you. But when that delight was only for her, your pleasure only from her, well, he felt like something was being stolen from him."

William snorted. "You're awfully introspective on the matter."

"I've had a lot of time to think on it." Robert sat forward, leaning on his knees. "That's the difference between him and me. He simply sees people's actions, then reasons them out. But people don't work from reason. They work from whims and fancies, lust, hate. He must have thought if he presented you with a logical argument, you would, logically, have to agree. Certainly you would be miserable for a time, but then you would come to see him as your savior again and you could go back to being conjoined."

"But we never were conjoined."

Robert laughed sadly. "Name me a time—before the queen—where you ever made a decision without going to Daniel first." He paused, waiting for William to respond. Try as the king might, he couldn't think of anything. "Hell, you even asked him what horses to buy and he doesn't even like the animals."

"Well, I asked you first." William's smile wasn't without warmth.

"Fine then, you asked him second." Robert sat back again, folding his hands over his chest.

William went back to considering the fire. "I owe you an apology." He faced his cousin. "We both know you're a schemer, but something like this—I was desperate to find an answer to it, and you did not deserve my accusations, my wrath."

Robert nodded. "I don't blame you."

"That's overly generous." William winced. "And I wish the queen could feel the same."

Robert snorted.

"Will she ever speak to me again?"

"She'll have to at some point." Robert took a final guzzle of his wine.

"You know what I mean."

Robert sighed, dragging his gaze from the blaze to the king, his dark eyes dancing in the glow.

"I wish I knew, cuz."

CHAPTER 14

The Weight of Lies

I t had been a fortnight and the queen had managed to stay out of his sight, shut away in her chambers, calling upon Moltmann to give her and her ladies private mass. But he knew he would see her this day, at Daniel's trial. She wouldn't miss the opportunity to see the man squirm under the weight of justice.

Bryan too would be in attendance. After his recovery, the king felt so ashamed he made the man an earl, giving him Castle Beaubourg as a dwelling until Cate was of age, even making his older brother a lord. William still couldn't look Bryan in the eye. Perhaps he should make Bryan part of council, to take Stephen's place. The king turned it over in his mind as he walked to the throne room, now transformed into a high judicial court.

Every peer from one end of the realm to the other crammed in, filling the sides of the room, their body heat making the room humid. The council was seated at the dais base behind a long table, Robert as prosecution sitting apart in his red velvet chair, William as final word, in his throne above it all. The king, dressed in black for his son, walked wearily up the steps of the glaringly spacious dais. Only his throne and Anna's remained. He'd ordered Daniel's chair burned the night she threw William out of her cell, and its absence didn't cease to strike his heart.

They had heard Jane's and Margaux's evidence yesterday. Both would be tried separately, but their testimonies were of great import for this case. William sat, sparing a glance to Anna's empty throne, his whole body aching. Wretched man. He nodded to Robert to proceed as courtiers whispered to each other behind hands and fans, eyes flicking from king to council.

Daniel, shackled, was led to his seat facing them. He was sallow, sunken, dressed in plain jerkin and shirt. William steeled himself against the sight, reminding himself what Daniel had done. And all empathy vanished. He glanced at the door, willing Anna to appear. Even if she ignored him, just her presence, her essence beside him, would strengthen him.

Robert stood. "Duke of Cecile, thou hast offended against our sovereign the King's Grace and stand accused of high treason, regicide by proxy, conspiracy to harm Her Majesty the Queen, conspiracy to harm His Majesty the King, extortion of a peer, slander against the same, false imprisonment of Her Majesty, and torture of an anointed Knight of the King's service. By the King's mercy, you are allowed to plead. What say you?"

Daniel grunted, aiming his eyes at a white marble square in front of his feet.

"You've nothing to plead?"

Someone coughed, but otherwise the room was silent. Bryan stood near the council and glared at Daniel so hard it seemed his will was the force that bent Daniel's head.

"Will you not speak to save yourself?" Halforn said this, his face pained as they all were. Daniel smiled softly at the tile.

Bustling at the entrance to the Great Hall brought everyone's attention to the door. In walked the queen, head high, her ladies trailing, all of them in black. Anna's skirts were blood red, with her bodice and kirtle black as ravens. She wore a gossamer veil over her crown, covering her body entirely like a shroud. She strode past Daniel without a glance, made a quick curtsy before the king, and settled herself into her throne, never making eye contact with William. He was desperate to reach out and take her hand.

Daniel finally looked up, taking in the sight. His smile broadened, he shook his head.

"And to think I brought this about. Both of you, sitting there, so sure of yourselves and your place in the world."

William stole a sidelong look at Anna, who sat, staring straight ahead at the far wall, her face revealing nothing.

"This is no place for thou to pontificate," Robert said. "Thou may answer questions put before thee and none else."

Daniel laughed, swiveled his head to Robert. "And look at you, half-cuz, so formal, so full of regality. Finally where you want to be. Well, almost. Methinks you'd rather be a few paces up those stairs."

"You've been warned, Cecile." This was Ridgeland, stern, sitting straight as a rod.

"I ask again, doth thou have anything to plead, anything to speak in thy defense?" Robert said.

"If I am guilty at all, it is of serving my country and my king, no matter the consequence, no matter the moral discomfiture." He spoke without anger or self-righteousness, almost as if he were reporting the weather conditions for the next hunt. He shrugged. "I've done nothing but try to save the realm and the king from destruction. How you and others have construed that into treason is another matter."

Halforn spoke. "You claim to be serving your king, but how, in bringing false claims against his queen, is that in his service? For the results of such speak for themselves. We have lost our heir."

Anna clenched the arms of her throne, her jaw tightening beneath her black screen. William's arm jerked in reflex to take her hand, but he stilled it, cleared his throat.

"And how is it my fault the queen cannot hold her pregnancies?"

Anna inhaled and William shot to his feet.

"Bastard." Bryan hissed from the side, the angry scars on his face making him no longer a handsome young knight, but a fierce, grizzled warrior.

Daniel laughed. "You're absolutely right. I am a bastard." He met William's eyes. "Bastard of a king."

William ground his teeth, breathing heavy. He wouldn't

stand being mocked, Anna being ridiculed. He felt her finger-tips around his wrist then release. He looked down upon her.

"It's all right, my liege," she said, still avoiding his gaze. He nodded. Wanted to weep, wanted to rail, wanted to fling tables and chairs. Instead he sat, rallying to match the queen's dignity.

Daniel spread his hands. "There is no way to know whether or not the queen would have gone to term, regardless of the circumstances. Therefore, you cannot lay this regicide by proxy—an invented accusation—at my feet."

"And yet we have testimony from court physicians and no fewer than twelve midwives that unusual and sudden trauma most certainly leads to induction of labor." Ridgeland gave the king a triumphant glance.

"That is still conjecture."

"Laying regicide aside for the moment, there still be a litany of offenses, each one carrying punishment of death," Robert said, pacing before the table.

"And which are those? Imprisonment? I did not have Sir Bryan and the queen imprisoned. The king did."

"By your false testimony!" Ridgeland pounded his fist on the table.

"His Majesty was following the law, so to accuse *me* of false imprisonment is wrongheaded. None of these accusations you list as treason are any of my doing, and the rest do not come with a penalty of death. I'm sorry, Your Graces, but the crown has no cause against me." Daniel cocked his head at Robert, as if daring him for more.

Anna scoffed, rolled her eyes. William leaned his weight on the arm closest to her. They were in this battle together. Surely she would soften now, recognize him as doing everything in his power to bring justice for her, for their son.

"To purposely give false testimony to the King's Majesty in and of itself is treason. And that, dear Cecile, is not in question. We hath sworn testimony of the same from the woman you paid."

"Extortion of a peer and slander merely carry sentences of various fines or years in prison." Daniel's faint smile had returned. It was almost as if he were enjoying this as some mental exercise, verbal acrobatics.

"Not when that extortion involves slander against Her Majesty," Halforn interjected.

"The queen is only consort. If she ruled outright, certainly treason would be the case, but she is merely the wife of our Liege Lord, the King. One cannot commit treason against her." Daniel lay his hands in his lap, chains clinking.

The crowd's murmur grew louder, Robert having to pound his gavel to bring silence. For the first time in weeks, Anna turned her face to address the king.

"That can't be true. He can't get away with this," her voice was low, stern.

"Remember, my love," he reached and took her hand, squeezed it, savored its warmth and the fire it sent through his body, "I am final arbiter here. He will not get away with a thing."

She nodded, stole her hand away, folding it with the other.

"Thy words hath always been fine, Cecile," Robert said, "yet the false testimony you spoke directly to the King's Grace still stands."

"Does it?" Daniel tilted his head like a curious pigeon. "If my

Liege and King would recall, I merely wondered at the queen's actions. Never directly accused."

William shook his head, opened his mouth to speak, but Robert spoke first, his voice rising, patience and formality slipping. "You forget I was there too, Cecile. 'Incontrovertible proof,' you said. Then produced your paid accomplice."

"And it was she who laid the accusation."

"Given to her by you!"

"That is her word against mine."

"And you expect any of us here now to accept *your* word?"

Daniel shrugged again.

"I, for one, have heard enough," Ridgeland said. "There seems no reason to keep dragging this on."

Duven scratched his chin. "This testimony does give me pause. Cecile is wily, to be sure."

"Are you saying you wish to discuss it further in chambers?" Robert was incredulous.

"I simply want to be entirely certain before we send such a longtime servant and friend of the crown to his death." Duven frowned at Daniel, who nodded his appreciation.

"As prosecutor, I call for a verdict." Robert slammed his gavel again and called each man for his verdict in turn. All asserted guilty, save Duven who abstained, Daniel watching idly.

"The court finds thou, Daniel, Duke of Cecile guilty of said charges, the law of the realm being thou deserves death. Thou shalt be burned on Traitor's Hill or else have thy head smitten off, as is the King's pleasure."

Robert came before the dais and bowed. "Your Majesty, doth thou affirm or deny said judgment?"

William closed his eyes, seeing him, Daniel, and Robert scampering about as boys, Daniel listening to him babble late into the night as young men in exile, Daniel counseling him to marry Anna . . . with the many times his heart had been ripped out in these last months, he was surprised it still beat. Opening his eyes, he found the queen, and all the rest, looking at him with silent, tense faces.

"We affirm the judgment."

"And what is Thy Majesty's pleasure?"

William glanced once more at Anna, steeling himself, then turned to Robert. "Take off his head. And may God have mercy on his soul, for I cannot."

The throne room erupted in chatter and some claps. William saw Bryan, staring death at Daniel, the crowd swirling about his still form.

The guards pointed their axe heads toward Daniel, symbolizing the verdict and his fate.

"Mark my words, Wills," Daniel said, stumbling to his feet. "You shall see this realm crumble, and there will be no one to blame but yourself."

They removed him from the throne room without a fight, though his eyes were ablaze, focused solely on the king.

Courtiers broke apart, exclamations and breathless conversation sending them filtering into the Great Hall, far behind the condemned. Anna rose, descended the stairs, and made a deep curtsy to the king.

"Majesty," she said. He nodded at her with a sad smile, she returned it, and quit the room with her ladies in tow.

Robert trod up the stairs, sat on the edge Anna's throne.

"'Tis done, cuz." He handed William the death warrant. "You just need sign it and set a date." The sorrow in Robert's voice echoed his own.

"I cannot believe it has come to this. Of all people on this earth, *Daniel.*"

" It boggles the mind, wearies the heart." Robert wiped a hand down his face, tugging on his goatee. "But you know there is no recourse. He knew what he was doing, knew the risk. You cannot show mercy. Not if you wish to be with the queen again, not if you wish to appear strong against all comers."

William sat back, his head hit the velvet cushion of his high throne. It could have been Anna's life he was signing away today, if the truth had not come out . . . He shuddered.

"Come for it before supper. I'll have done it by then."

Robert stood and rested a hand on the king's shoulder. "You've no choice, Wills. I, for one, shan't hold it against you."

William nodded and waited for the throne room to clear of all but his guards. He hoisted himself up, tucking the warrant under his arm, and headed to his empty chambers to contemplate the deeds that must be done.

William took a quiet supper with Duven, Ridgeland, and Robert, all of whom tried their best to avoid discussing the day's events, being extra buoyant and jovial, mainly teasing each other, recalling winning days of battle and nail-biting tourneys. All this talk of the past made William think of Daniel. For Daniel was always there, in the background, or at his side.

Now the king sat alone, letting the fire mesmerize him, wishing desperately for sleep, the creak of a door not even stirring him. But a scent, of lavender and cinnamon, faint hints of almond and roses, filled his very veins.

"Anna," he breathed, turning from his seat on the chest, taking her in. She was still awash in black, her red skirts winking beneath, but gone was the veil, the crown, her stateliness.

"I'm not ready to be reconciled with you," she said. "But I know what it feels like to think your dear friend shall meet death in the morn. And no matter how tangled my feelings for you have become, I could not let you stand vigil alone this night."

God, how he wanted to run to her, take her in his arms. But he wouldn't betray this small olive branch she extended.

"You are more gracious than I deserve," he stood, gesturing to her chair, unable to stop his glimmer of joy at seeing her settled there.

She took the wine he offered, raising it in thanks. "Regardless of my opinion of him, he was your friend. Someone you trusted, who has turned out to be a devil."

"I didn't realize until now how similar it is to what you must have felt about Bryan all those years ago." He took his own chair, nursing his wine.

"Ah, but at least the weight of putting him to death myself was not upon me."

William nodded. "And I have no hope of someone above taking the decision out of my hands."

"There's always the flag." She frowned into her lap. William grunted. Of course he'd thought of it, but then what good was his word, his rule, if he couldn't carry through? Would Anna think he had once again chosen Daniel's cause over her own?

"You would advise it?" He watched her staring at her hands, cup clutched between them.

"I would not. But I would understand your desire to do so."

"As you once said, I shall never forgive him for trying to take you from me."

She smiled into her wine. "But would you kill him on the spot with your bare hands?"

"I very nearly did," he said. Her eyes flicked to his. "What pains me most is that even his death will not cure the rift between us."

She shook her head. "Let's not speak on it, Wills, for I wish to be a comfort, not dissolve into more accusations, more pain."

"Say it again," he said, holding her gaze.

"I wish to be—"

"No. My name. Say my name."

She flushed and looked away. "Wills," she said, quiet. They were silent as he continued to peer at her, amazed at her presence, the grace she was giving him.

"It was good of you to give Bryan a title, let him live in Castle Beaubourg."

He shifted, sitting up, elbows on his knees. "I was thinking of giving him a seat on council, Master of Horse like your father perhaps."

She met his gaze again. "I don't know how he would take to being in your presence so much of the time, when he has been ill-treated."

"I can't forgive myself for what I did to him. I see in his eyes he knows it."

"What did you do? He won't tell me." She relaxed back, toes curled in silk slippers on the edge of the chest.

"Again, more than I deserve." He shook his head, unable to face her. He sighed. "I ordered him tortured."

"That much I surmised, for I heard him." She closed her eyes. "Oh those hours of his moans, his screams . . ."

"God, I'm such a fool."

"You're a king."

He felt her eyes on him, though he didn't meet them. "I was not a king then."

A need to confess it all to her erupted in him, as if she could somehow absolve him, if he told her everything, he would somehow be cleansed, made whole again.

"I went to him. I railed at him, poured out my hate, my vengeance, my anger. I punched him, twisted his already broken parts . . ."

She inhaled sharply. "Put him on council. Tomorrow. Let him refuse it if he may, but I will advise him against taking the post."

"You still see him?" It wasn't an indictment, yet it pierced to know she'd sought solace in another.

She nodded and their eyes met. "We Beaubourgians stick together."

"For kings come and go, but Beaubourg will remain?"

She smiled, melancholy. "Something like that."

"And what shall I do with Jane, with Margaux?" He went to fetch more wine from his desk, bringing the pitcher and some bread and cheese back to the chest.

"Margaux is a strange case indeed. For once she knew of the stable incident, she did not reveal her involvement. Though how could she know that was the whole of it? As far as I can tell, we ladies only knew that someone said *I* had been with Bryan."

"She was certain to know more than she let on, hearing all from her brother." He broke off a bit of bread and a hunk of cheese, chewing thoughtfully.

"But she was so decent during the labor. And then she took it upon herself to make sure Robert heard Jane . . . I've no idea what came over her."

"No idea?" He smiled. "It seems you forget your attendance at her births, from saving Frederick's very life, to the concern you showed at her own miscarriage. Surely there was something awoken in her."

"Perhaps." She sighed. "I still would never have guessed it of her."

"We are in a world of wonders." He pulled off more bread, if only for something to do with his hands.

"I would send her to Mohrlang, indefinitely. He is sure to dote on her, and she can concentrate on her boys."

"Now that *is* merciful."

"She did what was right, in the end."

"And will you say the same for Jane?"

Tears welled in her eyes. She dashed them away. "I—"

He was out of his seat and on his knees before her, catching the last of her tears with his thumbs, caressing her soft, pale cheeks. She trembled beneath his hands, reached hers up to cover his.

"I don't know how to forgive her," she said. "I don't know how to forgive you."

"I don't know how to forgive myself."

She took his head in her hands and tucked him to her chest. They held each other, each in their separate griefs, silent tears blending in sympathetic fellowship.

Dawn broke cold and gray, a low ceiling of clouds hung, almost touching the top of Traitor's Hill. Robert's wolf cape whipped in the wind, his chain of office weighty upon his chest. Unlike Helena, this execution was private, with only peers allowed admittance. William didn't want more attention brought to the whole fiasco.

Drums echoed from Stone Yard. Robert took one last look at the flag above the palace. The griffin flew. There would be no quarter for his old friend.

Anna sat on a small stool, in a small room reached by a rickety ladder. There was a round, unwashed window with a view of Traitor's Hill. She squinted to try and make out the crowd, the scaffold. She heard muffled drums over the wind, which howled around the nest of a room. She looked to the man standing with her, then into her lap at the folded red and white flag of mercy. The flag bearer arched his brows.

"If you wish to raise it, 'tis now or never, Highness."

Anna bit her lip.

Before dawn William rode with three guards into the woods,

the opposite direction of Traitor's Hill. But he could still hear the drums, loud as if he stood at the scaffold. He heeled his black steed, urging him deeper, farther into the densest trees, blocking out all thought but of the galloping beast beneath him, the frigid air lashing his face.

Robert saw Daniel's stark head appear at the crest of the hill. Daniel studied the path in front of him until he came among the courtiers. He craned his neck to look at the palace, surely seeking the flag, then he turned to the stands, desperate eyes searching for the king, but the royal box was empty.

"Do you have children?" Anna asked the man.

"Yes'm, two strapping boys and a little girl, sweet as pie."

Anna nodded, put a hand to her empty womb, and let the flag fall to the ground, red and white pooling at her feet.

William halted, allowing his sweating horse to drink from a stream, his men to stretch their legs. He was still in view of the castle's south side, but hopefully he was far enough not to hear. Yet he knew being out of earshot wouldn't keep his mind from treading well-worn paths of regret.

Robert wanted to look away, but knew he owed Daniel this. Even though he was a traitor, he was no different than Robert. Many times Robert's head had deserved to roll, but he hadn't been caught.

Moltmann and Bartmore stood stoic on the scaffold. Daniel took a trembling breath at the bottom of the stairs, then ascended, his whole body shaking by the time he reached the top. Bartmore performed his pompous duties, giving Daniel last rites. Then Daniel shuffled to the front of the scaffold, his chains now loosed.

Anna couldn't see, for the window was too dirty, the scaffold too far away. She didn't want to see anyway.

"Majesty, you've a good heart. That yer even here speaks to it. I won't fault you this day. And you shouldn't fault yourself."

"Thank you," she whispered.

"Good people of Troixden," Daniel said, his voice clear, crisp. "I ask you to pray for my soul and that of the king. He is a noble and fair Liege Lord, always after the best purpose of our realm, with you constantly in his heart. I too only sought to serve you and him, with all of myself. And if by dying this day I serve him all the more, then it is my pleasure to do so."

He made the sign of the cross over himself and went to kneel behind the block. He said something to the executioner, which caught on the wind and floated away from Robert's hearing. Robert tried and failed to steady himself. The axe swung.

William mounted and rode his horse at a slow walk, idly looking about for game of any size to occupy his thoughts. From the quiet burst a tumult of hundreds of birds launching themselves from the palace walls, screeching their displeasure as they raced overhead, a murder of crows.

William knew it was finished.

With her father passed and Daniel dead, Anna felt obligated to attend council when her schedule allowed it. Though, if truth be told, she also hoped being present would curb any further outlandishness in court. It was a month past it all, and Anna wanted to make sure justice was served and the whole incident tucked away. If only it were so easy to dispatch with her heart.

It seemed the men were too stunned with the recent events to care about seating arrangements, so Anna sat at the far end of the table, opposite the king, who sat frowning down at his hands, barely listening to the proceedings.

"With the Countess of Mohrlang under house arrest, we still have the matter of Lady Jane," Robert said. His duties as prosecutor still stood, though he eschewed the king's attempts to thrust Daniel's rank or responsibilities upon him, a development that surprised her.

"I have her death warrant here," Robert continued, "but we are still not unanimous."

"What is to happen to the boy?" Halforn said.

"He would become a ward of the crown, staying here at court," Robert said.

"Well that's quite lenient," Bartmore scoffed.

"The child had nothing to do with his mother's actions," Anna said.

"He's still a heretic."

"He is but seven years old, Your Grace," Anna said, trying to sound authoritative rather than annoyed.

"And cannot a seven-year-old believe improper, immoral things?" Anna could have sworn Bartmore jeered at her. "Indeed, it seems even five-year-olds have quite active theological minds, if the princess is any indication."

"Enough, Your Grace," William said, still not raising his gaze. Cate had just celebrated half a decade, and was even bolder about sharing her visions, perhaps motivated by what she'd witnessed between her parents.

"I merely point out that perhaps the child should be somewhere less resplendent."

"Losing one's mother is horror enough for a child," Anna said, "then to thrust him from the only home he knows? It's abject cruelty."

"Leaving aside for the moment any pity we might bear for the child," Halforn said, "it seems that to send him away would only breed anger and vengeance in the lad. If he stays here, we might keep him as a loyal supporter."

"What's one boy's anger against the crown?" Ridgeland said.

"If these past months are any indication," Halforn said, "quite a lot."

"If she dies, we'll keep the boy here," William said, finally addressing the council.

"But—" Bartmore raised a finger.

"That is final." William only flicked his eyes to the archbishop, but the fire that burned there clamped the man's mouth shut.

Robert cleared his throat. "And what then of the mother?"

Anna met William's eyes, questioning. She said, "As for the lady, if her son is lost to her, she may as well be dead." William winced and turned his face away.

"All the more reason we should send him away then," Bartmore said, "further punishment for her treason, knowing her son is far off and—"

"I said the boy stays." William pounded his fist on the table, cups and quills jostling in response.

"And the lady?" Robert watched the king, but William shrugged and went back to studying his hands.

"As it was Her Majesty's person that was most offended by the lady's actions, perhaps she might advise us?" Halforn said.

All faces turned to her, including that of a lifeless and taciturn Bryan, newly filling her father's shoes as Master of Horse.

Anna spread her fingers wide on the table and took a deep breath. "I think we send the lady and her son back to Cecile. Keep the lady under house arrest as the Countess Mohrlang is, but knowing that, unlike the Countess, the lady shall never be received at court and her arrest shall never be revoked."

Snorts of protest sounded around the table, Robert having to hit his gavel to silence them.

"You would allow the woman who wreaked such havoc, whose words have brought such ruin, be shown such latitude?" Bryan said, breaking his silence, voice still strained from the screams of his torture.

"Have we not had enough death?"

"I also find it too merciful," Ridgeland said. "If she is to live, certainly it should be in the confines of Stone Yard."

Anna looked at her hands. "I was asked my opinion and I gave it. You as council decide."

"Do as the queen says." William stood. "We are adjourned."

He stalked from the room, leaving behind a baffled and bickering council. Anna saw Robert fling the death warrant into the fire, the parchment overtaken by flames.

She left to follow the king, catching him at the top of the stairs that led to their chambers.

"Majesty," she called, stopping him.

He spun, shaking his head. "I don't understand it. It has been a month and still you spurn my company."

Her eyes grew, incredulous. "You expect that all would be forgiven and forgotten in such a short span?"

"You give your accuser such kindness, yet still you lay our son at my feet?"

"It wasn't her fault."

He stepped toward her, reaching out a hand, but then dropped it. "Not her fault? She knew all she needed was to sound the alarm to you against Daniel and she and her boy would be safe."

"It would have been her word against his. And we both know how that would have turned out."

"Don't keep throwing Daniel in my face."

"If you want to know why I can so easily offer her forgiveness and still hold offense against you, it's because you had no reason to believe such nonsense. Had you come to me, you would never have believed it, but instead you hid yourself away to stew in some twisted fantasy of Daniel's making."

A man cleared his throat behind them. Anna whipped around to find Robert, head bowed. She straightened.

"Begging your pardon, Majesties, but there are orders to sign, and then I will be out of your way."

"We were finished, Norwick," William said.

Anna opened her mouth then shut it again. She dropped a quick curtsy and retired to her own rooms, flustered.

She found Mary cleaning out her medicinal stores, Yvette mending shirts, and the rest of her diminished retinue in various states of relaxation. They jumped to attention at her arrival.

Amelia brought her a glass of wine and went back to her nee-
dlepoint. Anna sat on her favored chair for sewing, exhausted,
though she'd just been sitting for an hour.

Bernard entered, also sedate, and announced Bryan.

Mary stiffened at Anna's side. Her nurse had lectured her
enough about the time Anna spent in Bryan's company, especially now that she'd been accused of abusing such company. If
people wished to talk, so be it. Nothing anyone could say or do
could hurt her now.

But that wasn't true either. A small piece of her stung every
time William looked at her with those solemn, disappointed eyes.

"My Lord," Anna said, reaching a hand to take his in greeting. "I still must get used to saying that."

His lately absent smile touched the corners of his lips. "And
I must get used to hearing it."

"Have you also come to berate me over my clemency toward
Lady Jane?" She released him and he sat in the window seat,
either oblivious to, or ignoring, Amelia's blushes next to him.

"I've come to see how you fare, Madam."

She picked up one of the king's shirts and set to embellishing
the cuffs, a hint of clove and wood smoke wafting up from the
fabric. She ignored the flutter in her chest and stomach that his
smell produced.

"I fare as well as can be expected, but I am only wounded of
heart—you are wounded in body as well. How is your arm today?
I noticed you flexing your hand in council. Do you need more
treatment?"

He lifted his left hand and fluttered his fingers. "They're a
bit stiff, but as I was unable to fight before, 'tis not such a loss.

I can still feel fine flanks." Amelia's blush deepened. "And I don't need much more in my current position."

Anna lowered her voice. "And how is it with the king?"

"Miserable." He frowned at his hand, letting it drop.

"Oh, Bryan, I so thought this appointment would be a boon to you. I was foolish to expect you to interact with the man who had you tortured."

Bryan chuckled, looking at her under his brow. "*I'm* not miserable, he's miserable. Though it was admittedly difficult at first, to look him in the eye, to have any respect . . . but you know how he is. He wins one over eventually."

"Well, he's got quite a climb with me." She scowled at the shirt. Maybe if she embroidered these tiny swirls into snakes it would momentarily help.

"And that's why he's miserable. Which makes it miserable to be around him."

"If he is cruel to you—"

He laughed. "God in heaven, it's like I'm the princess he's so magnanimous to me. No, he's just gutted, hollowed out." His sky blue fixed upon her in candor. "We two are not the only ones struggling to come to grips with what has happened."

She shook away her prowling tenderness for the king. "I don't need yet one more lecture on how woe the king be. He's done it to himself."

Bryan shared some unspoken communication with Mary behind her. He nodded and leaned over on his knees, his blonde hair coming down like a curtain on the side of his face. A desperate desire to touch it, to feel its silken softness, kept her watching him. She shifted, her husband's smell drifting again to her nose. Damnable lust. Yvette had always told her that when she felt this distracted by her admiration of the male form, she was nearer conception. She was desperate for another child, but even this internal instinct, this underfed hunger, wouldn't drive her to William's bed. The very thought of it chilled her blood. Yet she couldn't stand being this close to her former flirtation.

"I feel I should lie down, if you'll excuse me, My Lord."

Bryan jumped up, his flexing thigh much too close to her grasp. "It is I who should be excused. Was it something I said? I don't wish to drive you to further despair."

She smiled, took his hand, tried not to inflame at the feel of its rugged maleness. "I always enjoy your company, friend. 'Tis nothing you've done. I am still recovering and need more rest than before."

"Of course." He bowed, kissed her hand all too quickly. "I would not tax you for my life."

He left and she took to her bed, images of William's scowl, Bryan's hands, the warm embrace of the king's bed melding in her exhausted mind.

Robert leaned into Yvette's kneading knuckles with a deep groan. "Ah, right there."

He carried all his worry where his neck met his back. Her expert hands tenderized his knotted muscles. He tilted even farther back in his desk chair, pushing into her pressure. She switched to using an elbow.

"Better?" she asked. Robert moaned. "I fully expect you to start thumping your leg upon the ground like a hound."

He circled his head. "I've other things I'd rather thump."

She sighed, rolled her eyes. "You're an incorrigible glutton."

"And you're an irresistible siren." He drew her hands to his mouth. "And speaking of irresistible." He slung an arm over his chair back, looking her over. "It's been more than a month. Why is the queen still giving our king nothing but cold sheets and bitter drink?"

She combed her fingers through his hair, swirling it, pulling gently. "You cannot expect her to jump merrily back into his arms so soon."

"It's her duty, I care not for her feelings on the matter." He stopped himself from purring outright at her ministrations.

"But he does." She left his hair, trailing a forefinger down his nose, placing it on his lips for a kiss. "If he had simply imprisoned her, perhaps this length of time would have healed her more fully. But 'tis the child she cannot forgive. You must realize she's not only mourning her marriage, she's mourning her son."

"So is he! They should be mourning together. Trying to make another son."

She laughed at this. "And since when do you want the king to have a son?"

He ran his hands down her sides, her shift pulling tight, hinting at what lie beneath.

"Now that I've seen the effects I wish him *bon chance*."

"This does not meet with your ambitions."

"Damn my ambitions." He pulled her to his chest. "I just want my friend back."

She smiled. "So you do have a heart after all."

He bit her chin. "Let's not have that getting out."

Christmas Day. Anna didn't feel like celebrating. All this talk of the Virgin Mary and her divine boy-child ripped open Anna's scabbing wound, dumping salt in as if to preserve it like dried trout. After a full day of services she would be forced to feast and look merry, dance with the king, and here she'd barely touched him beyond ceremony since the night before Daniel's execution.

She had closeted herself in her chambers after services to garner strength for the coming evening, attempted to read St. Paul, but kept flipping to Lamentations, wishing she could see her way out of this fog.

Her main doors burst open, Cate shouting as she came. "Mama, Mama! I've a gift for you!"

Bernard hustled behind her. "Now princess, no running!" Bernard tried his best to look stern, but even he couldn't resist this bubble of ribbons and velvet, and dimpled, bright red cheeks.

The queen opened her arms and Cate ran to her lap.

"Open it, Mama!" She thrust a small golden box under Anna's nose.

Anna did as entreated and found an oval locket, Troixden's griffin engraved upon it, amid a forest of curling vines.

"It's lovely, dearest." She kissed Cate's forehead. "I shall wear it to the feast tonight."

"But look inside," she said, eyes wide.

Anna obliged. The locket opened, each side displaying a curled lock of hair.

"This is mine," Cate said, indicating the left with her finger, "and this is my baby brother's."

Anna's heart caught in her throat, her own finger stroking the glass overlay. "But how—?"

"Uncle Robert gave it to me," she said, matter-of-fact. "He said we might fashion it for you."

"Uncle Robert did this?" Looking at the fine, curled hair the color of William's, something in her thawed toward this uncle.

"Do you like it?" Cate looked at Anna, eager for approval. The queen nodded. She had no words. "And look!" Cate took the locket and unsnapped another clasp Anna hadn't seen, revealing two empty displays. "For my other brothers."

Anna's breath stopped. She lowered her voice. "Catey, you must not speak like that."

"Why ever not if it be true?"

"Because it is worrisome to others. Worrisome to me."

Cate frowned. "But I thought you would be cheered by it. They said you would be."

Anna didn't want to know who "they" were. With Bartmore's thinly veiled comments, the princess's imaginings and dreams needed to be curtailed.

"I adore my present. Will you help me put it on?"

Cate snaked the chain around Anna's neck with marzipan-soft arms. They smiled into each other's eyes.

"I love you, princess-pie." Anna wiggled a forefinger at Cate's belly and her daughter laughed. "Now, will you stay with me until the feast? You may help me pick out the rest of my attire."

Cate clapped her hands and they set to work.

William's stomach had churned all day. Sitting mere inches from Anna for hours at mass, yet knowing he could not, should not, touch her, had done him in. Not simply the agony of her disdain, but the pent-up madness of his unquenched thirst. He had never seriously considered taking a mistress. Certainly, there was the occasional fantasy, a wide-eyed, fresh beauty at court, the temptation of fluttering lashes and pink bosoms, but Anna had always sated him, and he'd had no need to stray. Even at the beginning, when she'd refused his bed and Margaux had tried to ply her craft, he hadn't succumbed, even if to tame his dragon, as they say. But things were becoming unbearable.

Thus, the feast would be a double hardship. Not only would he be lusting for his wife who would give him no quarter, he also would be surrounded by ladies, plumped and pressed and dressed to impress.

He met up with Anna and Cate in the throne room. They glowed like Christmas candles. He caught his breath without breaking stride, bowed to the queen, took her hand and kissed it. Cate gave a regal curtsy and he tapped the tip of her button nose.

"Shall we?" He held up an arm for Anna to take, Cate jumping to her place in front. Anna held her arm slightly above his, laying her fingers on top rather than lacing them through his. He snaked up his fingers, pulling hers down to curl into his hand. He felt her flinch, barely. The heat that spread through him made him weak-kneed, and reminded him how long it had been since he'd felt this much of her touch. How ridiculous to be so aroused at such a minor interaction this far along in their life together.

A horn trumpeted their entrance and the court cheered and bowed and curtsied, all made merry by an excess of spiced wine. The royal family had to make their circuit of greetings before sitting down to eat. Anna entrusted Cate to Cariline and went to the opposite side of the hall, William following her with his eyes like a hungry dog. Robert startled him out of his pining.

"How goes the war?"

"See for yourself." He gestured at the queen.

"Something tells me she may be more softened this eve." Robert bounced his brows.

"For heaven's sake then, send her some wine. And keep it coming."

Robert laughed. "If she be not biddable, you know I can always find you a discrete outlet for your pains."

"Always at my service, ay?"

"With that in mind . . ." Robert led him to Halforn, who was surrounded by his daughters and another woman William didn't recognize. She was lithe like a willow, with deep-blonde curls waving down her back.

"Majesty," Halforn said with a bow, "may I present my niece, the Lady Marie?"

As she curtsied low William took her hand, kissing the soft, smooth surface.

"Enchanted," he said.

Robert smacked the king's shoulder. "Enjoy the evening, Majesty."

When William looked to give Robert some fitting response, he caught the face of the queen gone ashen, Yvette leaning to her, whispering furtively. When Anna saw him staring she hurried away, Yvette and Mary at her heels. He shrugged mentally and turned back to the docile beauty before him. She was fluttering her fan, talking about the castle decor. He nodded, not really listening. Good Lord, what was he doing?

He excused himself and finished his rounds, heading back to the high table. The queen was nowhere to be found. He sat, ordered his cup filled, and gazed about the court, eyes helplessly landing on women's chests, curves of their necks, slender fingers. He groaned and shifted his weight.

The chair next to his pulled out and the queen unceremoniously sat herself in it. She grabbed his wine and gulped it, dabbed her mouth with a cloth, and smiled, sheepish.

"I don't know what has me so thirsty. I could not wait."

His face remained unmoved, but a hope sparked within him. "All that is mine is yours, my queen."

She nodded, took another pull as her own cup was filled. She relaxed back, elbows on her armrests.

"'Tis a beautiful feast."

He leaned to her, eyeing her. "Must we?"

"Must we what?" She smiled, but he knew it was only for show.

"Must we make talk of the feast and the people?"

She cocked her head. "And what is it you wish to speak of, my liege?"

"Anna, don't. Please." He looked away, his eyes inadvertently finding Marie. "We're well beyond false niceties."

"I didn't think you'd want to have it out in public." She took up her own cup. "And I certainly do not wish to feast in complete silence."

"Those are the only two options then?" He sighed. "Argue with me or speak about the hard sauce and the holly and ivy?"

"By all means, Majesty, pick some topic that pleases you." Her tone hardened. Why had he not said, "talk to me like my Anna"? She was trying to be softer and he'd ruined it.

"I hear Catey shall take part in the masque."

That brightened her. "She gave me a private performance this afternoon. Along with this." She pulled out a gold chain, an engraved locket dangling on it. He had to bend to her as she didn't remove the necklace. Lavender, rosemary, and almonds filled his nose and his yearning for her heightened. She placed the opened locket in his hand.

"'Tis her hair." She let out a shaky breath. "And his. Justinian's."

"My God." He touched the glass over his boy's hair, the only part of him the king would ever see. Guilt, shame, and grief washed over him. He swallowed, releasing the tightness in his throat. She opened it farther, unfolding it like a bellows.

"She says these empty places are for her brothers to come." He felt her gaze upon him. He rubbed the blank glass, nodded once.

"She does have her theories, doesn't she?" He sat back and watched Anna tuck the locket beneath her corset, the same place she used to keep his ruby. "Thank you for showing it to me."

She dipped her head and they fell quiet as the food was served. Throughout the meal they spoke to those on their sides, Halforn, Robert, Duven, and a smattering of other gentry who needed attention. Before he knew it, it was time for him to lead the queen in the first dance.

His hand crackled with her touch as he accompanied her to the floor. She curtsied, he bowed, and the music began. Who on earth had chosen a volte? And there was Robert, bouncing on his heels next to the musicians, clamping down a mischievous grin.

Anna looked as horrified as William was annoyed, but there was nothing they could do. They lurched toward each other as the dance required, and he wondered if she was remembering their first dance at their wedding feast. She had a similar look on her face, but no fear or timidity now, only regret.

Grabbing her thigh and waist, he thrust her into the air, she now truly an angel descending back to his arms. She slid down his front, breathless. Again and again she came to him, again and again he sent her flying, both their hearts pounding. All too soon the dance ended. She curtsied and he pulled her up into his arms, searching her face.

"Come to me tonight."

"I'm not ready." Her eyes flit away, but he didn't release her.

"You once said you would never refuse me."

"And you once said you'd never force me." She met his hot gaze.

"I'm not forcing you, I'm asking you." *I'm begging you.* "I realize your grief is not yet healed—"

"It feels it never will be—"

"Nor will mine." He shook her in his impatience. Not hard, but it got her attention. Her eyes flared. "We must get on with living."

He could feel her heartbeat slow against his chest, even through his layers of finery. She nodded, eyes wet, and broke from his arms, heading straight to her chambers.

Now he'd done it.

She's not coming. Just go to bed and forget it. The king's eyelids drooped while he sprawled in his chair by the fire, fixing all his waning energy on the private door. It was nearly two in the morning and his chamber remained empty.

He sighed and heaved himself up to take his own advice. His knees cracked, his legs sore from all the dancing. After Anna left, he'd decided not to let the night go to waste and carried on quite well with Marie and many other partners. But who was he kidding? The only woman he wanted was on the other side of that stone.

He pulled off his shirt, scratched his chest, and wondered if he should have one more drink to send him off to sleep in a hurry, when a creak of hinges sounded. Soft light spilled on the floor and she was there. His angel.

Her hair cascaded over her shoulders, a dark veil, her silk shift barely hiding her curves. His groin hardened. She set her candle on the bedside table and brought her hands in front of her, finally raising her eyes. She sucked air when she saw his chest, then raised her chin higher.

"I am here to perform my queenly office," she said with no hint of play.

He put his hands on his hips, conscious that it showed his chest in its best light. "You know I don't want you like this." He gestured to her. "As if you've come for me to do surgery upon you."

Her eyes flashed. "Every time I see you, my heart breaks anew. For us, for our child. I'm sorry, but I can't offer you more."

He strolled to her. "And does my heart not ache as well? Every time I look upon you and your face is filled with scorn and despair? Every time I see your flattened corset it's like a fire iron thrust into my gut." He rested his hands on her shoulders, rubbing them with his thumbs. "I know you think me the author of your pain, your grief, and perhaps I am, but Anna, neither of us can get through this without the other."

"But don't you see?" Her voice was barely above a whisper, cracking with emotion. "That is what makes it all the worse. For you've ripped apart our sanctuary."

"Then we'll have to rebuild it, stone by stone."

She opened her eyes and a single tear escaped. He caught it with a soft kiss. She winced, but then threw her arms around his neck, pulling him down. She shook with soft sobs as he ran his hands up and down her back.

Slowly, he brought his lips to her temple, his hands moving to her waist. He grazed her cheek, her jaw, as she trembled beneath his hands. He drew back and she stilled. She lifted a hand to his cheek, caressing his stubble. Bending, he kissed her mouth with soft, gentle pressure. Her breath hitched, her hand slipping behind his neck, drawing him down. He groaned deep in his throat.

"Wills," she said against his lips. A cry and plea all at once.

Taking her face in his hands, he felt the dampness of her cheeks and moved to lick away the tears, only to find his own cheeks sodden. She clung to him, pulling his mouth back to hers. He stooped, picking her up, so light, so easy, and strode to the bed, lips never parting.

He placed her down as if she might break, their eyes holding as he removed his trunks and hose. He hesitated at the foot of the bed, one brow raised in question, heart pounding against his ribs until they were sore. She gave him a small, somber nod.

He came to her, nipping here and there, but his pent-up desire overtook him, and she responded. She too must have needed his physical comfort, felt this hunger. But her cries of pleasure were indistinguishable from those of pain, his yells of anguish and blessed release.

They held each other, bodies wet with sweat and tears, neither saying a word, finally succumbing to an exhausted sleep.

When the birds started their morning song, the light barely breaking the horizon, she slipped from his arms, tucked the sheets around him, kissed his brow, and was gone.

In his half-awake haze, he wondered if it had all been a dream.

To say the king and queen were anywhere near their old ways would be stretching the truth beyond decency, but after their night together, Anna made extra efforts to be less gloomy and reticent in his presence. They had only come together once more, him finding her in her chambers late in the night. He climbed into her bed, pulling her warmth against him. She found she could not, indeed did not, want to resist. But they weren't back to speaking freely, spending long nights in companionship by his fire. As desperate as she was to be near him, guilty even for being so intractable, every time she felt herself loosen, images of Justinian leapt to her mind's eye and she had to begin all over again.

For the last week she'd felt ill and weak, her breasts aching. She knew these symptoms well, and even with her struggles to conceive, she had no doubt she was pregnant. It must have been Christmas. Though she was barely along, she knew she had to tell William. Perhaps this new babe could move their hearts back to each other.

She hurried to finish her present for the king, took one last look in the mirror, and set off to his chambers. He was finishing up some conference with Duven and Norwick, so she took her regular chair by the roaring fire.

"'Tis not any slight to you, Duven," the king said. "I just want to be sure we've looked at all the possibilities before we start carving up Cecile's duchy. You would, of course, be the first of the share."

Duven bowed his head. "'Tis an honor to even be considered, Highness. I simply wish to be of service to the whole of Troixden, and worry over my part when the dust is settled."

"So contrite and politic, Duven," Robert said. "Quite at odds with our King of Misrule from last year."

"Is that a challenge, Norwick?" The men continued their repartee into the hall, leaving king and queen alone.

William came to her, leaned over, and kissed her cheek.

"You look glorious this evening, my dear," he said with a sweet smile.

"And you majestic as always." She smiled back. "Cate adored your present. She will not stop talking about her miniature warhorse just like Papa's."

"It was really all Bryan. He saw the pony and knew Cate must have it." He sat, elbows on his knees. "I heartily agreed."

"As long as you don't get her a sword to go with it."

"Oh no?" He grinned. "You would not have your daughter be as mighty as any man?"

Anna laughed. "I believe she shall slay men much quicker with her tongue."

"Just like her mother." He kept his smile as he considered her face. She felt her pulse quicken, so turned from him.

"Would you like your gift?" She held out a plain wooden box with gold hinges that fit in the palm of her hand.

"Certainly." He sat in front of her on the chest, his legs straddling hers. He picked up the box, rattled it, then peered at it from all angles. "'Tis quite small."

She was unaccountably nervous. "Just open it, Wills."

He stopped his inspection. "I like it when you call me that."

A smile fought its way to her lips. He flipped the lid. With a confused look, he pulled out the locket Cate had given Anna, opened to reveal the empty spaces.

"Did you not want to keep it?" His eyes were on her again, that glaze of sadness and regret seeping in.

She touched his arm and smiled. "No, Wills. The idea is that we shall fill it." He shook his head, brows furrowed. "I hesitate to tell you as it is so early, but . . ." His face transformed from one of concern to one of disbelief. "All the signs indicate . . . it seems Catey is right again."

He enveloped her in his arms, hugging her to his chest. "It's a miracle!"

She laughed into his shoulder. "I can hardly trust it myself, but the symptoms are so precise and distinct." He drew back, hands cupping her face, shaking his head in amazement. "My courses were due two days ago, but it was only a day or so after Christmas that I felt a change. When I woke and was starving, yet nauseated at the thought of food . . ."

"We must keep this quiet at court until you're further along."

She nodded. "It will be our private knowledge."

"Oh, my Anna." His smile could break rocks. He kissed her and held her again. Her heart softened even as it constricted. This new child reminded her of the one she had unjustly lost. And by his hands. She drew back with a sheepish smile.

"And I have something for you." He reached in his pocket and took out a velvet purse, piped in gold. "It may be too early, but it means nothing to me if you do not have it."

She unfolded the flap, feeling a familiar weight in her hands. Sure enough, she pulled out the ruby on a chain—his heart—and stared at it glowing in her palm.

"Wills, I—"

"Just please say you'll take it. Take care of it."

She knew he was asking for much more than for her to preserve a piece of jewelry. She fingered the engraving: *Locked fast thou art, within my heart.*

He closed her fingers around the necklace and held her fist, rubbing her knuckles with his thumb. She didn't wish to break this tender peace, this newfound joy, but she knew she couldn't wear it. Not yet.

She met his eyes, deep blue pools of hope. Placing her other hand on top of his, she said, "Thank you, Wills."

He nodded, withdrew his hands. "Shall we have a toast then, to our secret babe?"

Her smile was genuine as she raised a glass, toasting the new life inside her, and new prospects for all their futures.

CHAPTER 15

Birth for a Nation

Anna came out of the stable flushed and happy. Her new palfrey was the purest white she'd ever seen, like a summertime cloud, with eyes like the sky itself, looking for all the world like the unicorns on her tapestries. Perhaps she would give it a horn for May Day celebrations, let the children ride her as Bryan led in the ring. She smiled, imagining the scene and nearly ran right into the king.

He stood, hands in his pockets, watching her frankly.

"Highness, here is the posy from the child who—" Bryan's smile faded and he tripped to a halt.

"My queen," William said, "I had hoped we might discuss the dispersion of lands, but I could not find you."

"I was testing my new palfrey." She gestured to the stable.

"As I see. She is beautiful and full of grace, like her rider."

Her hands went carelessly to her blooming belly. Nearly half-way through her pregnancy and there had been no issues, no complications, other than the fact that tension remained with the babe's father. Whether or not he deserved her forgiveness, he was still her king, still Cate's papa, still that damnable hand-some and charming man who'd won her heart so completely, the scarred tatters of which screamed to be healed by him alone.

"Have you made your decisions? May I hear of them?" she said.

He bowed his head, swung a welcoming arm toward the cas-tle. "By all means."

She nodded and followed his lead, but not before she caught him give a pointed, yet quizzical, look back at Bryan.

Once inside, he made an effort at pleasantries. "So you wish to keep the horse?"

"She rides like a dream, almost as well as Sheba. I feel like a fairy princess when I ride her."

He smiled. "And does a queen need to feel like a fairy princess?"

"Every woman, no matter how old, wishes to feel like a fairy. It makes me remember what it was like to be a girl, without a care in the world."

He made to take her arm but stopped himself, hiding his desire by fishing for a kerchief. "I wish I could give you that."

She stopped, placing a hand on his forearm.

"I know you tried. And I am grateful."

He nodded and they continued in silence. Guards opened his chamber doors, revealing Robert, Duven, and Halforn seated around the king's desk. They rose, bowed, kissed her hand in turn. A page situated a tufted chair for her next to William's seat.

"I trust you've all had time to review my proposal?" William said. The men nodded.

"I've no need of more lands, Your Highness," Halforn said with a good-natured swipe of his hand. "Are you sure you want to carve up Cecile rather than appoint another duke?"

"I'm not sure your eldest grandson would be as generous as Your Grace," William said, with a smile for Halforn. "And regardless, I am decided that you and Duven shall have at least double the lands that our expansion of Havenside gobbles up."

"And what of the rest?" Robert cocked a brow, looking from man to man, avoiding the queen.

"The rest I wish to see again." William turned to Anna. "Well before Her Majesty's lying in, I would like to take a small retinue back to Foxhall. Once the highest heats have passed."

Anna's stomach clenched. There was too much history there. She wasn't sure she could manage it, being among Daniel's personal belongings, remembering how even then he'd begun to brew distrust, claiming she'd hidden a pregnancy from the king.

"Then I will decide if I rule it by proxy until another duke is fit, or if I divide it." William absently patted her hand. She hoped he couldn't feel her cold sweat. "What do you think, Highness?"

She could only nod, and kept silent for the rest of the short meeting, fiddling with the ruby on its chain in her pocket. Soon the men left and she and the king were alone again.

"I should leave you to your work as well." She rose abruptly, her finger catching on the necklace in her pocket as she drew out her hands to curtsy. It made a dull plunk as it hit the thick woven rug. William reached down, picked it up, and with gloomy eyes, handed it to her.

"I believe you dropped this."

"I-I just—"

He shook his head. "It cheers me that it is anywhere near you." But he looked as though she'd punched him in the kidney with an armored fist.

She took the necklace, hurriedly wrapped it around her fingers, curtsied again, and fled.

Back in her chambers, she feigned a headache and took to her bed, but Mary wasn't fooled.

"What be the matter, dearie?" Mary hovered, fluffing Anna's pillows, readjusting the sheets.

"It's just all too much." Anna covered her eyes with her forearm, willing herself not to cry. "He wants to ride with me to Foxhall, to survey Cecile's lands. I can't bear to see that place again."

"Well at least yer putting the blame where it belongs."

"Excuse me?" Anna hoisted herself up on her elbows.

Mary clucked her tongue, waving a knobby finger at the queen. "When are ye gonna stop making the king mope about, boxin' his ears every time he tries to be sweet to ye?"

"I'm not boxing his ears. And for heaven's sake—"

"'Tis more 'n half a year, dearie. You must relent sometime."

Mary shook the feathered overlay. It floated on top of Anna like the underbelly of a mother goose nestling her chicks.

"How can you say that? After you held my dead son?"

Mary bustled to Anna's face, lowered her voice. "I've held my fair share of dead sons, many of 'em your very brothers. You're not the first woman in the world to lose a babe. Stop feeling so damned sorry for yourself and get on with loving the living. Including your husband."

"I've no need of your service this afternoon, Mistress Mary," Anna said, chin trembling with self-righteous rage.

But as Anna watched the dust circle in a sliver of light, Mary's words haunted her

William rode beside the queen, feeling like a lovesick knave, chancing quick glances at her, using any opportunity to brush against her, guide her horse, adjust something with her skirts or mount. Only a handful of guards followed and Anna kept craning her neck to see them, for what reason William couldn't tell. They were at Foxhall again, headed to his hallowed pool. He hoped their visit could heal the slowly closing maw between them.

"If you don't stop fussing about me, I will give you something to fuss about," she said with an exaggerated pout and sparkling eyes.

"'Tis my duty to keep my wife and child snug and happy," William said.

"I've been all too snug as of late." She bathed her face in the sun. "I want to feel the wind in my hair, the ground beneath me roaring past."

He sidled up to her, removed his riding glove, and reached a hand to her hair. "I'm not sure I can condone my pregnant wife roaring anywhere." He drew out a pin, the red strands sprinkled through her hair flaming as a curl rolled to her shoulder. "But I can help you with wind in your hair."

She smiled as he released her carefully crafted coif. "'Tis improper to show my hair loosed in public."

"Then let the guards and the birds blush." He laced his fingers through her soft waves, marveling as they glistened, like a parched man at drink.

She brought his hand to her lips then gave it a pat. "And what of the wind?" She arched a brow and in the time it took him to blink, she had kicked her horse into a startled run.

"Anna!" Digging in his heels, he shot after her, dodging between trees, her laughter trickling back to him, his heart pounding with both fear for the babe and thrill at the chase. "You don't know where you're headed!" Her laughter only increased, as did her speed.

He caught her by the small clearing that led to the pond. She was breathing heavy, her smile its own beam of sunlight.

"I should be angry at you for riding so hard so far along with the babe." He tried to hide his grin in a scowl. She waited for him to dismount so he could help her down. She slipped into his arms, her belly round and hard against his own. "But I'm really just angry you beat me."

She laughed again, patted his cheek, and sauntered toward the water. "You must always be on your guard, my liege."

He grabbed a saddlebag full of refreshment and a blanket, and followed her, admiring her as she walked, a slight waddle to compensate for her belly. He grinned again. He couldn't take her seriously when her gait was that of a slightly drunken oarsman.

Quickening his pace, he came beside her, taking her arm. "I must say, I do worry this much exertion might be harmful." A cloud drifted over her open expression, closing him off, threatening rain. He knew she was thinking what he was. In a fortnight she would be in seclusion. The exact time their son was lost. He swore at himself inwardly. "But I do hear swimming is beneficial to all, in fact lulls the babe to peaceful contemplation."

She pursed her lips, but didn't pull away. "You're making that up."

"You accuse your king of making up proven science? I am aghast!"

She yanked on his arm to quicken his pace. "Only one way to find out."

They walked to the pond's edge, green water lapping the bank in tiny ripples. William spread the blanket, letting the saddlebag fall to the ground, a rosy-red apple rolling out. Anna reached behind her neck, unlacing her ties.

"Help, please," she said, chin tucked to her chest with her striving.

"Anything to get you out of your clothes the quickest." She didn't laugh, but he strode to her anyway, gently pulling ribbon through holes, a light swishing sound breaking the silence.

"Thank you, Wills." She took a great gulp of air. "Mother Mary these corsets."

He rested his hands on her rounded waist, cheek to the side of her head. "Shall I ban them for you?"

She rotated in his arms to face him. "And have me sagging like a crone? No thank you." She pushed out of his arms to extricate herself from her troublesome attire, taking his hand to step out of her skirts. She stood in her shift, one arm across her breasts, grabbing the opposite elbow, bottom lip in her teeth. She looked younger, like he imagined her before she came to court.

"You could never be a crone, my dear, no matter if you lived to be one hundred."

She nodded, turned her back to him, and removed her shift over her head. He stilled, as though watching a deer he didn't want to startle, blood thrumming in his ears. She put a tentative toe into the water's edge, shuddered, then looked over her milky shoulder at him.

"What are you waiting for?"

He needed no further encouragement. In a moment his clothes were around his ankles and he took a running jump off the baked, flat boulder, directly into the deepest part of the pool. His body shocked with the initial contact, his eye shooting open. As he pushed toward the sun, above him he saw the shimmering, distorted image of Anna, his own Lady of the Lake, hair disheveled and curling beneath her breasts. He broke the surface, gasping, staring. She smiled at him, her head to the side as if they hadn't a care in the world.

"And now, what are *you* waiting for, *mon coeur*?"

"You're like a fish."

"And you are like a woodland fairy conjured in a dream."

She laughed. "Poetry was never your strong suit."

He swam to the edge of the rock, holding on as he kicked. "Then come here and silence me." He splashed her and she yelped.

"I surrender!" She minced to the shallow edge.

He made his way to where his feet touched the silky bottom. "'Tis better if you just get in all in one go." She made a face. "Shall I help you?"

"Oh, I know what kind of help you'll be, thank you very much."

He laughed, slowly walking out, water cascading down his frame. "What if I carry you in? I promise not to plunge." She winced. "Come now, after that ride? Surely you're aching for a dip."

"Fine." She held her hands above her head. "You may carry me."

He climbed out, grin wide. She looped her arms around his neck and he hoisted her. She was so smooth, so deliciously pink.

"My queen, afraid of neither man nor beast, intimidated by a little cool water?" She pointed her nose in the air. He laughed and marched into the pool. She sucked in her breath when her bottom hit the lapping waves, then he fell to his knees, covering them both to their necks.

"Wills!" She went to thwack him, but he caught her hand before it reached its mark and kissed each finger. When he finished, he met her eyes.

"You see?" he said. "All at once, and in moments you are acclimated." He released her legs and she held his hand, moving to a place she could stand without crouching, water licking below her sternum.

"It's as if this place is full of magic." She put his hand on her cheek. "I was so worried, so fearful coming here—all the memories, being surrounded by his things, his scent." William brought his other hand to cup her face, rubbing thumbs over her cheekbones. "But coming here, to this place, this hidden emerald gem. It's as if all of it is washed away." She rested a hand on his chest. "As if the entire world is just this place and us in it." One of the horses nickered, breaking the spell. She grinned. "And the animals."

He wrapped his hands around her back, drawing her to him, her body as silken as the pond floor.

"We can bring this magic back with us, Anna. We don't have to leave it here." He kissed her forehead, her nose, her cheeks, her chin, and at last her mouth. She caved for him. Her hand ran up his torso and into his hair. He felt himself harden, heard her soft moans, her skin warm and slick. Taking her face again, he forced himself from her.

"With all I have I wish I could be with you now like we were the time before." He searched her perplexed face. "But this close to your lying in . . ."

She nodded, something in her eyes closing like a visor. He was too fearful of what might happen to the babe, and to his heart, if she rejected him after this. He wrapped her in his arms once more, kissing the top of her head.

"Oh, my Anna."

"Shall we eat then?" she said, with a quick kiss to his shoulder. "For I find I'm starved."

He led her to shore, ensconcing her in his summer cloak. He unpacked cheese and bread, fruit, wine, and some dried meat—a filling, if plain, picnic. They ate, making minor comments about the weather, Cate, gossip about her ladies and his groomsmen. When they were dry he helped her dress in silence.

Collecting the saddlebag and blanket, he strode back to her. "Now, that earlier race was not fair. I wasn't ready. But I shall race you to the horses, with my heavy-laden sack, and even give you a head start."

She laughed. "You would have to be pulling a bear to make it even close to fair. I can barely walk a straight line in this state, let alone outrun you."

"One—"

"William, you can't be serious!"

"Two—"

"And you know the path better—"

"Three!"

She lifted her skirts and ran, albeit lumbering, her laughter again filling the air. "You better not have started yet, I'm not even three feet away!"

His smile grew and he started out in a trot.

"And what if you can't find me? Do I win then?"

"Ah, so it is to be a hunt then!" He hastened his pace, surveying the forest she had disappeared into. "I doubt there be a tree big enough to hide you though."

He heard a snort coming from his left and when he neared, she squealed and set off in the opposite direction.

"You forget I am an excellent tracker." He waited, listening for the crack of branches, heavy breathing. He picked his way through the underbrush in the direction she'd gone. Rounding a tree, she darted again, heading straight for the meadow where the horses chomped contentedly at thick clover.

"Oh-ho, you've not won yet." He sprinted after her and she yelped.

"Stop, William!"

"None of this trickery, now—I shall win fairly or not at all." He was ten feet away, she was clutching her belly, clearly winded. "So you concede?" He made to chase her again, but she held up a hand, holding him back.

"I said stop it!" The iron in her voice froze him. "Or do you want to kill another of our sons?"

All blood drained from his face and he watched her wince in pain. "Guards!" His men responded instantly. "Get the queen back to Foxhall immediately—do not jostle her."

He went to her side but she pushed him away, wouldn't even look at him.

So this was how she still felt. That his touch was poison. His presence more than an unwanted nuisance, a danger even. He drew back, helpless as his guards lifted her, cradled her in their arms as he had so recently done. She laid her head on the shoulder of the man who would escort her back, face twisted, eyes clamped shut. He watched them ride away as a thick gray cloud covered the sun, the meadow's magic transformed back into reality.

The contractions stopped by the time Anna reached Foxhall, but nevertheless, the king sent her back to Havenside the next morning. Not wishing to take any chances, he arranged for her to go immediately into seclusion, all this with hardly speaking to her. She didn't blame him. The ugly words she'd said haunted her, and with no way to speak with him other than through a door, surrounded by perked ears, she was condemned to wait.

She sent him letters of contrition, his responses brief and too far between, lacking his usual good humor, yet still respectable, still concerned for her well-being and that of their child.

It was only the end of August and more than a fortnight before she'd even start to look for signs. Yet she was gigantic, like a sow at market, ready to burst. Her energy waned, though she didn't know if it was from the pregnancy or being confined. Thus her overwhelming need to rest, coupled with her exponentially increasing back pain, had her begrudgingly seeing the wisdom in her captivity.

She requested Margaux's return to help with the birth, remembering how stalwart the woman had been with Justinian, how she'd confessed her own doings with Bryan, without regard to her own punishment. But now, with the countess's smug, perfect grin floating about, Anna wished she'd not been so forgiving.

Any time the ladies returned from court Anna was desperate for news: how did the king appear? Was he well? Did he entertain anyone? Who did he see in his chambers? And it was always Margaux who provided the vague answer, some hidden delight dancing in her eyes. Yvette told Anna the blunt truth: he appeared haggard, distracted, he was thinner. He kept to his chambers with Robert and Duven, women continued to throw themselves in his path, but it just made him more ornery. And he always asked about Anna.

Her fears weren't allayed. She remembered her confinement with Cate, but this time there were no pebbles pelting her windows, no hovering king trying to sneak his way past sleeping ladies and changes of the guard. No jewels or trinkets. Just an occasional note. *I hear you are hale, and it cheers me. Be brave and strong, dearest. ~ W* or, *The princess says I should send for more sweets, do you agree? For you know I can't refuse her* . . . Nothing of his love, nothing of his pondering, nothing even of policy. How was she to respond? What was she to think?

Her head hurt, her ankles swelled, and she could barely support her own weight. "Surely we can open some windows in this stuffy room," she said, grumbling like Cate at an etiquette lesson. "'Tis as if we are living in the hellscape on an altar piece."

"Tush, tush," Mary said, bustling over. Anna sat near the south windows, hoping to catch even the slightest breeze that might blow around the tapestry. Mary handed Anna a plate of cold meat, setting ale on the sill. "You must keep your strength for the endeavor to come."

"I'm fat as wild boar already." Anna frowned at the offering.

"But you must keep your fires burning." Mary folded her hands over her apron, taking on the tone she'd used when Anna was a girl.

"Burning is not the problem." She gestured to the window. "Can we at the very least damp the fire?"

Mary's brows bounced.

"Out with it." Despite her protests, Anna stuffed a thick slice of roast beef in her mouth.

Mary's smile bordered on patronizing. "It wouldn't surprise me if that babe of yours makes an early appearance."

Anna rolled her eyes. "That is to be expected with a, well, fourth child."

Mary shook her head, still smiling. "Aye. But ye've all the signs."

"None that I can tell." Anna took a gulp of ale, letting its bubbly coolness soothe her insides.

"With all the babes carried to term by your mother, and with Catey to boot, acute ill-temper was always the sign of impending labor." With one last smirk, Mary left before her theory could be fully tested.

"Well good," Anna mumbled to herself. "At least then I can open a window."

She saw Yvette return from court, closing the doors softly. Anna made a feeble attempt to rise and hear any scrap of news, but found her back and her legs wouldn't allow it. While she pondered whether or not it was uncouth to shout for Yvette's attention, the lady approached, a gold box in her hands.

She curtsied, handing the box to Anna. "From the king."

It was about the size of thick-sliced bread, but ornately carved, shimmering in the dull light. Opening the lid she found a folded note and beneath it a flat, gray stone, perfect for skipping across water. Disgruntled, she read the note.

My Anna,

While this stone does not shine with the same luster as you, nor as the jewels you rightly deserve, 'tis more precious to me than any diamond. My mother clasped this stone whilst birthing my sister and kept it ever on her person after. I

*remember it clunking inside her pockets, with other hidden
treasures for us children to find. I hope it brings you comfort
and strength at your own time. Know prayers for you and
our child never leave my lips.*

> *Your humble husband,*
> *WR*

She picked up the rock, fingered its well-worn surface. One
slash of white across the top gave it a sort of halo. How many
times had Matilda stroked it, how many times had William
turned it over in his boyhood hands while resting in his mother's
skirts? She clutched it, letting its cool hardness seep into her, trying to sense the souls of those who'd held it before, not just the
Queen Mother, but perhaps thousands of generations, cradled
by the earth itself. It did give her strength, resolve. She wanted to
stand, to move. She looked wistfully to the king's door, recalling
how she'd paced the cool hall while waiting for Cate to arrive.
But the ache in her very bones kept her rooted to the chair.

*Oh, Matilda, what am I to do? How am I to repair my marriage?
How best to love your son? If only stones could speak . . .*

Her desperate prayer was answered, just not in the way she
expected. A tearing, kneading pain sprang from her sacrum and
clamped down on her womb like a blacksmith's vise.

Yvette's eyes widened, watching the queen gasp in pain.
"Mistress Mary! Ladies! Help Her Majesty up."

Before another contraction could take her, Anna's ladies
had her surrounded and hoisted to her feet. Her legs nearly
collapsed beneath her, but their straining arms held her aloft.

"I know gravity will help," Anna said between exhales, "but I'm too weak to stand."

"We shall walk you then," Mary said, shoving floor pillows and sundry furnishings out of their path.

"Shouldn't someone inform the king?" Margaux asked. Anna brought Matilda's stone to her chest as another contraction hit, in too much agony to care about Margaux's motives.

"Send Bernard," Anna managed.

"Let's get to the bed," Mary said to the ladies, "then I can check Her Majesty's progress."

The lot of them looked like a ponderous octopus, squishing its way across the floor. Tangling tentacles up the bedpost, they finally deposited Anna to the end of the bed, easing her on her back, her legs dangling over the edge.

Mary wasted no time in bustling beneath the queen's skirts.

"Take these clothes off," Mary ordered to the room at large. Anna was set upon by fingers unlacing, yanking. She groaned out the next contraction and all work stilled. The contractions were faster, harder than she'd remembered, even with Justinian. It felt as though the castle cook had shoved a spoon inside her, determined to scrape every bit of her internal organs out to make a stew. She was truly surprised to see Mary's face reappear unscathed.

"This will be blessedly fast, dearie."

She wanted to weep. The pain was unrelenting, the pressure more than she could bear. No matter how fast, she wasn't sure she could endure it.

It had only been two hours since Bernard informed the king. He had been to mass with prayers so fervent he could have been mistaken for a monk. Now, he prowled his bedchamber, unable to sit, unable to concentrate on anything, even Robert's attempts at humor.

"I think you need a change of scenery, cuz," Robert said, perusing William's sideboard.

"There is no way in hell I'm leaving." His jaw clenched.

"Whoa!" Robert backed up. "I only meant a change of venue for your pacing. It's unnerving, like watching the caged animals at the park." William growled, proving Robert's point. "Let's simply walk to the throne room. You can stalk around there unfettered by furniture. Besides, it's more airy."

William stopped, grunted, then headed to the door. Robert followed, almost skipping. When they reached the top of the stairs, William heard a shout, then a howl from the queen's chambers. He strode to the door, her guards' eyes as frightened as he felt. He went to knock, but hesitated. This wasn't like with Cate. She wasn't yelling for him. Didn't want him anywhere near her. She'd made that more than clear.

Another unearthly wail penetrated the thick wood. He cringed, wishing it would end soon, for all their sakes.

"Majesty?" Robert said, eyes full of concern.

"You're right, Norwick." William clapped Robert's shoulder, leading them both back to the stairs. "I need a change of scenery. Perhaps even so far as the gardens would do me well."

Anything to keep him far from her screams and his mind from his own wounded heart.

"William! Oh Jesus, save me!" Anna was beyond caring what flew from her mouth. All she wanted was her husband's strong arms and this baby out of her body. It had been about three hours and she could feel the crown of its head cresting.

But William wasn't there. She had asked. More like she had wailed, desperate to know if he had come, was waiting outside her door.

"Tell him of my love, tell him to pray!" She had said, but Bernard told Brigitte through the door that the king was nowhere to be found.

She thrashed her head back against her pillow, using her hands to try and lift her hips. "Ahhhhnnggg!" She let out her breath as the contraction passed, another already starting its grip.

"I must push, I must!"

Mary's face was in a permanent frown. "Where's the rest of that oil, Countess?"

Margaux hurried to Mary's side, offering up the famous soothing balm. "Ye can push soon, dearie, I swears it."

Anna had no time to sob as the next contraction bore down. She squeezed Matilda's stone as if to break it.

"I must . . ." It was a whisper, for she didn't have strength for volume. As the next round of pressure grew, Anna strained so hard she felt something in her face pop.

"That's it, dearie!" Mary's face was inexplicably elated. Anna thought she'd be censured, but with this blessing she pushed again. There was a sucking then vacuity, followed by a tiny, indignant cry. "It's a prince! Oh praise heaven, a prince!"

Mary held up a red, squirming, screaming boy, the spitting image of Justinian, the spitting image of William.

"Let me have him," Anna said, struggling to sit up, arms outstretched.

"We've got to cut the cord first," Mary said, wiping her cheeks with her free hand.

Anna's womb clenched again, the urge to push rising up once more. She knew she must rid herself of the afterbirth, but she'd never known it to hurt before. She must have torn. Panic gripped her, images of the prostitute she'd helped deliver all those years ago in Beaubourg floating unbidden through her mind.

"Mary," she said, voice shaking. "I feel—I don't feel well, I ah—" A cramp, as painful as any other, split her right side. Mary handed the baby to Yvette and crouched down. Anna heard her suck in air, then pop up, eyes huge, and crossed herself.

"By all that saints above," Mary said, "there be another one!"

"Wha—ahhhhh!" As if Mary speaking it aloud sparked the action, Anna's body took over, hammering down. She pushed with everything she had left, caught between disbelief and urgency.

"Breathe, Highness!" Margaux yelped, bringing a fresh wet cloth to Anna's face, then climbing behind her to bear the queen's weight.

"Unnnnngggggggg!" Anna tried, so hard she tried, but her strength was gone.

"The nose is almost out," Mary cried. "You've got to give it one more and I can do the rest."

Anna sobbed, shaking her head. "I can't, I can't." Margaux wrapped her thin arms around Anna's torso.

"We'll do this together, Highness," Margaux said, with a determination Anna rarely saw. The queen nodded as Margaux counted. On three, Margaux hugged and bore down, urging Anna to do the same. They even yelled together.

"You've done it! You've done it!" Mary sang as the rest of the ladies whooped. "The head's out and here comes the rest!"

But there was no responding cry.

"Oh Lord, have mercy on me," Anna said, turning her head into Margaux's shoulder. Brigitte giggled and Anna could have strangled her.

"Well, look at that," Mary said. Anna peered down the side of her body at her ladies' fascinated faces. "I think he smiled at me."

He? Smiling?

"Is it, is—?"

Mary held the second child up, eyes wide and curious, mouthing his forefinger.

Anna couldn't believe it. "Two boys—two *living* boys?"

In a breath she held them both in her arms, two tiny Williams, one with an abundance of thick, brown hair, cow-licked about his head like a crown, the other bald as a plucked hen. She knew one likely wouldn't survive, probably the one with hair, as he was much smaller than his brother, but she wouldn't think on that now. Now she would marvel at the two princes snuggled at her chest, their diminutive hands reaching out at the air, feet tangled together as they had recently been in her womb. Then she laughed with joy. Laughed so hard, tears streaked her face.

"Where is the king? Find him, tell him. We have heirs in spades."

As was tradition, all at court joined the king for the Feast of Waiting. Despite his clenched stomach, William was hungry, having eaten barely even bread since Anna's pains had begun. The second course was just served when Bernard appeared at his shoulder. His elaborate bow was the most convoluted the king had yet seen. Either something had gone very, very badly or very, very well.

"Majesty," he said, eyes gleaming, near brimming. "The queen has been safely delivered of an heir—" William jerked out of his chair, unable to form words. "Begging your pardon, Majesty, but there is more."

"A son?" William clamped Bernard's arms to his sides, edging on hysteria. "I have a son?"

"Majesty, if you would—"

The king hooted, nearly silencing the entire Great Hall.

"Majesty, 'tis not one son, but two. Twins."

William's mouth popped open. He hoisted Bernard, stiff as a soldier, and swung him in a circle while shouting, "Huzzah!"

Bernard attempted to hide his terrified look and grabbed hold of the queen's chair when William eventually put him down.

"A toast!" the king called. "To our heir and our spare!"

The courtiers laughed, clanked drinks, and began their ecstatic gossip. William pounded Bernard's shoulder.

"Can you believe it? Ha! Two boys! Did you ever hear of such?" Bernard was still trying to regain his composure and simply nodded. "I shall go to them, to the queen."

He glanced about the court for someone to take his place as host and realized, with an ache, he was instinctively looking for Daniel. All of the horrors of last autumn overwhelmed him. *Look what your cowardice and vice and false heart hath brought,* she had said, and *do you want to kill another of our sons?*

"Actually, 'tis probably best to let Her Majesty rest a while," William said, avoiding Bernard's questioning expression. "One birth is hard enough, but two? She is bound to be asleep already."

"As you wish, Highness." Bernard bowed again, then withdrew.

She wouldn't want to see him now, not while she reveled in her redemption, her vindication . . . He turned back to the feast, wiping the regret from his face.

Anna heard the bells peal their joy. William would join her any moment now. Her ladies had cleaned and primped her, all taking turns holding and cooing over the boys, and now she reclined against the headboard, a baby in each arm, marveling at the miracle of it all. She made sure the ruby necklace was prominently displayed at her bosom, Matilda's smooth stone resting beside her on the bed.

Bernard returned, reporting that the king didn't wish to overtax her and that he would come after the next course. He'd made no such excuses with Cate. Perhaps he was waiting until she was asleep, so he could see his heirs without having to speak to her, see her. She swallowed the lump in her throat and went back to adoring her sons.

"Do not fret, little ones, your papa will be here soon." *Surely.*

Mary had ordered food be brought from the feast and Yvette placed a full golden plate on Anna's side table.

"Highness, you should eat." Yvette smiled at the babies. "It will not be a hardship for any of your ladies to hold the lads while you do so."

"I wish to be ready for the king." She traced the eyebrows of the bald baby, who she was secretly calling Stephen.

Yvette took a deep breath. "It may be quite a while if they've only begun the second course."

Anna tried to sound sunny. "Oh, he won't stay much longer." Stephen spit out a bubble.

"I would wager you have time for sustenance." Yvette too was trying to brighten the situation. They all knew his excuse was a farce, knew he wanted to avoid the queen. Dear God in heaven, what had she done?

Anna smiled, lifting the arm that held Stephen. "You just want to get your hands on these babies."

Yvette carefully peeled Stephen from Anna. "You've caught me." Her face lit up as she curled him to her. "Aren't you just the sweetest boy? Yes you are!"

Mary was right behind her. "This one's mine." She unceremoniously plucked up the twin, bringing him to her shoulder, rubbing his minuscule back. "There you are, my little prince. Auntie Mary's got you."

Anna's whole body warmed as she watched such love

surround her children. She took her plate, eyes never leaving her sons, even as she ate ravenously. Food had never tasted so good. Finished, she let her head fall against the headboard, plate held loosely in her lap. Her eyelids drooped, mind fuzzy, and no amount of will could keep her from sleep.

She startled awake to find her room quiet, her ladies' soft breathing telling her it must be well into the night. On either side of her lay a son, each swaddled up to his chin, dreaming. She couldn't resist taking them back in her arms. They made little grunting noises but didn't wake. She hummed softly, enraptured by every little detail—soft, dark lashes, puckered lips, ivory skin soft as down. She wondered if William had come and gone while she slept but pushed the sorrow away. She kissed her sons' silken foreheads and kept humming.

William pressed his ear to Anna's private door. All was quiet. He hadn't planned on staying at the feast so long, but it seemed everyone from the chief steward to Halforn wanted to express their long-winded congratulations. He had to admit, it pleased him. He loved Catey with all that was within him and wouldn't trade her for a fleet of sons, but to finally have the throne secured, by not one but two heirs . . . well, he was full to bursting. His only hesitation was Anna. Would she still disdain him?

No time like the present to find out. He cleared his throat and pushed the door slowly, a high-pitched creak announcing his presence. The fire burned low, and two candelabras lit each side of the bed. He crept in, stopping a good ten feet away.

Finally, he dared to look, and what he found stilled his hammering heart. There was Anna, two tiny bundles in her arms, ruby shining against her shift, smile beaming to break the walls.

"Wills," she whispered, "come see your boys."

He was to her in three strides, climbing up the end of the bed and kneeling beside her. "My God, they're—they're astonishing."

He didn't think her smile could get any bigger, but it did. "Aren't they perfect? They will make their papa very proud."

"They already do." He roved over them both, hungry to take them in, count each finger and toe. "But not as proud as I am of their mother." He met her sparkling eyes, reached to touch the ruby.

"I'm so sorry, Wills," she said, her voice catching.

"Whatever for?"

"I've been a brute. I would blame the pregnancy, but it was just my own stubbornness and fear." He cupped her chin.

"What were you afraid of?"

"That we—that we wouldn't be the same. That we couldn't. And if I could seal myself up from it then it wouldn't hurt so much. But all it did was hurt worse."

He searched her face. "Of course we can't be the same. I lost your faith, lost our son—"

"Don't say it."

He moved a forefinger to her lips to hush her. "But such sorrow, such challenge, it can make us stronger. And I will never, ever doubt your fealty again."

"Don't doubt my love, either. For my heart beats only and ever for you, my king."

He kissed her, slow and soft, releasing her lips with a gentle pop.

"When I was shouting for you in labor, when I thought I truly would die—"

His heart sang. "You called for me?"

"About ten thousand times."

He smiled, astonished. He thought she didn't want him there.

"Now don't interrupt when I'm trying to give you my full, groveling apology." She grinned. He chortled and the babies startled, but didn't open their eyes. The one with all the hair snorted, crinkled his nose, and persisted in dozing.

She continued. "When I thought I would die, it all became clear. We've both hurt each other deeply, but the worst sin of all would be to continue even one more minute in disharmony. Why soak in the misery of the past when there be such joy for the future?"

"Oh, my Anna, how I've longed to hear those words."

"The thought of never seeing you again, of leaving you, Cate . . . I've never felt such terror."

"Well you need feel it no longer." He carefully climbed behind her, cradling her and their boys. She relaxed against him and his blood thrummed. She had come back to him.

"Tell me this isn't all a dream."

As if answering his request, the babe with hair like his own opened his eyes and started to wail. King and queen chuckled together.

"Well, now 'tis your turn to hold Stephen." She handed over the bald one and pulled down the front of her shift. In one graceful movement, the bawling boy was at her breast, sucking contentedly.

"You've chosen to feed them?"

She shrugged. "We certainly don't need another child any time soon, and with two, all the milk we have available the better." He kissed the scoop of her neck, careful not to squish Stephen. "And I'll admit, I was loath not to with Cate. Now I have an excuse."

"I will not be one to advise you differently."

Gazing at her, something stirred in him. It wasn't sexual, but rather a bond, an attraction, an urge to protect, to claim. Something about the vulnerability of her exposed breast, their child taking his sustenance from her, he was overcome by the fierceness of this devotion. He trembled so with it that he looked away, lest he alarm her.

"So you've named this one Stephen have you?" He said after clearing his throat. The boy had the exact same look of seriousness her father wore at council, brows slightly furrowed, lower lip extended.

"Oh it was just for convenience, I wouldn't think to name them without you."

"I say keep it. He has your father's chin. And heaven knows we don't want to name him after my father."

"But isn't it tradition?"

"Hang tradition. I'll not have that man's name ever uttered again in these walls if I can help it." He gently pressed his pinky on Stephen's pout and the babe sucked it. Any second he'd be sure to wake in protest. "And what of our hairy beast?"

"William to be sure, for he is the first born."

"Bah. So boring."

"It will be an honor for him to have your name. For there was never a king like his father."

"That's putting it judiciously." He could tell she wanted to swat him but her hands were full.

"You know what I mean." She unlatched miniature William. "Trade, please."

She scooted around to face the king, handing over his name-sake. He did look like William, down to the cleft chin. For a moment, the king wondered if this was what Justinian had looked like, but he buried the thought as quickly as it had arisen.

The prince's clear blue eyes were open now and he considered his father. Finding the picture wanting, his hand clamped the king's nose and squeezed with a grip that belied his size.

"Ouch!" The king laughed. "This one certainly likes to be in charge."

"I shall make no comment."

Little William yawned, his eyes rolling into his head then closing. Soon Anna was finished with Stephen as well. She took the future king from William's arms and nestled the two boys next to each other. Then she curled herself around them, creating a nest. William followed suit, mirroring her on the other side. He reached across the babes and took her hand, stroked it with his thumb.

"Sleep now, my love," he said, his own lids heavy. "And we shall wake to a new dawn."

She smiled, closed her beautiful brown eyes. "I love you so, Wills."

"I love you to, my Anna."

CHAPTER 16

Time Waits for No Man

obert stood by the open windows of his study, the early August breeze cooling him as he studied the royal family cavorting in the gardens. William was bent over his counterpart, forefingers grasped by pudgy hands, while stubby, unsteady legs propelled them both over the gravel, matching smiles of wonderment on their faces. The queen held Stephen on her hip, carrying him like a peasant would hoist a basket of apples, the child reaching up to capture the fractured light created by her jewels. Cate clapped, urging her brother to walk, the whole family blissfully unaware of their voyeur.

Margaux sat on Robert's settee, observing him as he watched the brood.

"When will she send you back to Mohrlang?" Robert said, eyes narrowing as Prince William's legs finally buckled. "It's been nearly a year."

"So eager to be rid of me now, brother? I can't see why."

The king threw his prince into the air, catching him just as easily.

"I'm simply making conversation." He sighed. Why was she in his study anyway? Disturbing his peace. He knew darning his shirt collars was some veiled excuse and he wished she'd get to her business and be gone.

"I suppose all is settled then," she said, glancing out the window. "There's nothing more to be done. He's had his sons. He has his queen."

"I've never known you to be so defeatist." He frowned at her.

"Oh, perhaps he'll tire of her at some point, but then I'd be nothing but a temporary plaything. I wouldn't have any real power. Any respect."

He chortled, turning from the domestic scene. "Well haven't you changed your tune?"

She harrumphed, absently picking at threads.

"Actually, I have you to thank for that."

"Oh do tell, for I love to be lauded." He crossed his arms, waiting for her assault.

"Eustace has proven to be quite the—how shall I put it? Attentive husband." She flashed a new sapphire-encrusted bracelet as she smoothed over her again pregnant belly. Catching Robert's glance, she added, "He prefers to give me sapphires, says they remind him of my eyes."

"Then he should shower you in topaz. It more matches their color." To Robert's surprise, she blushed.

"Kind of you to observe it, brother."

And here he'd meant it as an insult to her husband's intelligence. But no use picking a fight.

"He's certainly prodigious in his virility, I'll give him that much."

Her blush deepened. "Never you mind about that."

"You started it." He almost stuck out his tongue at her.

"All I meant to say was yes, my ambition for higher office has cooled. Though perhaps, if I play my cards right, the king might give Eustace the dukedom of Cecile."

"First you wanted a crown, now you want land. My, my, how you've grown." He strode to his desk and picked up a correspondence at random. "But the land will never again be in the hands of a bastard."

She stood, lay his finished shirt over the settee arm, and sauntered to him. "Just you wait, brother mine."

He leaned back, propped his feet on his desk. "As always, I'm delighted to see you try."

"I surrender!" William held up his hands as Cate wrapped herself around his leg. It was the tenth footrace he had been content to lose. "Your papa is not as young and spritely as he once was." He continued on to the fountain's lip, hobbled by a giggling Cate still attached. "Now let me loose or I shall fall into the water, my dear."

She obeyed then climbed up beside him, placing her hand in his. He had long since removed his jacket and vest and now had sweat through his shirt in the late summer heat.

"Perhaps I would like to take a dip and cool myself. Will you join me?" He grinned at Cate, pretending to tackle her.

She let out a laughing scream. "No, Papa!"

"Well, since you've been so good to your brothers today . . ." He hoisted her to his lap. She lay her soft head against his shoulder, not minding the damp.

"But I am good to my brothers every day."

He laughed. She picked up his loose shirt laces and fiddled with them, looping them around her fingers, plaiting them together as he breathed her in, fresh green, sunshine, lavender, and that sweet, salty mixture of all children, tangy yet pleasant.

"You know you're my favorite, don't you?" He pressed his lips to the crown of her head. "Don't tell the boys."

She arched to look at him, eyes blinking back up in wonder. "Don't you love the princes?"

He ruffled her hair. "Of course I do! But well, I always wanted a little girl. I told your mama that if all we had were you, I would be content."

"But then there would be no heir, no one to rule the realm."

He chuckled, thinking back to something Anna once said. "Tell that to England's Elizabeth."

She covered her mouth with her hands, and he could see the twinkle in her eye, the delight. She pushed up, wrapped her arms around his neck, and kissed his cheek.

"Thank you, Papa." She slid off his lap, gave a very proper curtsy and said, "I shall make us each a daisy crown."

"No finer thing will have graced my head." He nodded, solemn.

Anna approached him, watching Cate flit off to the lawn. The queen laid Stephen down in the grass and joined William on the fountain ledge.

"Care for a swim?" Her smile was full of mischief and memories.

"That is just what I threatened Catey with."

She covered his hand with hers and sighed.

"Are you as exhausted as I am?" He looked at her sun-flushed face. How was it she didn't age but he couldn't make it through an afternoon frolicking in the gardens?

"I didn't eat as much at dinner. Methinks your gut calls you to your bed."

He wrapped his arms around her and nipped her shoulder. "Methinks something else calls me to my bed." Then he belched.

"That last bit did not help your case, my liege." But she smiled nonetheless. "Perhaps an afternoon snooze is in order."

He belched again. She frowned at him. "I'm sorry!" He laughed. "Truly! They're just coming up."

"It's no wonder. I think you ate an entire goose yourself." She smacked his thigh.

He gnawed on her shoulder again. "If you recall, some dainty queen who only wanted 'a few bites' ate her fair share. I believe she even shoved away the hand of the server who dared touch her plate before she had finished."

She put her nose in the air. "But I am feeding three, with the boys not yet fully weaned."

"Yes, I'm sure a morning feed for our princes doth take the

goose out of one." He moved on to her earlobe. "Let us retire, my love, and find out how much goose you've got left."

He saw her jaw twitch, caught her looking sidelong at him, and he knew he had her.

"You win." She turned her head and kissed his nose. "Cariline, Mary? His Majesty and I shall retire for an afternoon respite." Her ladies bowed, sharing knowing glances. "Please have the children back in the nursery well before supper."

William stood, his legs aching more than he'd expected, and held his hand out for Anna. She took it with a conspiratorial look, and they strolled back to the palace, shadow finally replacing the sun as they retreated to their precious solitude.

Anna laid her head on William's bare chest and fiddled with the sparse, soft hairs, a handful of gray scattered throughout. She could hear his heart slowing after its exertion. He rubbed her back through her shift and sighed.

"Sometimes I think I will blink and all of this will disappear," she said, watching his chest rise and fall. "That I will wake up and it will still be the middle of the war, or when we were at odds—"

He caught her hand with his free one, brought it to his mouth, lips caressing her knuckles.

"I assure you this is no dream. What happened is we woke from a nightmare to find this reality."

"That's a beautiful way to put it." She kissed him, right over his heart. "I love you so, my Wills."

He squeezed her in a tight embrace. "And I you, my Anna."
He hugged her again, but it felt more like a shudder than an act
of endearment.

She laughed. "Wills?'

He made a queer gurgling sound, his eyes shut tight. Her
face, pressed into his chest, could feel his heart pounding.

"William?"

He winced and inhaled. "My Anna—" Then he went limp.
She sat up. "Wills?"

His face had settled into the serene and handsome smile she
had seen so many times before. She cupped his cheeks, feeling
the soft tickle of his stubble.

"Wills!"

He must have fainted with the day's heat and exertions. She
shook her head and lightly slapped his cheek. Nothing. He
would have to take it easy from now on, whether he liked it
or not. She laid her hand on his chest, seeking his breath, his
heart. She found only terrifying stillness.

After Margaux left him, Robert had decided to clear his head
with a ride out to the south forest. Was his sister, of all people, right? Should he leave well enough alone? Would being
"Uncle Robert" to the princes be enough to move them away
from Catholic rule? Maybe there was still a chance for the king
to warm to the idea—a way to regain Laureland, and with the
mess the Low Countries were making of themselves, perhaps a
chance to gain more lands . . .

He rode across the meadow, the palace to his right, and that was when the sky darkened. Then eerie silence. A pause. As if God Himself closed His eyes, took a breath and held it. And when He released, birds were His exhale, hundreds of doves and crows, finches and robins, took to the sky from the castle walls, their wings beating with fury, their sharp cries piercing his ears. He saw men running on the ramparts.

Good God. What had happened?

It had been three days. Annelore sat in William's leather chair, wrapped in his favorite black cloak, eyes red, face swollen. She stared at his empty bed. She wouldn't let the servants change the sheets, wouldn't even let them remake it.

She kept replaying the scene in her mind. Robert had dragged her from William's slack body, her wailing at him to let her go. Servants swarmed like bees as she screamed, *Don't touch him—don't you touch him! Stop this instant! William! William!* Anna tore at Robert's arms, leaving bloody gouges in his skin, trying to break free. Watching in horror, she saw Archbishop Bartmore yank William's signet ring—or rather, the king's signet ring—from his once strong hand and leave in a flurry of robes and lords. He was heading to the nursery. Even amid her sobs, she heard the faint echo float into the chamber from down the hall:

The King is dead. God save the King.

It was then that she sank into nothingness.

Waking in her own bed hours later, she sat up, wrapped her

rabbit robe about her, and went straight to their private hallway. She hadn't left William's room since, much to the consternation of Robert and the worry of Mary. Not even the twins and Cate could cheer her.

How could she have wasted so much time being so angry, so recalcitrant? She had frittered away a year in bitterness, when she should have been savoring every moment. How many embraces had she shunned, how many long nights of companionship had she lost, all because of her stubborn need to make him feel as horrible as she had felt.

She had given the country its heirs. The realm no longer needed her. And she couldn't bear to be apart from her beloved. She rose, walking to his desk, searching. Where would he have kept his seal opener? She spied the golden box where he stored his papers. It must be there.

Lifting the lid with a creak, she saw it, glinting in the sun. She grabbed it, stroking its sharp edge. Cradling it to her breast as she would a child, she took a deep breath. Opening her eyes, the top piece of parchment in the box caught her attention. It was her writing. Curious, she set down the opener and lifted the letter. It was dated during her confinement for Cate. *If I hear one more story about which courtier is carousing with whom, I shall scream. Oh, Wills, how desperate I am for you company! Your wit, your smile, your laughter, your embrace. Somehow, in all the worry about childbirth, I did not think what this long separation from you would do to my heart . . .*

An unbidden moan left her. Tears she thought could no longer fall rained down, blurring her perfectly formed words into a bleeding black. She let the letter fall, wiping away her tears. Oh

God, where was William, to erase them with his thumbs as he always did?

The next letter was one she had written after her father's death. One she had never sent, one of many Margaux was bid to destroy. And the next, from their early marriage, just a scrap: *My chamber or yours? – A.* She rifled through page after page; the entire box contained only letters from her. *Oh, Wills. What a fool I've been. My dear, dear love.*

She stopped at a letter folded in quarters and thin with wear, it was covered in unidentifiable smudges. It was a farewell letter from the first Laureland war. She held it to her breast and sank into his desk chair, sobs wracking her again.

Sniffing and wiping her face with his cloak, she clamped down on the opener. *Oh God, I can't bear it. Forgive me.* She traced her finger to its tip, gazing with longing. A single trickle of blood came from her finger. In a trance, she watched it roll down, red against ivory.

The creaking of the chamber doors and a stamp of the staff startled her and she clutched the opener and letter to her chest.

"Begging your pardon, Madam. I didn't know you were here," Robert said, looking anywhere but at her. "I'll just. Uh, excuse me." He bowed, making to leave.

Anna gave another great sniff and rose. "What is it you want? Come to claim his chambers while my son still nurses?" She didn't have the energy for malice, but she took umbrage at this intrusion into her grief.

"Majesty, I," he looked up at her and she saw his eyes were bloodshot, cheeks sallow, his voice scratched, hair disheveled.

She turned from him. Sympathy was the last thing she wanted

from Robert of Norwick, and it was the last thing she wanted to have for him.

"I just sought to be with him again. I thought . . ." He stopped then mumbled something under his breath. "Fine, just fine." His tone changed to anger so quickly it made Anna spin back around.

"He wasn't yours alone—he was in my heart too! God, even dead you can't let us have a piece of him!"

"How dare you, Robert?" Anna was in his face, trembling. "How dare you come here and try to tell me you were constant to him?"

"I would have died a thousand times over for him!"

"Not if it meant gaining the throne for your selfish schemes."

"You know I merely wanted William to lead us away from the pope."

"That may have convinced him, but I'll never believe it."

"That be enough!" It was Mary, speaking as she would to the children. "You two besmirch his memory, fighting—and in his own chamber t' boot! You ought to be ashamed. Both of ye."

Robert turned with a sneer. "I won't be disrespected in such a manor by such a woman."

"His Majesty would be grieved to no end seeing the two people he loved most in this world, besides the kidduns, at each other's throats. And I don't care who ye be, Robert a Norwick." At this dressing down, Robert turned heel and left without another word.

Mary moved to Anna, reaching out her arms. Anna fell into them like a girl, allowing Mary to pry the opener from her fingers.

"Let's get y' cleaned up. The king wouldn't want you all a mess. I know yer not allowed to go to the funeral, but you need to at least show your face in court."

Anna whimpered. If she left, it was the end. If she stayed here, stayed in the last place he drew breath, stayed among his things, handled the same objects, inhaled his pillow, clothed herself in his sheets, she could keep him alive.

"I can't leave, Mary. Don't you see?"

"I see very well, dearie." Mary wrapped William's cloak even tighter around Anna. "You can't keep him here, my love. He's in a new paradise. And he wouldn't want you to be in this hell."

"How do you know what he would want?" Anna tore from Mary's arms.

"We all loved him, dearie," she said, voice soft, breaking. There was a pause.

"Lady Yvette?" Mary called. In walked Yvette, the baby king on her hip. He was awake and squirming for his mama. "The king needs you. And so do the prince and princess."

"And so does Troixden," Yvette said, handing the precious bundle to Anna. Looking into his blue eyes, the same as his father's, something in her stirred, awoke to her duty, to her privilege. She wouldn't make the same mistake of frittering away precious time. She smiled for the first time in three days, cooing at her little king. And he gave her his father's smile right back.

Robert decided he would focus on how much his hose itched, not on what was happening in Piedmont Cathedral, where less than a year ago he'd held his gurgling godson. He wouldn't think on his role in this morbid ceremony, not on the hundreds of sparkling mourners dressed in black, only here for the pomp, for the feasting after. For William would have a feast. No moping about. Yet how could they feast in the face of their king cut down before his time? How could Robert, when he could barely put one foot in front of the other?

The Latin spouted by Moltmann and Bartmore floated over his head with the incense. Bryan stood across from Robert, facing him over the coffin, his blue eyes hard.

Robert felt, more than saw, movement around him, sensed the lowering of the gold-encrusted coffin to its resting place beneath the stone. He wondered, absently, who had been commissioned to make the tomb, then realized, as regent, it was his job. Certainly the queen mother wouldn't do it. Unbeknownst to anyone, William had appointed both Robert and Anna to rule as co-regents for King William III. Surely his cousin was having quite a laugh about it in heaven.

Duven, who stood next to Robert, cleared his throat. Robert looked at him blankly. Duven gestured with his chin toward the sunken coffin, eleven staffs of service broken on top. It was tradition for the men of council to do so, showing their duty fulfilled. And now it was Robert's turn. He gripped his staff, frowned, and gave a minuscule shake of his head.

Duven leaned over to him, whispering. "Your staff, Norwick. Everyone's waiting."

"No," he said. Bryan lifted one brow, and Robert thought he caught the glimmer of a smile.

He stared at his counterpart, unwilling to face the rest,

unable without breaking down like a woman. He would not dishonor himself so, but he also would not break his staff. He had vowed to serve William unto death. As far as Robert was concerned, that meant his own death as well.

Men shifted their weight, someone in the congregation coughed. Moltmann walked down the line to stand next to Robert. He placed what was meant to be a calming hand on Robert's shoulder.

"I know you still grieve, Your Grace, but we must go on with the service."

"Get your hand off of me," Robert bit out.

"'Tis only symbolic, Your Grace, it only—"

"Damn you and your trappings!" Robert didn't realize he was yelling until he heard the lords and ladies whispering below. "'Tis not a symbol to me! It's my word—my word to my blood, my friend, my king."

Moltmann nodded, slow. "But we need you to serve the new king now."

"I will serve them both!" He tore away from the priest, stumbling mindlessly down the altar stairs, staff still in his hand. Avoiding the gentry's stares, he looked to the balcony as he hurried down the aisle. Three women stood there, draped in black, faces veiled. But Anna, standing in the middle, clutched her veil in her hands as if to turn it to dust. Traditionally the queen wasn't allowed at the king's funeral, for some superstitious reason Robert couldn't recall. All these insipid rules and ceremonies. Their eyes locked. She opened her mouth as if to speak, but he kept moving through the nave, into the narthex, and finally out into the blinding August sun, where he dropped to his knees and wept.

Anna left the funeral with Mary and Yvette after Robert had made his peculiar exit. She didn't know what to think. Could she have been wrong this whole time? Did Robert truly love William? She hoped to God he did, and that his antics weren't some stunt to turn attention to himself.

Whatever possessed William to make them co-regents? As if even in death he would get his wish, to make partners in governance of them, if not friends. She had to give Robert credit for not attempting to move into William's chambers. With the new king still so young, she decided to keep him in the nursery, thus the king's grand chambers sat fallow. That is, if one didn't count the number of times she'd crept in, whether to sleep there or to handle his things, trying to feel his warmth, his essence.

She hadn't spent any time in the throne room since his death. She couldn't bear to do so. But now, she stood before that mighty chair of his, silent tears caressing her cheeks. She recalled the first time she had seen the throne, touring the palace with Bernard. She'd been desperate to touch it, thinking somehow, something of William's character, his spirit, would be imbedded in that chair, as she did now with his belongings in his chambers. She walked up the dais and bent to her knees with the solemnity of someone taking communion. Reaching out, she grabbed the golden arms and laid her cheek against the soft velvet, wetting it with her grief.

"Oh God, Wills. I can't do this without you."

She didn't care that Mary and Yvette stood silent and still below her. There was so, so much she no longer cared about, politics, gossip—everything seemed so trite, so meaningless. She closed her eyes, imagining her head was on William's lap, his soothing hand drawing fingers through her hair, a soft chuckle in his chest.

A clanging of a scabbard had her eyes open again, the fantasy dissolving. She almost wished this fast-approaching man was here to take her life. She didn't move, turn, rise. Whoever this was wasn't worth her effort.

Anna could tell he stopped suddenly, probably shocked by the scene he'd encountered.

"Your Grace," Mary and Yvette said with rustles of fabric.

Anna closed her eyes again as she did when she was a child, when she believed if she couldn't see, others couldn't see her. Or perhaps just to keep the living out.

She heard slow steps ascending the stairs.

"Your Grace?" This was Yvette.

The lord stopped behind Anna, his breath uneven. The leather of his boots made a sigh. Large, sinewy hands curled around the throne arms beneath her hands. She felt the warmth of his body stretch along her back, his head resting at her shoulder blades. His quiet sob reverberated through her torso. This masculine yet gentle touch soothed her more than she could have imagined.

"How are we to go on without him?" Robert said, in a whisper so low Anna wondered if he meant for her to hear.

From that moment in the throne room, things changed between Anna and Robert. She found unexpected solace in his company, often seeking it out just to hear stories of him and William gallivanting about as boys or in exile. These talks must have cheered him too, as he asked for more frequent audience with her, the two of them often talking well into the night.

They always met in William's chamber, Robert in her old chair, her in William's. If she let the fire and wine lull her, she could almost imagine those leather arms were his. His scent still lingered, imbedded in the fibers, and every time she sat, a waft of him enveloped her, as if his spirit sat astride the chest, joining them.

She told Robert this on one particularly gloomy evening, rain lashing the windows, wind whipping down the chimney, setting the flames to whirling.

"Sometimes," Robert said, watching the fire, "I could swear he's right behind me, right about to clasp my shoulder as he always did." He turned his eyes to her, his brown matching her own. "Can feel him breathe . . . and when I turn, the room is just as empty as before. But there's a whiff—wood smoke and leather." He swallowed. "It's probably my imaginings, my creating my own wish."

Anna gave a half-smile. "And Cate would say it was him, it *is* him." She shook her head. "But I can't decide what's better—letting him go, or constantly looking for these little hints, little comforts that, when they're gone, hurt all the more."

"I feel the same." Robert leaned forward, elbows on his knees, eyes earnest. "These meetings between us, they leave me wrecked."

The lurch in her heart at his words surprised her. She swallowed. "If you'd rather not—"

His brow furrowed and he shook his head. "But I would be more aggrieved without this. Without . . . you." Their eyes caught, she held her breath. He laughed and shook his head again. "In what world did I ever imagine I'd want to spend a lazy evening with the likes of you?"

She laughed as well. "Or I you."

He rose, striding to the sideboard. "Would you like more wine?"

She peered into her glass, finding it almost empty. "Yes please."

He sauntered back, tipping the pewter pitcher to fill her cup. He let a forefinger rest on her shoulder. She closed her eyes, grabbed his hand, and squeezed. He squeezed back and bent to kiss the top of her head.

While it was incredibly satisfying to feel even the light touch of a man, she felt only the caresses of a friend. There had always been sparks between them, but with William's death, she well and truly knew no one, no matter how handsome, no matter how charismatic, could ever stand a chance against such a man as her husband.

Besides, she would never hurt Yvette so. Nor would Robert.

"I had always wanted the first princess Cate to be my sister." He returned to his seat, tilting his head to consider her. "And while you are wholly different, when I'm with you like this, I feel my long-lost sister has returned to me."

"That means more than you can know, Robert."

He nodded, smile sheepish. "I aim to please."

She sighed, bittersweet longings tugging at her.

"That's what he used to say."

But where one thing was concerned, Anna and Robert would never be reconciled: religion.

And to that end, Anna, Cate, and the twins, followed by Moltmann, Bartmore, and reluctantly, Robert, were headed to the palace gate balcony. Cate, just nine, carried herself like a queen, grown impossibly serious in the wake of William's death. Her wild imaginings or visions were tempered, though occasionally she would mention a dream she had, saying things that would stop Anna's blood and bring her to private tears. "Papa told me he wishes you'd enjoy the stone work in the library," she would say, or, "Papa wants his Anna to put away her widow's weeds. He says there's too much fabric."

Anna wore black from the day William died until Cate shared this. Of course, it could be the musings of a child wishing to see her mother more colorfully bedecked. But the phraseology she'd used . . . Anna wore black not so much to remind herself of his death—for she thought of him, missed him every minute, every day—but to remind others, to remind the court, the country, of what a great man, what a great king they had lost. Whether this was a message from beyond the grave or Cate's own fancy, Anna knew William indeed would not like all that black. Instead, she now only wore blue. The color of Troixden, the color of his eyes, his favorite, with his ruby proudly outside her corset now, for all to know she still carried it, still cherished it.

Robert, being pulled along on each side by William and Stephen, sidled up to Anna. "But, Madam, the pope here . . . If we ever hope to regain Laureland and then some, the papal presence—"

"Norwick, we've been rounds on this," she said, not unkindly. She relieved Robert of the young king, bending to adjust his miniature chain of office. "If His Holiness wishes to bestow Defender of the Faith upon our king, and in doing so would also like to make a tour of our fair lands, we cannot refuse."

Robert twitched. "I know you think his coming here will finally rouse him to order standing guards at Calais, but he has larger countries to think on."

"Apparently not," she said, rising and taking William's hand. Robert sighed. "I know you don't like it, and I know you'd rather be anywhere but at court when he arrives, but how ever would I host a feast without your renowned hospitality?" He looked sidelong at her as they continued on. "Come now, I can't very well throw open the doors to all Havenside, pauper to duke, without my dashing co-regent. It would be like a feast without wine."

She heard Bartmore cluck his tongue in condescension at the "unruly mobs of the filthy," as he termed the city dwellers, but she ignored him.

"Uncle Robert," Cate said, taking his now free hand, "Mother is correct. A feast is a chore without your good humor."

Robert smirked. "Is that so?"

"Yes, Uncle Robert," the tiny king said. "Besides, I order it.

Robert's grin was full and wide. "If my king doth demand it, I've no choice."

"Just so," said William with a decisive nod. Robert ruffled his hair.

"Now you've gone and mussed his cowlicks." Anna halted again and attempted to smooth William's hair, but he made a face and kept dodging her hands.

Robert chuckled. "Oh, my king, you are so like your father."

"Stubborn you mean?" Cate said. Robert kissed the top of her head.

"That too." Robert smiled, eyes filled with bittersweetness.

Anna cleared her throat to tamp down her own memories and straightened. "Well now, my noble brood, let us open these doors and tell our waiting countrymen they'll soon have a pope to greet."

"Don't forget the free food!" piped Stephen.

"And the free wine," Robert said.

She pursed her lips to keep from grinning. "I must be dignified, as must you all, my dears." She nearly lost her breath at the sight of her radiant, obedient children. "That's right, stand up tall, for you are the sons and daughters of Troixden, the heirs of a mighty king."

She turned to Robert, his face now all regality as well. He nodded. She nodded back.

The doors were pulled open and the queen walked out into

the sun, a sea of her son's subjects below, sending up their cheers. Beside her, King William the Third stepped up on his royal viewing stool and waved stoically to the crowd. Cate dipped into a low curtsy and the multitude followed suit, doffing caps, taking to their knees. And in that moment, whether it was a cloud passing the sun or a trick of the eye, a blaze of light ignited the ruby at Annelore's chest, making it glow as though her lover's heart beat once more.

This is how we go on, Wills. This is how we go on.

The End

Historical Note:

In Crown & Thorns, more so than the previous books in the series, I have utilized actual historical people. I have taken some license with dates and places as we historical writers are wont to do. My use of Sir Walter Raleigh in particular is of course completely fictional, although history is hazy on his whereabouts after he fought with the Huguenots in France in 1569 and then registered as a student at Oxford in 1572 followed by Middle Temple in 1575. As our story takes places during his enticing absence from history, I placed him in Troixden, doing what he did best in life: writing, flirting, exploring and fighting.

Acknowledgements

This is the end, my friends. It was a long journey, but I hope a satisfying one.

I am again nothing without my editing and design team, Renni Browne, Shannon Roberts, Amanda Bauch, Morgana Gallaway, Jane Ryder and a fourth gorgeous cover by Kelly Leslie.

This series has been near ten years in the making, from the time I first spied a trembling bride in my minds eye, headed toward a resigned king. My closest friends and family have put up with me the entire way. Thank you for reading, advising, cheerleading and plying me with whiskey, chocolate and British dramas. And to my husband and my children, I too lose my breath when I think of your love, grace, kindness and good humor.

And heartfelt thank you, readers. Thank you for believing in me and these characters, thank you for pestering me to finish Crown & Thorns already, and for all your support online. You are my tribe and I can't do any of this without you.

They say authors believe a book is never truly finished. This is true for me, for the story, and the people of Troixden continue in my head as I hope they continue in your heart.

Author's Note

It always amazes me that people not related to me will pick up my book and read it. Thank you! If you enjoyed the book—or not—please take a minute or two to review it. Authors thrive from word of mouth, and the largest mouthpiece you have is the Internet.

Thank you for coming with me on the journey of Anna and William. . .

STAY CONNECTED:

Sign up for J. L. Spohr's newsletter at **www.jlspohr.com** to stay up to date on all the Troixden news and new books.

Connect on social media: Twitter/Instagram **@jlspohr, facebook. com/jlspohr,** and get a peek into Troixden's inspiration on Pinterest: **pinterest.com/jlspohr.**

About the Author

J.L. SPOHR has studied the trials and tribulations of royals since Princess Diana took that long walk to the altar. Her series *The Realm* has received rave reviews and rankings. She brings an informed perspective to the sixteenth century, having focused on the Reformation extensively for her master's degree. She is an ordained minister and lives with her brood in Seattle, WA.

www.ingramcontent.com/pod-product-compliance
Lightning Source LLC
Chambersburg PA
CBHW021833010726
47493CB00005B/1375